THE CHUC

"Satin-smooth mystery novel in a family fracas which starts with acts of malignant mischief and leads to murder. . . . Ingenuous manner for some ingenious matter—expert timing and mechanics and pleasant romantic asides. Velvet."

—*Kirkus Reviews*, starred review (September 1941)

Praise for the novels of Mabel Seeley

"What a find! I'm so happy to have discovered Mabel Seeley. You will love her feisty heroine and the delightful cast of characters who live in the mysterious Listening House. I changed my mind a dozen times about who I thought the killer was, but I was wrong every time!"

—Victoria Thompson, *USA Today* bestselling author of *Murder on Wall Street*

"Like her tenacious heroine, Seeley's writing showcases intelligence and a razor-sharp wit. This exceptional reissue is certain to win Seeley a whole new generation of fans."

—*Publishers Weekly* (starred review)

"Miss Seeley is to be welcomed as a very promising author of detective fiction."

—*Times Literary Supplement* on *The Listening House*

"Miss Seeley, with a good story to tell, ingenious plot and counter-plot, character diverse and clearly seen, lifts her book into the first class." —*Observer* on *The Listening House*

"Blood-curdling . . . especially good."

—*Saturday Review of Literature* on *The Listening House*

"The Crime Club have discovered a genius in Mabel Seeley. The author's style is unusual: she tells her story in natural everyday language, but she puts it 'right over'—and what a climax!"

—*Manchester Evening News* on *The Listening House*

"So packed with weird thrills that it grips from first page to last . . . should take its place as one of the best thrillers of the season."

—*National Newsagent* on *The Listening House*

"First rate whodunit, with enough of romance to give it a Mary Roberts Rinehart appeal. . . . This is a newcomer in the field—a good 'un."

—*Kirkus Reviews*, starred review (September 1938) on *The Listening House*

"Beautifully told by a writer who is expert at finding horror in commonplace settings. Recommended for highest honors."

—*The New Yorker* on *The Crying Sisters*

"*The Crying Sisters* is the Crime Club selection for this month, and it is an excellent mystery novel of the 'atmospheric' type. . . . it holds its interest from the beginning as it rises in crescendo toward climax."   —*The New York Times* on *The Crying Sisters*

"Another superior job of atmosphere, character and suspense."

—*Kirkus Reviews* on *The Beckoning Door*

MYSTERIES BY MABEL SEELEY

THE
CHUCKLING
FINGERS

Mabel Seeley

BERKLEY PRIME CRIME
NEW YORK

BERKLEY PRIME CRIME
Published by Berkley
An imprint of Penguin Random House LLC
penguinrandomhouse.com

Copyright © 1941 by Mabel Mysteries / Elsewhither Publishing, LLC

BERKLEY and the BERKLEY & B colophon are registered trademarks and
BERKLEY PRIME CRIME is a trademark of Penguin Random House LLC.

Library of Congress Cataloging-in-Publication Data

Names: Seeley, Mabel, 1903–1991, author.
Title: The chuckling fingers / Mabel Seeley.
Description: Berkley Prime Crime trade paperback edition. |
[New York]: Berkley Prime Crime, 2021.
Identifiers: LCCN 2021012428 (print) | LCCN 2021012429 (ebook) |
ISBN 9780593334560 (trade paperback) | ISBN 9780593334577 (ebook)
Classification: LCC PS3537.E2826 C48 2021 (print) | LCC PS3537.E2826 (ebook) |
DDC 813/.54—dc23
LC record available at https://lccn.loc.gov/2021012428
LC ebook record available at https://lccn.loc.gov/2021012429

Pyramid mass-market edition / 1973
Afton Press hardcover edition / 1988
Berkley Prime Crime trade paperback edition / September 2021

Printed in the United States of America
1st Printing

Book design by Daniel Brount

This One
For Gregory

To the eternal glory of Minnesota, there is such a place as the North Shore. Otherwise this story is entirely fictitious; there is no such estate as Fiddler's Fingers, and the people I put there, the events I have happen there, are entirely imaginary.

SETTING

FIDDLER'S FINGERS, *a remote and pine-grown private estate on the North Shore of Lake Superior.*

DRAMATIS PERSONAE

ANN GAY, *stenographer in an insurance office, twenty-six. If trouble was a lake, she'd dive into it headfirst.*

JACQUELINE HEATON, *Ann's lovely cousin, whose second marriage precipitates crime.*

TOBY SALLISHAW, *not yet three, Jacqueline's daughter by her first marriage to Pat Sallishaw.*

BILL HEATON, *lumberman, Jacqueline's new husband, whose Heaton inheritance includes the Heaton luck.*

FRED HEATON, *Bill's brash nineteen-year-old son by his first marriage.*

MYRA HEATON SALLISHAW, *Bill Heaton's cousin, and mother of Jacqueline's first husband, Pat Sallishaw.*

PHILLIPS HEATON, *who believes the world owes a Heaton a very good living. Myra's brother.*

OCTAVIA HEATON, *so often unseen and unheard, younger sister of Myra and Phillips.*

JEAN NOBBELIN, *Bill's business partner, French Canadian.*

MARK ELLIF, *just out of college, engineer of one of the Heaton-Nobbelin pulpwood freighters.*

BRADLEY AUDEN, *old friend of the Heatons, and owner of an estate east of Fiddler's Fingers.*

CAROL AUDEN, *Bradley's impulsive eighteen-year-old daughter. Her hair is red.*

CECILE GRANAT, *man's girl, but also something else.*

ED CORVO, *owner of the resort west of Fiddler's Fingers.*

ELLA CORVO, *Ed's wife.*

LOTTIE ELVESAETTER, *Ella's sister, occasional maid at the Fingers.*

DR. RUSH, *physician and coroner, who has work on his hands.*

PAAVO AAKONEN, *tenacious sheriff of Cook County.*

THE HEATON FAMILY

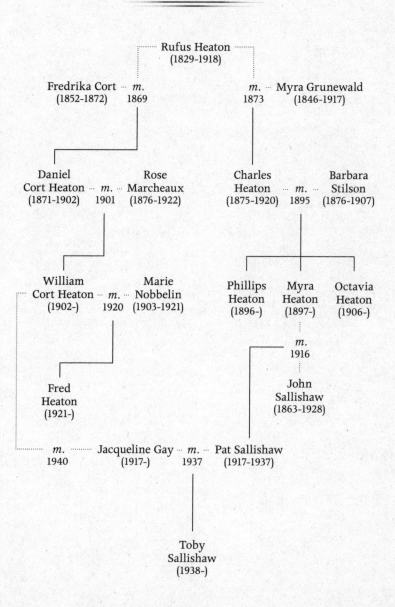

Rufus Heaton
(1829-1918)

Fredrika Cort — *m.*
(1852-1872)   1869

m. — Myra Grunewald
1873   (1846-1917)

Daniel
Cort Heaton — *m.* — Rose
(1871-1902) 1901 Marcheaux
                   (1876-1922)

Charles
Heaton — *m.* — Barbara
(1875-1920) 1895 Stilson
                   (1876-1907)

William
Cort Heaton — *m.* — Marie
(1902-)   1920 Nobbelin
                 (1903-1921)

Phillips   Myra   Octavia
Heaton   Heaton   Heaton
(1896-)   (1897-)   (1906-)

m.
1916

Fred
Heaton
(1921-)

John
Sallishaw
(1863-1928)

m. — Jacqueline Gay — *m.* — Pat Sallishaw
1940   (1917-)   1937   (1917-1937)

Toby
Sallishaw
(1938-)

1

OTHER PEOPLE MAY THINK they'd like to live their lives over, but not me—not if this last week is going to be in it.

Out of what has just happened at the Fingers, both Jacqueline and I got something worth keeping, but heaven defend me from ever again having to stand helplessly by while it becomes more and more apparent to almost everyone but me that the person I love most in the world is murderously insane. Heaven forbid that I ever again see a car moving like Frankenstein, of its own power and volition, carrying a secret burden into a lake. Or that I ever again grasp an arm and feel that rigid marble chill, or that I ever again have to look on while a blood-drenched shirt is ripped away from the terrible red hole a bullet makes in living flesh.

I never again want to know the panic of facing the evil of a mind so much more skillful than mine that even the signs we did see—the acid in a bride's toiletry bag, the burned matchsticks under a bed, the word scrawled with a child's blue chalk on rock—all just bogged us deeper in error and despair. I never again want to have a flying figure come hurtling at me from an unlit staircase, or wake in the morning to find my bathrobe slashed, or stand endless hours facing a door, fighting a vicarious fight. Any time in my life is going to be too soon for me to want to feel again that I'm a member of a looming last-man's club, with death walking hooded in the night, relentless and remorseless and successful.

Someone, I suppose—some Heaton—will live on at Fiddler's Fingers. But it'll be all right with me to be away from that particular slash of water, that particular brush of wind, that near-inhuman chuckle that came to sound like laughter.

THE FUNNY THING IS that even on the day I rushed up to the North Shore from Minneapolis, I was expecting trouble. Not the kind of trouble I got—just nice, ordinary trouble I could smooth over in a wind. Smoothing over my beloved cousin Jacqueline's troubles isn't entirely new in my life; we'd lived together since she was four and I seven. This second marriage of hers to Bill Heaton was bound to take adjustments, I thought, considering that she had a daughter of two and he had a son at the university.

Undercurrents of restraint had run through Jacqueline's recent letters, and then there'd been that out-of-the-blue note from Jean Nobbelin which had catapulted me in to ask my boss for a week's vacation. Two days after I got Jean's note—eleven fifteen on the morning of the Fourth of July, to be exact—I was clinging to the guardrail of the North Shore bus as it slowed for its Grand Marais stop. My neck cricked so I could peer through a window, my feet ready to get me through the door the moment it opened. One glance at Jacqueline, I thought, would tell me what was wrong and how much.

That girl on the bus seems awfully simple and unsuspecting to me now.

Just before the bus jolted still, I had an instant's glimpse—against a backdrop of sun-dazzled white cement, filling station, and blue lake—of what looked like a completely normal family group: Jacqueline in the fuzzy blue sweater and white slacks I'd given her for her Bermuda honeymoon, Bill in all-white flannels and almost terra-cotta skin and, down below, holding Jacqueline's hand, the pink, small, bouncing mite that was Toby.

Then the bus door folded open, and there was nothing between us but a heavyset woman with several suitcases. In an instant, I had Jacqueline's shoulders in my hands.

That was when dismay slid all the way down my interior like a liquid silverfish.

Over Jacqueline, like a fever, was what looked like shivering expectation—no, worse than that, fright. Her eyes were full of it, eyes so lovely you couldn't usually see anything except their loveliness, brown flecked against a green as dark as pine needles.

She laughed, she hugged me, she cried lightly, "Ann! We're so delighted! Your wire surprised us so!"

She didn't mean it.

I said stupidly, "What's wrong?"

Through all the insecurity of our childhood, we'd been almost one person; even that brief and tragic first marriage of hers to Pat Sallishaw hadn't separated us. But she was shut off from me now; she moved out of my hands, her eyes avoiding me.

"Wrong?" she repeated as if the word had no meaning. "But nothing's wrong, darling. Here's Bill and Toby . . ."

Her head, with its free-blowing dark hair, was thrown stiffly back. I stood caught in so much bewilderment that for an instant,

I didn't see or hear anything—foretaste of a state that was to become all too familiar.

Then there was a grab at my knees, and I had to tune in Toby, her hands puffing at my skirt, her small pink face impatient and demanding.

"Me! Me! I here!"

I bent to scoop her up.

Usually Toby can grab my attention and keep it—Toby, who's not yet three and who has funny, wispy, colorless hair sticking out in all directions like tangled petals on an aster. Toby, whose eyes are like Jacqueline's and who has the promise of Jacqueline's exquisite, full, bursting mouth. Toby, who's almost all that's left now of those five months when Jacqueline was Pat Sallishaw's wife.

The small arms gave me one immense return squeeze before the independent back inside the pink corduroy coveralls stiffened.

"I get down now," Toby decided, and slid.

A long brown hand slid in over her head as I looked up to the grin on Bill Heaton's warmly hued, imperious face.

"My turn." He shook my hand hard, the grin intensifying. "Ever thought about going in for pole vaults, Ann? You stepped clean o'er one fat woman and three suitcases, getting out of that bus. I'll bet I could get you in the next Olympics."

I babbled something.

Sunlight was blazing back from the white concrete of the filling-station driveway on which he stood; some of that light seemed to come from his easy, commanding strength. I suppose every woman thinks there must be a man like Bill Heaton somewhere if she could only find him. But when I looked closely at the face that was all smooth, brown-red planes meeting at the bold ridges of his brow and nose and chin I saw what was hidden under his jocularity. The corners of his wide, generous mouth were tight, and his eyes—darker and warmer brown than his skin—had been widened with shock.

Suddenly instead of seeing them as they were now, I saw them turning from the flower-banked altar in the living room of Myra's Duluth house on the tenth of May to face the people who had come to see them married. They'd stood caught up in a kind of shining, supreme content.

Eight short weeks to make this change.

AS WE DROVE EASTWARD the twelve miles from Grand Marais to Fiddler's Fingers, they made an effort to seem normal and casual, but I just felt more and more strongly that something strange was wrong. We sat all of us abreast in the one capacious seat of Bill's low old topless car, Bill driving, Toby's head bobbing at my elbow, Jacqueline at my right, staring silently straight ahead. With an impatient movement of his wide shoulders against the gray kid of the seat back, Bill began talking about the thousands of acres of cutover woodland he owned near Little Marais and near Hovland, about the crews he kept continually cutting the softwood as it reached the right size and the other crews who replanted. He bought wood from other pulp farmers, too, and what he could get from the government out of Superior National Forest; it was all dumped in Grand Marais Harbor to be loaded on his freighters, to go to Fort William and Duluth and Detroit, to become paper, matchsticks, laths, fence pickets.

I'd known he was a lumberman; I didn't listen very hard.

All my antennae hunted for the sources of disturbance. The countryside through which we passed drew little of my attention until after fifteen minutes of riding the car swung to the left, through the open wrought-iron gate of a tall spiked iron fence.

Jacqueline roused to speak the only words she'd said since we left Grand Marais.

"This is the entrance to Fiddler's Fingers."

Near the gate, round white birches grew in rings; after that, the car entered a grove of Norway pines so densely set that dusk seemed to close in. No green along the earth there—only the light brown of old pine needles halfway toward being resolved into earth again, dappled in moving patterns of light and shade. The pine stems swayed like huge black reeds, extending twenty and thirty feet upward before the branches were needled, in whorls like round green eyes against the thin blue sky.

My nose filled with the warm sun-heated pine smell that's as pungent as spice. When the car slowed to take the hairpin curves I heard for the first time over the hum of the motor the wilderness sound that was to be woven through all that happened—the rushing clash of treetops, the wind's rustle and swirl among pine needles, the crash of water against rock. The sound seemed in layers—overhead the roaring rush, down below an intense quiet, as if something in the forest listened for the sly, secret pouncing by which most of its denizens died so that others might live, listened for what might be a twig snapping under the paw of death, blood hungry and near.

Instinctively I reached across Toby for Bill's coat sleeve.

He grinned at me briefly. "See a bear?"

I answered idiotically, "I'd rather see than be one."

"Ann likes me." He patted my knee.

Jacqueline turned toward me, and for an instant there was contact; we'd long ago had a commune of perceptions—was my thought in her mind, too? But she turned away quickly; I couldn't tell. The car was swinging now toward the opening beyond a last rank of trees; with a suddenness of a picture whose covering has been ripped away, the Fingers and the lake were right in front of us.

I'LL NEVER FORGET MY first sight and nay first feelings about Fiddler's Fingers.

A clearing on the shore, with the restless silver-peaked blue lake filling the foreground, thick forest filling the background, with the huge square brown log house to the west and those dark rocks to the east. Those rocks—the five tall, jagged pinnacles from which the place got its name—dominated that first sight; they stood a little distance from the drive, crooked, looming, entirely too much like the grasping fingers of a gigantic hand.

I'd heard the legend from Myra—one of the Paul Bunyan yarns about a girl named Lily Lou whom Paul had favored. When Paul had gone on his long trips east and west, Lily Lou had found company elsewhere, so flagrantly that Paul at last had heard. He'd come back to find the girl at a lakeshore dance, waltzing in the arms of one of his own henchmen while his own favorite fiddler scraped out the tune.

What Paul had done was to beckon the fiddler to play on; he'd grabbed the girl from her partner and danced with her in a tempo quickening like storm, waltzed until the eyes of the watchers swam and the fiddler reached his breaking point. At the crest of range Paul had flung the girl, not even glancing to see who caught her. The fiddler, chuckling, had died in his last effort, falling, soaking into the earth like one of his own tunes. Only his right hand had stayed aboveground, the fingers reaching for the bow.

"Yaffs!" Toby pushed me, anxious to show off the marvels of the place, as soon as Bill stopped the car.

I'd heard that part of the legend, too, but somehow as I stood beside those rocks I didn't feel prepared for what I heard—the large, satisfied, silky gurgle that seemed to come from beneath the stones.

Bill, amused, said, "No need to look so startled, Ann. That's just an underground river bouncing around in its rocky caverns. It's not really Paul Bunyan's fiddler."

But what was making me look startled wasn't just the sight and sound of the Fingers—it was a feeling I had, a feeling of the wilderness, of which I seemed to be standing at the core; a feeling of being awed and exalted, because that wilderness was so beautiful, so mighty, so aloof. When I turned the lake was before me; this was Superior, the largest freshwater sea of the world; this steel blue water that lashed itself white against the harsh and rocky rim was water so old that it had brimmed lost glacial and preglacial lakes.

Much more clearly than in the car I heard the forest roar, the forest that began here along the lake and that I knew stretched from the head of the lakes at Duluth eastward and northward through all the great, lost, undiscovered reaches of the Laurentian Shield. This was the heart of what had once been an entire boisterous wild continent—primeval, bold, tumultuous, and dangerous. Wild animals were at home here. I could feel that only strong people ought to live here; weak people living here might find in their eyes the light, steady stare of the wolf.

This wilderness could rouse basic desires to be, to get, to do . . .

Perhaps in what was to happen, the wilderness was more important than anything else.

I managed to shake off some of that first overwhelming impression of the wilderness and its power, but through all that followed I was never quite to lose it. The house toward which we turned after a few moments was a huge square barrack of pine logs peeled and varnished until they shone like honey. Inset at the east side was one porch and across the entire front, facing the lake, was another. A terraced bank of flowers divided the lawn from the drive.

"That low building in back is the barn. Myra keeps cars in it now." Jacqueline pointed out two smaller buildings. "That other one west on the shore—there, half hidden by trees—that's the boathouse."

Toby had started on a run for the house.

"Gramma! Where is you?" she called as she went, and disappeared inside the front porch. When we reached there she was jumping up and down announcing loudly, "I go bafroom!"

Myra, rising, was hastily dropping her needlepoint in a chair and stooping to undo buttons with a practiced hand. She gave the exposed rear a small spank and came forward smiling as Toby scuttled into the house.

"Loveliest thing about Toby," Myra said, "she makes life so formal. Goodness, Ann, I'm glad you've come."

Wasn't there worry at the bottom of her dark eyes, too—a worry she was trying as hard as Jacqueline and Bill to cover? But what was uppermost as she took my hands in both of hers was her warm hospitality and friendliness; impossible not to like and admire Myra. She has some of the Heaton imperiousness—she's Bill's cousin—but it's an entirely feminine imperiousness; she's so delicate she might have been carved out of crystal by Lalique— white hair braided in a coronet around her small head, wide eyes that are deep and almost black, faintly pink-flushed skin. She's forty-three, young to be Toby's grandmother, but then Pat, her son, would have been young to be Toby's father—if he'd lived.

Young marriages, I'd learned, ran in the Heaton family. Pat

was nineteen, a sophomore at the university, when he married Jacqueline after knowing her exactly one week.

Making the best of things is one of Myra's characteristics.

Goodness knows she must have had long practice of it, being so long a widow and having her sister, Octavia, on her hands. The first thing I'd heard her say after Pat's marriage was, "Well, I can use more family," and she'd stretched that to include not just Jacqueline, but Aunt Harriet and me, too.

When Pat was killed that summer at the job he took—a dust explosion in a flour mill—Jacqueline and the coming baby became the core of Myra's life. Jacqueline is Toby's mother and has responsibilities such as discipline, but Myra and I just adore her.

Wry recognition of that weakness was in Jacqueline's eyes now as she glanced once again at Toby laboriously and hurriedly mounting the stairs inside. When she turned back, some of the smile had faded from her mouth.

"I'm *glad* you've come," she repeated, and it had an emphasis I couldn't mistake; she was worried and had an anxious hope that now I had come things might be cleared up.

"Not half as glad as I am to be here." I answered both the open and the hidden statements. I could see now what I must do—I must find out what it was Jacqueline hid before I could do anything else.

I asked lightly, "How's about helping me unpack?" It wasn't in Jacqueline, I thought then, to keep anything from me if I got her alone.

But the green-brown eyes just brushed me evasively. "We'll all help unpack. Toby loves unpacking. So does Bill." It was quiet, but it held her screened.

"Me, I'm a travel-bag addict," Bill said behind me, and I looked to see if he were being pleasant or helping Jacqueline evade, but this Roman-coin face didn't tell. He had one of my bags in each hand—bags he'd tipped a filling-station attendant to lift to the car at Grand Marais.

I'd have to play the game of casualness, too. "Hercules lifted the world," I said, "the Finns held off brute Russia for weeks, but *Bill* carried in *two suitcases*!"

"Remember this the next time someone tells you I won't even carry my own cigarettes." Bill started for the inside room, and I was following when Myra touched my arm.

"You remember Octavia?"

Hurriedly I glanced around, for the first time noticing the woman who sat in a corner bent above a magazine, but with her eyes lifted, watching.

"Oh, Octavia, I was hoping you were here!" I tried to make it warm and pleasant, going toward her to shake hands, but somehow the words came out too cheerful, as if she were a child I didn't know how to approach.

As usual when she was looked at, a spasm of agonized shyness contorted Octavia Heaton's face and the dark eyes so like Myra's sought wildly around as if for escape, then looked down at the magazine as if that were a refuge. I had to reach for her hand; she didn't lift it.

Poor Octavia! I'd never known anyone for whom I felt more thoroughly sorry. As far as I knew, there was nothing wrong with her, except that she was birthmarked—her upper lip was puffed and blue. She was somewhere in her thirties, fragile like Myra, and with smooth brown hair in an enormous knot low on her neck, not bad-looking, except for the disfigurement which seemed to have broken her spirit entirely. I'd never heard her speak as much as a word. Through the week I'd spent at Myra's Duluth house before the wedding Octavia had seemed to slide along the walls like a crumpled wraith, vanishing completely if any stranger came near. Only Myra treated her as if she were a person; other people found it almost impossible to remember she was around.

"Ann's going to have the southeast room while she's here," Myra told Octavia now. "The next one to yours. It's nice to have the house full, isn't it?"

But she expected no answer from the down-bent, still-agonized face. She turned, leading me back toward the door where Jacqueline waited. Bill had gone on upstairs to the pleasant pink-and-blue corner room I was to occupy during my stay.

Myra stayed below, but Toby, returning from the bathroom to be rebuttoned, joined Bill in nosing things out of my suitcase with the intimate, fascinated interest of a pup terrier. For her I'd brought a slate and colored chalk, for Jacqueline a black velvet evening cape with a hood and a scarlet silk lining—one I'd picked up in a clearance. With the surface gaiety she was using for her screen, Jacqueline put on the cape, pirouetting in it.

"Little Black Riding Hood," she said. "Does anyone like me?"

Bill should have answered—he didn't. Instead his eyes fixed on her, dark, inscrutable.

"I like you. I'll take you back if Bill doesn't look out," I began, and I wasn't just fooling, either. But she was standing still, pulling at the ribbons with fingers that shook, slipping hurriedly out of the cape and walking away down the hall with it, her head bent.

Bill turned abruptly to stare out the window until she came back, bright and animated again, to lead the way downstairs. I went, but what was growing in me then was anger. I was going to find out what the matter was, or else—

The upstairs at Fiddler's Fingers was to be fairly important in what happened. I can just as well show you its simple arrangement now.

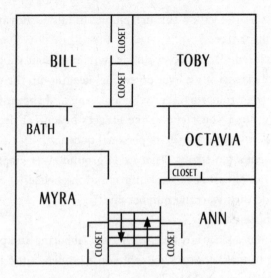

The moment we were downstairs Myra called cheerfully from the kitchen, "You're going to find out what a holiday's like at the Fingers, Ann. The maid's helping her sister at the resort, so we're fending for ourselves. If anyone would like to help set the table— and someone could go to the resort for roast chicken and ice cream—"

Quickly I grabbed at opportunity. "Let's you and I—"

But again Jacqueline was swifter, forestalling me, smiling her covering smile. "And leave Bill to set the table?" she asked lightly. "No, I'll do the table. You go to the resort with Bill, Ann. Toby can go along."

Frustration—another emotion that was to become familiar. I found myself, reluctant and mutinous, being maneuvered across the front porch where Octavia still huddled over her magazine, and on up the path toward the resort with Bill and Toby.

That resort path, which was to feel my feet so often, led across the narrow west lawn, past the boathouse, then up a little hill and down a little valley, through clumps of tall bushes and some ash and birch trees.

Bill offered, "Superior's cold for swimming, but we go along here to the resort if we ever do swim," keeping up the pretense that things were normal, but with a gloomy and absent face.

"Why don't you swim at the Fingers beach?" I detached a portion of my mind for the impersonal question.

"Current's too strong. That underground river empties into the lake out of that rock bank in front of the house."

"Wilderness warning number one?"

"Yeah. Don't try it."

Ours was a jerky advance, with Toby jabbering and pointing, stopping to look at a rocking robin on a branch, a red leaf on a strawberry plant, pebbles in the path; Bill paused once to wait, giving me a quick sidelong glance, and I got the feeling he held some pent-up question.

"Your parents," he said abruptly, "and Jacqueline's—they were drowned."

He couldn't have married Jacqueline without knowing that story. The antenna of my mind started hunting.

"Yes," I said, "on Lake Pepin. A quick storm came up."

"It must have been terrible. Young, happy people?" Not a statement; a question.

"Yes," I said. What I remember most about my parents and Jacqueline's is their laughter and their waving that day they drove off for the fishing trip, leaving Jacqueline and me with Great-Aunt Harriet, where we stayed.

"Remember your grandparents at all?"

Obscurely I roused to antagonism, as if my family were being attacked.

"Grandfather Gay kept a hay, feed, and grain store. He died in the odor of sanctity at ninety-two. Grandmother Gay was simply wonderful. Her barn had pigeons in it. We've got an uncle Frank running a mine down in Peru . . ."

Right then occurred the first of those incidents that were to add up afterward to such a heavy total.

Toby had pulled away from me when I stopped to glare at Bill. The next I heard of her was an outraged yell. She was about twenty feet ahead of us then, smack on her stomach, her heels kicking.

"I failed!" she wailed angrily. "St'ing falled me!"

I forgot about other things, running to pick her up. And then I, too, went to my knees, almost on top of Toby. Something had caught me just above the ankles.

"What—?"

Bill asked curiously over my head. "Why, it's a—"

"Wire." I'd twisted around to where I could see it. A thin silvery wire stretched tightly across the path, tied neatly and well to a tree on each side. "But someone must have deliberately—"

"Wire," Bill repeated. Then he was reaching for the snare, ripping it from its fastenings, stuffing it into his jacket pocket. His face—his whole head—had turned almost as dark as blackberry wine.

2

AUTOMATICALLY I GOT TOBY on her feet, brushing at the path dust that smudged her.

"Who would do that?"

He asked haughtily, "Don't you think I'd like to know?" As if his own question prompted him, he walked around first one tree to which the wire had been fastened, then the other, his eyes searching the ground.

"Not a footprint. This—" Then he seemed to swallow anger, striding away up the path, his back stiff. "Jokes like that make me see red. Let's get going."

I looked after him, confused. A joke, he called it. But he didn't himself think it was any joke.

A wire across a path—that seemed a kid's trick.

What leaped to my mind was the thought of Bill's son, Fred. He'd been at the wedding—a burly and unlicked young cub in his second year at the university. Apparently he'd felt toward his father's marriage the genial, worldly indulgence of a younger brother marrying off an elder. But jealousy is something that can grow . . .

I shook myself erect, telling myself that I must be mistaken. Whatever had happened must have some ordinary root, must be concerned with something normal, such as a jealous son.

I WASN'T TO WAIT long for fresh fuel for my confusions.

Toby and I got along slowly. When we reached the edge of the resort clearing Bill was striding along a row of small white cottages and then up a rise toward a porched white farmhouse set behind a few trees. As Toby and I emerged from the path I noticed a large boathouse on the shore, but its interior was dark.

We went on as Bill had toward the farmhouse, which had been made over into a summer inn by the addition of a wide porch. A few people were eating at its white-covered tables, but no attendant was visible. Toby, however, knew her way. She made straight for a door that opened into a kitchen, a dark room overfull of stove, kettles, tables, and two large pulpy women who stood facing Bill.

We were no more than inside the door before I sensed the distrust and wariness in that room. The elder woman—the one with a dark mole at her jawline and skin the color of sponge-cake batter—was jabbing with a poker at the burning sticks in the firepot. The other woman was basting six stuffed chickens in a long pan on the oven door. Her face was more firmly fleshed, and patches of red rode her cheekbones; she had a faded, somewhat frowzy youth.

Despite whatever their hands did, both women kept their hard China blue eyes fastened on Bill, who stood poised forward on the balls of his feet, his hands in his jacket pockets, his eyes fiercely questioning.

"What do you mean," Bill was asking, "you had something funny happen last night?"

No answer right away. The woman with the poker jabbed once more.

"Our boat got smashed," she said.

"Your boat," Bill repeated, and there seemed a heavy acceptance in it. "Where's Ed? I suppose he's down at the boathouse."

"He ain't inside here."

Bill left by the door through which we'd come. The women looked after him, quickly at me, and then at each other. The older woman lifted her thick shoulders in a shrug before she banged the stove lid down on its round hole and pulled a kettle nearer.

I began hastily, "I—we came over from Fiddler's Fingers for a chicken and ice cream. Mrs. Sallishaw—"

The chicken baster opened a grudging mouth. "Oh, you're the company they got. I'm the one helps over there—Lottie. I'll get the chicken ready."

As she bent to rummage for a kettle under a counter, I went on, hoping to get some reason into what I'd heard. "Superior must be a dangerous lake for boats—the shore's so rocky."

"Rocks didn't smash our boat." The older woman answered in just those few short syllables. Before I could ask anything more, they had me outside the door, the chicken in a lidded kettle in one hand, Toby by the other.

"You tell Mrs. Sallishaw I'll bring the ice cream and wash her up." Lottie closed the porch door behind me, definitely shooing me along.

But I found it impossible to go back, knowing so much and no more. "Ed will be down at the boathouse," Bill had said. Inside two minutes, Toby and I were at the boathouse door, staring in at the dim interior, which seemed lit only by water flashes glinting up from the slip and reflecting from the walls.

In some ways, it was like we'd come across a wake. Not quite as grave as that—perhaps more as if a beloved pet had died—a dog or a horse. Yet, of the four people beside Bill who were looking down at a boat in the slip, three were incongruously dressed for mourning; they were in bathing suits. Then I temporarily forgot the boat I'd come to see as the owner of one of the backs before me swung around, reached for a nonexistent handkerchief, and flushed from waist to forehead—visibly, since all he had on was trunks, and incredibly, because he was already so dark.

I didn't have to wonder anymore if I'd see Jean Nobbelin.

"Hallo, Ann," he said. "I heard you were coming. Nice seeing you again."

"Hallo," I said. "I remember—weren't you at the wedding?"

Very definitely, he'd been at the wedding; he was Bill's best man, a stocky young French Canadian, terribly black as to hair and eyes and very red as to skin, apparently overpoweringly fond of Bill and proud of being Bill's business partner. He was a good four inches shorter than Bill and much more heavily muscled, but in a good many ways, the two were alike—perhaps it was the wickedness of the slow white grins. Since I was Jacqueline's attendant, Jean had squired me to the wedding parties, and I'd been more nettled by him than by any man I'd known before; I'd felt I ought to wear armor when he was around—not too secure armor. But after the wedding I hadn't heard a word from him until that note had come.

Dear Ann, that note had read briefly, *Weren't you planning to spend your vacation with Jacqueline? Looks to me as if you ought to make it right away.*

As I looked into the black deep-set eyes so nearly level with mine, I was aware of two things: Jean still made me feel as if I needed protection, and he didn't want me to say anything about that note.

He asked, "What do you think of a job like this?" stepping aside, so my vision of the boat was unobscured. As he spoke, the two other people in bathing suits had turned inquiringly, a girl and a man. I recognized Bradley Auden, who'd also been at the wedding and who greeted me briefly. The girl was a stranger. All my attention had gone to the boat toward which Toby was running excitedly, pointing.

"Boat b'oke! Boat all b'oke!"

She was right—no doubt about that. The sides of the boat were shining and varnished. At first glance the boat had looked all right, but when I moved closer, I saw that its leather seat cushions were ripped to shreds, the seat springs and stuffing were scattered like chaff, the motor cover was bashed to splinters, and the uncovered motor dented and crumpled.

No lake had done that damage.

Malicious, willful destruction. What was going on here? What connection did this have—what connection did that wire across the path have—with what I'd sensed in Jacqueline and Bill? Because there was some connection—that was apparent in Bill now as he stared down at the boat with what looked like perplexity and despair.

"Who could have done it?" I asked. Fred was again in my mind, because Fred might explain Bill's attitude.

No reply—just a silence becoming thick and embarrassing.

Then a man's slow drawl came. "I'd sure like to get who did it, that's all I say."

The speaker was the man halfway down the boathouse—a man with a sword-thin, pale, harsh face and eyes the color of dark water, whom I was later to know as Ed Corvo, owner of the resort. He was sitting bent forward on an orange crate, his gaze on his hands. It was from him the emanations of mourning had come.

Subdued words from the girl in the South Sea–print bathing suit. "We were out in it yesterday. That was a darn swell boat."

"It's going to cost a lot to get her fixed." The boat's owner kept his gaze on his hands. "And she won't ever be the same."

He waited as if he expected some answer to come, but none did.

"I'm going to get the sheriff on this. I don't care who did it." This time the drawl carried, very faintly, almost respectfully, a threat.

To that, after another small silence, an answer did come. From Bill.

He said quietly, "That's right, Ed. Call the sheriff."

THE GROUP BROKE UP then; Ed Corvo, as if he had waited only this permission from Bill before he acted, going at once crosswise up the sand toward the inn; Bill, with his air of wrenching decision made, turning as if he were shaking off nightmare.

"Oh, you're here, Ann. Of course you know Jean and Brad. But Cecile—Ann, this is Cecile Granat."

Introducing her to me but not me to her.

The girl said, "Hallo," distantly and without glancing at me, as if she expected me to be unfriendly. She was definitely a man's girl—sleepy blue eyes, suntan, silky flaxen doll-like hair blowing around.

"Another girl is wonderful," I said. "Next time you swim, could I go along?"

As usual, an attitude like hers made me react perversely; only a girl who's been pushed around is that unfriendly.

"If you want to." She made it indifferent, linking her fingers with Bradley Auden's. "If we're going to eat before the food gets impossible—"

"Sure." Bradley Auden came awake with a jerk from his staring at the boat. He smiled at her, a recklessly handsome man of forty or so with a thin, slightly sunken face and graying brown hair thinned in two Vs like devil's horns at his temples. At twenty, he must have been a heart-cracker, but now there was a disillusioned look over his debonairness, and his eyes were tired—from looking at his own life perhaps. I couldn't imagine him turning down a pleasant temptation such as Cecile.

"See you tonight, Bill." The fingers linked with Cecile's tightened as he moved toward the door.

Bill went out with them. For a moment, I was alone in the boathouse with Toby and Jean, who moved with awkward hesitance toward me, as if he had something unpleasant coming and could just as soon get it over.

"I got the note," I said, low, and waited for the explanation. Surely some light should be coming now.

Reluctance seemed to writhe in him. "I just thought you ought to be here. Couple things happened I don't like."

"What things?"

He gestured toward the boat. "Stuff like that. I don't see any sense in it. I just don't like it."

"But what has this to do with Jacqueline? Is it Fred?"

I'd almost never seen him without the grin, but his mouth was a straight grave line then.

"You don't want any prejudices I might give you. Just keep a lookout."

"KEEP A LOOKOUT." WHAT was this? Added to my confusion and frustration there was now a growing sense of fright. There was something in Jean's tone, something in his eyes . . .

Quickly he was stiffening his shoulders and walking out.

When he reached the door and bright sunlight, his head ducked, as if the light was water he dived into. Bill stood alone outside; Bradley was walking toward one cottage, and Cecile toward another; Jean broke into a spring that caught him up with Bradley.

Bill told me curtly, "Don't say anything about the boat. I want to handle this." Then, as if he'd waited just for that, strode up the path toward the Fingers.

He walked so swiftly, Toby and I were soon left behind again, Toby chattering in a steady stream and making such strenuous efforts to help carry the kettle that we almost dropped the chicken on the path every twenty feet. As we went my mind seethed, but I didn't know enough then to get anywhere; I couldn't see the ends that must meet. Not until we reached the porch and Bill came to open the door did he notice the kettle and in swift compunction reach for it.

"Good lord, I didn't mean to let you carry that. I forgot it."

"We carry fine," Toby said for me tactfully, and burst off toward the kitchen where Jacqueline and Myra were. Octavia was still in her corner.

"Boat b'oke!" I heard Toby announcing intensely. "Boat b'oke!"

Jacqueline came into the living room to meet her, brushing her walnut-brown hair back, not glancing at me.

"What's Toby talking about?" she asked, and then, without waiting for an answer, began talking about clean hands for dinner. Toby kept on sputtering about the boat as Jacqueline took her upstairs, but Jacqueline, I think, didn't even hear. I followed Bill to the kitchen.

"Goodness, we thought you must be eating at the resort, you stayed so long." Myra looked up from the potatoes she briskly mashed. "Was Jean around? He could have had dinner here."

"Jean and Bradley Auden and a girl named Cecile Granat," I answered when Bill didn't.

"You don't know it, but you're gossiping," Myra told me. Then to Bill, "I'm glad to see that chicken. Just put it on the table. And hurry washing—we can eat right away. Ann, if you want to help you could wash at the kitchen sink . . ."

So I turned to the homely details of getting dinner on the table. One of the things I'll remember about those days is the way the necessary routine of life—meals, sleep, getting up in the morning—went on as a background to the other activities that held us. I even remembered Lottie's message and got in one question I'd wanted to ask.

"Is Fred up here this summer?"

Apparently Fred wasn't connected in Myra's mind with the trouble. She answered at once, "Oh yes, didn't you know? He won't be here for dinner though. He's out on a hike with some other young people."

The Fiddler's Fingers kitchen was big and dark, but what could be done for it in the way of working space and gray and watermelon paint had been done; the effect was homely and pleasant. I was at the linoleum counter, dishing up the mashed potatoes, when the bulk of an extremely short, thick man showed formless against the light glare of the side door.

Myra said, "Oh, Phillips. Ann, I don't think you've met this last member of my family—my brother."

Phillips came in, preceded by an aroma of leather and tobacco I recognized as a well-advertised man's perfume. He wasn't much like Myra and certainly he wasn't like Octavia. Maybe he had nice bones underneath, but it was hard to imagine him having bones; his pink, glistening skin looked full to bursting. White hair stood out all over his head like an unpruned bush. He didn't seem to look at me, but I got the impression that his browless round gray eyes had managed to take me in pretty shrewdly before he thrust a pink soft hand at me.

"Just a brother. No one bothers to say I'm a Heaton," was what he said negligently, in a thin, almost feminine, voice. "Bill's the only Heaton that counts nowadays."

I murmured something. What he was really looking at was the stuffing-plumped chicken Myra was lifting to a platter. He moved toward that as if the steaming, delicious fragrance pulled him with strings.

Myra commanded sharply, "Do let's for once have a whole bird on the table," as she held the kettle over the gravy boat, pouring out the thickened gravy.

He answered comfortably, "Don't be mean, Myra," and, with suddenly deft, quick movements of his hands, picked up the butcher knife to sever a wing.

At Myra's silence and compressed lips he chuckled, lounging to the doorway to lean against the casing, where he stripped the meat from the wing with dainty, snapping bites. When he was done, he threw the bones toward the sink. They missed, but he turned and went out the door, not even shrugging, just letting them lie there.

Ugh, was what I thought. So Myra didn't just have that sister on her hands—she had this brother, too. He looked like a beach-comber to me.

WHEN AND WITH WHAT results Bill would bring up the story of the smashed motorboat and the wire that tripped Toby—that question filled my mind as we gathered around the table set on the side porch. As the meal went on, however, it seemed that again I was to get little light on what I wanted to know; instead, I was to hear about the Heatons.

The atmosphere of personal withdrawal and strain wasn't diminishing; I could feel it in Bill at the head of the table, in Jacqueline at the foot, in Myra across from me, even in Octavia, who, to my surprise, slipped, wraithlike, out to sit at Myra's right—in Duluth she'd always eaten in her room. Only Toby and Phillips were exempt, and Phillips had an atmosphere of his own—apparently he set out to be deliberately annoying.

We'd no more than sat down before he began what for a startled moment I thought was going to be grace.

"For what we are about to receive we thank Thee, Lord— Heaton." He sat back in his chair looking at Bill, the crow's-feet of a smile indenting the padded corners of his eyes.

Pink deepened in Myra's cheeks. I guessed Bill must be paying at least part of the household expenses, but why shouldn't he, staying here for weeks?

"Don't let me spoil your appetite, Phillips." Bill remained cool, taking up his fork.

"Honestly, Phillips!" Myra controlled her exasperation.

Then to Bill, "You know how delighted—"

The grin appeared briefly. "Don't say it, Myra." It was affectionate, and he glanced at me.

"Has Jacqueline told you the big news—why we're here?"

Jacqueline hadn't told me anything. "No," she said.

"Myra and Phillips and Octavia have sold me Faraway." Some of the lines in Bill's face smoothed at the thought. He leaned forward to talk with the same enthusiasm he'd had about life at his wedding.

"Fiddler's Fingers is Myra's, you know. It was her husband's. Faraway is the Heaton estate—old Rufus Heaton's own. It's right east of the Fingers. Not a pine on it's been touched. Did you know there are just three private estates left on the North Shore, where the original white pines still stand, and those three estates are the Fingers, Faraway, and Auden? Wait till you see the lodge I'm going to build. That's why we're staying here this summer—so I can watch the building."

"It's going to be wonderful." Myra, too, lifted to animation. "Heatons living at Faraway again, and Toby and Jacqueline staying where I can see them every day."

With no idea in the world I was crossing a line—after all, it was the thought that would come into anyone's head—I said, "I suppose the original house has fallen to rack and ruin if no one's been living there."

Short dead silence in which everyone except Toby—even Phillips this time—stared down at the table.

Curtly then from Bill, "That house burned."

Jacqueline began explaining gently, "It was a tragedy, Ann . . ."

The stillness on Phillips's face broke into a chuckle as he resumed eating.

"Hear the music of a family skeleton rattling, Ann? You see, old Rufus Heaton, that most honored of our ancestors, married when he was forty or so and had a son. That son's name was Daniel, and that wife died. Rufus married again—this time what was, by all we know of her, really a very clever young—All right, Myra, I won't use the word. That wife had a son too—Charles.

"Somehow or other, Daniel got disinherited when he was sixteen, and, considering that Rufus had ripped half the trees of Minnesota from their outraged stumps, that was supposed to have put Daniel out about two million bucks. So, everything went along swimmingly until the year of our Lord 1920—old Rufus and his wife had died before that—when the house at Faraway burned down. Charles burned to death in that fire, and Daniel died soon after."

"He was burned, too, saving the pines," Bill added savagely, and I felt my mouth opening. *What about saving Charles?* was what I wanted to ask, but even I couldn't ask that. Under every word Phillips had said, there had been crosscurrents of hidden meanings and old stresses.

"In case you're a little at sea," Phillips went blandly on, "Daniel was Bill's father, and Charles was the father of the other lovely Heatons you see before you. Retributive justice, isn't it? Bill, of the disinherited Heaton line, comes up in the world, while we, of the favored line, go down."

"We aren't exactly starving." Myra obviously didn't like the conversation.

"But, ah, I remember the old days." Phillips paid no attention, smiling dreamily across the table. "Grandfather's heyday—what a heyday it was! I can remember the old boy standing on the banks of a flooding St. Croix. I was just a kid then. Grandfather was all of seventy. The river was full of logs and log rollers, with Grandfather yelling what he thought of them. After a while, he ran out himself. He was the best of the lot even then. He kept his log on the roll and himself on his feet. He had on patent leather shoes as I remember, and his thick gold watch chain dangled, and the cigar didn't even fall out of his triumphant, grinning face—a grin just like Bill's."

He went on to tell of a long glittering table at which he'd sat as a moppet of ten or eleven. Teddy Roosevelt had sat at his grandfather's right, the famous Roosevelt smile out-glittering the crystal. He told of the winter his grandfather had taken him east—Myra, too. They'd stayed at the Waldorf and seen the plays; the best hadn't been good enough for Grandfather.

As he talked, I began to get the feeling of the Heatons, what they'd been and what they were—proud, imperious, bold, lavish, a little remote, and scornful of lesser people. I could feel that,

whatever divisions there had been, there was also a family likeness and solidarity.

Against that union, Jacqueline was an alien, as I was, in spite
of her double relationship to it, because Pat Sallishaw, too, had
been a Heaton just one more generation removed than Bill. Toby
was listening, her eyes big. For the first time I realized with a
pang that Toby wasn't all Gay; she also was a Heaton; this past
of which Phillips spoke was part of her heritage.

"Well, hi-ho, *sic transit*." Phillips ended his recital with a
shrug. "We were punkins in those days."

The moment he quit talking, Toby straightened, anxious to
add her bit to the family conversation.

"Boat b'oke." She nodded her head violently. "Bill, didn't it
b'oke?"

Impossible not to notice her, with no one else talking.

Myra asked, "What does she mean, Bill? Boat broke. She's
been saying it ever since she got back from the resort."

"Oh," Bill said. He laid his fork across his plate, sitting back,
letting an expectancy fall before he told them.

"Some time during the night, some—person—smashed Ed
Corvo's boat. With an ax. Ed's getting in the sheriff."

3

AN INSTANT OF SUSPENSION, in which forks halted halfway toward plates, in which shoulders held taut, in which the sounds of the wild wilderness swept through the porch, and I seemed to hear, even at that distance, the chuckle of the Fingers. Only eyes moved from face to face—Jacqueline and Myra looking as if they wanted to cry out, denying that such a thing could have happened, Bill's eyes lit by fierce demand, Octavia's for a moment clear and open but quickly sensing my glance and retiring behind that contortion of embarrassment, Phillips's covert and small in his stuffed pink face, as if a drawstring had puckered the lids.

That was almost the only reaction. Eating resumed. Only Phillips asked a few politely interested questions: when had the damage been discovered, how bad was it, had Ed any suspicions as to who'd done it. Bill answered shortly and informatively, his downcast eyes dreary.

What had he gotten from that abrupt announcement? I couldn't tell.

My necessity to get to the root of things only grew. As soon as we rose from the table, I turned on Jacqueline.

"So far I haven't had a word with you." No reason why I shouldn't make it open. "I propose we go for a cousinly walk."

Quickly she began stacking ice cream plates, her eyes avoiding mine. "Wouldn't you rather just—? We could get up a table of bridge. Myra loves to play."

Quick awareness and approval of my purpose from Myra.

"Nonsense! Why don't you go blueberrying? Thrifty of me, but the berries are lovely this year—they're fun to pick. I'll get Toby to bed and help Lottie."

The men had stepped outside for smokes. I hadn't even seen Octavia vanish, but she was gone. Resistance stayed on Jacqueline's lovely mouth. She started to object again but then she looked at me and saw her stand was useless.

"All right. But we'll have to change to rougher slacks. We'll take Toby up."

Toby expects to be captured for a nap. She and I were both breathless by the time I had her high over my head where she could wriggle and squeal but didn't dare jump. Jacqueline had gone upstairs.

"Toby goes in the northeast room," Myra told me over the hubbub.

One door on the hall upstairs was closed, the center door on the east, which I thought must be Octavia's. Jacqueline was also in the northeast room, changing.

I began, "Toby could sleep in my room while I'm here."

Jacqueline held back her answer for a second. "Oh, we're not crowded. Fred and Phillips have rooms over the boathouse."

In the pause before she answered I had time to see that in addition to Toby's crib near the window, the only other bed in the room was a single bed, and that on the dresser were Jacqueline's tortoiseshell dresser set, her manicure things. None of Bill's things.

JACQUELINE WASN'T GOING TO proffer anything. She moved aloofly and dispiritedly on the way back up the drive toward the highway. Before I asked any questions, I set myself to quicken her pace, talking of Toby and Aunt Harriet, anything to loosen her mind from its fastness. By the time we'd crossed the highway and traversed another belt of pines, she was at least stepping and breathing faster. Beyond that second stretch of pines there opened a bumpy section of hillocks and swampy pools where the ground, the rocks, the hillocks were covered with low plants as dark and shining a green as holly, clustered with frosty blueberries until they looked like violets. For an instant, I felt dissociated. This must be the reality—this beauty and the sun warmth that lay along my skin like a flush, with the exhilarating chill air under the warmth. But tight beside me was Jacqueline's cold quiet to remind me of the other.

I swung on her. There'd never been any need for finesse between us.

"Look, Jacqueline, don't you think I can see there's something terribly wrong? What is it?"

She drew into herself as if her skin were contracting. "Bill and I've got to handle our own troubles. I'm sorry, Ann. I know you want to help."

"This isn't just ordinary trouble—I can feel it. How does that boat today possibly affect you? And that wire Toby tripped over—"

She made a wordless exclamation, her hands reaching for me. She demanded fiercely, "Wire? What was that about a wire and Toby?"

"If I tell you, will you—" But her eyes were so openly frightened now I couldn't bargain. I told her the whole incident.

"Against Toby." Desperation in her tone. "There's never been anything against Toby before . . . No, that must have been an accident. No one could know Toby would be along that path."

She started sitting down. Luckily there was a rock under her—she hadn't looked to see.

I sat down on my legs beside her. "If you won't tell me, let me guess. Is it something to do with Fred? Is Bill angry because you think Fred's up to these malicious tricks?"

She twisted her face aside. "Don't ask me. Please!"

"Or Phillips Heaton—it's not hard to see he's jealous of Bill. But why should that affect you so much?"

"Don't ask me."

I hunched closer without rising. "I won't stand for your being like this. Silly and—insane."

She gasped, "Ann! Don't say that! You don't know—"

Horror on her mouth then, but I drove on relentlessly. "Whatever it is, it's trouble enough to frighten you, to separate you and Bill."

"Don't ask me," she begged again, and suddenly her face went down to hands that rose to meet it. "I can't stand this! I can't tell you!" She began sobbing, her entire body shaken.

Emotion she couldn't control now.

Uncertain, frustrated again, I got to my feet. Where did I go from here? I wouldn't give up, because I couldn't, but I could see I'd have to get my information elsewhere.

I said gently, "Look. I'll walk one minute away and one minute back. Then we'll pick blueberries."

WE DID PICK BLUEBERRIES after I got back, scrambling over rocks, standing, squatting, sitting, even lying down, Jacqueline still wrapped in what held her, I in my resolves, although we talked casually enough. It must have been nearly five when, our pails filled, we started back toward the Fingers and the incident which was an unguessed mainspring for what was to come.

Jacqueline and I had worked eastward as we picked. Instead of going back to the driveway, we struck directly south through the pines, reaching the lakeshore some rods east of the Fingers beach. We followed the shore then, scrambling over rocks again, pausing to look out over the tumbling, pointed water that was darkening and dulling to gray now that the sun had swung westward, pausing again to pick harebells growing from the rock crevices. We each held a big bunch of the delicate lavender blue flowers when we rounded a rock and came abruptly upon the Fingers.

A long shadow flung out from the five jagged pinnacles now. As we walked into that dimness, the shadowed coolness closed around us; to my ears it sounded as if the chuckle underground were somehow allied with the bewilderments which seemed all that the brief six hours since my arrival had brought me.

When we passed the Thumb, the last of the Fingers, we came in sight of the group on the lawn.

Sometimes there's a way light strikes down, some contrast of color and shadow, that makes a scene in real life look too brilliantly set, like a play. That scene on the lawn of the Fingers was like that. The thick gold light of the late-afternoon sun came on a long slant, burnishing every object it struck but leaving behind those objects long, dark shadows, so that everything was in high relief. Behind were the encircling pines, merged by this light into a unified dark mass. At the side loomed the brown darkness of the house.

In the center of the half circle of golden-green lawn were the people, a bright, urban-looking group, lying or sitting on the clipped grass or reclining easily in beach chairs. Almost all there, the people who were so soon to go into the crucible.

Myra in white, leaning back in a chair of brilliant green-and-orange stripes, her needlepoint in her hands, but her dark eyes hovering lovingly over Toby, who sat cross-legged on the grass nearby, her head bent over the slate I'd brought, her hands busy with the chalk. In the next chair, Phillips lay with his hands clasped over his abdomen, his bushy white head turned toward Cecile Granat, who sat easily upright in another beach chair, her hand trailing within tempting distance of Bradley Auden at her side. A little apart, Bill and Jean Nobbelin on the grass, their knees hunched, their arms around their knees. Facedown on the grass in attitudes of collapse lay three more figures—two strangers. One I recognized as Fred.

Jacqueline called to the group, "Hallo!" Her voice, too, was brittle, as if, entering this scene, she had to play a part. "Blueberries! Flowers! Look!"

Toby, in a short yellow dress that made her look like a buttercup, bounced toward us across the grass.

"F'owers!" she squealed. "Me! Me!"

Jacqueline gave her some of hers. Toby flew back to push the flowers at people's noses—Myra first, then Bill. Jean, when she got to him, bit off a flower and chewed it, to Toby's halted bedazzlement.

Again that surface appearance of calm. Calls and questions as we more slowly approached.

"Get your pails full? Aren't the berries wonderful? What're

the flowers for?—Queen of the May? Come on and collapse—it's almost time for supper."

We lifted our pails to show the berries, wagged our flowers, called answers back. Bill had risen to get us chairs, and the three who lay facedown on the grass lifted their heads.

Fred asked lazily, "What's the commotion? Oh, hallo, Ann!"

"Hallo right back." I made it pleasant but brief, noting that he didn't greet Jacqueline. His face seemed sullen; the genial man-of-the-worldliness he'd displayed at the wedding was definitely not there.

The girl beside him had lifted herself to her elbows. "Hallo—you didn't see me at the wedding, but I saw you. I'm Carol Auden. You'll get to know me now." She was as bright as a zinnia, with a rust-print kerchief over sun-tangled red curls and flushed, bright cheeks. I guessed she could be a long-legged imp.

"Don't mind our lying around like this," she chattered on when I'd indicated knowing her would be no grief. "We three got up at six this morning and hiked. Now we're wrecks. Twelve-mile wrecks." She dropped her head on her arms again.

The other young man said, "So you're Ann Gay. I wondered who rated a name as nice as that." He ducked his head in a bow, still lying on his stomach. "Hi, Ann. I'm Mark Ellif."

Brown, smooth hair and a lean, pleasantly masculine face and body, someway mathematically clean and humorous.

"Engineer?" I made a guess.

"How'd you know?"

"That's what you look like."

"Not bad, Ann," Bill came in. "Mark engineers the insides of one of my boats. Does all right, too."

Myra offered, smiling, "Lovely how people have to introduce themselves up here. I'm ashamed but not ashamed enough to stir."

Octavia, I noticed, wasn't there; she'd be hidden from this company.

"Something should be done to greet the ladies." Fred was slowly pulling his bulk upright. There was a lot more flesh on his bones than there was on Bill's and more width in his heavy, mobile, unformed face. I could see what he might be like in middle age—portly and perhaps a trifle gross.

"Let's see now—what do I have to offer?" He went on heavily, as if he forced himself to it. "Queen of the May—no. How would Ophelia be? Or maybe Robinson Crusoe?"

Bill had returned to Jean Nobbelin's side. He straightened as Fred rose, his brown eyes flicking warningly over his son.

"Twelve-mile limit, kid," he said.

Fred paused, glancing at his father, but then he swooped up the white shawl that hung from the back of Myra's chair and the flowers I'd dropped on the grass. Mincingly, he stepped across the lawn toward the Fingers, where he struck a magniloquent pose, the scarf over his head, the flowers in the crook of his left arm. His voice came in a falsetto chant:

I'm monarch of all I survey!
My right there is none to dispute;
From the centre all round to the sea,
I am queen of the fowl and the brute.

There was a sudden immediate stillness against the slash of the lake, the brush of trees, the near-inhuman chuckle underground.

"*Queen* of the fowl and the brute"—that was Jacqueline he meant. Clumsily, foolishly, but with some strong inner compulsion, he was trying to express resentment. I was on my feet, but so was Bill, his whole face and body constrained and knotted, powerful and spurred to spend itself. Then in that instant, the anger was gone, swallowed in mastery of himself and the situation.

He didn't even take a step forward; he just spoke quietly. "You and I've gotten a little out of touch lately, Fred. I'd like it if we had a talk tomorrow."

Fred dropped his pose as if it had been peeled off. He stood still, bracing his shoulders back, his face smoothed from its hard smile. Then he flipped the flowers over his left shoulder and pulled the shawl from his head. He came walking naturally toward the group of us, his eyes on his father, as if only the two of them existed.

"Sorry, Dad," he said. "Talking to you tomorrow is fine by me."

It was then I found myself still on my feet, all my muscles ready for some kind of action, when the time for it had passed. With my first outraged resentment ebbing, I could see that Bill had done not just what was best for Fred, but also perhaps what was best for Jacqueline.

Jacqueline. Quickly I looked toward her, expecting her to be shrinking and stricken, as she'd been all day. Instead she was sitting bolt upright in her chair, awake and taut. I could almost see feelers reaching out from her toward everyone in that group. Startling, the change in her; she wasn't downcast at all.

I, too, looked then at the others—at Jean, staring flushed and embarrassed at his knees; at Cecile and Bradley Auden, with their lips still parted by amazement; at Myra, uncomfortable but with some of Jacqueline's speculativeness in quick, questing eyes; at Phillips, slyly watching as if he enjoyed a play. Carol's uplifted face stared at Fred with something of disgust, and Mark looked as if he wished he could hurry away.

More strongly than ever I felt the pull of concealed stresses and strains. It was as if all the hands there gripped a network of crisscrossed threads. Why didn't I feel that the trouble was explained now, that this was all there was to it—a jealous and resentful stepson? I couldn't. More surely than ever I felt there was something else, something deeper . . .

I was facing the house; in the center window upstairs something moved—not anything visible—just a play of light and shadow. Then Phillips spoke, his bushy wide head cocked amusedly.

"Better be careful, Fred. Good old Heaton custom—son of the first wife gets kicked out."

Bill swung on Phillips then. It seemed odd that anyone so imperious would hold his anger at that sly poisoned barb.

"If anyone besides Fred is interested, I've never made a will. I never intend to make one. Fred doesn't have to worry about being disinherited." Then he turned on the rest of us.

"That'll be enough of this. Fred's just a little upset. I can understand how he feels. Lottie should have supper ready. Let's forget this."

NO ONE CAN SAY we didn't try. Again there was one of those concerted efforts to make things look serene. As we all of us— except for Octavia, who stayed hidden—filed around the table Lottie had set for a buffet supper on the side porch, anyone watching us would have said that here were leisurely well-to-do people—lucky, enviable people—being gay and charming, not having a care in the world. Yet the stresses remained; Fred was no more than back on the lawn before he was in another skirmish— this time a small one with Mark Ellif.

When Carol Auden came out with her filled plate Mark was behind her; he'd been next in line. Fred was waiting behind two chairs, his plate on the seat of one.

"Got a place for you, Carol," he invited.

Carol answered casually, "Oh, sorry, Mark asked me to sit with him." She went past Fred to stand waiting, her chin lifted, while Mark hustled more chairs from the porch. Either she hadn't liked Fred's recent exhibition or else she just preferred Mark.

"Look at the gal," was all Fred said. "Gives me the go-by." He turned to Jean Nobbelin, the last to come out. "Chair here."

Jean quickly took in Carol, Mark, and—I was pretty sure—me.

"We ought to get in some tennis this week, kid," he offered, and sat down in Fred's chair.

Mark and Carol had a twosome conversation; Bradley Auden and Cecile made a chaffering pair, but over the rest of us talk passed like desultory hail.

"You girls missed something," Myra began, although the moment the words were out she looked as if she wished they weren't. "The Case of the Smashed Motorboat. The sheriff was here this afternoon—not that he got anywhere."

Phillips, again amused, looked over from the chair where he was rapidly emptying his plate. "Good old Paavo Aakonen! What you'd expect up here, isn't it? A Finn for a sheriff. Hot on the trail. Said his men were getting fingerprints."

"Don't undervalue Aakonen." Myra made a crisp return to that. "I've found them shrewd people, the Finns."

Bill began telling me about Finnish saunas which began with being steamed in a family or neighborhood bathhouse and ended with a jump into cold water—an ice-fringed lake if nothing else offered. Jean came in with hilarious reminiscences, but when that subject was wrung dry, talk again limped.

I said, "We ought to play games." Action is my bulwark against social discomforts.

It didn't meet with much approval. Cecile said, "Ouch!" and

Phillips seconded her with a chilly, "I never play games." But Jacqueline took me up swiftly.

"Yes," she said strongly. "Ann and I know a game. Ann can see blindfolded. She could pick out any one of you that came near her."

I gave her a look. Why should she choose, so instantaneously, that particular game? The year I'd been ten, I was zooming downhill on a toboggan—typical of my activities at that age—when the toboggan flipped me into a tree. The next year I'd gone around with my eyes bandaged, expecting to be blind. Jacqueline had spent that year at my heels. I can still hear her anxious, urgent voice, trying to keep me from looking at blackness. The game was one we'd played because my ears and nose had sharpened so I could tell people by scent and sound.

Fred's comment was, "Cats see in the dark." Apparently some of his animosity extended to me.

Cecile seized a pretext for being provocative. "I've often thought I felt things in the dark."

Bradley Auden came to attention with, "Who, for instance?"

"Cecile wouldn't know," Jean said. "In the dark, all cats are gray."

Carol Auden was watching her father with obvious displeasure as he laughed upward at the girl whose jade sweater gave the old answer to the old conundrum as to why girls wear sweaters. She got to her feet.

"I'll play." She undid the kerchief from her hair. "This'll do for a blindfold."

"It's not much of a game," I apologized, explaining. Jacqueline had risen, too. Together she and Carol arranged me in a chair back toward the trees, with the kerchief over my eyes. The spattering of grumbling and amusement died to whispers, and then there was only the lake's rush and the river's gurgle and the wind's sweep—and those other undercurrents.

"Ready now," Carol Auden called gaily. "Here comes the first."

It wasn't hard guessing no one else there would be wearing a French perfume which, if I'd been naming it, would have been called *Ouvrez la Fenêtre*. After Cecile, Myra—she'd be the one who used expensive lavender soap. No one strode over grass as swiftly as Bill. Jean Nobbelin smelled clean and warm, surprisingly like rock and earth; the boys were hotter, dustier, damper—Fred more so than Mark.

Then Toby said meekly, quite close, "Is me," and was hauled back to laughter. There was still an echo of a giggle following Carol Auden. Bradley Auden used Houbigant's. Then spice—that was Jacqueline. I'd forgotten until then that she used pomanders—small bags of spice—for sachets in her clothes. When I had only two senses, the scent came faint but clear, like a plum tree in blossom a block away.

I'll never forget that scent again.

Phillips came last. I remembered the aura of leather and tobacco in which he'd entered the kitchen that noon.

Carol came then to take off the kerchief, and there was a burst of clapping, with derisive guesses as to what my nose had in some instances told me. "Ann's smelling game," Bradley Auden dubbed it.

The moment the kerchief was off, I looked to Jacqueline, who was smiling a small, successful smile.

She said, "I think it may be comfortable having a detective in the house, don't you?"

4

FOR WHOM WAS THAT remark intended?

Her gaze was directed at no one, and no one answered her. Fred was sitting now beside Carol and Mark, the sullenness gone from his face, leaving it amused, awake, lazily curious. Phillips Heaton, at the back of the group of chairs, was glancing speculatively, not at me, but at the others—Myra indulgent, Cecile negligently tolerant, Bradley joking. Only Bill and Jean seemed to feel any meaning behind Jacqueline's remark; they were frowning slightly, and the dark eyes under brows were quick.

Almost immediately, there began a second, more decided brush between Fred and Mark over Carol, who had remained standing after the game, retying the kerchief I returned.

"Mother'll be waiting for me," she said. "I usually read to her in the evening. Thanks, Myra. Thanks, Bill and Jacqueline. It was a lovely supper."

I remembered that I'd heard Bradley Auden's wife was an invalid, crippled by arthritis.

Fred was quickly on his feet. "Here, I'll walk home with you."

"I am." Mark put it briefly, but there wasn't any doubt about his intentions. He bent to pick up two weather-beaten leather jackets from the grass. "Thanks for me, too, everybody."

"The hell you are!"

Fred's head was lowering pugnaciously on his neck. "I invited Carol on this hike. I saw her first."

Carol snapped, "Mark's taking me home!" She turned her back to march across the lawn toward the Fingers and the shore, her zinnia-bright head high and obstinate. Mark followed with long strides, catching her elbow to help her down the terrace.

Bradley Auden grinned, boastfully paternal. "No one pushes redheads around."

"That—" Fred didn't fill it in. He'd stepped a pace or two forward but halted, his face thunderous. Then he turned, shrugging.

"Don't lay any bets on Mark. I'll take care of him."

His father said evenly, "That should be simple. Your two hundred pounds to his hundred fifty."

Slow, chanting sarcasm. "But surely his strength is as the strength of ten, because his heart is pure."

Myra asked ruefully, "Oh dear, what will you other people think of Heatons?"

IT WAS SOON AFTER that we found the blue chalk gone.

Jacqueline turned to Toby with a cozy, "Lovely, it's bedtime," and Toby begged only to finish drawing a wriggly red line down the colorful tangle on her slate.

"I put in box," she agreed when that was done.

While she was rounding up her chalk, Bill and Jean were having a business discussion—I can remember that. Something about whether they should hold some pulpwood stock for a likely price now the Nazis had the Scandinavian countries out of the market. It was a warm argument, both men so lost in it they noticed nothing else, both of them sitting up fierce and quick, marshaling arguments like battalions. Yet they seemed without animosity, as if they'd follow amicably any decision made.

"One gone," Toby complained after a moment of hunting. "B'ue one gone." She held up the box, showing where one more chalk belonged.

"It must be under a chair, ducky," Jacqueline told her. "Mama'll look, too."

So first Jacqueline, then I, then Myra joined in the chalk hunt. Even Jean and Bill, Cecile and Bradley looked around where they sat; Fred had disappeared. The chalk stayed missing.

When, at Jacqueline's nod, I carried Toby off she was wailing at the top of her lungs.

"Need!" she kept insisting. "B'ue one gone!"

"If we don't find it, I'll buy you another in the morning," I promised rashly in that chalkless spot, but Toby clamped an inconsolable face in my neck and wept on. We tendered her a fancy bath with rose-geranium salts and a spongy Jiminy Cricket toy I'd brought for a later gift, but she slung the Jiminy Cricket at the bathroom water tank and later sobbed herself to sleep.

"It is odd about that chalk," Myra said then. "There were blue marks on the slate—she must have just had it. But no one would take Toby's chalk."

We were to find out about that.

JACQUELINE DIDN'T GO DOWNSTAIRS again after Toby was asleep.

"I think I'll go to bed now, too," she said. Her upper lip was stiff with fatigue, and her eyes under the long dark lashes were almost glazed.

Myra said good night and left, but I sat for almost two hours on the foot of Jacqueline's bed, talking. As soon as she sensed I wasn't going to ask questions, most of her aloofness went.

"I'll sleep now," she promised at last. Her arms came up to give me a quick hug. "Oh, Ann, it is good to have you here! Forgive me for being—unpleasant."

"Things'll come out somehow," I promised myself as much as her. After I'd dropped a kiss on her cheek I switched off her light and went along the hall to my own room, past the closed door behind which Octavia seemed to live her solitary life.

Undressing, I had my first chance at solitary thought. Through the day, one incident had seemed to succeed the other. Now I was alone it seemed again that what I felt so strongly in the presence of Bill or Jacqueline must be wrong; what was going on couldn't be odd and mysterious; it must be Fred that was the root of difficulty. Wouldn't his behavior on the lawn this afternoon support that? He'd been my first thought in connection with the wire across the path. Suppose he had some grievance against Ed Corvo that would make him smash up the boat—wouldn't that explain everything?

But why had Jacqueline been unwilling to admit Fred was the source of difficulty? And why did I feel things were so *serious*?

I went to bed but the moment my backbone hit the sheet I knew I wouldn't sleep. Through my head milled everything that had happened since I'd come, the words that had been said, the looks on faces . . .

In the end I sat up, inactivity becoming unbearable. I hadn't been able to get anything out of Jacqueline, but there was one person who should be made to see he owed me an explanation. Bill.

Moonlight lay in a long rectangle on the floor, and the air was chill. In slippers and robe, I padded out into the hall. Thin lines of light showed under two doors now—Octavia's and the room across from mine that I'd guessed was Myra's.

At the remaining door there was only the vague opacity of moonlight.

"Bill," I said at that door, low, so as not to rouse the others. When there was no answer, I felt for the light switch and turned it. The room sprang into color and solidity: big carved oak bed, with the spread still smooth, towering wardrobe against the north wall, wisteria-chintz draperies and chairs, nothing but two military brushes on the dresser. Undoubtedly that was Bill's room, but he must still be downstairs. So much the better; I'd rather talk to him there.

As I turned the light off, one detail caught my eye: the covers of the bed had been folded back at the top, revealing a bit of the board along the side, blackened and charred, as if at some time a careless occupant had set the bed afire with a cigarette.

But I wasn't interested in that then. Noiselessly I went on downstairs, glad now that the stairs were solid maple planks and didn't creak, into the black well of the living room. Only toward the front veranda was the darkness fringed with light, a faint echo of moonlight from the roofed and screened porch. Under the murmur of water and forest was the murmur of human voices, one of which I thought was Bill's.

But it was Cecile Granat who was talking when I got within hearing distance. Cecile, in anger.

"And you have the right to tell me what to do, too, haven't you?"

Then Bill, certain and cool as ever. "Maybe I just don't see you as a stepmother-in-law for Fred."

I LEFT, OF COURSE, as quietly as I'd come. It was no business of mine how well Bill had known Cecile before he married Jacqueline;

he'd never pretended to be a saint. Just the same, that bit of insinuated information didn't make me feel gentle toward him.

Grimly I waited at the foot of the stairs, interrupted but not deflected. A car started up. Quite soon after that Bradley Auden called, apparently from the driveway out front:

"'Cile, you on the porch? Ready to go?"

Three is a crowd. I moved back toward the veranda.

Cecile's answer was, "I can't wait!" Footsteps rushed across the porch; the porch door slammed.

My mind went over what I'd heard. It hadn't been hard to guess that Cecile was making passes at Bradley Auden; now it appeared she hoped to make those passes legal. "Mother'll be waiting"—Carol had hurried home after supper to the crippled woman who waited at Auden, but Bradley hadn't.

Crippled wife against Cecile Granat. And what attitude did Bill take? "Maybe I don't see you as a stepmother-in-law for Fred."

I was so busy thinking, I didn't hear him come; Bill almost knocked me over. He, too, lost balance, clutching at me to right himself.

"Who—?" His hand passed over my face. "Oh, Ann. Good lord, what're you doing here in the dark?"

"Looking for you," I told him levelly. "I'm Jacqueline's cousin, in case you don't remember. I'd like to ask a few questions."

He said quickly, "Come out on the porch where we won't wake people." He piloted me, with a hand at my elbow; apparently he, too, knew his way in the dark. On the porch he turned me to face him.

"All right. What is it?"

"That's what I want to know. What's making Jacqueline sick and frightened?"

He stood silent, the moonlight faintly etching his face—skull outline, bold socket arch, nostril flare, mouth. When he spoke, it wasn't to answer me.

"Listen, Ann." His tone was slow, uncertain, low but still intense, as if he were hungry for the answer. "There hasn't been—the people in your family have always been—*all right*— haven't they?"

Nothing happened in my head. My family *"all right"*? My mother, laughing as she packed the picnic basket . . . Aunt Ellen and Uncle Dick leading Jacqueline down the front steps of their house . . . Why did my mind go back to that day of disaster? Aunt Harriet, a little remote because she was so old, but gentle, holding my forehead when I had the whooping cough . . .

"All right?"

Then in one instant, I knew, knew I'd been sensing right all day, knew what he'd meant when he started asking me about my family on the way to the resort, knew what the sickness was behind Jacqueline's eyes.

I went up like a rocket. Bill didn't think Fred responsible for those tricks—he thought . . .

"You!" I said. "You dare to think Jacqueline strung that wire, wrecked that boat!" I was talking before I could possibly have thought out what to say; words spouted—I didn't know what words. When I slowed, Bill was backed against the railing at the west end of the porch, my right hand flat against his chest.

"I suppose you think Jacqueline has to *stay* married to you!" Fresh anger spurted in a geyser. "She's leaving here this instant! We'll divorce you so quick you won't even know what—"

"Ann, wait!" He managed to get his voice above mine. "I don't suspect Jacqueline. I just want the reassurance—can't you understand that? I've been faced with the most impossible—"

"My family is so sane," I said, "Jacqueline is so sane—"

I couldn't think of any comparison. "There's never been any

but the most levelheaded people in our family from the days of Magna Carta on. We—"

"Ann, I believe that's true. Of course. I feel it's true—" What I said might have been manna out of heaven. He put his arms around me, hugging me, all the hard strength of his body tight against mine.

Behind us a gasp. Myra, with long white braids hanging down the shoulders of a dark robe. She asked in stupefaction, "Bill—Ann—I heard your voices upstairs—what's—?"

Before I could pull myself free Bill was already answering her.

"Jacqueline. I'm sure now she isn't responsible for what's been happening. I'm going to get to the bottom of this business." He was like a projectile ready to be loosed.

"But that's what I've been telling you all along." Relief loosened Myra's face. She came closer to shake Bill's arm. "That's what we've got to start from—the belief that Jacqueline *isn't* responsible."

"All right," he said. "You get any new explanation today?"

She spread her hands. "How could I? You know I don't—"

My fury hadn't died. "I don't suppose it's entered your heads that Fred might be responsible. He's only too obviously jealous."

"Fred?" Bill asked as if he couldn't believe his ears, and his stare grew hard. "Look, Ann, Fred may be jealous, but there's no small meanness in him. He's no more capable of playing tricks to put Jacqueline in a bad light—"

At that reminder that Jacqueline had somehow been made to look irrational, I boiled again. No wonder she'd cried out when I'd used the word *insane* that afternoon.

"Jacqueline isn't staying here to be put in any bad light," I said through my teeth. "I'm taking her home to Minneapolis now. This minute. Even if we have to borrow your car. We're leaving!"

Every muscle in Bill leaped to battle. "I won't have my wife taken—" But then he just looked at me, his body relaxing. "Of course, that's the thing to do. Take Toby and Jacqueline away. Not tonight—they're asleep. I'll drive you in to Duluth tomorrow."

Abruptly he jerked his head back and walked off the porch.

LEFT TOGETHER, MYRA AND I stood watching his shadow recede swiftly toward the lake. The first sound was Myra's long exhalation of breath. Her arm came along my back.

"Ann, you're like new hope. Why didn't I think of that before? When Jacqueline's gone and things still happen, that will be proof she has no connection with them."

I was reluctant to wait until tomorrow but I saw reason in Bill's decision; Jacqueline had been awfully tired.

"Myra," I asked, "what happened before I came?"

She answered hesitantly, "I think perhaps Jacqueline should tell you . . . There've just been some tricks that will turn out to be nothing but silly malice—I'm sure they will. And don't think too badly of Bill. It's going to be terrible to have Toby and Jacqueline gone, but do as you say. It must be done for safety."

No one had to beg me.

We went together back toward the beds from which we'd risen. At the head of the stairs Myra's door was open on her lighted room, and the thin line of light still showed from Octavia's room.

Myra gave a small exclamation, walking forward to her sister's door.

"I almost forgot." She turned a key, which was outside the lock. "Octavia sometimes walks in her sleep. She likes to have me lock her in. Even out here where we're alone, it wouldn't be safe for her outside her room, with the current and the sharp rocks along the shore."

She came into my room with me to tuck me in. It was while I was sliding my feet out of my slippers that I noticed my window was closed and turned to open it. That window gave on the Fingers and the east lawn. I paused a second, looking out through the pearly night to the vague loom of those five tall rocks. As I did so, I became aware again of the reach and pound of the lake, the brushing clash of the pine tops, the ceaseless low chuckle of the river underground. In this light the rocks were distant, curtained as if by veils . . .

In that vague distance, something moved, something as dark as the rocks but smaller.

Suffocation in my throat, my body stiffening—how quick fear was to rise!

"Myra!" I whispered. "Look!"

She was beside me, her eyes following where my finger pointed. Unmistakably I saw again that curiously elongated form moving, merging with the Fingers.

Myra said, "Why, there is someone!" And in her voice, too, was quick fear of the thing that walks unknown in the night. But then she gave a little gasping laugh.

"It's Bill. We know he's walking around somewhere."

Slowly the tautness eased out of my body. No sight of moving came again, but of course she was right—it had to be Bill.

"You don't know how *safe* things are up here." Myra was quickly over her first start, reassuring me maternally. "Into bed with you, youngster." She propelled me firmly to that haven, doing a thorough job of the tucking in, pulling up the extra blanket from the foot.

Even after that, I stayed long awake; the uneasiness I'd felt at seeing that dark figure wouldn't entirely die. It seemed an omen . . . And I had plenty else to think about, little of it pleasant.

Of one thing I was certain. The next night Jacqueline and Toby and I would not be sleeping in this house.

SOMEHOW ON THAT LAST comforting thought I fell asleep, to wake only hours later with the quick start you have at a sudden unexpected sound or movement in the night.

Was it sound, or was it movement?

As I lay waiting for realization, it seemed more a movement than a sound. As if my bed had moved.

I asked, "Jacqui, do you want me?" this time not frightened. The room was dark now, completely dark. No moonlight; nothing around, except the wilderness sounds.

Then again, the faint waft of motion.

5

―――――

"I'M AWAKE, JACQUI," I said again. "What is it?"

Again, I thought something moved, retreating. I was by that time sitting up, scrambling to my feet, drawn toward that retreating motion. "Jacqui, what—?"

Then it seemed the motion was gone.

I groped toward the door and the light switch. My room, as Bill's had, sprang into reality. Empty, except for me. The door beside me two inches from being closed.

Had Myra left it that way when she went after tucking me in?

I'd wakened so quickly I was still partly bemused, unsure. I looked in the closet, behind the chair. Had I even been certain the bed moved? Or had I been having a nightmare—a result of the state of mind in which I'd gone to bed? Why had I waked thinking it was Jacqueline in the room?

I could quickly find out if she had been.

Without further thought, slipperless, hugging my arms across my chest against the cold, I hurried down the hall where no lines of light showed now. Jacqueline's door was ajar as mine had been, but moonlight lay clear on the floor there. In the intense hush under the wilderness sounds, two near sounds of breathing were clearly audible: Toby's silken and slight, the inhalations quick and distinct, the exhalations slower, quieter. At my left Jacqueline's breathing was almost like a faint sigh. Soundlessly I moved to bend above her.

She lay on her side, cheek down to the pillow, one arm flung up around her dark tumbled hair, as if she'd cried herself to sleep. I caught the scent of spice.

I whispered, "Jacqui."

Surely she was asleep; she couldn't counterfeit that relaxed flow of breath.

As soundlessly as I'd come, I went back to my dark room. I called myself, going back, all the kinds of idiot there are. Once I had thought for them, I realized the maple planks were ice under my feet, and my skin was so contracted by cold it had difficulty holding my bones.

I shut my door tight, wishing it had a key, and then in surprise seeing it did have one. I turned it. Now if I went on hearing and feeling things I'd be able to give myself the lie. Then, with my fingers on the light switch, I halted.

Moonlight in Jacqueline's room, none in mine . . . I could see why. The pink-and-blue chintz curtains over the windows here were pulled snugly close.

Myra hadn't pulled those curtains after she tucked me in— the certainty was in my mind at one leap. Who had? Could she have thought the moonlight would make me wakeful and come back? What other reason could there be for closing them?

The room looked otherwise untouched. Certainly no one was

in it now. My dresses hung in the shallow closet. The dresser drawers were closed—I'd have surely heard a drawer opening. Along the foot of the bed lay my pink robe . . .

My teeth settled together, all ready to chatter. In one motion I turned the light switch and dived through the quick dark for the bed. From there I reached to pull the nearest of the curtains back so a little moonlight would come in. Myra, I thought, must have come back to pull those curtains—perhaps long before I waked. Then the movement had stayed in my mind and finally roused me.

Only—what had made me think it was Jacqueline in the room? Relaxing into my pillow, I shut my eyes, wakening my ears, my nose, trying to recapture that intangible message which approached, then eluded me. Almost as if—yes, almost as if there were still in the room some faint echo of spice.

What of that? Jacqueline had helped me unpack; reasonable the scent might linger. She might have slept here, even, previously. On that I sent myself to sleep.

So it wasn't until I woke again to the clear bright light of day—realizing sleepily that, with all the alarms and excursions of the night, I'd slept late and that I must hurry, because today I was taking Jacqueline away, and she didn't even know yet—that I reached rather blindly for my robe at the foot of the bed, and as it came toward me knew even before I looked at it that something was wrong. Then I sat stupidly staring.

The thing was in ribbons. Slashed. All that lovely salmon-pink woolly fabric cut as if with a razor—again and again, so that when I held it up the cut bands eddied out like pennants.

I threw on clothes, in my mind the most stumbling, incoherent thoughts I'd ever had in my life. Wanton useless destruction. Yesterday that boat, today my robe. And the person who'd done it had been in my room as I slept, ripping and slashing.

That dark moving figure I'd seen near the Fingers—suppose that wasn't Bill? Suppose—No, that must have been Bill.

The robe lay where I'd dropped it on the bed, a pink puddle among the blue tufts of the candlewick spread. The questions to ask were the reasonable questions. Who had been in my room, and why? I hadn't been injured; I hadn't been touched. Quickly I fingered over my clothes in the closet, the dresser. Nothing else had apparently been touched. Why cut that robe? It must mean something. What? A warning to leave? But I was leaving . . .

Bill and Myra knew, but others didn't. Fred didn't—Fred, who might certainly want Toby and Jacqueline gone.

As I zipped on a sweater, I tried to place Fred behind this subtle, menacing trick. Fred was a horned bull, determined but clumsy and blundering. Phillips might be subtle . . .

Suddenly I didn't even want to know the answer. I just wanted to get away, taking Jacqueline and Toby with me. As I sped down the hall, the morning chill seemed a part of some unwarming chill inside me. Octavia's door again was closed, but both Myra's and Bill's were open on empty, tumbled beds. In the bathroom the shower was running, an odd, ordinary sound.

Jacqueline's door, too, was open, the room empty, the blankets tucked around the hollows in the beds.

"Jacqui!" I called as if I expected no answer, but her voice came back from the bathroom.

"Ann? I'll be right out."

I took a deep breath, settling myself. No use going into a panic; we'd soon be out of the way. I called again, casual this time.

"Where's Toby?"

"Didn't she come in to you? She started for your room."

At the head of the stairs I called, "You down there, Toby?"

"I eat now!" came instantly and loudly.

"She's waiting breakfast for you." Myra's voice came up, too. "Don't be long."

Smell of frying sausages and buckwheat cakes, sound of Toby's running feet. Again I felt dissociated. That was the way the world was; it couldn't be that other way, with Bill asking about insanity, and my bathrobe slashed.

But it was the other way.

Jacqueline was still in the shower. Impatiently I went about her room, pulling up the blankets on the beds, hanging up Toby's sleeper, straightening the dresser top.

In the mirror, strangely, appeared my face. It might have been the face of a stranger's ghost—the ghost of a tall girl, thin and brown, staring at nothing out of brown eyes, her one hand hovering over the dresser top.

Then slowly I looked down again to what I'd seen. Jacqueline's manicure scissors. Caught where the blades joined was a tiny tuft of salmon-pink silky wool.

JACQUELINE'S VOICE BEHIND ME. "Admiring yourself, darling?"

She stood smiling at me through the glass, her hair the color of walnut wood sparked with light, her brown-flecked green eyes morning fresh, her blue robe that was the twin of my pink one snugly belted around her waist. Affectionately she brushed her cheek against my shoulder.

She must have felt then that I was trembling.

"Ann! What's the matter?"

I swallowed hard, fighting. *"Your family all right"*—it was a whisper in my ears to which I couldn't listen.

"Look." The word came harshly, because what I wanted to do was traitorous—I wanted to tear out that wisp of silky wool and roll it in a ball and not tell her, ever, about my robe. "Last night while I was asleep someone came in my room and cut my bath-robe to ribbons."

She said, "Oh," retreating, her face becoming a mask from which the eyes stared at me blankly. Then after a long time and as if the movement hurt, she looked down at the dresser top.

She said, "Your pink robe," and with one quick gesture caught up the scissors and ran to my room, where she held the scissors against the slashed fabric, her hands shaking so the scissors shivered against the pink. There couldn't be any doubt; the fuzz in the scissors was from my robe.

She dropped robe and scissors both, turning to me weakly, helplessly.

"Ann, I can't remember. Do you think I've—gone insane?"

Admitting at last the dark doubt Bill had held against her.

Suffocation in my throat again—not fear this time, but tight, swelling anger. My hands took her shoulders, shaking her.

"Get your senses back! You know you didn't cut up that robe! You didn't tie the wire across the path or wreck the boat! Some-one is—"

Stark dread shrouded her face. She gasped, "I do know. I know I didn't. It's only sometimes—"

When my hold on her loosened, she sank until she sat upon the bed, but her eyes stayed on my face. "It's been so awful," she said tonelessly. "I haven't known what to do." All the defenses, all the evasions she'd kept against me yesterday were gone now.

I commanded, "Begin at the beginning and tell me."

She said in the same dull voice, "It began on our honeymoon. In Bermuda. Bill went to a suitcase to get a pair of white shoes. When he took them out they were like"—her hand gestured to-ward the robe—"that. As if someone had cut the leather in strips with a knife. Bill was—he was furious. He likes his clothes. He likes everything he owns."

"So he jumped to the conclusion you'd ruined his shoes."

"Oh no. He thought it was a joke, because he was married. He thought someone at the wedding had done it."

Something on which I could pounce. Awareness rose—no use having her tell me things unless I could see through them to the motive and perpetrator.

"Then he hadn't looked at those shoes since he left Duluth."

She shook her head. "They were with some clothes he'd brought just for Bermuda."

"Anyone could have tampered with that suitcase. Go on."

"The next was worse." Still no emotion in the voice. "We were dressing for dinner. Bill went to the closet to get a suit, a gray tweed suit. It was one he'd worn, even there in Bermuda. It had just come back from the cleaner's. It had big holes all over."

"That must have happened at the cleaner's." Strength was getting back into me and a grimness that was something new for me in grimness. "Don't tell me Bill didn't—"

He had the hotel valet in, who said he'd hung the suit in the closet that morning while we were out; he said the suit was all right then."

"Lying. If Bill let it go at that—"

"The valet looked frightened, and Bill kept asking questions. He found the valet had his own dry-cleaning shop on the side. Bill talked to the other two men who worked there; they both swore the suit was all right when it left the shop. But they looked frightened, too, and Bill didn't believe them. The hotel manager made them pay Bill half the price of the suit. Then the next afternoon—"

Her voice dragged slower. "I'd been so happy. Those two things had happened but they hadn't really touched me. I was sitting at the dressing table putting polish on my nails. Bill sat by me, fooling with the bottles in my toilet kit, smelling the cold cream and saying it was lard and perfume, smelling the nail polish and saying it was varnish. Then he took out another bottle and held it to his nose, and his eyes widened in shock. He asked, "What's in this one?" and I couldn't even remember seeing the bottle before. He pulled out his handkerchief and tipped the bottle so a little of the clear liquid ran out, and the handkerchief turned brown, and most of it disappeared."

I said, "Jacqui," and my voice had become clipped and mechanical, too. "Acid. Someone must have put that bottle in the kit before you left. Like the shoes."

"But the suit—how did the acid get on the suit? Bill had been wearing it."

"You know you didn't put acid on any suit!"

"I said so, over and over, but Bill stayed white and—away from me. He went out of the hotel—he was gone for hours. When he came back he put his arms around me, asking if he'd done anything to hurt me or make me dislike him. He said I mustn't take—ways like that—to get even with him for anything he might have done. As if I were a child. And it wasn't true. He'd been—I'd been so happy I sometimes thought I couldn't be alive."

There was a grief I couldn't bear under her tonelessness. "There has to be an answer. Who did you know there? Who came into the room?"

"The valet. The chambermaid. The bellboys. Some people we knew casually. After a few days, Bill got almost all right again. He said he believed me—he said it must have been a trick or an accident. But when we left he gave that money back to the valet. Without saying anything, as if it were a tip."

"You're certain no one from here was there. Fred or Phillips—"

Again the shaking head.

Cold air swept at me. "One other person was there. Bill."

That roused her. "Oh no. It wasn't Bill. If you'd seen him you'd know."

I had seen him—when we found the wire across the path, when he looked at the motorboat. No, he hadn't looked as if he were seeing his own handiwork. He'd been angry, bewildered, hurt, as if someone he loved were torturing him.

"Besides," she went on forlornly, "why would he want to?"

"No," I repeated. "Why would he marry you just to—? It wouldn't be sane. And Bill is sane. As sane as you are."

I caught her hands. "Anyway, it's over. You and Toby are—"

She interrupted. "But it isn't over. That's what I've begun to feel. Ann, I have the oddest feeling, as if—"

She was looking at me steadily, and, as so often in our lives, our connection brought unspoken understanding, but I felt a different emotion as well. It swept over me, overwhelming; I felt as I had yesterday when we drove in through the pines, as if I were in a shadowed forest. Only now the dark shapes bore no leaves; they were the strange, incomprehensible forms of happening and circumstance. I felt that same waiting, as if somewhere in that dark forest something waited for the pounce, as if soon a twig would snap under the poised foot . . .

Then the emotion broke, because Jacqueline was talking again, quickly, as if she wanted to get the rest poured out.

"That's all until we got here to the Fingers. Then—"

"Wait." I couldn't make the transition that fast. "You mean nothing happened on the boat coming back? And you spent a week at Myra's in Duluth—"

"Nothing happened there."

"Did you or Bill tell about the incidents when you got back?"

"Bill jumped on Fred, wanting to know if he had been responsible. On Jean, too, and Phillips and Bradley Auden. But on Fred the most."

"I take it no one admitted anything."

"That's what seemed to start Fred being difficult. He said to me afterward, 'Maybe you think you'll get somewhere setting Dad against me but you'll find out.' He'd been having other arguments with Bill, too. Bill wouldn't let him have a car, because he'd had an accident with one a year ago and hurt a little boy."

She looked down at her hands linked with mine.

"The next incident was the first weekend we were here at the Fingers—the weekend of June fifteenth. Fred hadn't come up from Minneapolis yet. Myra drove to Duluth that weekend, and Octavia and Phillips went with her. Bill, Toby, and I were alone here. Saturday night we went to bed about eleven o'clock. We were all in the room Bill has now, with Toby's crib in the corner. Bill made a joke and locked the bedroom door.

"About two o'clock, he woke me up. The room was full of smoke. I got Toby, and Bill pulled the door open. When we got out in the hall there was no smoke there. Bill ran downstairs for pails, and we filled them in the bathroom and came back and switched on the light. We'd been so bewildered we hadn't even thought of the light. When we could see, we found it was the bed that was burning—the mattress. Bill got it out right away—it was only a small fire for so much smoke.

"I'll never forget. Bill stood, with the pails in his hands, staring at the bed and the smoke still in the room. He said, 'There's no one here but us.' It sounded as if he were fighting for his life. And I felt as if I—didn't even want to fight."

She'd been bewildered and lost; she was that again, even remembering.

I said swiftly, my mind foraging, "That fire must have been set before the others left."

"They'd left Saturday noon. The fire was more than twelve hours later. If there'd been fire we'd have smelled it when we went to bed."

"Lottie."

"She was at the resort."

"The resort of Auden, if it comes to that. Anyone could have come in—"

"The bedroom door was still locked. Bill looked for marks of ladders under the windows or for signs in the logs if anyone had climbed. There wasn't anything."

"But it must have started somehow."

"Bill found two partly burned matchsticks under the bed. He said, 'And maybe they came from pulpwood I cut.'"

I sat helpless, wanting to see an answer harder than anything I'd ever wanted in my whole life but unable to see any light.

Jacqueline twisted her hands from mine. She said, low, "It is possible, isn't it, for people not to know what they do? I keep thinking, *suppose I should hurt Toby*—"

Suddenly she'd twisted around; she had my robe and the scissors in her hands; she cried, "Look, Ann—look, I could take your robe like this and push the point of the scissors through! Look, it cuts so easily, as if I had a razor blade!"

At once and on instinct I slapped the scissors out of her hands, grabbing them up, tearing out that telltale wisp, rolling it between forefinger and thumb until it was a characterless pellet, throwing it.

"That's enough! Your door was open last night—anyone could have walked in to take your scissors!"

But her voice was hysterical over mine. "I could have done the other things, too, couldn't I? I could have wrecked the motorcycle Fred got and I could have cut up Myra's dress and Phillips Heaton's pajamas and Octavia's magazine she hadn't read. Everyone's had something done, except me. I—"

I shook her to break it. "Listen! We're getting away from here! You're leaving with me today—you and Toby! We're going to Minneapolis! Can't you understand? There won't be any more of this!"

As quickly as it had begun her hysteria stopped; she was quiet in my hands, her eyes quiet but defensive, wary.

"Oh no. I won't do that. I knew you'd say that if you knew. That was why I didn't want you to come or know."

"But you've got to leave. Don't you see? When you're gone and things still happen—"

"No." Just the one determined syllable.

"Bill talked to me last night. He asked if there'd been any insanity in our family. You don't have to take that. You don't have to care what he thinks . . ."

I was strained forward, shaken with the urgency of my pleading but she looked coolly back at me, completely in control of herself now.

"That's your mistake, Ann. I do care. Really I know I didn't do any of those things. It isn't often I lose my head. I'll never lose it again. And I'm glad now that you're here. You can help find the answer."

She believed the explanation would have to come and that when it did, she and Bill would find the happiness they'd lost.

She seemed to have opened some reservoir of strength; finally and wearily I had to acknowledge temporary defeat. We went down to a subdued and worried Myra, who obviously knew of the struggle and its outcome—we'd been talking loudly enough.

"Over at Ella's, people eat their breakfast before it's noon." Lottie slammed bowls of chilled blueberries before us.

Myra took her place behind the coffee urn. "Toby got too hungry to wait. She ate and went to the resort with Bill. Jean's going out on one of the boats with Mark this morning, and Bill wanted to see them before they left."

When Lottie had stumped back to the kitchen, she made a direct plea. "Jacqui, you must go with Ann. You can't lose."

There was almost a quarrel, Myra insistent after she'd learned about my bathrobe, Jacqueline adamant. At last, Myra said, "But it isn't a question of whether you want to go. Bill agrees you should."

Jacqueline sat a moment longer, her face stiffening, then she stood up from her chair to run blindly, her hands over her face, toward the stairs.

"No, wait!"

Myra rose to halt me as I started after. "Let her think it over by herself, with no one urging her."

AND SO IT CAME about that I walked out of the house by myself.

Had there ever been a morning when trouble was so incongruous? Sun lay over everything—the grass, the rocks, the trees, the flat blue water—in an actual golden shimmer; the air was like cold water when you're thirsty; the forest and water sounds were the large, resonant, thrumming hums of bull fiddles.

I walked diagonally across the drive and the side lawn toward the Fingers. I thought I'd boost myself to the bend of the Thumb and sit looking out over the shoreless wide horizon, trying to get some perspective on what had happened.

But someone else was at the Fingers, someone who seemed to be lying on his back, looking upward; a man's feet in scuffed brown oxfords protruded beyond the base of the Thumb. I rounded the rock to see who it was.

Fred Heaton lay there, his shoulders and head propped against the base of the middle Finger, something bulky and white around his neck.

I said, "Hallo, Fred," and then my hands reached drunkenly sideward for support. The harsh sharp edges of the rock came under them, real and cutting, but there was no reality in what I looked at.

Fred's face was swollen and bruised, his eyes open and blank. Down the front of his bright blue-and-green-plaid flannel shirt ran a thick stain like the stain of a red fountain that had faintly trickled and stopped and dried.

6

NOTHING HAPPENED INSIDE ME; it was as if a switch had turned, shutting off thought and emotion. I had Fred's shoulder in my hand, shaking it.

"Fred!" I said. "Fred!" Still feeling nothing but hearing the thread of crying, unbelieving horror that ran through my voice at the contact with his shoulder, cold and rigid, like chilled marble under the bright plaid flannel shirtsleeve.

"You can't be—" I whispered, and then I was standing, running.

"Bill! Bill! Myra! Come help!" I ran by instinct, in darkness, seeing nothing; I think I must have shut my eyes, as if that way I could shut out what I'd seen. Sometime in that headlong plunge, someone grabbed me, shook me, shouted at me.

"Ann! What's happened?"

Bill. My eyes flew open to numbing light and his face, hard, expectant, armoring itself.

"It's Fred," I gasped. "By the Fingers—" Somehow I managed

to remember that this was Fred's father and that what awaited him was anguish; I grasped at him. "No, you mustn't go—" But he'd wrenched himself free before I got it said.

He was running toward the rocks, shouting, "If he's hurt, get a doctor quick!"

Still numb, I ran again. The telephone was in my hands and central's answer in my ear. "Get a doctor to Fiddler's Fingers! Hurry!"

Then I was looking at Myra.

"Ann! Who's hurt?"

There must be something we could do. I said, "Towels. Hot water. Quick! It's Fred."

Lottie must have been there, because she had the teakettle in her hands when we were running back across the lawn. Phillips, too, had come from somewhere.

But at the Fingers, all that frantic, useless hurry stopped.

Bill knelt below the rock, cradling Fred's head on his shoulder. Even his back, which was all I saw of him, was contorted with agony.

"No use," he was saying to himself. "No use. He's dead."

SOMETHING—TOWELS—FELL OUT of my hands.

The hush in which we stood, with Bill's tortured voice the only human sound, was an awful unmoving quiet in which the colors and shapes of people and rock seemed set and hard, as if they had petrified for eternity. Minutes fell past. But then slowly, like a wind sweeping up, the quiet was no longer a hush, but a great, inarticulate roar in which the chuckle of the underground river rose and swelled, in which the lake beat with rush and thunder, in which the wind-shaken forest clamored in a boisterous surge.

For this human evil, suffering, and tragedy, the wilderness had—

Laughter.

I heard it full. Huge, gargantuan, as old as Earth, the laughter of forest and water and wind.

SOMEONE WHIMPERED. "LOTTIE."

Phillips Heaton whispered, "He was killed, wasn't he? It looks like a shot. Police—we'll have to get the police."

Killed . . . shot . . . As if those words were a key to reality, I saw the group of us standing in our petrifaction—Myra paper white, caught up into incredulity and lost horror, Lottie in sick fright, her face fallen into lumps, Phillips Heaton for once unamused.

Bill said dully, "Go away, can't you? All of you go away."

"NO POLICE HERE." PHILLIPS seemed talking to himself as we stumbled back toward the house. "There's the sheriff. He's the one."

As we reached the porch door, there was the fall of light, scuttling feet on the stairs and in the hall above; I thought it must be Octavia, that she'd heard the echoes of catastrophe and perhaps been at the porch door watching; against any crisis I'd expect her to run. Octavia—but there was someone else, too, upstairs. Jacqueline, thinking only that she might have to leave . . .

Phillips went at once to the phone, where he talked low and quickly. I walked toward the stairs as if I were walking against swift opposing water. Telling Jacqueline was the last thing I wanted to do, but I must . . .

In the hall upstairs, only two doors were closed—Octavia's and the one to which I went. On the other side of that door, Jac-

queline was folding a blue nightgown to lay in the suitcase open
on the bed. Beside the crib was Toby on the floor, the slate and
yellow chalk in her hands, drawing.

My Jacqueline and my Toby, against whom lightning must
strike.

Toby lifted her face. "I need a b'ue one. Ann, today you get
me a b'ue one?"

Jacqueline said evenly without turning, "Bill sent Toby up
when he got back from the resort. Well, I'm packing."

"Come outside," I said.

Her face changed when she looked at me; she came at once,
closing the door behind her.

"Ann," she whispered, "there's been something else."

"Yes." I wouldn't have to give her many words.

"Another—trick."

"Worse than that."

Her face set in the mold of anguished expectation. "Bill."

"No. Fred."

"Hurt?"

I nodded.

"Ann, he's dead," she said, only eyes in her face. She whispered, "Someone killed him. I should have felt it coming. Something as terrible as this."

When I told her where Bill was she ran out to him at once.

I went in to Toby; that was where I should stay, keeping Toby
away from what had happened. I couldn't stay, yet when I got
downstairs, with a subdued Toby clinging to my hand, the group
below was almost as I'd left it: Lottie cringing alone near the
kitchen door, Myra holding to the back of the davenport, Phillips
with his hands on the phone.

"I wonder when it happened," Phillips said. "I hope it was
while I was in Grand Marais." He was thinking of himself again.

When motors hummed, Myra jerked toward the door, but her brother gestured her aside.

"No, I'll go."

Through the side windows, we could see two cars stop beside the Fingers, spilling men. Phillips reached them. Loud muted exclamations drifted back . . . Two figures emerged to come toward the house: Jacqueline escorted by a stranger.

There was that moment then when Jacqueline stood in the door, the tears of pity on her face, the shadow of a sheriff's deputy behind her.

Murder. I'd gotten to the place where I could think that naked word.

Murder is something more than someone dead and someone a killer. I couldn't get Jacqueline away now.

Murder is a trap.

EVERYTHING ELSE THAT MORNING seems disconnected and dimmed. Small incidents stand out . . .

. . . The deputy who had brought Jacqueline saying at the phone, "That you, Gus? Aakonen wants you at Fiddler's Fingers right away. Boy got shot here. Bill Heaton's kid. Yep, news, all right." Words threaded by the fire of excitement.

. . . Jacqueline whispering, "It's so awful for Bill," sinking to the davenport, her hands to her face, Toby running toward her asking, "You cry, Mama?" A note of beginning fright behind her voice, and Jacqueline's head jerking back. Jacqueline and I sitting on the floor, cutting snowflakes out of paper in a frantic effort to keep Toby lulled while Myra called a friend of hers in Duluth. "Caroline, I'm going to ask a great favor of you—I must. We've got to get Toby away. Something frightful has happened. If you could come . . ."

Myra remembering as she turned from the phone, "Oh, poor Octavia!" Her quick ministering feet on the stairs and her distraught return. "She's in bed. I can't get her up. She has the blankets pulled to her eyes. Whatever happens, I won't have Octavia harried—I won't." Just as I wanted to shield Jacqueline and Toby, Myra would want to shield her timorous, unworldly sister.

. . . Cars coming and going. A short, crisp man in shirtsleeves pausing in the doorway to say cheerfully, "Biggest scoop I ever had, Mrs. Sallishaw. I'll phone it in to the big-city dailies right away," as if we would rejoice in that broadcasting.

Myra on the floor with Toby, staring after him, white lipped. "Joe Moe, from the Grand Marais *Bugle*. We'll be overrun. Aakonen will have to put a guard at the gate."

. . . Newspapers. The realization that Aunt Harriet must be prepared against shock; that phone call and her staunch old voice repeating, "I depend on you to look after Jacqueline, Ann— Toby, too. Remember you're the oldest." What she'd said to me since I could remember.

. . . A gray hearse by the Fingers, and when it was gone, Bill walking in alone through the door, walking into the litter of our cut paper and our silence; Jacqueline rising to meet him, and Bill stopping to rest his face against her hair for a moment before he said thickly, "Stay with the others," and went upstairs.

. . . A tall, stooped, bulky man asking, "Mrs. Sallishaw, could I have lunch here?" Myra answering, "Of course, Sheriff Aakonen."

The trap isn't enough, is never enough; sooner or later must come the step of the hunter.

HORROR WAS WHAT WE walked in—horror that Fred should be so suddenly dead, horror that one human being had killed another. The fear I had then was vague, obscure, unreasoned, a sick weight at the pit of my stomach. It wasn't until later, when I was taken to look at the Fingers again, that the fear became defined.

Only Aakonen and Phillips ate lunch that day; even Toby left her food untouched. She was fascinated by the sheriff, by the thick blue vein that ran diagonally across the brown bald dome of his forehead; her hand kept stealing to feel of her own brow. Bill and Octavia hadn't come down.

As soon as he shoved back from the table, Aakonen moved purposefully, speaking the words that were to become the focus of our days.

"After a murder only one thing is important—to catch the murderer. I will want to see you one by one, please."

He moved heavily; the fall of his weight showed as it shifted from foot to foot, but he quickly had the wicker living room table pulled near a window, a chair behind the table and himself in the chair. He sat hunched, a man of great dignity and benign sadness, looking us over with light, unshifting eyes as we huddled after.

"Mrs. Sallishaw, you first, please. The rest go on the porch."

Jacqueline said, "It's the little girl's rest time."

"Oh, sure. You take her upstairs."

When I went along his eyes noticed, but he didn't object.

"Mr. Bill Heaton," he said to Myra, as if he were establishing a foundation in a morass before he started building. "He's your cousin, correct?"

UPSTAIRS I SAT WITH Jacqueline, thinking nothing, doing nothing, held by that vague, formless fear, not seeing any reason or pattern in what had happened. The wire over which Toby had tripped, the wrecked boat, my bathrobe—all were gone out of my mind. Nothing existed except Fred's murder and Jacqueline's being here—held.

An hour or more until the knock at the door.

"Aakonen wants to see Ann." It was Bill, whose eyes stared at nightmare.

Jacqueline asked achingly, "Did he question *you*?"

"He had to." The answer was wooden. As if he couldn't bear our pity, he crossed quickly to his own room, closing the door.

I got downstairs, where Aakonen leaned forward over the table, pointing with a thick forefinger at a chair facing him and the light. There was another man beside him now, a brown little man like a curled and weather-beaten wood shingle.

"You're Miss Ann Gay?" The question came while I was sitting down.

"Yes."

"Mr. Bill Heaton says you found his son's body."

"Yes."

"Why'd you go out to the Fingers this morning?"

Why had I? Numbness still held me, but around the edges of the numbness, there was a loosening, as if soon now it must break.

"I just—walked out. I was going to sit on the Thumb. I wanted to look at the lake."

"You have any idea who killed Fred Heaton?"

"No. Oh no." Numbness retightening.

"You hear any shots during the night?"

Floundering through the night in which so much had happened, my mind could grasp at nothing.

"It's so noisy here . . . the lake . . . I don't remember."

"What time this morning was it you found the body?"

"I don't know. Maybe nine o'clock—nine thirty."

"Nobody say anything about Fred Heaton not coming for breakfast?"

"People here seem to eat anytime they like." Could I go on like this, just answering automatically?

He leaned forward, pausing. "You walk out of this house alone this morning. It's a nice morning. You go out by those rocks. What do you see?"

Everything inside me shivered. I'd have to remember now.

"I saw his feet—Fred's feet . . ." I heard my words, limping, setting that scene again, saw the swollen, bruised face, the stain on the shirt, the white bulk around the neck, felt again that cold rigidity under my fingers. Aakonen and the brown man listened as if they held their breaths. When I finished, there was again a pause.

"When we got here, Mr. Bill Heaton had moved the body. Where were the harebells when you saw him?"

"Harebells?" The scene was in my mind, but no harebells.

"Mr. Bill Heaton says he took some dried-up flowers out of Fred's hand. Then that stuff you saw around Fred's neck—that this?"

He reached toward the brown man, who took from the chair beside him a white mass and set it on the table. I stared at it, my skin creeping.

That was Myra Sallishaw's shawl—her white hand-knit wool shawl. The thing had been slashed like my bathrobe, cut and pulled into a heap of raveled, crinkled yarns.

"That," I said, "it's been—"

"Yes?" he urged.

"Cut."

"Was that what you saw around Fred's neck?"

"I didn't look closely."

"And the word on the rock," he said, "you didn't tell about that."

I tried again to picture the scene by the Fingers, but my mind was hastily building a wall against something that confronted it. Harebells, shawl, a word on the rock . . .

I asked, "What word?" My voice loud and toneless.

He nodded. "So you didn't notice. You can walk out there with me now."

He led the way, lumbering before me, across the living room, halting to hold the door for me. The porch was populated. White, strained faces turned quickly toward the door as it opened, all the eyes asking a question—Bradley and Carol Auden, Cecile Granat, Phillips and Myra, the Corvos, Lottie—sitting together, but with a curious effect of isolation. Against the porch rail leaned a strange man, watching. No one spoke as we passed, crossed the lawn toward the rocks that my very bones protested against nearing. The long, loose man who'd brought Jacqueline in stood there on guard. Only gravel now where Fred's body had lain, dark, thin, gray pebbles as smooth as lentils, with the huge gnarled Fingers bent above, and, underneath, the incessant chuckle. Aakonen pointed, and my eyes lifted.

On the face of the middle rock, the one against which Fred's shoulders had been propped, letters were scrawled in blue chalk.

Blue chalk. Then that was what had become of Toby's chalk!

Suddenly, thoroughly, my mind came alive. No place for formless fear now, no time for cringing behind walls. I knew now what Jacqueline faced.

Monarch. That was the word on the rock.

That scene of Fred's clowning on the afternoon before—harebells in his hands, Myra's shawl, the stanza he'd recited.

Here at the same spot the scene of his death had been made to look as if Jacqueline had retaliated.

I felt cold and hard, sitting in the chair in the living room to which Aakonen returned me.

Aakonen said, "Now, this is the first time you have been here at the Fingers, is it?" There was a tightening in him, too.

"Yes."

"You came yesterday. You're a cousin of Mrs. Bill Heaton's. Why did you come?"

"Jean Nobbelin sent me a note. He said he thought it would be a good idea for me to get here."

"Jean Nobbelin?" His voice lifted. "Tell everything you saw or heard happen after you got here."

"That's quite a lot." I fenced for time, chaos inside my head. Why hadn't I spent the time since the discovery of the murder sorting out what I'd want to tell? How could I hide what had been going on? He'd be sure to find out from others. No, best to tell everything, coloring it as well as I could.

So I began, feeling in tight throat muscles the effort to keep my voice level. Perspiration came out all over my skin; I was soon cold with its chill. The one important thing was the effort I must make.

I told of my arrival and, since the chalk had become important, even of the gifts I'd brought. Told about the wire snare and the smashed motorboat, leaving out Bill's reactions; surely he must have the decency to conceal what his doubts had been. Told of berrypicking and then, choosing my words as if they were stepping-stones over a torrent, told of Fred's behavior on the afternoon before—minimizing and softening it.

"Apparently a little jealousy of his father's second marriage," I said. "No one took it seriously."

Just the same, he made me go through it a second time, my tongue burning every time it touched a fatal word—the harebells, the shawl, the stanza. Only too open now the links between that scene of yesterday afternoon and the scene of the murder.

When I finished the second time, he leaned back, his eyes like the points of ice picks. He asked another question, but I didn't hear it. My hands were on the arms of my chair, raising me.

That group of us on the lawn—Myra, Phillips, Cecile, Bradley Auden, Bill, Jean, Mark, Carol, Jacqueline, Toby, me. We were the only people who had seen that act of Fred's.

Only someone who had seen that act could have arranged the carefully fantastic setting of the murder.

AAKONEN REPEATED SHARPLY, "YOU then went in for supper?"

"Yes," I answered breathlessly, but I was lost in thought: Myra, Phillips, Cecile Granat, Bradley Auden, Bill, Mark, Jean, or Carol—the murderer is one of them. Or Lottie—Lottie might have seen and perhaps told the Corvos. And hadn't there been a glimmer at Octavia's window? Yes, it was just possible that Octavia might have seen—or anyone else who had been watching . . .

That dark figure I'd seen near the Fingers.

Again, I automatically lifted myself. "Good heavens! I saw someone—Myra and I both did—out near the Fingers. In the night. Suppose it wasn't Bill—"

He was nodding. Relief so intense it hurt excruciatingly, like blood going back into a foot that's been asleep. I tried to hide it, but he pounced.

"You are overjoyed at remembering this figure by the Fingers. You were afraid the murderer was someone you know."

"Oh no." I could fence easily now. "It's just that—I wouldn't want to have to think anyone from here or Auden or the resort— It must have been an outsider."

"This outsider, who would he be?"

"Anyone—a tramp. Fred might have surprised him—"

"You think a tramp would put a shawl on Fred's shoulders, dress him up with flowers and a word on the rock?"

Some of my relief ebbed. "A prowler might have watched yesterday noon and thought he'd throw suspicion on us."

Aakonen shook his massive head. "Miss Gay, I have been sheriff of Cook County many years. Every once in a while, a man gets killed. Two men drink and fight, and one man sticks a knife in the other and runs away. I wish I had that kind of murder here. There might be a man hiding out, hoping to steal food or money or a car—sure. He wouldn't stop to dress up the dead body fancy."

"But you can't rule that out."

"Fred had money in his pocket. It was still there when I looked him over. He had a watch and ring. You had two cars here and you still got two cars. No cars gone from anywhere around."

Persistently I clung to hope. "Fred's been away at school—he was quite overbearing. Suppose someone came to get even? Or Bill Heaton—men important in business have enemies."

The lower lip thrust out. "Enemies? Bill Heaton?" When his voice came again it was gentler, changed.

"Miss Gay, I can see you do not know about Mr. Bill Heaton—who he is. You do not know how things were in this country before Mr. Bill Heaton changed them. The lumbermen had taken all the big trees. The summer is short, and the nights are cold. There wasn't enough to feed the people on the sandy farms or in the towns that had grown up while the trees were going out. Many left. But there were some people too poor to leave. There was little tourist business then—only trapping and fishing. It was that way when I was a boy."

He paused, waiting.

"When Mr. Bill Heaton took over his father's small business, he was very young, but in a little while he got this idea—that farms here should raise crops of trees as other farms raise corn. It seems easy now, doesn't it? It wasn't easy then. Trees take a long time growing. I have heard Bill Heaton talking for hours, angering men into doing what he wanted, forcing them through debts, bullying them. But after a while, it was different. When the first growths were cut, there was food in the stores. Children came to school, because they had shoes. Bill Heaton would be away, planning with the railroad to get vacationers here. Bill Heaton would be in St. Paul fighting for the North Shore road, so the automobiles could come."

The big mouth twisted. "I think all the first money he had was spent on bribes. You see, no murderer could kill Bill Heaton's only child, because this country, too, is his child."

Again he waited. In spite of my turmoil over Jacqueline, I could feel his reverence. Inescapably my own attitude toward Bill was colored; I could see why Jacqueline felt about Bill as she did, why Myra admired him so much and had been so delighted when he married Jacqueline.

The sheriff went on slowly, "You can see now how important this is, how heavy my responsibility is. Go on, please. You were beginning to tell me what happened as you ate supper yesterday."

Subdued, I went on with yesterday's incidents—supper, the first brush between Fred and Mark over Carol . . .

"Fred was angrier than Mark," I tried to judge. "Fred might have wanted to beat Mark up, but I didn't think Mark was equally angry. Why should he have been? Carol picked Mark."

Aakonen grunted as if for once he was pleased, and gestured me on. The game in which I'd been blindfolded, Carol's departure . . . It wasn't until I told of Toby's missing chalk that he interrupted again.

"Who was there when you found that out?"

"Mrs. Sallishaw and my cousin and myself. We three took Toby in to bed. Bill Heaton and Jean Nobbelin—they were arguing about something. Cecile Granat and Phillips Heaton and

Bradley Auden sat together talking. Fred had left before that—I didn't notice him go."

"So the chalk could have been taken during supper or the game . . . When did you next see Fred?"

I hadn't seen him again until I saw him dead.

"You perhaps heard someone speak of him?"

Fred had been in my mind last night; I'd thought him an aggressor, thought him perhaps responsible for the tricks, for Jacqueline's trouble—when he was a victim, perhaps already lying dead.

"No."

"Tell me what you did through the evening."

I told of going down to talk with Bill. What had Bill's account of that talk been? "We agreed my cousin and the little girl should leave with me today."

"Why?" The word leaped at me.

"Because we didn't like the looks of that smashed motorboat and a few other things that had been happening."

Apparently he accepted that. He went over the glimpse I'd had of that figure near the Fingers again and then how I had wakened in the night, found my bathrobe slashed. I left out my trip to Jacqueline's room and the scent of spice, left out the tuft in Jacqueline's scissors—no one knew about those things except me and Jacqueline. I told of telling Jacqueline about my robe and her recital of the previous tricks but left out her hysteria and fear.

His eyes were like leeches, but I thought he surely must see the incidents I told were no more connected with Jacqueline than with anyone else who might be a familiar of the house.

When I was done, he nodded at the brown man. He asked me, "You have a gun here?"

I braced to the new attack. "Oh no, I've never had a gun— never so much as held one."

Dryly, "You'd recognize one?"

"I suppose so. I've seen pictures."

"Seen any guns here at the Fingers?"

No answer to reaching thoughts. "No."

"Mr. Bill Heaton says he had an automatic in his room. On top of his wardrobe. Now he says it's gone."

That big carved-oak wardrobe I'd glimpsed in Bill's room—at some time, there'd been a gun hidden behind the raised scrolled front, up high where Toby couldn't reach it.

I said, "I've never been in Mr. Heaton's bedroom."

The man like a wood shingle curled closer; Aakonen grunted.

"That gun and the blue chalk seem still to be missing."

"Then I should think you'd be looking for them." The words slipped out tartly.

The wide mouth smiled, but the eyes didn't. "It has now been many hours since the murder. The murderer did not wait until I got here to hide what he had to hide, nor to say what had to be said. If that were not so, do you think I would let two of you sit alone together upstairs?"

Then when he had me following that line of thought, he thrust sharply, unexpectedly.

"Why is it you and Mr. Bill Heaton and Mrs. Sallishaw all work so hard to get me not to pay much attention to your cousin, Jacqueline Heaton?"

7

I'D FAILED. BY MY very care, I'd made his suspicion greater.

I said, "You can't think my cousin committed this murder."

The words welled, resounding, in my head. "I've known her since she was born. She's never even done anything unkind."

I'd been three years old; I'd worn a white embroidery dress, sticking out in a ruffle over my long, thin legs in black ribbed cotton stockings. I'd stood with my nose against plate glass, staring in at the top of a dark-fluffed head in a hanging white canvas basket in a row of hospital baskets. My mother said, "That's your cousin— that's Jacqueline. She'll be the sister you never had, and you'll love her very much." When I took my nose away, my breath was still on the glass—mist.

I said steadily, "I haven't worked to keep you from suspecting my cousin. I've told you things as they really were."

He smiled at me wearily, as if he didn't expect much truth from humanity. "As you saw it perhaps."

I escaped to anger, remembering who he'd said had tried to

protect Jacqueline and those he hadn't mentioned. "I suppose you think Phillips Heaton is the one who tells the truth. That malicious, envious, fat *bedbug*!"

He laughed, a short yelp like a coyote's. "I've known Phillips Heaton a long time . . . If you'll ask your cousin to be next, please."

As I walked toward the stairs, my ears were too thickened by emotion to hear what he was saying to the warped little man; my heart was hot, swelling so it pushed against my ribs.

Jacqueline next, not knowing what she faced.

She stood up when I came in, expecting to go next.

I told her without preamble—the harebells, the shawl, the word on the rock. But I wouldn't have had to; she already knew.

She said, "I saw them." She smiled lightly, touching my arm, and walked out of the room.

Mary, Queen of Scots, they say, once walked out like that . . .

Toby was awake, playing on the floor. After a while, Myra dragged listlessly up to join us. She, too, knew where Aakonen's suspicions tended; the knowledge was on her face like a blow taken.

"We must do something. We must find out who that person by the Fingers was."

I stared at her, and suddenly strength poured into me like a river. I didn't just have to sit by watching things happen.

"Of course! Myra, who could that person have been?"

"Ridiculous now to think it was Bill." She sat down at the bedside. "It must have been one of the others." She'd seen the same small circle of suspects I had.

"I've been sitting watching them—most of them—there on the porch, thinking until my head feels ready to crack. Why would any one of them want to kill Fred? That's what I can't see. *Why?*"

I said slowly, "There was one other person Fred showed resentment against yesterday—"

She said, "But Mark's such a boy. He isn't down there . . . I don't know what to think."

I left her with Toby. As I went along the hall, Octavia's door was still closed; I could picture her cowering in bed still, the blanket pulled to her eyes, as she'd been when Myra had gone up to her that morning and been again at noon when we'd set a tray beside her bed. Aakonen would have a hard time getting anything out of Octavia.

He was talking when I descended but stopped at the sound of my footsteps. Jacqueline sat as I'd sat in the wicker armchair, facing him, and I knew a little relief; she was braced against him, but he seemed to be treating her as he had me—as a witness.

I asked, "Is it all right if I go out?"

"The porch," he answered. "Do not try to leave the place." He waited for me to be gone before he continued questioning.

Except that Myra was gone, the people on the porch were as they'd been when I walked through with Aakonen. Mark was still missing—Mark and Jean Nobbelin. The guard pointed to a chair.

"You can sit there. No talking."

Aakonen's voice rumbled inside; Jacqueline answered, but it was too far away for words to be audible. Gradually I saw the differences in the people on the porch, under their common tension. All were turned toward me now, the Corvos and Lottie sullen and frightened, Phillips with recovered aplomb; he rested back in his chair like a Roman senator viewing Christians about to be divertingly eaten by lions.

I asked him, "Where are Mark and Jean?"

He gestured toward the lake. "Out there."

Cecile said, "They left early this morning on one of the boats."

It was a defensive answer; sullenness was heavy on Cecile's lipsticked mouth and in the blue eyes flickering toward Bradley Auden. Lipstick had been becoming to her the day before, but now pallor made too sharp a demarcation at the lip line.

Carol swallowed a gulp. "I could have pretended I was in love with him." It was a meek and pitiful voice to be hers; impishness was gone from her now-woebegone triangular face. When I looked at her, she bent double, her face to her lap.

"I was so mean to Fred yesterday—just as mean as I could be!"

She cried aloud, unashamedly, crying not only her shock that a boy she'd known was dead but a second tearing grief over her own lack of love.

Bradley Auden proffered a large handkerchief. The girl gave an enormous gulp and straightened, to sit swallowing recurrent fits of sobbing, dabbing at her cheeks.

Over the back he patted, Bradley Auden asked me, "Have they decided yet if it was murder?"

"You ain't supposed to answer that," the guard cut in sharply before I could reply.

Bradley Auden brushed a hand across his forehead. "Poor Bill. I don't suppose he wants to see anyone. We were told only that Fred was dead and murder is suspected. Surely it must have been an accident."

"Bill's upstairs. I don't imagine the sheriff would let you see him." I answered as much as I thought was permissible.

"Interesting, isn't it?" Phillips Heaton asked blandly. "Except for Bill, little Carol here seems to be the only case of grief."

He let words drift out lazily. "Even more interesting, isn't it, to think that behind one mask of careful shock, someone might be glad?"

"That's enough there!" The order was sharp, but every pair of eyes leaped, and I felt my muscles contracting. Someone here—

yes, was there a pair of hands here from which blood had been washed? Had someone here been the figure that skulked at the Fingers, waiting?

A car's motor hummed behind the house, grew louder, stopped. Footsteps on the gravel and low voices.

Three men came around the corner of the veranda—Jean Nobbelin, Mark, a tubby and important stranger.

Two exclamations rose, one mine, one Carol Auden's.

Mark Ellif carried his head forward, tipped, as if he had difficulty seeing. Both his eyes were blackened; a bruise on his left cheek spread, swollen and magenta, far below his cheekbone, and a ragged cut ran from the right corner of his mouth to his chin.

Carol was on her feet, running to meet him at the porch door. "Mark! You've been hurt! Fred's dead! Is everyone going to get hurt and killed?" The cry came hysterically.

Under the flamboyant color of the bruises, Mark's face was ash gray. He raised his eyes to the rest of us, over Carol's head. The look on his face was one of stoicism and despair.

"I heard Fred was dead," he said. "I guess I must have killed him."

EXCITEMENT AND CONSTERNATION BROKE loose in a flurry that the two deputies could not quell.

"I never meant to." The boy seemed in an advanced state of shock. "I didn't mean to."

I'd thought of Mark as a possible murderer, but this didn't make sense. "Whoever killed Fred meant—" I began, but a big hand clapped harshly down on my shoulder.

"No talking here!" It was a bellow from the tubby, important deputy. "I got to get these men to Aakonen."

"In the living room," from the deputy who'd been guarding us.

The tubby man shouldered his charges to the door and inside it. Carol had fallen back, looking as dazed as Mark.

"He couldn't have. Mark couldn't kill anybody."

Her father put his arm around her, leading her back to a chair. "We don't know anything, Carol. We've got to wait."

Then I forgot them; Jacqueline stood in the door.

"Was it Mark?" she asked. She looked taken aback, but that's all; my heart jumped like a minnow in a pail when you grab for it.

If it's Mark, it isn't you—how could I even think that? I sprang to sit by her. She asked where Toby was; I answered, but all that mattered was that Aakonen had let her go.

I asked, "What did the sheriff say when Mark came in?"

"Aakonen said no talking here." That command again.

Impatience burst. "What difference does talking make?"

"Suppose somebody knows something he ain't been told?" Professional contempt. What did I know about hunting murderers? All I had was my necessity.

From inside the house came a hoarse shout—Jean's voice talking for a moment loudly. Then the voices sank again. My ears strained, but it was no good against the sounds of nature.

Mark's "I didn't mean to" made no sense in context, when the murder setting was so deliberate. Yet why should he have admitted that he must have killed Fred if he hadn't? What sort of farce could lead to that final scene, with Mark not knowing what he did?

We had to sit for twenty minutes in that suspense; Jacqueline quiet and aloof, Carol running the hem of a soaked handkerchief between forefingers and thumbs, Bradley Auden alertly waiting, Cecile with more color in her cheeks so that her lipstick blended naturally, Ella and Lottie hunched like rabbits, Ed sitting up fierce and straight, his water-dark eyes watchful and wary, his face sharper than ever.

At the end of twenty minutes, Mark Ellif walked out weakly, behind him Jean's dark shadow.

What looked like great relief showed in every line of Mark's face and every relaxed muscle of his body. Jean had a hand under his arm, supporting him. The boy's cheeks were wet. He said, "I didn't kill him."

The rusty man even then wouldn't allow a question.

THE INTERVIEWING FROM THEN on went quickly. When Ella Corvo came out—she was the last—there was an interval in which Aakonen must have gone up to do his best with Octavia, because thinly from upstairs came a sound like a shrill, protesting child's cry, and I guessed that for the first time I was hearing Octavia's voice.

Jacqueline rose. "I suppose Myra—"

But Toby's small feet were already running across the living room; she appeared in the door, pausing in sudden shyness at seeing so many people, until Jacqueline picked her up.

"I stay you now. Gramma said."

"That's fine. We're all glad you're down."

Undoubtedly Myra had gone with Aakonen into Octavia's room, but, whatever he got out of that colloquy, it didn't last long. Within ten minutes, he was in the doorway, brooding over us like a sphinx.

"Come in, please, all of you. Take chairs here in the living room."

What was this to be—a public accusation? My heart beat faster as I followed Jacqueline in; I couldn't touch or look at her, because that would be an open confession of the fear that leaped in my chest. Myra was on the stairs, looking toward Toby anxiously.

"Must Toby—?" she began, and Aakonen jerked around.

"No, of course," he answered, and made a gesture at the long, rusty deputy.

That man at once walked toward Toby, fishing a jackknife from his pocket. "I got a good knife here," he said. "I whittle wood dolls for my little girl. I guess I could make a pretty good doll now if I had a stick."

Toby, in Jacqueline's arms, slowly started sliding to the floor, her eyes glued to the knife.

"You know where there's any sticks?"

No answer, but the seduction was complete; Toby went out with him, hand in hand, and Jacqueline looked after them with a sigh.

"He looks as if he'd be responsible . . . I wonder when Mrs. Foster will get here. It's only a hundred and twenty miles from Duluth."

Then she forgot even Toby. Bill was coming downstairs with the wood-shingle man, erect, not hiding his grief but looking nowhere for consolation. Jean Nobbelin started to his feet but halted. Through the room ran a current of sympathy so strong you could almost feel it with your hands.

AAKONEN STOOD BEHIND THE table, facing us, bent, so that his fisted hands rested on the table. His big head was forward like a bull's, his eyes steadily grave.

Aakonen said, "There are fourteen people who may be mixed up in this death. Those people are Mr. Bill Heaton, Mrs. Jacqueline Heaton, Mrs. Myra Sallishaw, Mr. Phillips Heaton, Miss

Octavia Heaton, Miss Ann Gay, Mr. Bradley Auden, Miss Carol Auden, Mr. Mark Ellif, Mr. Jean Nobbelin, Miss Cecile Granat, Miss Lottie Elvesaetter, Mrs. Ella Corvo, and Mr. Ed Corvo."

Of the fourteen he named, only one wasn't looking at him now. He must have been unable to get Octavia up, or else he thought her presence unnecessary.

He went on more slowly, "I believe that one of the people I have just named murdered Fred Heaton."

Stirring breath, tension that was already tight growing tighter, the trap walls closing in.

"I am not going to say who I think might be that murderer. However, I will say that among the fourteen of you all are thirteen who are not murderers. From those thirteen, I want help."

Breath released, bodies moving forward.

"Someone with a grudge seems to have been working hard around here. Things have been smashed and cut up. I know Mr. Bill Heaton's son, Fred, was jealous of the stepmother, but I have asked Mr. Bill Heaton and all of you, and you all say you know no reason why anyone would want to kill Fred."

Again a pause.

"Yesterday afternoon I was out here, talking to some of you about Ed Corvo's boat. About four o'clock I went back to the resort with Ed and stayed for supper. So I know Ed and Mrs. Corvo were at the resort until maybe eight o'clock, when I went home. They say they stayed there all evening. Lottie got there about nine o'clock, and they all went to bed."

A change in stress between what he knew and what "they say." Only the word of the Corvos and Lottie that they'd been at the resort through the evening and night. Ella Corvo's soft bulk moved as if a hand had shaken her shoulder.

"Here at the Fingers you were together for supper at six.

About seven, Mark took Miss Auden home. He says he stayed at Auden until eleven."

A rising, "Mother will tell you—"

"There is nothing here to be proved. Fred Heaton was killed long after eleven." The quiet resumed.

"So. After Mark Ellif and Carol Auden left, Fred walked from the front of the house toward the boathouse, as seen by his father, where his bedroom was. Only Mark Ellif will say he saw Fred Heaton alive after that."

Again a pause, in silence.

"That was around seven, or a little after, when Fred Heaton went to the boathouse. Lottie came out and took the trays in to wash the dishes. The little girl got sleepy and was taken off to bed by her mother, grandmother, and Miss Gay. The little girl was crying because she had lost a blue chalk. We have not yet found that blue chalk but we know for what purpose it was used.

"Left on the lawn were Mr. Bill Heaton and Mr. Nobbelin, talking. Mr. Auden, Miss Granat, and Phillips Heaton also stayed there, talking. It got cool, and the mosquitoes began to come out. Miss Granat picked up Mrs. Sallishaw's shawl from where it had been left in Mrs. Sallishaw's chair and wrapped it around her shoulders. In another few minutes, the five people moved to the porch, taking the chairs along. After a while, Mr. Phillips Heaton left to drive to Grand Marais."

Had that been the car I heard when I came downstairs?

Fear and waiting over the room; from our piecemeal testimonies, Aakonen had built this carefully dovetailed account.

"Miss Granat says that when she left, she dropped Mrs. Sallishaw's shawl in the porch chair in which she was sitting. No one of you will admit seeing that shawl after that. Mr. Auden took

Miss Granat home. Mr. Auden's car was at the resort. He says he left in it at once."

That shadow at the Fingers wasn't Bradley Auden, then, unless he lied.

"When Mr. Auden got home, his daughter told him that Mark Ellif had just started walking back along the shore. The Audens say they then went to bed.

"Here at the Fingers, Mr. Bill Heaton bumped into Miss Gay in the living room. She says she was coming downstairs to see if anyone was up. They went to the porch to talk. Mrs. Sallishaw heard the voices in her room overhead and came down to join the talk. Mr. Bill Heaton decided that his wife and the little girl should go to Minneapolis with Miss Gay until the person who had been up to tricks around here should be caught."

Did his eyes touch me obliquely? Had he guessed the real reason for the decision? If he had, he gave no sign.

"Mr. Bill Heaton then went for a walk, Miss Gay and Mrs. Sallishaw returning upstairs, where Mrs. Sallishaw locked the door of Octavia Heaton's room from the outside as a precaution against her sister's habit of sometimes walking in her sleep. I may say now that it is hard to see how Octavia Heaton could be the murderer, since she was there behind that locked door when Mrs. Sallishaw unlocked it this morning."

Yes, no wonder he hadn't forced Octavia to come down. She seemed to be out.

"While Miss Gay was opening her window about ten o'clock, she saw what she thought was some dark figure lurking near the Fingers. Mrs. Sallishaw also saw this figure and decided it must be Mr. Bill Heaton, since he was out walking. Mr. Heaton, however, says he did not go near the Fingers—he was on the lakeshore near the boathouse.

"There is a chance what the two women saw was Mark Ellif,

coming home from Auden. Fred Heaton was probably not killed until closer to midnight, but of course that does not mean someone could not have lurked by the rocks, waiting."

I shivered, seeing again that dark, curiously elongated shadow.

"Mark says he got to his cabin at the resort about ten thirty, he thinks. Fred Heaton was sitting on the doorstep. Mark, I would like to hear for a second time what happened then."

A glisten of sweat stood on Mark's forehead, but the eyes inside the bruised circles seemed steady.

"That's right. Fred was sitting on the step. He stood up. He said, 'You had a nice long evening with my girl.'

"I said, 'You haven't any mortgage on Carol.'

"He said, 'Come on down to the shore. I want to talk.'

"So I went down to the beach with him. The minute we were there, he swung on me. He didn't say anything—his fist just got me in the jaw. He had a ring on—it cut. I couldn't just stand there and let him beat me up. We rolled all over the beach. He got me on the side of the head, and I went out. When I woke up, I was still there on the sand. I was icy cold and wet. I don't know how long I'd been out. I looked around for Fred. There was enough moonlight so I could see he wasn't there. So I thought he'd gone home. I was still punch-drunk. I went back to the cabin and woke Jean up."

Jean spoke quickly. "It was about two then. Mark told me what had happened. I gave him some whiskey, washed him up, and put him to bed. This morning, when Bill came over—"

"Wait!" The order was Aakonen's. "At the Fingers, too, things were happening."

He described how I'd wakened in the night, my morning discovery about my bathrobe, my visit to the Fingers. As he described the scene of the murder, I watched faces—apparently, it was the first real information about the murder that most of them were getting. Bradley, Carol, Cecile, Jean, Mark, Lottie, the Corvos—they all sat immobile, as if mesmerized by their own imaginations.

"There is no sign the body was dragged or moved," Aakonen went on. "Apparently Fred was shot right there at the Fingers. I will know more later, but Dr. Rush thinks the death was some-time between midnight and two o'clock."

Phillips Heaton said quickly, "I'm lucky. I was at Hanson's until three o'clock this morning."

He sat forward, his entire body looking plump and cheerful, like a rubber ball all ready to bounce. Of course that was all he would think of, I thought—his own safety. Animosity against him rose in my chest, and I guessed mine wasn't the only one. Out of all of us, he and the quailing Octavia were the only ones who apparently had an alibi.

Aakonen said abruptly, "That is all. For you who are inno-cent, remember this. No one of you is safe while a murderer is uncaught."

Swift blaze of realization, like a fire following a kerosene trail. Into that awareness, he sank his next words.

"Someone here is lying. If any of you recognize anything not true in what I have told, it is best to say so now."

Silence so strong it seemed lifting us on currents of air. How many half-truths had I told? Either he knew them for what they were, or else Bill and Myra had made the same evasions.

"Very well. I shall expect the innocent among you to work heartily with me. Anyone who finds a gun or a piece of blue chalk is to bring them to me. Now I will look at your feet, please."

He went around examining our shoes, top and bottom. I won-dered if it would be possible to tell, as long afterward as this, if shoes had been dew wet. "You, of course," he said to Mark. It was his only comment.

When he was done he gestured at the wood-shingle man, and the smaller figure warped after him upstairs. They must be going to search the house.

Movement returned to the room, people breaking out of the trance into which Aakonen's account had thrown them. Bill went over to rest his hand a moment on Mark's shoulder, then walked upstairs.

As if Bill's gesture of belief were a signal, some of the others, too, circled around Mark. Carol was there, clasping his hand; the boy looked back at the sympathy gratefully.

"I thought maybe I hit too hard. I thought maybe he got away and died. The man who came out in the motorboat wouldn't say anything except that Fred was dead. Then when I heard he was shot—"

His words stopped, as if he couldn't express his gratitude that he wasn't a murderer.

WE HAD THE SMALL hustle and bustle of getting Toby off soon after that. Mrs. Foster came.

She looked buxom, indulgent, and capable; Myra had chosen well. Toby and the long, rusty deputy were found on the ladder leading to the boathouse bedrooms, the deputy working on a wooden Mickey Mouse, and Toby delicately cradling a long-legged doll with a remarkable likeness to Cecile Granat.

When Jacqueline and I went upstairs for Toby's things, Aakonen and his men were just coming out of Octavia's room. He nodded with what looked like relief when we asked if Toby could go and followed us to the room, where he stood talking aimlessly while we packed. But he didn't miss anything that went into the suitcases.

When we got down, Mickey wasn't yet quite done, and we

had to wait until he was. And when the car drove off, it wasn't Jacqueline or Myra that Toby wept to have along, but the long, rusty man.

As we walked back toward the porch from seeing Toby off, I got my first glimpse at what Jacqueline's life was going to look like from then on. Ed Corvo and his wife were on the porch, asking the guard for permission to return to the resort.

Jacqueline just brushed Ella Corvo's soft bulk, and Ella, turning, saw who'd touched her. Her body drew back, and her butter-pale, sagging cheeks mottled with an unpleasant blue. What was on her face was unmistakable—loathing. Either Ella Corvo, after hearing Aakonen's summary, believed Jacqueline to be guilty, or else she was giving an awfully good imitation.

Ed Corvo, too, swept Jacqueline with truculent, distrustful eyes. Then the two of them hurried out the door and toward the resort.

I gasped, "Jacqueline, they're just—"

Her face was just quiet.

Myra said, "The Corvos are trash. You mustn't pay attention to what they may think," as helplessly caught in anger as I.

The people in the living room had been talking, but as we came in they stopped. Almost all the eyes seemed to come toward Jacqueline with a furtive, morbid interest. Not certainty in those eyes perhaps, but heavy doubt.

It was into that suspicious silence that Aakonen came down. I heard his heavy footsteps on the stairs and looked up to his ponderous descent. He was carrying something in his hands—something that looked like a soft puddle of silky black.

With a knife thrust of foreboding, I knew what he had—the evening cape I'd brought Jacqueline yesterday—the black hooded evening cape.

8

AAKONEN COMPLETED HIS DESCENT without speaking and walked all the way across the living room through the quick hush to hold the velvet out to Jacqueline.

"This thing," he said. "Miss Gay told me she brought you an evening cape yesterday for a present—is this the one?"

The brown-flecked green eyes flashed me a stricken glance, but there was no panic in her straight shoulders or level voice.

"Yes. I didn't have any before."

"It was a new cape when you got it, wasn't it? It hadn't been worn?"

"Of course."

"You didn't tell me you went out last night, wearing this cape."

"Why should I? I didn't."

His left hand took the garment by the shoulder, letting the fabric fall until the cape hung its full length in soft folds. His right hand held out the creased ribbons at the neck.

"These have been tied."

"Sure, she tried the cape on to show her husband and the little girl—" I couldn't keep out of it.

But he ignored me, keeping his heavy eyes on Jacqueline.

"You say that is all you wore it?"

From Jacqueline, staunchly, "Yes."

"Then how," he asked, and his voice was sharpened to a point, "—how do you explain this?"

The clumsy right hand dropped the ribbons to gather in the bottom of the cape. The velvet pile at the bottom was spotted, plastered down—dry now, but at some time it had been wet, as if it had swept over dewy grass. Unmistakably that cape had been worn outdoors.

THAT FIGURE BY THE Fingers, that oddly long shadow . . .

In that instant, I did all I could do to keep from screaming. Myra and I had been together when we saw that shadow; Octavia had been behind a locked door, and the only other woman in the house was Jacqueline . . .

But I couldn't follow where that thought led. Someone else must have taken that cape last night. Through the roaring in my ears, the sheriff's voice came again, still questioning Jacqueline.

"Perhaps you now remember going for a walk last night?"

"I didn't. I stayed in my room after Ann left."

"It is nothing against you if you went out last night—and can explain."

"I didn't go."

"Perhaps you loaned the cape to someone."

"No. I hung it away yesterday morning. I didn't see it again."

My tongue loosened. "Her bedroom door was open all night. She was fast asleep. Anyone could have walked in there to take the cape out of her closet—anyone. I'll bet the house wasn't even locked."

The eyes did come to me then, perplexed and sharpened.

"How do you know your cousin's door was open all night?"

He'd caught me short. My trip to Jacqueline's room in the night was one thing I hadn't told.

I got the pieces of myself together. "I was in Mrs. Heaton's room until probably ten o'clock. She was dropping off to sleep when I went. I was the one who left the door open."

It wasn't good enough; he waited.

I had to push on, improvising. "Then when I couldn't sleep—before I went downstairs—I walked back to the door of her room. I thought if she was still awake I'd talk to her again. But I could hear by her breathing she was asleep—both she and Toby."

"You walked into the room?"

"No."

"You could hear from the door that two people slept—by the breathing?"

"Yes."

"You have good ears."

"Yes. You heard about the game we played last night."

"Hm." Aakonen was almost glaring at me. He pulled in a violent breath.

"Perhaps you borrowed the cape to wear down on the porch."

"I had my bathrobe on—it was still whole then. I haven't seen or touched the cape since I gave it to my cousin yesterday."

"No," Jacqueline said, "of course she hasn't. It's ridiculous to mix Ann up in this."

He shook the stained bottom folds of the cape at us. "Were these stains on this cape yesterday noon?"

"No," Jacqueline said.

"They got there, then, sometime between yesterday noon and

now. Certainly it is reasonable to think they got there during the night."

Abruptly he turned from us to glare at the room's other occupants, who stood watching in arrested postures as if they'd been playing statues. Bradley Auden held a blackened match halfway between pipe and ashtray; in the kitchen door, Lottie stood with a bread knife, patently forgotten, upraised like a pikestaff.

Aakonen looked at them all, then back to Myra, beside me.

"Was there anything about that figure you saw out near the Fingers to prove it was wearing this cape?"

Myra's dark eyes seemed hypnotized by the black velvet. "No. It was just a shadow."

"Did you know Miss Gay had brought this cape?"

"No. I wasn't there when she unpacked."

Already Aakonen was leaving her, swinging swiftly across the room to Lottie, still standing in apparent blankness at the kitchen door, the bread knife in her hand.

"You know this cape was in the house?"

"Ya." It came faintly, stiffly. "I see it when I fix little girl's bed after she sleep in afternoon. I look and hang it away."

A small pause, then fostering indulgence. "Now, Lottie, if you borrowed this cape to wear to the resort last night, Mrs. Heaton won't be angry. Just tell the truth."

"No. I just take off hanger, hold up, and look at red inside. Is so pretty." From fright, her tone had slipped to a Scandinavian singsong.

"When else did you take out the cape?"

"Didn't take out again. Didn't even look again."

"Maybe you told someone about it?"

Lottie froze again. Then slowly, as if the words squeezed through a tight throat, "I tell my sister Ella." Tears began sliding down her cheeks. "But Ella don't come here! We stay to resort all night!"

Vehement, desperate. With a last threatening glance at her, Aakonen swept on to the others in the group—Cecile, Carol, even the men. No one would admit having seen or heard of the cape. When he'd scanned the whole room, he came back to Jacqueline and me, his eyes focusing on us like searchlights, their penetration almost insupportable.

Yet he said nothing to us; when he finished that second wordless inquisition, he nodded at the long, rusty deputy.

"Mr. Bill Heaton is upstairs. Get him down here."

Silence, except for the deputy's footsteps going upstairs. Aakonen walked across the room to stand close to the stairs; Jacqueline and I followed. Silence still, with the footsteps coming back doubled; Bill descending, in the dark, untouchable shell in which he'd cased himself.

I knew then what the coming moment must bring—decision for Bill. Yesterday he had wondered or feared that Jacqueline might have strung a wire across a path, wrecked a boat . . . Now he must choose whether or not he would believe she had killed his son.

Powerless to help or hinder, I stood beside Jacqueline, we, too, statues in that room of waiting statues.

Aakonen held out the cape to Bill. "You have seen this before?"

"Why, yes." The color of Bill's face had dulled since morning; his eyes had retired behind a glaze of grief. "It belongs to my wife. Miss Gay gave it to her yesterday."

"Someone wore it in the night."

Bill stood staring at him; obviously, at first he didn't know what Aakonen meant. Then he saw.

He said rapidly, "You mean you're suspecting—"

Bill looked now as I'd felt when I saw the word on the middle Finger. Who acted then was the Bill that Aakonen had portrayed for me—the Bill who could be a great man.

He walked toward Jacqueline, who drew away from me, drew away from him, bracing, but then stood proudly still.

"Oh, my darling, I never really believed about those other things—it was just that I was afraid. I know you had nothing to do with this."

His arms went around her, drawing her tightly, desperately close; his face went down to her hair.

"Forgive me. Help me to bear what's happened."

That's Jacqueline's face as I want to remember it. Glory breaking over it before she hid it against Bill's shoulder.

I DIDN'T KNOW WHAT repercussions that decision of Bill's would have. All I felt then was triumph. Bill had shown the others what he thought of their suspicions, and his leadership was strong enough to sway them; they turned decently aside, and I felt a perceptible lessening of their antagonism.

Aakonen's eyes stayed on Bill, perplexed and baffled. Whatever he had hoped to get from calling Bill down, patently it wasn't this. He went upstairs again, the cape still over his arm.

EXHAUSTION FROM TOO MUCH emotion set in. As I helped Myra and Lottie make sandwiches and chocolate a little later, I was suddenly done in. For the rest of the evening, I just remember the bare outlines of what happened—people filing past the kitchen counters to fill plates, they, too, dragging but clinging together as if they'd become parts of a whole and couldn't break away.

Aakonen returned after a while, the remnants of my bathrobe

added to the cape over his arm. He and his men searched the downstairs, moving us from room to room. Bill went upstairs but stayed for a few moments only; he spent the evening at Jacqueline's side. The phone rang many times but once to give a message he wanted—Toby and Mrs. Foster were safely in Duluth.

Phillips told Myra, "I'll bed here in the living room, if you don't mind. I don't fancy sleeping in that boathouse alone." His regained aplomb had abated a little as evening darkness settled.

Myra started wearily upstairs for blankets, but Bill stopped her.

"Phillips can have the room Jacqueline was using."

So that was what he'd done on that short trip upstairs, I thought, and I was right; when I went up to help Myra, there was nothing of Jacqueline's left in the northeast room.

When we returned downstairs Aakonen was waiting. He got sheets of typewriter paper from Myra and a blue wax crayon that had been Toby's. He had each of us, standing, print the word *monarch* in capitals, first with the right hand, then with the left. He made no comment, and we made none. When we were done, he stacked the sheets, folded them lengthwise, and stuck them in his pocket. He picked up a newspaper-wrapped bundle into which my bathrobe and the cape had been wound.

"I am stopping at the resort," he told Lottie. "Would you want to ride?" Then to the rest of us, "I am leaving a man here. It should be safe for you to sleep. If you leave, you will be followed. Do not try to run away."

The group dispersed then—broke—with no good-byes given. Jacqueline went upstairs with Bill.

Maybe the others depended on Aakonen's man, but I slept behind a door whose key was turned, and with the window locked tight.

Like so many of the things that happened, the efforts we

made next morning to solve Fred's murder seemed to get us nowhere, and yet they all had their places in the final pattern.
When I woke in my barricaded room to the day that was to begin
with striving and end with new disaster, I saw through the window a thick grayness of fog so heavy that mist distilled from it
to hang in flat beads on the glass.

For a time I lay in a half state between sleep and waking, my
body so weighted that my strength seemed too small to lift a
finger. From the shrouded world outside, the wilderness sounds
boomed dully. The house was as quiet as if no one in it lived.

I had to do something to find out who had killed Fred, but
inertia lay as heavy as the fog. Where could I begin? Pebbles took
no footprints; rough rock took no fingerprints; if there'd been
any clues left near Fred's body, I'd heard only of the damning
ones I couldn't believe—the harebells, the shawl, the word.

I managed to get up, to dress in the chilly dampness. The four
other doors on the hall were still closed as I tiptoed to the bathroom. When I got downstairs, the rooms were as they'd been left;
Lottie hadn't come yet.

At the cold kitchen range, I stuffed paper in the firepot and
kindling on top of it. Twin sweaters were buttoned to my chin,
but the chill struck in, and my mind seemed as congealed as my
blood. The fire was just beginning to crackle, sending up spears
of heat to my hovering hands, when footsteps sounded on the
stairs—Bill and Jacqueline, their pale faces smudged by weariness, as if they hadn't slept at all.

"We heard you come down, so we did," Jacqueline told me.
"We've been talking—"

"Trying to decide what must be done," Bill said. Grief still
held him, but it was harder; he'd begun to think; he'd take
charge of this as he would of anything else. "People will want
coffee. Ann, I want to talk to you."

"I'll get breakfast." Jacqueline gave me a small, pale smile, accepting.

When I followed Bill to the living room, he closed the door, standing with his back to it.

He said, low, "All those tricks, looking as if Jacqueline had done them. And now Fred—looking as if Jacqueline had done that, too. Do you see it as I do?"

I nodded.

"The amount and the kind of planning," he went on. "It's diabolical. Someone—for some reason I can't see—wanted Fred dead and began planning as long ago as the wedding that Jacqueline should be made to look responsible. That must have been the reason for those tricks—to make Jacqueline look unstable."

Exclamation rising in my throat; as soon as he said it, I could see it—that terrible devising. In the light of morning—even this gray, sightless morning—fear had lessened, but now it thickened again like the fog.

"Who could it be?" he asked. "Who, Ann? All that cunning— and what's the motive behind it? No one benefits by Fred's death." The tumult of dark, struggling thought was on his face. "There must be something I can't see—"

"No one can see," I said.

"We've got to start work—and, Ann, you mustn't tell Jacqueline—she mustn't see this so nakedly."

But when we opened the door and Jacqueline came in with silver for the table, I didn't think she needed telling. Looking at truth, she quietly made toast.

Almost at once, most of the group that had broken up so late the night before was together again, as if it were drawn by some unbreakable cohesion. Myra and Phillips came down from upstairs, Myra strained and drawn, Phillips at least in this early part of the morning subdued. Octavia, of course, remained unseen. Jean came with Mark; the impact of what had happened showed on Jean's dark face only in heavy soberness and gravity; he looked as if he'd slept. Mark held himself aloof, quiet, but he had clearly been thinking; the alertness of his gray eyes contrasted oddly with the swollen, discolored bruises that still covered most of his thin, thoughtful face.

"The inn's locked this morning," Jean told us. "Owens was on the porch—he waved us away."

Myra roused. "You can get breakfast here."

"Thanks." Jean continued looking at Bill. "Do you think the inn's being locked could mean anything?"

"What could it mean?" Bill began a restless pacing.

"It could mean Ed Corvo." Jean stood solidly still. "Have you thought of that? Aakonen was there in the inn when I went to bed."

"Ed?" Bill asked. "He couldn't have handled this."

I set down the cups I'd brought in; any possibility was something to grab.

"You mean you think Ed Corvo—?"

Jean turned then to me. "Well, you don't know it, Ann, but Fred had an accident with a car a year ago—ran into Ed Corvo's nephew near Lutsen."

Bill said heavily, "That was why I wouldn't let Fred have a car." He turned aside, his mouth twisting.

I remembered that Jacqueline had said something about a car and an accident.

Jean went on to Bill, "The kid just limps a little, and you gave his father all that dough in a trust fund. Just the same, they kicked up a row about wanting the cash instead of the fund."

"I can't see it." Bill's reluctance held. "I can't see Ed Corvo managing that acid on my suit and the fire in the bed. If Ed is the answer, then the tricks are one thing and the murder is another. I can't see it."

Bradley Auden and Carol also came; before we'd finished our brief breakfast their car was in the drive.

"Thought we might be of some help. Any news?" Bradley Auden, too, was nervous and strained, his eyes flickering from face to face with a sort of hunger as he lit a cigarette. Carol, like Mark, was quiet outside, alert inside; she moved as if unconsciously in Mark's direction. I noticed she didn't look at Jacqueline, any more than the others did.

Bradley talked rapidly on. "No guard at the gate this morning. Was one last night. Who's around besides the man at the Fingers?"

We all quickened to that, realizing the man at the rocks was the only guard we'd seen that morning. Jean told Bradley about the locked inn.

"Don't blame them." Bradley gave a short laugh. "I locked my own house last night—first time in my life."

Bill got up from the table. "I'm not interested in fright. I want to see this thing cleared up. Jean, if you'll wait a second, I'd like to send you in to the office. Two of you could go over the barn and boathouse again. How about you, Brad, and Phillips? It was dark last night when Aakonen searched."

Bradley nodded like a workman relieved to get orders. Phillips asked, "Outdoors in this weather?" But he went, too.

"Everything but Fred's room," Bill went on. "Ann and Myra, would you take that? I can't make myself. Bring me anything that could have a bearing. Then, if the gun were hidden in the rocks—"

"We'll look around the rocks, sir!" Instantly from Mark.

"Thanks. I need to make a lot of calls. If you'll help me,

Jacqueline . . ." He was keeping her under the protection of his presence.

Myra, pausing only to take a breakfast tray up to Octavia, came out with me into the gray clouded landscape in which the five rocks and the guard by them loomed almost as obscurely as the shadows had on that significant night.

"It's a relief to have Bill take control." Myra voiced my own thought. "I spent the night trying to see what we could do but feeling lost and helpless."

I, too, had a feeling of direction under Bill's orders. But when I stood in the door of Fred's room above the boathouse, a hand seemed to clap across my nose, shutting off breath. I knew then why Bill couldn't come. Fred was gone into the dignity of death, and here were the pitiable, ridiculous leavings of the living—two chewed pencils and a gum wrapper beside a tray overflowing with cigarette stubs, detective magazines littering a cot whose brown crash cover was pitted and awry with the twisting and turning of a living body. On the wall above the cot, hanging like a picture, was a football jersey with the number 47 on its back.

Myra's eyes went first to that. She said, "They were hoping Fred would make the team next fall . . ."

Her voice shook, and I had a moment of my own, knowing all the hopes and ambitions that room had held, all the restless beating desires, all the hungers and resentments.

Myra said, low, "A boy doesn't bring much to a lake for the summer." In her voice, too, the subdued and humble knowledge of our pitiable humanity.

Slowly we began going over what personal possessions the room held—tennis rackets, fishing tackle, golf clubs, more magazines, a college geometry and English textbook from a table near the window, a limp half-emptied cigarette carton, and matchbooks from Grand Marais and Minneapolis. In the closet, slacks were folded over wire hangers alongside one wool suit, heavy jackets, and some shirts. From the dresser drawers, which might as well have been stirred with a spoon, we took out each article, refolded and replaced it.

It wasn't until we were leafing through the magazines that we found anything at all. Myra shut one magazine hastily, thrusting it under a pile.

"What was that?" I asked.

"Nothing important. He drew faces—I didn't like them."

I pulled out the magazine she'd thrust away. All around the title of the first story, a familiar face had been drawn in—Jacqueline's. He'd put a witch's hat on her head. He'd tried to make her malignant and evil, but he hadn't succeeded. He'd drawn her mouth big and out of proportion, but it had stayed soft. Along a margin, he'd drawn mouths that had no face; he must have been trying to find the meanness that wasn't there.

"I wish you wouldn't look," Myra said. "It's like—" She burst suddenly into fierceness. "People should know when they're going to die so they can destroy what they wouldn't want seen. Here we're prying in the secret places of Fred's life!"

"We're doing it for a reason," I reminded. I leafed on through the magazine, where more sketches appeared, up and down the margins like illuminations: Cecile as a centaurette, her slender waist emerging from the body of a sleek and dappled horse, her fingers spread wide over her breasts, her blond hair billowing from a coyly lowered head. Bradley Auden as a centaur, pawing the earth. Bill in a beard, unmistakably the Lord God, Jehovah. Carol Auden as a mermaid, combing out her hair. Carol Auden as a hollyhock, her hair the petals. Carol Auden in a bride's veil. Jacqueline again, this time with her eyes tipped upward, and horns.

Not much doubt what Fred had thought of people. I laid that magazine aside to show Bill.

Going through the contents of the suitcase under the bed, we made the next find. The suitcase held notebooks, textbooks—summer-school work Fred would never do. But under a sheaf of papers, something bright showed—travel folders. I took them out. Then I sat back on my heels.

"Myra—look! These are for steamship lines! Here's the line Bill and Jacqueline took on their honeymoon. What do you suppose—?"

Myra reached over to take them. "Imagine his keeping those," she said. "He must have been following each place they went. Here are the times of leaving and arrival—marked."

I said slowly, "Suppose he did follow—actually follow? That would explain that suit with the holes in it."

"But that's impossible! He was at school—how could he?"

"It's one thing we can find out." I laid the folders aside with the magazine.

An hour later, we stood with dusty hands, having taken up the rugs from the floor, the bedding from the bed. There was nothing to say whom Fred had met that dark midnight by the Fingers or why he'd died.

Bill was silent over the magazines, looking soberly at each sketched face. Jacqueline looked whitely at what Fred had thought of her, she, too, not speaking.

To the travel folders—and my idea—there was a more vehement reaction.

"That's impossible. Fred couldn't have been away from school in late May. I saw his grades." But Bill rose to get the housemother of Fred's fraternity on the phone, tracing her all over Minneapolis until he found her in summer residence at a daughter's home.

From the receiver, when he got her, came a staccato rush of questions.

Jacqueline whispered, "The news must have been in the Minneapolis papers this morning." Yesterday Bill had walked in a shell; today she was in one, as if her emotions had become so strong, she'd had to insulate herself. I went to hug her head against me, feeling unbearably the solitude in which she sat.

But she smiled up at me. "Everything's going to be—We'll soon know. Bill will find out."

She thought Bill could do anything.

Bill asked clipped questions at the phone, turning from it with finality. "That question's settled. Fred was in residence at his fraternity from the day he got back from the wedding until school was out. He didn't miss a day."

I asked, "Then what do those folders mean? They must mean something."

He took them up, his voice roughening. "I'm not so sure. Poor kid, he looked grown up, but he wasn't. It was the first time I ever took a trip without him. Here!"

He pushed the folders at me as if he couldn't bear them. I still had them when I went upstairs with Myra to wash while he went on with his interminable telephoning.

Jean was in my room when I walked in, and I didn't notice what I did with what was in my hands. Later, I was to find I'd absentmindedly left those folders on my dresser.

"Sorry," he said. "Bill's orders." He refolded a slip neatly and placed it back in a drawer. "Not that you'd hide anything, but something might have been planted on you."

It was no time for personal sensitiveness. "Learn anything you can," I said, and went on to wash.

When Myra and I got back downstairs, Phillips was there,

standing in the exact center of the living room, his heavy white head cocked, on his mouth the pleased triumph of the news bearer.

"We can quit our hunting. The murderer's caught. Aakonen made the arrest this morning."

9

FOR ONCE, PHILLIPS HAD everyone's attention, and he loved it. At the immediate questions, he preened and pivoted, dragging out his answers to get the full drama.

It was Ed Corvo that Aakonen had arrested.

The moment the name was out, Bill was facing him like an antagonist. "How much does Aakonen have to go on?"

I noticed then that Bradley Auden was there, too, standing back, letting Phillips do the talking, and that Jean had come down. Phillips couldn't talk without elaboration; the gist of the story was that Aakonen had stayed at the resort the night before, hammering at Lottie and the Corvos.

Lottie had been trapped into an admission—after going to bed the evening of the Fourth, she'd thought she heard someone going downstairs. Ed always got up if a car drove in or at any unusual sound; she hadn't worried, and had promptly gone to sleep.

Ed, cornered by her admission, had admitted he'd been up. At about ten, he'd said. He'd made the rounds of the cabins and the boathouse, his wrecked boat on his mind. You couldn't, he'd said, tell what such a vandal might do—he might burn everyone in his bed.

"You stayed up all night?" the sheriff had suggested.

"No." Ed Corvo had been insistent in that denial; he'd gone back to bed again, hadn't again gotten up. Ella had corroborated, saying her husband was back within an hour, but she'd been unhappy and confused. Ella, who yesterday had made such an open display of loathing Jacqueline.

"Big chance you were taking, walking around in the dark." Aakonen had made an adroit suggestion.

"No, I—" Ed had caught himself, but too late. He'd been forced to admit he'd taken his gun along.

"It had been fired recently, too." Phillips closed his complacent recital. "Couldn't tell when—but lately. Aakonen said he'd know for sure when he got the bullet out of Fred."

Behind me Jean asked, "Where you get all this?"

"From Owens—the tall deputy. Brad and I went over for cigarettes. Owens is still there."

Bill said, "You mean to tell me Ed Corvo planned this whole business of throwing suspicion on Jacqueline? He wasn't at the wedding—"

"Lottie was," Jean said. "If Corvo did it, he must have had help. Lottie saw that act on the lawn here, too."

"Even then, I can't see it. Can't see a strong enough motive. Can't see Ed being clever enough."

"Owens figures it this way," Phillips came in again. "He thinks Aakonen thinks Fred was mad at Ed Corvo because he'd kept Fred from having a car. Aakonen and Owens both were right there after the accident last summer, when Ed said that a kid like Fred shouldn't have a car, and, Bill, you said that from now on, Fred wouldn't.

"Aakonen thinks maybe it was Ed who wrecked Fred's motorcycle, and when Fred guessed it, he went over and smashed his boat. Then on the night of the Fourth, Ed might have heard Fred fighting with Mark and gone out. Maybe Ed charged Fred with wrecking his boat and Fred just laughed. Maybe Ed got mad and shot him."

"There wasn't any sign Fred's body had been removed."

"Ed's got a wheelbarrow," Jean said.

"My gun—why's that gone if Ed Corvo used his?"

"Red herring," Jean said.

As if that last were a signal, everyone moved and spoke, Jacqueline coming forward to stand beside Bill.

"It must be *someone*, Bill."

"Yes," Phillips repeated, "it has to be someone. If not Ed Corvo—who else had any reason for wanting Fred out of the way?"

Sly and poisoned—another barb. Why look for a motive?— that's what people would say. Fred didn't have anything, but his father did. The second Mrs. William Heaton, that barb insinuated, wouldn't be sorry the boy was gone.

Bill said harshly, "There is another motive. We can't see it, that's all. But we're going to see it."

Myra said slowly, "Can't we believe it must be Ed Corvo? I suppose this explains why only one man is left on guard here. We'd all rather it was Ed than anyone else. That's brutal but the truth." She could be forthright even about murder. And this let Jacqueline out.

Bill said, "Get on with your hunting."

SO THE DOGGED EFFORT of that Saturday morning continued, flogged on by Bill. At the phone, he was calling a detective in Duluth, ordering a search of Fred's possessions in the Duluth apartment. He called friends of Fred's, asking always the same questions—had Fred spoken of anyone who had it in for him, had he gotten threatening letters, had he been in debt. Phillips and Bradley Auden had finished searching the boathouse before going to the resort for cigarettes. At Bill's suggestion, we went over the house again, Myra doing Octavia's room, and then on to the barn. Mark and Carol were still out hunting among rocks.

As we walked toward the barn, the grocery bus came into the drive; Myra left to pick out meats and vegetables.

"Lottie'll never turn up now," was her grim parting. "You go on with the men, Ann. I'll start lunch."

Bradley Auden had been working spasmodically, varying between feverish energy and gloomy thought. He said now, "Maybe you haven't noticed, but we haven't seen Cecile all day. I'm going over to see how she is." He, too, left.

So only Jean, Phillips, and I went on to the second searching of the barn, which held Bill's big old car, its top still down, and Myra's newer sedan. Back in a corner was a mass of twisted metal. Phillips went toward that, to stand before it musingly, his head on the side.

"The trouble with Bill is he's always right." Jean was still grumbling over Bill's reaction to the Corvo arrest. "If he thinks Ed Corvo is out, Ed Corvo probably is out."

"This business of the wrecked motorcycle now." Phillips kicked at the twisted mass. "That was an interesting little incident, too. Fred and Bill went over this wreckage—I don't see what I could learn from it now."

He turned to me as I went through Myra's car; Jean had tackled Bill's.

"It seems someone started the motor of that motorcycle one night while we all slept. Got it going across the lawn toward the lake—there's quite a grade. Thing rolled right into the lake. Current did the rest."

Jacqueline had just mentioned the wrecking of the motorcycle. I lifted my head.

"How do you know that's what happened?"

"Suspicious kitten, aren't you? Fred found the tracks across the flowers on the terrace next morning. Went out in a motorboat and hunted along the bar until he found it. All North Shore rivers have bars at their mouths, you know, except the Temperance."

When I didn't answer, he went over to Jean. "Working hard, aren't you?"

He seemed to have lapsed into being as provoking as he'd been before murder struck. "I can see why. If Corvo is out—as Bill so gallantly thinks—that leaves just one person behind the eight ball, doesn't it?"

My hand stopped in the act of opening a car door, every muscle wanting to leap to battle. But before I could open my mouth Jean had swung around, his jaw outthrust.

"So I have a hard time believing Bill's wife killed Fred," he said. "What's it to you?" Then his eyes half closed, and his tone became soft. "Aren't you just a little anxious to remind us about the suspicions against Jacqueline? Where do you come in?"

Phillips didn't retreat against the advance.

"Me?" he asked negligently. "I come in under the head of loving truth. Let's see, didn't you take Jacqueline out a few times before she met Bill?"

"Louse!" Jean said, and knocked him down with a punch to the jaw.

Phillips Heaton got sweetly up, cocked an eye at me, smiled, and strolled out.

Jean said furiously, "Jacqueline was the prettiest girl I'd ever seen. Sure, I dated her. I liked her. I was the one who introduced her to Bill. I wasn't in love with her. I'm glad Bill married her."

Each sentence was like a shot. He went back to hunting.

So there was that, too. I'd found there was one more person who didn't suspect Jacqueline, but . . .

If I could have wished the murder on anyone, I'd have wished it on Phillips Heaton.

Of course I told Bill and Jacqueline. Before lunch. Myra didn't ask Jean to eat with us; he left, going toward the resort.

Bill took my account with utter incredulity.

"I thought Phillips came in looking—" he began, then, "*Jean?*"

He stared at me and suddenly, discordantly, he laughed, a laugh that sounded as if it drifted up out of hell. "Does Jean have to be suspected in this, too? My friend that's my brother?" He walked away to the windows as if what he faced was intolerable.

Jacqueline had risen wonderingly from the phone book with which she'd been working. "But Jean wasn't interested in me," she said. "Myra met him one day and asked him for dinner. He took me to a movie. That was the only—"

Bill at the window, "Jean came back to the apartment that night. He was staying with me. He almost knocked me across the room. He said he'd met the girl I'd marry." He swung around. "No. That's ridiculous. Jean has no personal interest in Jacqueline, and he isn't jealous of me. Jean's square from the ground up."

Bill was the one who was always right.

"There's still Jean's question," I said, low, so that Myra, upstairs giving Octavia her lunch, shouldn't hear me. "Where does Phillips come in? He seems to have an alibi, but—"

Bill shrugged intolerant shoulders. "What does Fred's death put in Phillips's pockets?"

MYRA HAD MADE A fire in the fireplace and set the table before it. Toasting as I ate, it seemed to me that, although I hadn't stopped to notice, I'd been cold and wet all morning.

Until then, reporters hadn't bothered us. But as we ate, the vanguard arrived, skidding to a stop in the drive. Two men got out, one of them coming to the door.

"Mind if we take a few pictures here?" he asked pleasantly. "We're from the Minneapolis *World*. Been in talking to Aakonen. He seems to have the murder sewed up."

Bill answered curtly without rising, "I don't suppose I can stop you."

"You're Bill Heaton, aren't you?" The question came smoothly. "I'm Chris Paxton. You may've seen my name. We don't want to get in your hair, Mr. Heaton—we know this is hell. You agree with Aakonen's ideas?"

"He's in charge of the investigation."

Mr. Paxton nodded, still pleasantly but with an air of getting at some more malleable person later, and strolled off toward the Fingers, where a cameraman was already setting up a tripod. Later, I learned that a piece of brown paper had been fastened over the chalked word as a protection against fog and wind; otherwise the rocks were now unguarded.

Phillips said sourly, "The Minneapolis *World* is going to list what we had for lunch. Pity it won't do the family more honor." The corner of his mouth was purplish where Jean had hit him.

"Getting nowhere." Bill rose impatiently from the table where he'd eaten so little. "Fred's friends say he has no enemies; he wasn't in trouble with any girl; he didn't owe any gambling debts; he hadn't been spending heavily—it's all too far afield.

What I'm after must be here. *Right here.* There's someone *here* who wanted him dead . . ."

He walked the room from end to end, unseeingly, his eyes seeking inward for the dark clue he desired.

Unobtrusively, Phillips melted away. I was to notice him later in what was by that time a knot of reporters near the Fingers. Chris Paxton got the news source he wanted.

At loose ends now that Bill's rush of effort had flagged, Myra, Jacqueline, and I did the dishes and then called Toby, who said she was ready to come back now, and Aunt Harriet, who asked why we didn't all just leave. About two, Aakonen called—there'd be an inquest Monday morning at ten in the Grand Marais town hall. Of Ed Corvo's arrest or any other clues he might have, he would say nothing.

Jean was back by that time. "Inquest," he said. "Aakonen must figure he has something. I wonder what he figures about your gun being gone, Bill. I've been thinking about that and I don't like it."

There'd be only one reason the murderer might want to keep the gun. I looked at the others and watched realization strike—in Jacqueline's eyes, quick but steady, in Myra's. Bill and Jean already knew.

Bill said, "Carol and Mark got back here just before Ann came in. They'd looked all morning and didn't see anything."

"Forty thousand acres of hiding places around here," Jean said.

But my mind fled over those surrounding miles of wilderness, then pulled in close. "The murderer had to reach the hiding place—if there is one—between the time Fred was killed and morning. He had to cut up my bathrobe while it was still dark, too."

"Good girl!" Jean said. "Well, I thought I'd start on the patch of woods between here and the resort. Anyone want to come along?" He looked at me.

Bill chose his words slowly. "I think I'll get farther staying here as headquarters. Mark and Carol said they'd go out this afternoon again, too. I want to do some thinking. And Jacqueline had best stay with me."

Myra got to her feet, but she was only too obviously all in from sleeplessness and strain. I sent her to bed for a nap and went with Jean alone—through the pantry window, to avoid reporters.

BILL HAD SAID JEAN was above question, but as I walked with him toward the resort path, some apprehension quickened; suspicions can't be settled with a word. The fog that had swathed the morning had lifted only slightly; it hung heavily—within touching distance, it seemed—overhead; the lake dashed angrily, the color and apparent consistency of geyser mud; the chuckle of the Fingers echoed distantly, as if mocking our frail, unproductive efforts.

"Look for any sign," Jean told me. "Broken twigs, a scrap of fabric, leaves or mold disturbed—anything."

At first as I stumbled back and forth between trees, half my attention was for him. Inside a house, he sometimes seemed hesitant and clumsy, but out here, he moved easily and swiftly, covering much more ground than I but keeping near me.

We'd worked perhaps half an hour when I thought I heard a rustle from somewhere near the center of that patch of woods.

I didn't speak, but Jean straightened from a rock he was overturning to look at me. More certainly this time a small rustling, not continuous but intermittent, as if someone moved, stopped to listen, then moved again.

"Stay here, close to the path," Jean whispered, and instantly was gone, melting into the trees and grayness like a shadow. He made no more noise than a panther, but as I strained my ears, that other sound of movement stopped; when it began again, it was much louder and coming in my direction. Whoever it was had heard Jean coming and was cutting directly into the path. Straight at me.

For the first time in my life, while waiting for the unknown rustle to resolve itself into a human being, I wished I had some weapon of defense. I moved backward until I was on the open path.

Then a figure became visible, and relief washed up. Cecile Granat.

Seeing her there, her own words flashed in my mind—her words to Bill on the porch. "And you think you have the right to tell me what to do, too, don't you?" Inimical words—she'd been angry. What little I knew of her was none too good; what little I'd guessed of her was none too good, either, and still, perversely, I was relieved. What I'd expected was probably a man—huge, uncouth, unknown—to leap at me, snarling and slavering.

I said, "Oh, hallo, Cecile! I couldn't imagine who was there in—"

"Hallo yourself. You all alone out here?"

"No. Jean's along."

No surprise on the gold-tanned, exotic face over which caution was now laid like an enamel.

"I was out looking around," she said. "Thought I might stumble across the hiding place of that gun, if it is hidden. Bradley Auden told me it hadn't been found. That what you're doing, too?"

It was a little too prompt, but I nodded. Jean had heard her change of direction and was coming back, threshing noisily this time.

To him she repeated her explanation. "I was getting the shakes, sitting in that cabin all alone."

One of Jean's thick brows went up an infinitesimal fraction, but he seemed to accept her words at face value.

"We could use another hunter." He spaced us so we stomped through the woods like a dragnet. Birds flew up under our noses; rabbits fled; we even flushed a young fox who sprang with a liquid, angry bark from a secure thicket, then stopped thirty feet off to look back at us with disdainful incredulity before he trotted daintily away. The fog began lowering, so that we worked in progressive gloom.

Whatever her purpose in the wood lot, Cecile was playing up to her part; she hunted with apparent thoroughness. Before long we were dusty, twig scratched, and—in spite of the chill dampness—hot.

Cecile stuck until perhaps five o'clock before she stood upright to rub a rueful hand along her back.

"We're nuts." It was disgruntled and sulky. "What we're hunting might be under the one leaf we don't turn. This is where I quit."

I stood, too, to ease back muscles that yelped.

Jean cajoled, "It's only a few hundred feet to the road. Come on, Cecile, stick with us."

"Too much is sticking to me. My clothes. I'm getting back to the shower before it freezes—which wouldn't surprise me any minute."

She left, and Jean bent again to his task, but he wasn't really hunting—he was listening to her audible passage through the woods.

"No, she's too clever," he said when the sounds ceased. "She went straight to the resort. Come on. I'm going back to the spot where she was when we heard her first. I marked where it would be."

So we went back to the center of the wood lot, ground we'd already covered. We turned over practically every bush leaf. There was nothing.

Jean didn't give up until we'd been at it an hour. "She was in here for some reason. What?"

"If she was hiding the gun—"

"Aakonen searched her cabin. And we agreed the murderer had plenty of time to hide the gun the night of the murder."

"She might have come to see if it was safe or to move it to a safer hiding place."

"Possible. If she did, she did a damn good job." He kicked at the soft leaf mold. "The trouble with this damp, crumbly ground is that it's hard to see if it's been disturbed. Sprinkle a few leaves over it, and a dug-up spot would look like all the rest."

I said slowly, "We've got to remember a girl like Cecile might have something else she'd want to hide. Something she mightn't want to burn or throw in the lake, but would want tucked away if she thought the hunt might get too close."

"I said Aakonen searched her cottage."

"He didn't search me personally."

A grunt. "He slapped me over. And Mark. The kind of clothes you girls wear makes a personal search unnecessary. So either she came to see the gun was safe or to hide something flat and small enough that she could have had on her person. Or something else we haven't thought of. All right, let's get back to that strip of woods we haven't covered."

I followed without demur, but I'd seen the impossibility of what we were attempting. If the wilderness hid anything we wanted, we were doomed never to find it—the hiding places were too many, the space too great.

It was perhaps eight when we emerged on the highway after a more and more cursory search. Jean, too, was accepting impossibility. By the time he quit, he was muttering to himself in anger; evidently unsuccessful physical effort had the same effect on him that unsuccessful mental effort has on me.

"We should have stopped before," were Jean's first articulate words. He grabbed at one of my torn and aching hands and began a brisk trot. By that time, the darkness was so heavy we automatically followed the highway around to the Fingers drive instead of cutting through the woods. The moment I'd stood still, I'd begun feeling chilled; it was a relief to run in the freshening wind; the big breaths I had to take were clear and sharp in my nose. When we passed the gate among the pines, the treetops were knocking together in that wind, the bare branch nubs clashing.

"Sounds like a thousand skeletons being jangled," I said. Lulled by his dedication to the search, my suspicions of him were gone; I was warm from running, and my muscles were as smooth as oil.

"A little less of those skeletons," he said, but he grinned at me.

We got to the lodge at the end of a sprint so speedy that I grabbed at the screen door and stuck to it, panting.

"That was fun." He was breathing heavily, smiling. "Let's do it again sometime. The trouble with civilization is that you have to be so all-fired decrepit the minute you're grown up."

"I'd say that's not true of you . . . Heavens, the house is dark!" It was a darkness that was quickly reminding, sobering. Yesterday morning I'd discovered murder and now I ran and smiled.

"Here, I'll get a light on." He led me across the porch and inside the living room, his fingers groping for the nearest lamp. Then he pulled a chain, and a warm cone of light swam up.

"Everyone must be out," he began, but we both saw at once that everyone wasn't.

A limp arm hung over the arm of a chair near the fireplace.

I ran, fear gripping my chest like a cold steel wrench. But when I got to where I could look down on Jacqueline's dark head, relief came out of me in an audible gasp. She was sleeping normally, soundlessly, her head fallen against her shoulder, her whole body relaxed and easy.

Jean said low, beside me, "Bill must have gone out."

I tiptoed backward. "Let her sleep; she needs it. The others must be around. Maybe Myra's still asleep. I'll run upstairs to wash. If you'll stay I'll get you something to eat."

He hesitated, looking at me. "No, I'll drive in to Grand Marais—I understand we're being allowed that much rope—if I can't get anything at the inn. I'll see you later tonight though."

"Check on any news they have there—especially if they've found out if that bullet came from Ed Corvo's gun."

Jacqueline stirred, sighing. Jean nodded agreement and left as I tiptoed the rest of the way to the stairs and up. On the way, I felt the impression of movement ahead of me; I thought again that Octavia had probably been in the hall listening and had scurried to her room.

It was easy, except when Myra took her food or spoke of her, to forget that Octavia was even in the house, she succeeded so completely in effacing herself. What, I wondered as I passed her door, was her existence now? Was she, like the rest of us, apprehensive that the person who had killed Fred might strike again? Was that why she hid so completely, cowering and waiting for a footfall? Did she, like the others, suspect Jacqueline? Or was it merely the exposure of her infirmity from which she fled? Certainly she was puzzling. If she hadn't had that alibi . . .

The key was no longer on the outside of her door. She must be locking it herself on the inside.

Myra's door, too, was closed; I hoped she was asleep.

Not knowing the hurry there was, I dawdled. I was in the bathroom perhaps fifteen minutes, some of the time with the clanking faucet open; the bathroom window was closed. Leisurely I went back along the hall to my room, where I got out slacks and a fresh sweater and stood in front of the dresser putting them on.

It was then I made that small discovery so soon to be brushed from my mind.

The travel folders I'd dropped there were still on the dresser top; when I pulled the sweater over my head, I scooped them up to throw them into the wastebasket. Like everything else we'd worked on that day, they seemed just a dead end. But, curiously, before dropping them I looked at them again. Only some of them were marked. The steamship line which Bill and Jacqueline had taken was marked for times of leaving and arrival; some of the passages of descriptive fluff were also underlined—rapturous accounts of life aboard ship.

"No Marco Polo, no Cortés, no Balboa, no other explorer silent upon his peak in Darien ever thrilled to more exotic, more exciting sights and sounds than you'll thrill to on these South Sea trips of the Island Line," one folder began. "For you we have planned . . ."

That passage had been underlined in an odd, disrupted way. A line under a word here and a word there—a line under *no*, a line under *more*, a line under *trips*, a line under *for you* . . .

Stupidly I stared at it, knowing I had something but not able to see what it was. Then I did see.

The underlined words were a message—*No more trips for you*.

A message Fred had gotten perhaps while Bill and Jacqueline were on their honeymoon. A taunt.

Quickly I went through the folders again. In some, the passages underlined were just the more glowing accounts of the fun to be had on the boats and the islands. But there were other messages.

"Take it and like it."

"You'll keep . . . your nose on the grindstone." Out of a passage adjuring the opposite.

Peculiarly, with those folders in my hands, I could feel as if I were Fred getting them. Envy coming on. He'd been getting a lot of ribbing about his father's marriage. There'd be the possibility of baby brothers and sisters at his age. He'd been manfully throttling his natural jealousies. And then these had come, arrows turning in the wound. I could understand now that scene of his clowning . . .

Automatically, staring at myself in the mirror, I reached out my hand to my powder box on the dresser and flapped the puff against my nose.

Then in a great gasp of stinging pain I ran groping for the bathroom. Pepper. Someone had put pepper in the powder! Sneezing, coughing, weeping, I threw water on my streaming eyes; it was minutes before I could even see myself. Then as pain subsided, broken by recurrent fits of sneezing, anger began rising. I looked as if I'd had a three-week crying bout. Of all the nasty tricks . . .

Tricks. This was another.

Anger got too big to hold. I bounced down the stairs to wake Jacqueline, but as I stood furiously staring at her chair, I thought that my blinded eyes were telling me lies. I even put my hand on the cushion.

She wasn't there.

I looked for her in the shadows of the room, calling her. "Jacqui! Where are you?"

"Ann!" As if in distant answer, her voice came calling me, mingling with the lake and forest roar. From somewhere outside.

"Ann!" My name again. Far away, but wild and urgent.

Instinct got me across the front porch, stopped me to listen.

"Ann!" From the direction of the Fingers. Sightlessly I ran, caught my toe in a plant on the terrace, fell, was up again.

She wasn't calling any longer; she heard me. "Hurry! Get Bill's car!" She was commanding, weeping.

I got to the Fingers, stumbled again, went down against something that my hands groped for and found—a man's legs on the gravel, right where Fred's had been.

10

———

JACQUELINE'S SOBBING WAS CLOSE to my ear.

"Ann, hurry! It's Bill. I've got to get him away from here. His car. Hurry!"

Senseless thunder and chuckle in ears, all around and through me. I rose to obey, running sightlessly and thoughtlessly.

"No! Ann, wait! Come back! The keys—"

She must have been groping in Bill's pockets for them, because she had them ready when I got back. Again I ran across the lawn, still hearing her weeping mingled with the chuckle of the river and the boisterous pounding rush of wind and water, sweeping up again its loud pagan exultation.

I could remember where Bill's car was in the barn. I was in the seat, the wheel under my hands. The car moved as if it were rehearsed—back, around in complete darkness. The lights went on, twin beams flashing across the lawn, arcs of light fringing into blackness; my eyes stung, but I could see. Ruthlessly I drove

across the lawn and the flower bank. The lights picked up Jacqueline sitting with Bill's head and shoulders on her lap; even the
colors flashed up, unforgettable—her blue dress, her white face,
Bill's long brown shadow. When I swung the car to stop beside
them she was rising, trying to lift the man in her arms.

I saw Bill clearly then—over the front of his white shirt a red
stain, wetter, redder, wider than that other stain. His head lolled
limply on her arm, the ridges of cheekbone and nose and chin too
sharp, too bold.

"He's dead," I whispered. Ice, as if the cold of an entire winter
flowed out from my heart.

"No!" she denied me fiercely. "I shouldn't move him—it's all
wrong to move him. But I've got to get him away." She struggled,
panting, crying, moving him closer to the car. "Ann, help me—"

All our lives, I'd been the leader and she the led, but now she
whipped commands at me, and I obeyed, taking Bill's knees, lifting, tugging, dragging him to the car.

She said when we had him on the seat, "I'll hold him. You
drive. Hurry!"

All the way in to Grand Marais that was all she said.

"Hurry." The car could go any speed. Forest rushed by on
both sides; we were in a streaking tunnel. A car came up; white
faces flashed behind a windshield; it was only a glimpse.

"Hurry, Ann, hurry!" It had become toneless, a whisper.
"There's a cottage hospital. I'll show you."

And then to Bill, she said, "Bill, I didn't mean to. It was all
my fault."

SMALL SCENES IN THE jumble of those next hours. A big white
house that looked like a dwelling but that smelled of disinfec-
tants inside and had a woman at a table inside the door.

"Hurry! Bill Heaton's been hurt. We've got him here. We need a doctor—any doctor."

A man running, getting a stretcher, Bill being lifted to the ground, four of us carrying him, and then the stretcher lying on a narrow table in the hall, the shirt too red for horror in terrible bright light, the face with its driving intensity gone, looking dignified and majestic, as a dead king should look.

A second man coming out of a side room, pushing up his shirtsleeves.

"Good lord! It *is* Bill Heaton," he said as if he couldn't have believed. Then he shouted, "Scissors!" and scissors were in his hand. There in the hall he slashed twice at the shirt the blood-soaked fabric folded back from Bill's chest and the awful jagged hole under the collarbone.

Jacqueline whispered, "Hurry!"

The doctor's eyes swept over her, over me like fire passing.

"Get me Miss Bolles," he told the doorkeeper, and to us, "You can't come."

The orderly trundled the table with Bill on it quickly down the hall, the doctor following. A door slammed behind them. The doorkeeper ran upstairs. In a minute a second woman in white came downstairs, running. The door closed behind her, too.

"He's got to live. It was my fault," Jacqueline finally said. The entire front of her dress was red-soaked. She'd forgotten I was there. She walked up and down the hall, grinding her palms. Repeating.

"He can't die. It was my fault. He can't die."

The doorkeeper came back, telephoned. Before anything else happened, Aakonen was there, bulking in heavy and huge, his somber eyes distraught.

He asked, "What happened out there?"

I stammered, "I don't know. I found—found them—"

"No—Mrs. Heaton. How did Mr. Heaton get shot?"

Jacqueline asked, "Is that important now? What's important is that he's got to live." But she was looking beyond us. She said, "I don't know. There was someone. I think he must have gone behind the Fingers. I heard the shot when I was coming out the front door. I ran, calling. And something moved. It must have gone behind the Fingers."

She stopped, as if anyone could understand.

Aakonen took her arm. "Mrs. Heaton, if you would get calm and tell it all, I want to hear this from you."

"It was my fault. I went to sleep. I wasn't going to leave him. I thought if I stayed with him all the time, then nothing could happen to him. No one could shoot us both at once. Don't you see? But I fell asleep. And he went out."

Again she stopped, as if that could be all.

My own thoughts had scarcely more coherence. So that was what she'd meant by it being her fault—that Bill couldn't have been shot if she'd been with him. The skin loosened a little over my bones.

I said, "She and Bill were in the living room this afternoon when Jean Nobbelin and I went out. When we got back about eight thirty Mrs. Heaton was in the living room alone, asleep in a chair." No fencing, no concealment now; I didn't realize enough of what I said to know what to conceal. I told about the travel folders and the pepper in my face powder, told of running downstairs, of hearing Jacqueline call . . .

"So," Aakonen said when I was done. "Mrs. Heaton, try again."

"That's the way it was. We were in the living room this afternoon, Bill and I. He was thinking out who could have killed Fred. I was watching him. Then suddenly I was waking up, and there was a lamp lit. Bill was gone. I knew where he'd be—outside, walking. I ran out, calling him. He shouted from over near the Fingers. And then there was the shot. Not very loud. Dull. I ran there—"

"That shout—what was it?"

"It didn't say anything—it was just a shout—a warning. I got there, and someone moved right in front of me. It was very dark—black. Bill was on the ground. I tried to carry him but I couldn't. I called for Ann to come—"

Swiftly—"This something that moved—"

"I'm sure it went behind the Fingers. But then it went away while I was calling Ann. Toward the east. Away from the house."

"You didn't try to catch this person?"

"I was thinking about Bill."

"You saw nothing of him?"

"No. It was black."

I said, "It's dark outdoors tonight."

"Yes," he said, repeating to Jacqueline, "This person moved away when you got there but not until you were close."

"Yes."

He said to me, "Would that make it about nine o'clock when Mr. Heaton was shot?"

How long had I been upstairs? What time had it been when Jean and I got back?

"It must have been about that time."

He left us abruptly to go down the hall to the telephone. We heard him there, guarding his voice with his hand.

"Can't they know soon now?" Jacqueline asked me, as if I could hurry the doctor's hand.

How much was there of that waiting? I don't know. Eternity. The doors of the hall going by until they became as familiar as the beads of a fingered rosary.

Then the door at the end of the hall opening, and the doctor coming out, a blunt man, thick; there was black hair on his arms. The world rocked and waited as he walked toward Jacqueline.

"He's alive, Mrs. Heaton," he said. "It'll be touch and go. I think he'll fight."

Jacqueline fell back against the wall.

Aakonen asked, "You get the bullet out?"

"Kept it for you, Sheriff. It missed the heart. Went through the apex of the left lung. Some internal hemorrhage. God's hands from here on."

Aakonen asked, "Would there be time for you to call if—?"

The doctor nodded. "There should be."

Jacqueline gasped, "Oh no! I'm staying right here with him. I want to be in his room. Can't I go there now?"

Aakonen had her arm. "No," he said. "I am putting a guard at his door and another under his window outside. Until I know who shot him, no one is to go in his room except the doctor and the nurse, unless I, too, am there."

Jacqueline became still, all over. "But I've got to be with him."

Aakonen repeated his command.

"Very well, then," she said. "No one is to see him at all. No one is to carry anything in to him. Food or flowers. No one from—out there—is to come near the hospital." As if Aakonen's order were her own, and she were amplifying it.

Aakonen wanted us back at the Fingers. He was like a river in flood, propelling us out to his car, driving as if some of the car's impetus came from himself.

"Suppose they should call now," Jacqueline kept saying, "now while we're on the road? . . ."

Even when we walked into the living room at the Fingers, her mind stayed at the hospital; apparently she felt nothing of the emotion sweeping out from the huddled people. Myra was there, her dark eyes seeming to quiver in the pallor of her face. And yes, in the shadows behind her there was a gray dress and gray face—Octavia, shrinking behind Myra as if that frail body must cover and conceal her. Phillips was near, staring and ash gray. Bradley Auden had a face as stark as if death had touched him, too. Carol crouched, white, beside him. Apart and alone sat Cecile, and in another spot Ella and Lottie sat, trembling so I saw their bodies in a shimmer. Mark and Jean looked to be fighting against the terror but held by it.

After Fred had died there was terror because murder and a killer were near, touching us. But now there was a different terror, the horror of people in a trap who knew for sure now that the killer would strike again, knew that any eyes at which theirs looked might be a killer's eyes . . .

Aakonen herded Jacqueline and me closer into the light; as he did so a concerted gasp of horror went all over the room; eyes centered on Jacqueline, fascinated and fearful. I remembered then the red ruin of her dress; to them it looked a symbol. That was Bill's blood staining her.

"Come upstairs with me." I knew she must quickly get into another dress.

She remained impervious to their stares, walking with me toward the steps.

Jean was on his feet, asking harshly, as if he dreaded the answer so desperately he could hardly form the words, "Bill— is he—?"

"He's alive," Jacqueline answered. "They'll call me if I'm needed."

"Thank God!" Surely that was honest prayer. Over the rest of the faces, too, passed a relieving stir.

When we came downstairs again, Aakonen was talking to men not a part of the group: Owens, the wood-shingle man, others.

"You go over there and sit," Aakonen told us, gesturing. Somehow the chairs were in a rough order, facing forward toward Aakonen and the wary-eyed men who stood beside him. Unmistakable again, the drawing away from Jacqueline as she went toward one of those chairs.

"Now." Aakonen said the word with a deadly chill and paused. "I want to know where every one of you was and what you did tonight. I'm going to make you talk in front of everyone, so that you'll be caught if you lie. Before I leave here, I'm going to know who shot Bill Heaton."

He shouted suddenly, thrusting forward a violent finger. "You! Where were you at nine o'clock tonight?"

It was Mark Ellif his finger singled out; pallor increased under Mark's livid bruises, and there was pallor in his voice.

"I—I—" And then nothing. Mark just stared, transfixed, at Aakonen's finger, as if his tongue had refused motion.

Carol rose out of her crouch to stand at bay, words racing. "Mark was at Auden! With me! He isn't the murderer, and you know it! We hunted that gun all afternoon and couldn't find it! We came here at six o'clock and told Bill. Then we went to my house and had dinner. Mark was with me every minute!"

Aakonen roared, "I don't want you talking! Mark!"

Mark moistened his lips.

"He was at Auden!" Carol screamed.

Bradley started to his feet. "She doesn't lie—

"*Where were you at nine o'clock?*" Aakonen towered over Mark.

"I was at Auden." Mark at last found tongue.

"Why didn't you say so?"

"I—didn't know when nine o'clock was."

"I looked at the clock!"—Carol.

"How do you know now when nine o'clock was?" Aakonen still beat at Mark.

"And when I looked at the clock it was almost nine thirty." Carol was beside Mark now. "And Mark had just gone out of the door."

Aakonen turned then to flail at her, but she was fiery, standing to her guns. There was a clock in the hall at Auden. Mark had gone out the front door. She'd looked at the clock on her way up to her mother's room. Twenty-seven minutes after nine exactly. Aakonen couldn't shake her.

Bradley Auden next. "You—where were you at nine?"

"He was visiting with me at the resort—I don't suppose he'd want to say so himself." Quick answer by proxy again, this time from Cecile Granat, bent a little forward, her eyes glowing. "He was still there when Owens came for us. Ask Owens."

"That right?" Aakonen swung on Owens.

"Yep."

Back to Bradley. "When did you get to Miss Granat's cabin?"

Quickly again, "After eight."

"How long after eight?"

"Twenty-thirty minutes."

"You!" The pointing finger darted now at Jean.

"At nine o'clock I must have been coming from the resort toward the Fingers." More steadiness in Jean's voice, but steadiness under pressure. "I had a sandwich in my hands—I was eating it. I heard a car starting up, here at the Fingers.

"But when I got here, no one was around. I looked in the living room—the light was on. After a while, Phillips came in. We thought Bill and Jacqueline and Ann must have driven in to Grand Marais for dinner. We looked upstairs, and no one was there but Myra, asleep in bed, and Octavia in her room. Phillips and I were waiting around downstairs for the others to get back when your deputy got here."

"So." Ominously. "It would be easy for you to have gotten here *before* the car left—"

"Lottie gave me that sandwich. It must have been nine o'clock then."

A swing to Lottie. Lottie thought maybe it had been nine o'clock. She and Ella had been at the resort all day, unlocking the doors only when they knew who knocked. They'd given Phillips Heaton some sandwiches, too, about seven o'clock.

The finger pointed at Phillips. "You—do you have an alibi for this shooting, too?"

Phillips, palely, was afraid he didn't. After he'd eaten he'd gone to his former room over the boathouse to pack.

"I was carrying a suitcase when I walked into the house and found Jean here. I was over the boathouse when the car started. I heard it, too."

"Hm. But you heard nothing else." The ominous tone again.

"You've got to remember how noisy that boathouse is. Lake right under that room." He seemed to be holding himself in abeyance, waiting for something, but although Aakonen beat at him, he got nothing. He went on to Myra, who said she'd vainly tried to sleep in the afternoon; about five she'd risen, taken two sleeping tablets, and gone back to bed. She'd still been asleep when the deputies came.

"I was asleep," she repeated. She seemed lost in the chaos into which life had fallen. "Bill always made things happen," she said inconsequently, but I knew what she meant. Bill, the ruler, hadn't ordered these last days.

"You!" The finger was on Octavia now. Like the eyes of the rabbits we'd flushed that afternoon, her wild dark eyes darted, frantic for escape; her misshapen face took on its stricken, tortured grimace. Myra at once forgot everything else to spring to Octavia's defense.

"My sister hasn't been out of her room since Fred's death, until your men took her out by physical force tonight. Sheriff, you could have talked to her in her room. It isn't necessary for her to be subjected to this."

Aakonen took no notice except to let his voice soften slightly.

"Mrs. Sallishaw, can you prove your sister wasn't out of her room this time?"

"Of course I can. She doesn't want to be out of it."

Behind Myra, at that, Octavia began a frantic, vigorous nodding.

Into my memory came the recollection of the sound I'd heard as I came up the stairs that evening on my return from the useless hunt. I opened my mouth to speak but closed it. Perhaps Octavia hadn't actually been out of her room; she might just have been standing at her door listening. It seemed inhumanly cruel to tell of that slight incident before the agonized face that nodded such hopeful, helpless agreement to anything Myra said.

"No, tell me yourself," Aakonen insisted. "Miss Heaton, were you out of your room this evening?"

The nodding changed to a vigorous denial.

With a short pause, as if he were still unsatisfied but didn't know what else to do, Aakonen came on to me, making me tell again what I'd already told him at the hospital. After me he went on to Jacqueline.

"Bill must be doing all right, or they'd call me." She said that first before repeating, as if by rote, how she had run out to the rocks. Attention had been tense before; now it became painful. Again that awful converging suspicion.

When she was done Aakonen moved back, his head forward, staring at us, picking out one face, staring at it until his gaze became insupportable yet had to be borne. Passing on to another face.

When he spoke at last, he was completely quiet, and I knew the shouts and bellowing had just been something he put on to shout someone into panic, into telling the truth.

He said, "There is not one of you who could not have shot Bill Heaton. Mrs. Sallishaw, you would only have had to be awake for a few minutes instead of sleeping. Octavia Heaton, there is no real proof this time that you stayed in your room. Phillips Heaton, no one saw you in that boathouse. Jean Nobbelin, Lottie cannot prove when she gave you that sandwich, and I cannot know within a few minutes when that shot was fired. You could easily have done it. Lottie and Ella, if one of you lied for the other—"

His shoulders rose and fell. "The same is true of you, Mr. Auden, and of Cecile Granat. True of you, Mark and Carol. One could lie for the other. You, Ann Gay, you would only have had to come downstairs a little before. You, Mrs. Heaton, you even say you were right there by the Fingers when the shot was fired."

In the imperfect light and the fog that seemed to swirl in circles even inside the room, he was like an aimed projectile, a projectile with eyes and a blue welt diagonally across the dome above them.

He catapulted himself upon us, beating at us again, shouting, demanding, trying to force confession by power and vigor, throwing himself again and again at people who paled and crouched tighter into themselves and were helpless under his on-slaught but who always, consistently, persistently denied.

It went on almost all night. When he stood back again at last, we were just the shreds, the remnants of people.

It was then that the long, rusty deputy, Owens, stepped toward Aakonen.

"I—I guess there's something you ought to know. I just thought. When Mr. Auden and Mr. Heaton—Mr. Phillips Heaton—were over there at the resort talking to me this morning—"

Slowly the remnant of Bradley Auden wavered up, clinging to a chair back.

"Get on with it!" A hoarse reflection of his roar from Aakonen. "If there is anything—"

Owens was pale, swallowing over a jerking Adam's apple. "You see, I was sitting there on the resort porch, and Mr. Auden and Phillips Heaton came, and I let 'em in. They got some cigarettes out of the machine. So then they started talking, and I told 'em about you arresting Ed. You never—"

"It was no secret! What about it?"

"So then there was that bundle, lying on a table—"

Through Aakonen the galvanic movement of shock and memory.

"That package . . ." He moved softly forward on Owens.

"Sure," Owens said. "It had the pieces of that bathrobe in it and the black cape. You'd left it there, and I thought—seeing if the murderer was Ed Corvo—they wouldn't be very important . . ."

He'd given the bundle to Phillips Heaton to take back to the Fingers.

11

INESCAPABLE, THE VISION OF a Thing again walking the night and the dark, hooded against sight.

Someone screamed, "Let me out! I ain't going to stay here with her! I know she did it! She got the cape back!" It was Ella Corvo, her hysterical eyes on Jacqueline as she plunged toward the door, dragging Lottie with her, panting, sobbing, fighting back at the men who tried to stop her. The two women were almost carried back and dumped into the chairs they'd left.

"You can't go until I say so!" Aakonen roared at them, and then advanced on Phillips.

"So you have the cape." His tone had softened again.

Phillips wasn't a spectator now; he was scrunched almost like Octavia and he spoke in a rapid, husky whisper. This was what he'd waited for.

"Oh no. Owens said he guessed you didn't want the cape. He gave it to me. So I brought it along back here. I dropped it on the porch in a chair. That front porch right there." He pointed. "I didn't see it again. Anyone could take it. Brad and I came into the room here where some of the others were. We told them Ed Corvo had been arrested. I never even thought of the cape again."

Descent on Bradley Auden, still clinging to the back of his chair. "You see him leave that bundle on the porch?"

Again a tongue moving over dry lips, under set eyes that stared. "Yes. That's true. We brought that—terrible thing—back here. Phillips dropped it on the porch. I remember."

Swiftly Aakonen was out the door; porch lights flashed up.

He found only newspapers, string, and the tatters of my bath-robe, crumpled in a corner behind a table.

He came back into the living room with the bathrobe, the paper, the string. He set them on a table. We all looked at them.

Phillips said shrilly, "Don't forget, Aakonen, I couldn't have shot Fred. Joe Hanson will tell you where I was the night of the Fourth if you don't believe me."

Shortly, "I have seen Joe Hanson."

Aakonen looked around at the rest of us, and drive was gone out of him almost as thoroughly as it had gone from Bill.

He said slowly, "A cape is a big thing to hide. Owens!"

Owens straightened, taking the order that wasn't put into words.

"You can all go," Aakonen dismissed us. "I'm done with you."

Jacqueline stood up. "If I can go to the hospital—"

Out of my beaten weariness I looked at her, marveling. She stood quiet and aloof, as if she didn't know that the hand of al-most everyone there was now against her; her only anguish was that Bill might die.

NO USE GOING INTO detail over that Sunday; it will always be a nightmare. We did nothing but wait for the outcome of Bill's

battle between life and death. Everything else—even the knowledge that suspicion was tightening so desperately against
Jacqueline—seemed secondary.

Later I learned that only Lottie and Ella—escorted—went
home that night; the others slept exhaustedly in the beds or on
the sofas of the Fingers. Crews of men were set to combing the
buildings and the wilderness for the cape and the still-missing
gun. Then I knew only that Jean, Jacqueline, and I were driving
to Grand Marais in Jean's car, with a deputy's car following, and
faint yellow-pink light along a far eastern horizon, with the black
sky overhead.

A nurse rustled out to meet us in a corridor still electric lit;
she gave us the emotionless words nurses use.

"Dr. Rush says Mr. Heaton is holding his own. It's impossible
to make any prognosis."

Through bleak early-morning hours we walked the corridors;
it was then I learned Jean still kept his first bulldog decision as
to Jacqueline's innocence. Soon after, I was to learn that Myra,
too, had stayed on our side, but then it seemed the three of us
against the world.

We sat in chairs in a cubbyhole that had a table. The next thing
I knew, my face in my arms on the table and hot sun beating on
the back of my neck. My head ached, and my mouth felt like the
inside of a ski boot, including the extra woolen sock. I woke with
a start, worried that Jacqueline was gone. But when I rushed down
a corridor where people stared there she was, with her back to the
wall near Bill's door, opposite the guard Aakonen had placed.

"It's noon," she told me "and he's still alive."

"I slept," I said. I was heavy and drugged with it. "Can't you?"

"I don't need to. Ann, Aunt Harriet will see about Bill in the
newspapers."

I called Aunt Harriet, hearing alarm quickening in the old voice. Couldn't I do anything? Couldn't I get Jacqueline away?

People, so many people, walked up and down the corridor. When I looked out a window I saw crowds of men, some of them in bright shirts such as Fred had worn, standing on the sidewalk. Jean was at the window, too, looking soberly out; he seemed held by a waiting second only to Jacqueline's.

"Bill's men," he said. "Did you know they call him Lord Heaton? They love him."

Phillips had called Bill that. It didn't seem like love.

I came to recognize Dr. Rush, the physician in charge of the hospital who kept his calm by never being flurried. He moved tirelessly, endlessly—hospital hours, office hours, calls, more calls, office hours, hospital hours. He lived there at the hospital. Miss Fleet, the woman at the door, told us how lucky we were that he had been in the hospital when we brought Bill.

Bill's condition remained unchanged.

Aakonen was there once that Sunday, looking at a table piled with packages: flower boxes, baskets with napkins, rude crumpled bundles from Bill's well-wishers. The warped little man was opening them, taking out hothouse flowers and tight small bundles of wildflowers and cakes and jars of soup.

"None of this is to go in his room," Aakonen reminded. "A pity so much food must be thrown away."

At nightfall, Dr. Rush told Jacqueline, "Mr. Heaton is still holding his own. You'll have to get some sleep, Mrs. Heaton. I know you had none last night. I'll give Miss Gay some sleeping tablets for you."

Pink under a transparent cheek. "Does that mean it's safe for me to leave?"

A hesitation. "It means I count on Mr. Heaton's not becoming suddenly weaker."

———

JEAN DROVE US BACK to the Fingers, saying good night at the door. Even Jean wove a little with weariness, walking. I was long past sensing or knowing much of anything. In the Fingers living room, a strange man unconcernedly played Canfield. "I'm on guard here," he explained.

"That's nice." Nothing was important now except bed.

At the head of the stairs Myra met us, and I saw that she, too, balanced on the thin edge.

"Bill's all right. He must be all right, or you wouldn't be here," she begged. "I've been calling the hospital . . ." She caught at my arm, and I felt her trembling.

"Thank heaven you've come! The others were here all day waiting for the news but then they left. Phillips went to Auden for dinner. I stayed with Octavia. I keep thinking—" She was shaking more now. "Suppose it's happened again? It might be happening now . . . someone I know, someone I love, being killed, and I sit here helpless to stop it. And maybe it's my turn to go next . . . For the first time in my life I've wished I could run away."

"Bill isn't running away," Jacqueline told her. "He's fighting."

Myra made an effort to stop her trembling. "I never thought I'd make such a spectacle of myself."

We put her to bed with one of the sleeping tablets Dr. Rush had given me for Jacqueline. More people than Myra, I guessed, would start falling to pieces if this strain kept up. Coming out of Myra's room, I heard a footstep and looked from end to end of the hall, but there was no one.

Of course!—Octavia. As usual, I'd forgotten she'd be there behind her closed door. But as I stood there now, so tired, it seemed to me I got a stronger sense of her presence, as if for once her personality was not negative but positive.

Poor Octavia, I thought. If Myra could come so close to being shattered, how terrible must be timid Octavia's waiting!

WAKING ON MONDAY MORNING was like crawling, weak and confounded but sentient, out of a cocoon. Sunlight lay fuzzily golden over the blue candlewick tufts of the spread; the window was closed and locked like the door, but faintly I could hear a hum and thrum; the wilderness sounds didn't stop for locked windows and doors.

Beside me Jacqueline still slept, her face tucked down into the blankets, away from light. Sleepy as I'd been, I'd had sense enough to make her sleep with me.

Thinly from below, something was ringing—the telephone. The moment it sounded, she was galvanically awake, tumbling out of bed, running as she was, in pajamas. I stopped just long enough to get into slippers and my polo coat and grab up her robe and slippers. A phone call might mean . . .

The Canfield-playing guard had taken the call.

It wasn't about Bill. As he talked, he shook his head at Jacqueline, waiting tensely at his elbow.

"That so? You got her, huh? That's good," was what he said.

"Bill—is it about Bill?" Jacqueline kept asking in spite of the headshakes.

He hung up the receiver. "No, that was—"

But she had no time for anything else. At once she was calling the hospital, feverishly putting her question.

Bill, Miss Fleet said, was still holding his own.

"I'll be right there," Jacqueline told her, swaying against the wall, weak with relief. "I'll be there as soon as I can get there."

Something—this was Monday morning. What was connected in my mind with Monday? Then I remembered.

"The inquest. It's to be this morning. We'll have to go to that." I held out the slippers and the robe.

"In case you'd like to know"—this time, the guard's drawl held a note that made us listen—"Cecile Granat tried to run away last night. That call was to say she'd just been caught."

SO WE HAD THOSE short hours when most attention was focused on Cecile, where we wondered aloud if she was the killer and that in sudden convulsive fear of being caught, she'd run away.

Again there was a gathering at the Fingers. Every eye went to Bradley Auden when he came in, harassed and uncertain.

"But I don't see why she'd run away," he kept repeating. "No one was suspecting her particularly. You weren't, were you, Aakonen?"

Aakonen admitted he hadn't; he, too, was there, waiting for Cecile to be brought in. I remembered suddenly that I'd never told him about seeing Cecile in the woods that day Jean and I had hunted for the gun. When I told him now, he just grunted.

"She said she was looking for the gun, too," Jean contributed, his black brows drawn low with thought.

Carol was openly, almost viciously hopeful. "That Cecile! I hope she is the one. I never could stand her."

Myra, however, was torn by doubts. "I wanted to run away, too, last night. I can't suspect anyone just for wanting to run away." She was still tired, but she'd slept and was able to hold herself together again.

A detective from Duluth brought Cecile just before ten o'clock. She walked into the living room, truculent and sullen.

"All right, so I tried to get out of this hell trap," she said harshly. "Who wouldn't? It's not because I've been doing any shooting. It's because I don't fancy myself getting shot. And I don't fancy hobnobbing with a murderer, either."

Aakonen took her off to the kitchen. The sound of the voices came through for half an hour. Around me as we waited, I could feel the sway and pull of opinion. Soberer second thoughts were suggesting that if Cecile was the murderer, then she had planned and executed all those tricks to make suspicion point so sharply to Jacqueline. Skill as cunning as that would hardly reveal itself by going childishly out on the highway at night and thumbing rides to Duluth.

Yet temporarily, Cecile's running away was lifting some of the weight of the distrust against Jacqueline; no one came near her—I realized that from the time of Fred's shooting on, no one had made one friendly gesture toward Jacqueline, except Jean, Bill, Myra, or I—but the difference was perceptible in glances and attitudes.

Aakonen came out of the kitchen in a thick rage. "For this, we had to postpone the inquest a whole hour! Get there now, all of you! If any more of you try running away—" He dropped it there, perhaps because an implied threat was stronger than any he could voice.

THE INQUEST WOULD BE about Fred's death. As I drove into Grand Marais with Jean and Jacqueline, I wondered if we could even remember the circumstances of Fred's death; it seemed so long ago, so overshadowed by the attack on Bill and the question of whether he would live or die.

Again we stopped at the hospital where the guard sat implacably at Bill's door.

"Mr. Heaton's about the same," Miss Fleet said. "He's begun coughing a little."

I don't think Jacqueline knew what that meant, because she turned wordlessly away, but I caught the flicker in Jean's eyes and thought, with a quick stab, that it must be blood he's coughing—hemorrhage. The question was in my throat, but the flicker in Jean's eyes had turned to warning. Jacqueline had to go to the inquest, and the ordeal would be bad enough as things were.

Confirmation of that was to come only too quickly.

The town hall where the inquest was to be looked like a New England church, except that instead of a steeple it had a flagpole. No flag flew today, but the double doors were open, and people clustered on the wide porch and the sidewalk. Not friendly people.

As Jacqueline stepped up the one step to the building's vestibule, a voice spoke out from that cluster of people, a man's loud voice, heavy with vindictive hatred.

"There she is. If Bill Heaton dies, she'll get everything he's got."

BLIND THAT I HADN'T seen before the terrible change that the attack on Bill had made in the case against Jacqueline. If Bill died now, with Fred dead before him . . .

I was so stunned by realization, I stood helpless, turning, staring out over those inimical faces, seeing them only as a blur against the backdrop of Grand Marais's scattered, somehow alien houses and, behind the houses, the rising tree-dressed hill that was the rampart of wilderness. Jacqueline, too, must have halted, but the next instant Jean had us by the arm and was hurrying us on into the room where we must stand against fact.

Bleak light fell in that room through tall, unwashed windows. As we came in, the rows of hushed people turned so that antagonism struck us from a thousand eyes at once.

There she is, the fascinated eyes repeated. Our passage was like running a gauntlet of whips, so that just being able to sink into our seats in the second row, with the other witnesses around us and the eyes behind us, was like coming to a haven. Distrust surrounding us there was at least familiar.

Ed Corvo was there, sitting self-righteous and vindictive, his arms folded against his chest. Of course he'd be released now; he'd been in jail when Bill was shot; he had an unbreakable alibi. Ella and Lottie, beside him, seemed to feel his vindication included them; they looked around at us boldly, spitefully now. Mark didn't glance at us; he was leaning over to whisper to Carol Auden. Cecile was still sullen and nervous, glancing at us out of the corners of her eyes, then down at her hands. Bradley, too, just glanced; he seemed harassed by some goad that kept him in constant movement—hands, feet, head. Phillips held his short bulk forward, trying to resume his attitude of watcher at a play but cautious lest the play move too near him in the audience chamber. Only Myra managed a smile at us; she leaned over from her chair next to Carol's to squeeze Jacqueline's hand. Octavia wasn't there; somehow Myra must have managed to persuade Aakonen that, since her sister had been locked in her room, she wouldn't be useful as a witness.

Had they all before this seen that horribly logical motive against Jacqueline? Probably they had. I'd been the only one so certain of her innocence I wouldn't think it. *Jacqueline, how would she ever get out of this?* I sat still blinded, held by that terror.

OUTSIDE ME, THE INQUEST began.

Aakonen and the tubby, important man lumbered in to sit across the aisle. Behind them came Dr. Rush, harassed but capable, carrying a briefcase. Apparently he was the coroner, because he seated himself at once behind the table at the front of the room and proceeded swiftly to panel a six-man jury. The stocky, weather-beaten countrymen who responded paused conscientiously before replying that they had formed no previous opinion as to how Fred Heaton had met his death. No one of them tried to evade; each one advanced soberly and portentously to his task, as a citizen of a democracy now goes up to vote.

Dr. Rush addressed them. "It will be your duty to decide whether Frederick Heaton met his death by natural or unnatural means, and, if the latter, whether a known or an unknown person caused that death. First, I will ask you to view the remains of Frederick Heaton at the undertaking parlors."

The six men rose to file solemnly out, holding their hats against their shoulders, their eyes fixed stiffly forward. Nothing happened in the room while they were gone, except that Dr. Rush sorted papers from his briefcase. When the six jurymen returned they were harder, stirred. What they had been told had become real—a boy was dead.

My name was called first. I had to leave my absorption to go up, my heart pounding, my hands cold, to take the armchair between coroner and jury, facing the eyes.

"Miss Gay, do you know of any reason why anyone should have desired Fred Heaton's death?"

All that talking and hunting we'd done, what had come of it? The only logical motive was the one I couldn't believe.

I said steadily, "I know of no reason."

Bit by bit, questions drawing out of me what I knew.

Carefully I'd held to what I told Aakonen; his was the face I watched, a face intently waiting to pounce on any slip. I was dismissed as soon as I'd described the scene of Fred's death.

After me Dr. Rush himself talked.

"I arrived at the scene with Sheriff Aakonen. Frederick Heaton was, without doubt, dead, the death apparently due to gunshot wound, although considerable bruising of the face and upper trunk was also evident. Later, I established that death was caused by a bullet piercing the upper-left ventricle of the heart. The bruises had been received prior to the death and did not contribute to the death."

A long sigh, and a movement of Carol's hand toward Mark.

Aakonen went up next to describe in heavy, slow words how the scene had looked when he got there. Evidently, Bill had done nothing but pull Fred flat and snatch away the shawl and the harebells.

He gave after that Bill's evidence. I tightened, then relaxed. Bill had scrupulously shielded Jacqueline.

About that long series of tricks, Bill had said, "Until Fred was killed I thought someone must have a grudge—probably against me. But no one would kill Fred just to satisfy a grudge against me."

As Aakonen repeated the words, I could hear Bill's tortured voice saying them.

Could there be a grudge so great that it could extend to Bill's murder and to fastening the guilt of those murders on his wife? That seemed only less incredible than that Jacqueline should be guilty.

NOON BROUGHT A RECESS in which the jury went out to view the scene at the Fingers and in which Jacqueline, Jean, and I made for the hospital. Nurse Bolles, this time, came through the guarded door to see us.

"Mr. Heaton's still coughing, but his pulse and temperature are steady."

"You'll let me know at once if—"

"Yes, Mrs. Heaton." A peculiar inflection in the name, a peculiar watchfulness in Miss Bolles's eyes. She, too, suspected Jacqueline.

We went to Hanson's for sandwiches. There, sitting in a booth, I learned how much Jacqueline knew and how she was taking it.

She smiled at me, her eyes steady over the glass of milk she held. "Poor Ann, you're so worried. Darling, if Bill gets well, maybe he'll know who shot him. And if he doesn't get well . . . all this won't make much difference. You'd have to take Toby."

THE REST OF THAT inquest held little reality for me as I sat facing that stunning acceptance of possible defeat.

Jacqueline testified quite soon after the noon recess, testified well, her voice coming clearly, unfalteringly. "No, I know of no reason why anyone should have wanted to kill Fred Heaton."

But the people's enmity was too heavily entrenched; instead of lightening, it seemed to swell and grow. I wanted to stand and scream at those people, but something was tightening around my wrist—Jean Nobbelin squeezing so hard, my hand beyond his hold was dark red, purpling.

"Don't make it open, you idiot," he was whispering. "Don't you see that's the worst thing you could do?"

He was right; the case against Jacqueline had to go unacknowledged.

One by one after Jacqueline the others testified—Myra telling not only her story but also Octavia's.

"It is absolutely impossible for my sister to have been out of her room that night," she insisted. "She knows nothing of what has occurred."

After Myra, Aakonen passed along to the jurymen the harebells, the shawl, my bathrobe, telling about each one. The jurymen handled them as if they were alive and crawling. The last object he passed was small, misshapen, leaden—the bullet that had killed Fred.

"That bullet's been to Minneapolis and back. I asked the police there to run it under their microscopes."

He handed over another misshapen ticketed nodule. "There was just one other gun around the Fingers or the resort or Auden, and that was Ed Corvo's gun. I sent that in, too. The Minneapolis police confirm that there isn't a chance the bullet that killed Fred Heaton came from Ed Corvo's gun."

In the row ahead of us Ed Corvo turned to sweep us with a malignant, triumphant glance.

SO THERE'D BEEN MORE than one reason why Ed Corvo had been released. Ella and Lottie, too, felt newly absolved. Their drawn-up, formless bodies expressed the justification of the righteous.

Aakonen passed, last, the sheets of paper on which we'd printed the word *monarch*, but there was no excitement in him; the jurymen stared stolidly at each sheet but said nothing.

When he had finished Dr. Rush said, "That completes the evidence." Swiftly, concisely he summed it and dismissed the jury to consider its verdict.

The jury returned after only a few minutes, the first man picked remaining on his feet.

"We find that Frederick Heaton met an unnatural death at the hands of an unknown person or persons."

His eyes as he said it, the eyes of all the jurymen, were fixed soberly, almost sorrowfully, on Jacqueline.

And strongly in the people around me, too, I found the belief strengthening that Jacqueline was the one from whom they must recoil.

I knew, going out of that town hall, that something needed to be done. Fast.

YET WHAT WAS THERE I could do? No more clues, no more apparent motives than at first. Wherever I turned blank walls met me. I seemed bound by mummy wrappings of futility.

Jean, Jacqueline, and I made again for the hospital, waiting for Dr. Rush to see Bill. He came out of Bill's room with no emotion whatsoever on his face.

"Mr. Heaton's still coughing. There's a little more fever." He hesitated. "It won't be necessary for you to stay."

Jacqueline didn't want to go, but I knew what she'd do if she stayed—stand endlessly by Bill's door, pouring her strength into a vicarious battle. And the Fingers repelled and drew me—repelled because that was where death walked, but drew me because that was where the answer must be.

So I prevailed upon Jacqueline to leave. At least at the Fingers she could get dinner, and we could barricade ourselves again and sleep.

"I suppose you know," Jean said on the way, "that Aakonen found some fresh traces of blue chalk behind the Fingers Sunday morning after Bill was shot."

Attention leaped. "No! Does that mean—?"

"It could mean that, as Jacqueline says, someone did dodge behind the Fingers when she ran out."

He stopped the car almost where Bill had stopped that first day I came. The brown paper was gone from the middle rock now; the chalked *monarch* still showed faintly. I supposed the jurymen must have studied there any similarities in the same word on the sheets of paper. But I had little time for that thought, or to note that the rocks were again unguarded. Almost directly behind the middle Finger, ground in among the dark lentil-smooth pebbles, were a few blue slivers and particles of dust, as if a chalk had been dropped there and perhaps stepped on, and the rest picked up.

Jean said, "I figure maybe the murderer intended writing another word on the rock but didn't have time."

I exulted, "That chalk dust fits exactly. Bears out Jacqueline."

But she said slowly, "You forget I might have dropped the chalk there."

Silence, with the chuckle underground for punctuation. Was everything I grasped always to turn out unsubstantial?

Jean said solidly, "It's still corroboration. What gets me is this. Jacqui, you say you came running here as Bill was shot. The murderer hadn't yet made sure that Bill was dead but he—"

He didn't finish. Phillips came—running—from the lodge.

"The hospital's calling. They want Jacqueline to come."

12

"I SHOULDN'T HAVE LEFT—I knew it!" That was Jacqueline on the hurtling journey back. She willed it should be Aakonen arresting her, willed it should be Bill conscious and accusing her of having shot him—anything but that Bill should be dying.

Men in groups on the sidewalk again, quickly gathered. Withdrawal on the fact of Miss Fleet at the door.

"Dr. Rush and Mr. Aakonen are expecting you." Her heels tapped a quick muted rhythm, leading us down the hall. I could notice at a time like that that the floor was brown battleship linoleum and the day so late that lights already glowed fuzzily overhead.

When Bill's door opened Bill's voice immediately became audible—loud, toneless, insensible.

"Jacqui, Jacqui . . ."

Aakonen's bulk almost filled the door opening, but beyond him Dr. Rush was visible, bending over the bed—Nurse Bolles at the foot.

Aakonen said, "Only Mrs. Heaton, please." He took Jacqueline's arm, leading her in. Dr. Rush stepped back from the bed.

I saw Bill then for the first time since Saturday night. He lay staring upward at the ceiling, his eyes wide, his face thinned to the bone. Stone quiet.

"Jacqui . . ."

"I'm here. Darling . . ." Aakonen let her come close, let her sink to the chair at the bedside, let her reach for Bill's hand.

"Jacqui . . ." No awareness that she had come, no change in the loud monotone of the voice.

"I'm here, Bill." She bent forward to put her cheek against his shoulder, but Aakonen snatched her back.

"Stay where you are, please."

Dr. Rush came out of the room, nodded at the nurse.

"You can't go in, of course," he told me, and shut the door. He went off down the hall, the doorkeeping Miss Fleet following.

Even with the door closed, Bill's voice was audible, repeating Jacqueline's name. When Jean spoke it was so unexpected I jumped; I'd forgotten he was there, too, that he'd driven us in. His head was thrust forward in an intensity of listening.

"Aakonen must be trying to decipher if Bill means he wants Jacqui there or if he means it was Jacqui who shot him."

"Do you have to make that a question?"

He seemed as startled by my presence as I'd been by his.

"Oh, Ann. Here, let's talk to this woman." He went rapidly back down the hall to Miss Fleet.

"Mr. Heaton's talking—does that mean a change in his condition?"

She said coolly, "No great change."

His face loosened. "I wasn't sure."

He turned to me then, his head gesturing toward the cubbyhole of the waiting room. "Come on in here. If anything happens we'll know."

But when I mechanically followed, he changed his mind.

"No, it's late, and you haven't eaten." Again he turned to Miss Fleet. "We'll be at Hanson's. If Mrs. Heaton comes out tell her where we are, please. Or if we're wanted for anything, you can call us."

"But we can't leave!" It seemed disloyal to go, leaving Jacqueline there alone.

"Jacqueline can call us. I want to talk over some things we might do to figure this business out."

I hesitated, torn between the loyalty of staying and the necessity I'd seen that afternoon—that something must be done, and soon. In the end I went—at the hospital I could really do nothing but wait.

So it was at Hanson's that our next blundering efforts to think through the crimes were made—efforts in which there were many errors but which, like the few discoveries made after Fred's death, were to find their places in the final answer.

I said, "Aakonen and the jury couldn't have been able to tell from those sheets of paper who'd printed the *monarch*. If they had they'd have indicated it."

He nodded. "The rock's too rough." We were sitting in a booth, both of us bent over the table, Jean turning a water glass between thumb and forefinger. "I've come to the conclusion that, as far as Fred's death is concerned, we're sunk. We've got to start over again. With Bill."

Facing that prospect, I didn't think I could eat much, but Jean ordered chicken soup, hot, and after I'd eaten it I was suddenly weak with hunger and fatigue.

"If I'm this way, how must Jacqui be?"

"She's got something holding her up." But he ordered a sandwich and a thermos of coffee sent to her at the hospital at the same time he ordered dinner for us. The steaks and coffee were good. Some strength came back.

As soon as the plates were taken away he started. "The last thing we worked at was the hunt for that gun. Now Aakonen and his men have been fine-combing the country around ever since early Sunday morning. And this time they aren't just hunting for a small automatic and a bit of chalk—they're hunting for the cape. Still no go."

"The murderer must think the cape is necessary—"

"Yeah. He's had a chance to see how it strikes terror into the rest of us. That chalk business, too—that just looks like decoration to me. I wonder what the word over Bill would have been if there'd been time to write it."

Would we ever know? Weight pressing down, I said, "I wish we had Bill to work with. He seemed to know where to begin."

He smiled at me crookedly. "You don't mean that as hard as I do. I've worked with Bill eight years. It's seven eighths of my brains gone. That's why I hauled you over here—to talk at. I can't work alone."

He took a notebook from his coat pocket. "This morning while we waited for Cecile I did a little thinking. Not much, but—"

"More than I did. All I've done since Saturday is wait."

"I made a list of everyone who was near Bill when he was shot." He flipped the notebook to face me. Names ran down the page.

1. *Jacqueline.*
2. *Ann.*
3. *Phillips Heaton.*
4. *Myra.*

5. *Jean.*

6. *Bradley Auden.*

7. *Cecile Granat.*

8. *Ella Corvo.*

9. *Lottie.*

10. *Mark.*

11. *Carol.*

"This list leaves out Ed Corvo, who was in jail. It leaves out Marjorie Auden, who can't walk, and the Auden maid. It leaves out Owens and reporters who may have hidden in the underbrush. I'm sticking to people who were also around when Fred was killed and who can imaginably have any connection."

I took a deep breath of acceptance, seeing again the smallness, the closeness of that circle. "Eleven names now. And I know it isn't me and isn't Jacqueline. So that leaves nine."

"Not so fast. We've got to do this thoroughly." His thumb turned a page to more of his thick black handwriting.

> 1. *Jacqueline. She inherits if Bill dies. She has the only obvious motive. Bill's been a difficult husband—they've had a lot of trouble. The case against her, which would include all the bizarre tricks that have happened, is that she's subject to fits of insanity which have become homicidal—motivated by a shrewd sense of gain. This assumes that this combination of mental shrewdness and emotional instability is possible. Alternative explanation—that the craziness is deliberate and to be used in a plea of insanity to get her off the murder charge.*

Scourging words—horrible, unbearable . . . They disappeared; what I saw instead was Bill's thin, flushed face on the pillow, calling for Jacqueline, and Jacqueline telling him she was there, and Bill not hearing.

"It's not true. It's not true, and she isn't—"

He said harshly, "You're reacting emotionally instead of thinking. Don't you see, if we're going to get anywhere we've got to look at the thing straight. We've got to know what we're up against. And don't think I made this theory up—*that is what we're up against*. It's what is in Aakonen's mind now. Why do you think he watches her so closely? It's what the other witnesses are thinking. It's what was in the mind of the jury today. Didn't you see those men looking at her? You heard that man in front of the town hall. We won't get anywhere by shutting our minds."

True—it was all true, but each word still stung, whiplashed across my mind.

"Here," he said. "Maybe this will take your mind off that." He flipped another page, and my own name leaped.

> 2. *Ann. She's extremely fond of Jacqueline and Toby. Would she kill Fred because he was an annoyance, kill Bill because he was making her cousin unhappy—because she felt her cousin had to get free—yet keep the Heaton money?*

He'd written across it, *No soap*.

A short laugh shook out of me. "Should I be grateful?"

"No. But that's why I've picked you to work with—any of the others I'd pick might be the wrong one. Go on."

> 3. *Phillips Heaton* on the next page. *There was something about that Heaton fire. First chance I get, I'll tackle Brad Auden on that. Phillips has an alibi for Fred's mur-*

der which I've checked and which seems tight. No alibi for Bill's shooting. Motive—Phillips obviously hated Bill, but Bill always brushed him off like a fly. What bothers me about Phillips, in spite of his alibi, isn't his general unpleasantness—he's always been that way—it's his being a coward. The way I see it, murder is something a coward goes in for, whether it's one man or a nation. You're inferior and can't get what you want in open competition, so you bolster your weakness with weapons to give you the advantage your body, mind, and character haven't. With guns, the murderer or the statesman goes out to get what he wants cheaply at the expense of someone else.

He was blushing when I looked up from that philosophizing, a red so dark it was almost mahogany. "I was just trying to work things out in my mind. I work with the crews in our business. I get to know things—men—pretty well."

My mind slipped from what he was saying to Phillips Heaton at the table on the day I'd come. "For what we are about to receive we thank Thee, Lord Heaton." I saw Bill at the head of that table, strong, almost arrogant, assertive with the confidence he had because what he was, he'd made himself.

I said, "Phillips was talking about his life when he was young. The President visited his grandfather. Now he's nothing."

"Now he's a bum. His grandfather wasted most of the money he took out of this country, and his father was a heel—a charming heel with a little money. Phillips is a heel without any money, soaking Myra for what she has."

"If only he didn't have that alibi—"

"Let's hear for ourselves. This is where he got that alibi, you know." Jean got up from the booth to walk toward the bar at the front. When he came back, he was accompanied with a short, dark man who carried hairy arms thrust under a dirty white apron tied around his middle.

"Miss Gay, this is Joe Hanson."

"I guess you want to hear about where Phillips Heaton was the night Bill Heaton's kid got shot." No need to ask Joe Hanson questions. "Well, it's like this. The Fourth of July night—it's a big night, ain't it? Here like in any tavern. My place is full up. But I notice that Phillips Heaton. He sits in a booth right across from the bar. He's got a girl with him—a Grand Marais kid—one girl, and he's in a booth holds four. He won't let nobody in that there booth with him—it don't mind who it is—it don't mind how crowded we get. All he buys is a few beers. That ain't the money I ought to get out of a booth on Fourth of July night!"

"Couldn't he have gone out an hour or so that you wouldn't see?"

Joe Hanson took the hands out from under the apron to rest them against the edge of the table and lean on them.

"Lady, I don't like Phillips Heaton. I'd just as leave see him fry, only they don't fry in this state. All I got to say is he wasn't gone from that booth only maybe five minutes to the washroom until three in the morning. I wish it wasn't the truth, but it's the truth."

Doleful but decisive—there could be no doubt Joe Hanson thought he was telling the truth.

"Thanks, Joe, thanks for your trouble," Jean told him.

"Oh, no trouble," Hanson assured him. "I told this thing once, I told it fifty times. You, Aakonen, Owens, reporters, guys." He went back toward his bar shaking his head sadly. "Bill Heaton, too," he said. "A swell guy like Bill Heaton this had to happen to."

"Rock bottom," Jean said. "So because Phillips is a heel doesn't make him a murderer."

"Everyone agrees about Bill," I said. "What is it about him? He's charming. He knows what he wants and gets it. But he can be—"

Jean looked down at the backs of his hands on the table. "Bill's a giant in the earth."

"So we have nothing against Phillips except that he has a motive—he hated Bill. And he knew where the cape was."

The next page read:

4. *Myra. Same reasons as Phillips? She's seemed friendly with Bill though. Terribly fond of Jacqueline and nuts about Toby. I can't see her doing Jacqueline this deliberate dirt. And I don't see where she'd gain anything.*

He supplemented: "If Jacqueline got the money, she'd make Myra's life easy, but Myra wouldn't care for things secondhand. Anyway, she's not hard up—she just got a good big chunk of dough for Faraway. I think Phillips had long ago signed away his share, but the two women hadn't."

"Oh, Myra's impossible," I agreed. "I'm so close to her—I could *feel* it if she were the one, and she isn't." Then another thought struck me; quickly I turned back to the list Jean had made.

"You left out one person. Octavia."

"Uh." A small grunt of exasperation. "I have the toughest time remembering Octavia exists." In pencil, he made an addition after Myra's name: *4½. Octavia.*

He frowned over it. "Can you imagine Octavia setting out with a gun?"

I hadn't done much thinking about Octavia but I tried to then.

"I don't know much about hide-in-a-corner people. Is it just sensitiveness about her birthmark, or is it something else? If we're looking for oddness, we've got it in Octavia."

He still frowned. "I suppose Octavia is an example of some kind of decadence, but, anyway, we can't get past that business of her alibi for Fred's death. That morning, I was searching the upstairs—Saturday morning—I had a look at the doors. They fit tight to the door sills and the frames. I don't see how anyone could have worked any key tricks."

"I saw Myra lock that door, but if Octavia was already outside—"

"Don't forget Myra swears she unlocked that door in the morning and that Octavia was then *inside* the room. The only way you can break that alibi is by proving that Myra is lying."

"Myra'd do a lot to shield Octavia."

"This would make her an accessory after the fact."

"She couldn't have stuck to it after Bill was shot." I had to agree but I still brooded over that alibi. "Someone had an alibi for those tricks that were done in Bermuda, too. Anyone clever enough to have figured those out might have been clever enough to handle that locked door."

"You figure it out."

I said slowly, "Before Jacqueline and Toby, Octavia must have had all Myra's attention. Now she has just a little."

"You forget about Pat. Myra was wrapped up in Pat just as hard as she is in Toby. Octavia was never the only one."

I was still trying to see into that hidden life. "I wonder what her mind is like inside. Myra's doing things for other people all the time—seeing they get fed, keeping the house going, looking after Toby—there was never anything she wouldn't do for Toby, from changing messy diapers to standing by the hour ironing ruffly dresses. I've never seen Octavia do anything but scuttle and sit—how can anyone be so idle?"

"It's a way of getting out of life. She's doing the same thing now, hiding in bed."

I had the feeling there was more I ought to get, but Jean was impatient.

"No, I can't imagine Octavia pulling herself out of her beautiful oblivion to do anything, much less murder. Go on."

A little reluctantly I obeyed.

> **5.** *Jean Nobbelin*, the next page read. *Bill's partner. Fred might have been a possible later rival if he'd been good at the business. Then there's the jealousy-over-Jacqueline motive that Phillips so kindly brought up. Bill and I have had a lot of public arguments. If Bill dies now, I'll have to take over the business alone. I think Bill is the king of the earth, but who else knows it?*

Remembering that incident in the barn made me draw back; I'd almost forgotten it.

I said, "It must be fun, thinking up motives for yourself."

"This is for your benefit and to show me where I stand."

"I heard you arguing with Bill the night of the Fourth. I thought you were friendly. You and Bill always did things together, but Bill was always first, you second."

He was steady under fire. "You think the second might want to be first. Anything else?"

"You sent me that note suggesting I come here in the first place."

"Think Jacqueline hasn't needed the support?"

"Did you know she was going to need it?"

He snorted. "Didn't she need it even then?"

"You didn't want it known that you'd sent me that note."

"Can you imagine how Bill would like knowing I'd interfered in his affairs?"

I could see his point there. Slowly I turned the next page.

> 6. *Bradley Auden. Brad's known Bill since he was a pup. They've racketed around. Brad's only got Auden, could be jealous. Brad owes Bill some dough but certainly hasn't been pressed for it. Can't see anything else. Poor suspect.*

"It's always the least likely person who does murder."

> 7. *Cecile Granat. Her running away puts her in the spotlight. She's known Bill for years. Some private business dealing with him; comes to see him in the office. Funny attitude on Bill's part—knows what she is but, as far as I can make out, he's sort of paternal. Lead here—find out what relationship is.*

"Well."

The dark eyebrows pulled together. "No, I'm serious. There's something about Bill and Cecile I don't get."

"That may not be so difficult," I said grimly. "Apparently Aakonen didn't get anything out of her about running away or about what she was doing that day we caught her in the woods."

"It was too bad we forgot to tell Aakonen about that woods incident for such a long time. Anything else we haven't told him?"

"I told him about the pepper in my face powder—"

"Must have been done to keep you busy while Bill was being shot. Nice stuff."

"And I told him about the messages in the travel folders—" I sat up. "Those travel folders! They weren't on my dresser anymore!"

He exclaimed with exasperation and despair, "Of course not! They'll be safely burned by this time." He sat silent a moment, looking at his hands. "When you sit off like this and look at the whole thing—it's paralyzing, isn't it? So intricate. All that scheming, all the tricks, and hardly a sign. So successful, and we're so unsuccessful. It makes you feel it's useless to pit yourself against it." But then he shook himself, fighting the depression off, leaning forward to talk rapidly.

"Right now, we may have a chance. For the first time, the murderer wasn't successful. Don't you see? Bill didn't die—he's still alive. If he keeps alive that's a failure for the murderer. It must break up his plans."

I said, swept up in hope, "Bill's talking now—not conscious but he may be. If he could tell who the murderer was—"

Jean was not so sanguine. "We can't count on that. If the murderer wore the cape—" His shoulders lifted. "No, we've got something, but we can't overbid it. Bill alive means the murderer must be in a tight place. We can just hope he'll do something desperate to get out and be caught."

"But that means—every minute the murderer must be wanting to—"

"What do you think Aakonen's guards in that hospital mean?"

"I know, but suppose that isn't enough? Maybe the only important thing is to guard Bill."

He said slowly, "No, I think we can leave that to Aakonen. He may not be getting much of anywhere with the investigation, but he's guarding Bill all right. What else could we do?"

I thought of the guard at Bill's door, the guard under the window, the flowers and the food thrown out, Aakonen watching Jacqueline like a hawk at Bill's bedside. No, that seemed taken care of. Bill was guarded, but . . .

I started rising. "Jacqueline. How do I know she isn't next on the murderer's list? She isn't getting out of my sight again!"

He reached across the table to pull me down. "You forget," he said. "The murderer had a chance to kill Jacqueline and didn't.

She was alone with Bill for quite a while before you ran out. According to her own story, the murderer was right there behind the Fingers. If she'd been on the murderer's list, she'd have been killed then."

I could only stare at him.

"No," he said evenly. "Don't you see? The murderer is so anxious to have Jacqueline stay alive that he was even willing to risk Bill's survival rather than shoot her so he could make sure of Bill."

Still I stared.

"Don't you see?" he repeated. "That's the plan. Jacqueline isn't to be murdered. She's to be the murderer."

I DID PULL MYSELF together after a while. Enough to finish the list.

> **8.** *Ella Corvo,* the next page read. *With Ed out of the picture, Ella is a weak suspect. Question—Could Ed have killed Fred, then Ella have gone after Bill? Bit complicated. Fred did injure the nephew, but all they have against Bill that I know is that he wouldn't turn that trust fund into cash.*

"Ed Corvo waited for Bill to say he should go ahead before he even called the sheriff about his own boat."

"Yeah—that's where I put Ed, too."

> **9.** *Lottie. Unless she's crazy, poor suspect. Might have hated Bill because she served him, but, then, why didn't she pick on Myra? Anyway, most people jump to wait on Bill.*

I, too, thought Lottie unimportant.

> **10 and 11.** *Mark and Carol. I know Mark. He's a good kid.*
> *No murder in him. Same for Carol, I'd say.*

"Sudden rush to the head?" I asked, and the responsive color flooded up.

"They're kids. It's like suspecting Toby."

"They're a good deal older than Toby. Mark did fight with Fred. He worked for Bill—are you sure there wasn't any trouble? And Carol's rush to explain that Mark was at Auden until half past nine the night Bill was shot—that didn't sound any too solid to me."

"Look," he said impatiently. "Whoever is doing this shooting is pretty good at the devil's work. Those kids still trail their clouds of glory."

"He reads Wordsworth!"

Another wave of color came up before the last had had a chance to recede. He pulled out his handkerchief to mop the back of his neck.

I cajoled him; it was as if my mind couldn't stand the pressure to which I'd subjected it and wanted to escape into badinage. I heard myself laughing, forgetting, and then, with shock and self-reproach, remembering.

WE HAD TWO LEADS, we decided—two that might lead to others. First, see Bradley Auden about the feuds and grudges in the Heaton family. Second, try to find out where Cecile came in.

We went back after that to the hospital, where Jacqueline was waiting in one of the cubbyhole's mission oak chairs.

Now that I'd seen Bill, I could see how much more sharply

her face, too, showed the modeling of her bones, how darkly the shadows lay above the cheekbones, how strained the corners of her lovely full mouth were. But she could smile at us briefly.

"Thanks for the coffee. Bill became quiet, and I was sent out."

But even as she said it quick footsteps ran.

"Mrs. Heaton!" It was Nurse Bolles, and for once her face wasn't withdrawn. "Mr. Heaton—his pulse is . . ."

Jacqueline was running down the hall, I following. The man on the bed was quiet now; the skin seemed to be pulling back from his forehead, his nose, his chin, leaving them too sharp, too bare.

Jacqueline bent over him, calling to him.

Nurse Bolles shoved me out. Aakonen and Dr. Rush were both in the room. The door closed; the guard stared at us impassively.

Jean said, "He's dying. Bill." He groped blindly for the wall.

13

SO WE SAW NEITHER Bradley Auden nor Cecile Granat during that longest of all long nights.

It must have been half an hour before Miss Bolles opened the door to meet our mute question.

"He rallied," she said tersely, and went on swift feet down the hall.

Yet I felt no relief; there had been no loosening of tension in Miss Bolles. Jean's face, too, stayed strung.

"They must be afraid he'll go under again."

When Miss Bolles came back, she was accompanied by the orderly trundling a cart that carried canvas, a tank. The door opened for them.

"That was an oxygen tent," Jean said.

How many hours did we face that door? The orderly came out; the phone rang at the end of the hall, was answered by a voice too low to hear; occasionally a light went on above a door; another nurse rustled out of a side room to answer. Once I felt as if everything—the door at which I stared, the corridor—had begun gently rocking. Then Jean was walking me rapidly up and down.

He asked, "How much sleep have you had since Fred was killed? I'm going to get you a bed."

"No." It was as if I could help Bill by staying awake, as if I could fight off death by fighting off my own loss of consciousness.

For four hours then nothing happened. No one came in or out. No phone rang. No light went on. Only time passed, mercilessly slow, flowing down the hall like a river.

At two in the morning, Aakonen brought Jacqueline out.

Her face was shining.

She said, "He's fighting. He won't die."

"PERHAPS MRS. HEATON SHOULD stay," Dr. Rush said. "But you two go home. I hope tonight was the turning point. No pneumonia, though I was afraid of it. The oxygen tent is helping. Still touch and go, of course, but . . ."

He, too, was hopeful.

Before I left, I helped Jacqueline to a bed upstairs. When I came down Jean had been talking to Aakonen.

As we went out, I asked what Aakonen had said.

"He said Bill didn't recognize Jacqueline but that he seemed to know when she was there. When they took her away Bill would get restless, and his pulse would flag."

"Doesn't he realize what that means?"

"Aakonen isn't against Jacqueline. He's just helpless in the face of circumstance."

ARMISTICE LET ME KNOW how exhausted I was. I slept in the car going back to the Fingers, not waking until it stopped with a jerk. I opened my eyes to Jean half risen over the wheel, his whole body tensed to iron. A smothered exclamation, and he was out of the car, running.

It took me a while to pull myself from the dizzying currents of sleep enough to see that it was the Fiddler's Fingers barn before which the car had stopped and that Jean was tearing along the east side of the barn toward the pines at its back.

What was he chasing? I was out of the car myself, following. In the black deeps of the trees ahead of Jean, nothing was visible, but as I strained my ears it seemed to me I heard the crash of branches. Then that, too, was gone—swallowed in the brushing of the hundred thousand branches, the hundred thousand waves. Jean, too, became a shadow and was gone. In sudden unreasoning terror I cried, "Jean! No! Come back!" seeing that in the blackness what he chased might have halted, lurking, waiting for him . . .

My own feet halted their headlong plunge. Over me like a smothering blanket was the feeling of that evil opposite force that moved, covert, on that strip of shore, as if it were a malignant outgrowth of the wilderness itself, as if the calm, ruthless, impersonal destructiveness that the wilderness could wreak in storm or sunshine had here become personal and purposeful, showing itself only to kill.

Incessant, the beating chuckle . . .

In that moment I wanted so badly to run away it seemed impossible to withstand it. I wanted to fly, screaming, back to Jean's car. I wanted to drive like a comet through the night, drive anywhere, faster and faster, just so I could get away from the evil in that place. When I got any grip on myself I was standing by the car, shaking it, as if I were fighting it, as if it embodied the temptation I fought.

"It got away—I thought I saw something . . ." That was Jean, panting, beside me.

I whirled. I said hysterically, "I suppose now there'll be some proof that was Jacqueline, too! I suppose now there'll be someone else dead!"

He said, "Gosh, you poor kid—you were asleep and you woke up to that. Here, I'll get you inside."

He hustled me into the house, rousing Myra to help get me in bed. While Myra was heating milk for me to drink, he called Aakonen. There must have been sleeping tablets in the hot milk, because even as I lay waiting for Aakonen's men to come, I slept.

BLINDING LIGHT IN MY eyes when I wakened—sunlight. And Jean and Myra by the bed. I blinked at them stupidly.

"Well, there isn't a sign I really saw anyone last night," Jean told me cheerfully. "I sure thought I saw someone skulking back by that barn, but the woods were scoured and no one found. General idea now seems to be that I thought up the whole thing to make myself look innocent."

Myra had brought a tray with coffee, fruit, and toast which she insisted I eat in bed. She was bone-weary and jumpy but she fussed around, plumping pillows.

"Thank goodness Phillips and Octavia were in bed," she said. "The other people we know—Bradley and Carol and the resort people—were all in bed when the sheriff's men reached there, too."

"*Could* have made a dash and gotten there." Jean wouldn't quite give up.

"Thank goodness Jacqueline was at the hospital," I said. It didn't seem possible to drag myself back into the mess. "I hope she stays at the hospital all day. It's better for her than getting out here where she's suspected by everyone."

"I *still* think I saw someone around last night." Jean seemed to feel his honor was involved. "If I could have caught that guy—"

If he had, the whole thing might have been ended now. But even as I thought that it seemed impossible; I felt as if we were doomed to live forever in this half-life of distrust and suspicion and failure and fear.

Myra seemed to sense my depression; she said quickly, "Bill's doing all right—I just talked to the hospital. And Toby's fine—a little lonesome. I called your aunt Harriet this morning, too. She's worried, but I told her both her girls were safe in bed."

I was ashamed of myself; if Myra could maintain some courage after so many sieges then I surely should. I forced myself to eat the breakfast. It was nearly noon, they told me; I'd slept through the morning.

It wasn't until I noticed that they didn't leave so I could dress before I began to wonder if they were still holding something back, then I noticed that they were both dressed up.

I asked, "Now what?"

"Fred's funeral," Jean told me soberly. He'd been sitting on the foot of the bed; now he rose. "One o'clock. Bill had told the undertaker to have it the day after the inquest. We wondered— since Jacqueline's at the hospital . . ."

So I dragged myself from bed to represent Jacqueline at that brief private ceremony which only Bradley and Carol, Mark, Jean, Myra, and I attended beside the minister and the undertaker's men, but which seemed lit by flashlights and which a thousand people watched outside the church and outside the cemetery wall. It was an ordeal for all of us; we were all so quivery, we jumped each time a flashbulb went off, and Bradley Auden, getting out of a car at the cemetery, slipped and almost fell, hurting his ankle.

It was when we were back at the Fingers that Jean said carefully, thoughtfully, "I notice Cecile wasn't there." It seemed a long time ago, the evening before when we'd decided we must find out about Cecile.

"Cecile?" Myra asked, surprised. "But of course she'd know she couldn't go to the funeral." She'd sunk into a chair as soon as we returned, her strength inadequate to carry her farther.

"Why not?" Jean turned to her quickly.

"Well, really—she's been a friend of Bill's, and I've allowed her here for that reason—"

"She's a Grand Marais girl." Jean was frowning at her. "What do you know about Cecile, Myra?"

"Not much, except that she's illegitimate," Myra said with distaste. "Her mother was a waitress in a Grand Marais café. I never heard who the father was. You can't hold that against the poor girl, of course, but—it's not a good background: The mother lived until Cecile was about fourteen."

"Who'd she live with after that?"

"I don't know. Someone must have been giving her money, because I've never heard of her working."

Old scandal. Jean stood looking at Myra so thoughtfully her eyebrows rose.

"Surely you don't—Bill's thirty-eight. If you think he could be the father of a girl who's every day of twenty-four—"

"No," Jean answered, "I couldn't think that. You're sure you never heard who her father might be?"

"Village gossip didn't get to Faraway." It held a hint of the old crispness. "I heard the story at the time the girl's mother died. Bradley had heard it. He was wondering if we should contribute to the girl's care. Then when he inquired, he found she'd been sent to a girls' school, expenses paid."

Jean grunted. "*Brad* isn't her father—not so she knows it— not with the sort of play she's been making for him."

He maneuvered me after that out onto the porch. "I think our next play is to get hold of Brad and go into some past history. We'll have to sneak."

I could see why; we'd been followed home from the funeral. A camera was set up in the drive, and what were obviously two reporters lurked outside the porch door.

"You could ask Myra about the Heaton family," I suggested. "She'd know more than Bradley Auden."

He shook his head. "Ever hear a Heaton on the subject of Heatons? No, I want an outsider."

We paused only to call the hospital to make sure that Bill was holding his own—the report was that he was, if anything, stronger—and to tell Myra where we were going.

She started wearily to rise.

"If you're going to be detectives, I can go along . . . No, I should spend some time with Octavia—I've already left her alone too long. And I'm sure Cecile—"

"Why don't you lock yourself in your own room and get a rest?" Jean asked her. "By the way, do you have any idea where Phillips is?"

Phillips, too, I remembered, had been absent from the funeral.

Her face relaxed momentarily. "I think he's being a detective, too. Anyway, he was here this morning asking for a magnifying glass."

We saw Phillips ourselves when we drove to the resort for a quick stop at Jean's cabin. Phillips sat on the sand, his arms clasped around his fat gray seersuckered knees, talking to Cecile. They both stopped talking when they saw us, turning their heads to watch us with the secret distrust which these days looked out of almost every face which turned toward me. That was because I was Jacqueline's cousin.

AT ONE POINT ON the highway toward Auden, Jean gestured at a gaunt dead pine.

"That's the end of the Fingers—the place where Faraway begins. The land from here on is Bill's now."

The same thick luxuriance of pine, with a narrow road cutting toward the shore. Hard ruts with sand drifting into them. After that first day, there'd been no more mention of the lodge Bill was building; that had been forgotten with Fred's death.

"Already the tracks our trucks made are beginning to fill up," Jean said.

"Sometimes I can feel it wait," I said. "The wilderness. Waiting until it can blot us out."

He didn't answer, but there was between us in the car a common awareness of the wilderness power, its will to survive in this last stronghold against the holocaust of civilization. From such a stronghold as this, when the human race has finally destroyed itself, the wilderness will come . . .

AUDEN IS NOT AT all like the Fingers. The first Auden had built, not a log house, but a colonial dwelling. Seeing that white, wide-shuttered, strong house in its setting of pines, I remembered that the homes of New England, too, had been built in forest; it fitted. The Audens lived there the year round.

Bradley himself came limping to open the door, his face quickening at sight of us.

"Is Bill—?"

We stood in the hallway talking about the thing that was still more important than anything else—Bill's chances of survival.

"Carol's out somewhere with Mark," Bradley said after that. "They dropped me here after the funeral. Marjorie's having a bad day, what with this and that. I'm sorry, Ann, because she'd like to see you."

What arrangements, I wondered as he led us, still limping,

across the hall, did he make with his mind and his conscience? He talked now about his wife as any husband might talk of a loved and considered woman—yet how many times had I seen him laughing with Cecile? As if he were helpless, willingly helpless, laughing at his own weakness.

He took us through a living room which looked as if it had been set in a mold years ago, then never lived in, never touched. The glassed porch to which he took us was lived in, however—disorderly. Magazines in piles, a spaniel on the floor in the sun, cocking a sleepy ear above one opened eye. Filled ashtrays littered a low table.

Bradley settled us into a glider. There was a nervous expectancy about his movements, as if he waited and apprehended something. When he himself sat down, it was to busy himself lighting a pipe. The dog dragged its belly along the floor to lie where he could reach it.

Jean asked, "Soso out last night?"

"She's out every night. Rabbits." The long nervous hand went down to scratch Soso's head, and Soso's muzzle collapsed contentedly on her forepaws. Bradley cautiously stretched a leg whose ankle was badly swollen.

"Saw you twist that ankle," Jean told him. "You better take care of it."

"Oh, it'll take care of itself . . . You out detecting today?"

"We hope." Jean leaned forward, his attitude changing. "We want to know about the Heaton family. I can remember there was some sort of stink when Charles and Daniel Heaton were burned in the fire that destroyed Faraway lodge. Of course that was before my sister married Bill. I didn't—"

I straightened, aghast. "Your *sister* married Bill! You mean your sister was Bill's first wife?"

The dark face became darker still. "Didn't you know?"

I hadn't known, and my mind rocketed, trying to see what change this fact might make. Would a brother be so jealous of a second marriage . . . ? No, that seemed incredible.

I said, "Then you are—you were Fred's uncle!"

He asked, "What did you think I was in this for?—the ride?" His face was suddenly swift, fierce, with more emotion than there'd been on it even last night when he spoke of Bill. Yet at the funeral, his face had been impassive, stoical.

I hadn't time to think; he was going on to Bradley, "I was a kid about twelve at the time of the Faraway fire. But I remembered some hint Phillips made to me that a charge had been made against Bill's father."

The hand on the dog's head stopped scratching.

"You think Phillips is the murderer."

"Not yet. I'm trying to get at motives and causes."

"You ask Myra?"

"I want it from an outsider."

"You could find out about the fire from the file of old Grand Marais newspapers." He seemed oddly on the defensive.

"Then there is something about that fire."

"Why come to me?"

"Weren't you living here at the time?"

"I saw the fire. I don't know—"

"Don't know what?"

"Don't know who started the fire."

"So that is it!"

Bradley Auden's long body limped to the end of the porch. He stood for a long moment looking out over his lawn. Then he turned.

"It was hushed up. Phillips Heaton accused Bill's father of setting that fire. Some other people believe . . . maybe Phillips set it."

WE WERE ALL STANDING.

I said, "But Myra's father was burned to death in that fire—and Daniel Heaton died afterward, too. If Phillips is suspected of setting it, *does Myra know*?"

Bradley walked back toward us. "Wait. I didn't say there was any suspicion Phillips set that fire deliberately. He was drunk."

I sank back into the glider.

"Oh. You think he—"

"I don't think anything. I just gathered from Myra that what she believed was that Phillips accidentally upset a kitchen lamp and then went drunkenly in to bed, not knowing what he'd done. Anyway, she was the one who stuck up for Bill's father."

Jean had remained standing." Wait. How did Bill's father get into this?"

"He—" Bradley said the one word, stopped. "The whole Heaton history is wrapped up in it."

"It can't be too long for us."

Bradley dropped into his chair. "You know about old Rufus. He was one of the lumbermen who gutted the state. He filled this country up with emigrants, city clerks, bums out of jails—anything. He paid their filing fees on forty-acre plots in the middle of virgin forest. Then he'd go in and cut the timber for miles around. "Rubber forties, they called 'em. In the end he didn't even buy up the homesteaders—he just used names out of the Chicago directory."

The disillusioned eyes looked steadily at Jean. "Rufus had two lieutenants. John Sallishaw was one of them. My father was the other, but he was younger and never made much money out of it."

"I knew that." Jean nodded.

"Then you must know old Rufus disinherited his older son, Daniel, when Daniel was sixteen. Dan was crazy about trees—I know because it was to my father Dan went when he was kicked out. A lot of the ideas Bill used really came from his father. My father's friendship with Daniel lasted until Daniel died. In the summers, old Rufus and Charles and his family would be at Faraway. I'd play with Myra and Phillips. But in winter they'd go, and then Uncle Dan and Bill would come out from Grand Marais—to Auden, that is, not to Faraway. Uncle Dan never set foot on Faraway until after old Rufus died in 1918 and Charles found out how little money there was." He rose to knock his pipe ashes out against a tray and to limp restlessly to a window.

"Lord, I can remember as if it were this morning! July 1920. This same time of year. Uncle Dan came out one night to see Dad, excited. He showed Dad a letter he'd had from Charles—a letter asking Dan to make a bid for the Faraway pines."

Jean was behind me. "You mean Charles wanted to sell the pines from *Faraway*?"

"Yes. I hadn't realized it, but even if Uncle Dan had been disinherited, he must have felt as if the Faraway pines were partly his. He couldn't bear to have them cut. He talked—"

"You heard this?"

"I was twenty-two. Lord, it doesn't seem to be so long ago!" But his eyes were distant, looking back. "I can remember how I felt. Divided. There'd been—" He laughed suddenly, softly. "I'd thought I was in love with Myra—lord, how I was suffering! And she'd married John Sallishaw. A widower as old as her father. Charles Heaton thought the Audens didn't have enough money."

Air gasped into my lungs. "You were in love with Myra? But you never—"

He asked, "Does it seem odd anyone would be in love with Myra?"

"No, oh no. She's lovely and—But you—"

He shook his head at me, smiling. "Let me be a lesson to you. How I suffered! And then the minute I saw Marjorie, it was all gone."

For an instant, his face was what it should have been, the disillusionment gone.

"I suppose this is the important part. We went over it enough later. Uncle Dan left Auden about ten o'clock, the night of that fire. Sometime around eleven, Dad and I saw the glow over the trees. By the time we got to Faraway, the house was a charred frame. Terrible, like a black gallows."

"Dan Heaton was there?"

"He was running around like a crazy man, carrying buckets of water from the well to wet the ground along the first ranks of trees."

"Who saved Phillips?"

"Dan. He'd pulled him out."

"Hadn't he tried to get Charles?"

"He said he had. He said the stairs were gone. Phillips slept downstairs."

"No one else was in the house?"

"The girl who did the work slept over the boathouse. Dan had her carrying water to the trees, too."

I asked, "What about Myra?"

"You remember she'd married John Sallishaw. She was living at Fiddler's Fingers. Octavia had already gone to live with Myra, too. Myra and John Sallishaw got to the fire sometime after we did."

"Why did Phillips accuse Dan of setting the fire?"

The thin shoulders shrugged. "Trying to get out of his own hole maybe. The trouble was, Uncle Dan couldn't prove he wasn't there when the fire started. He'd stopped his car to walk in among the Faraway pines. Then he smelled the smoke and ran."

"Saved Phillips," Jean said. "Let Charles burn." He took his time to walk up and down the porch.

"Uncle Dan lasted three months," Bradley went on, "with Phillips trying to fasten an arson charge on him. If it hadn't been for Myra—" Again the shoulders lifted.

Jean said, "So that's the story. If I'd been hunting for a reason for Bill to murder Phillips, I'd think I might have it. But I'm looking for the opposite. And I don't see it."

Neither of us saw the real answer in that fire.

14

"IT'S ENTIRELY PLAUSIBLE," I said on the way back, trying to twist facts to be what I wanted them to be. "Look at Phillips. Maybe he upset a lamp in the kitchen. He was drunk. He wouldn't know. Maybe he actually believes Bill's father set the fire."

"So then he's out for revenge by killing Dan Heaton's son and grandson."

"Not to mention Bill's life was on the up while Phillips's went down."

"Okay," he said. "Something is better than nothing."

"What we should do next is—"

"Wait up. We set out to do two things and we haven't finished, either."

"I should think we'd have about cleaned up Heaton history."

He laughed. "Girl, a family lives, dies, suffers, hates for a hundred years—and you think you've heard it all in fifteen minutes."

"What do you think we should do next?"

Lowering darkness over the face already so dark. "Is there

any lamp in heaven to light up this mess?" He brooded over the wheel a moment, but then his face cleared.

"Look. Let's get back to the idea Bill had—his ideas are always right. Do you remember what he thought? He thought everything that had happened since the wedding—all those tricks—was part of one plan. If we could find out how those tricks were engineered and who engineered 'em—"

The car swerved drunkenly—my fault for grabbing at his arm.

Why hadn't I thought of that before?

WE WENT TO HIS cabin to talk out our plan of action. Mark, as he'd expected, was out. Nothing was in the one small room but the inevitable furnishings of cabins, plus what clothes and gadgets two men—two remarkably neat men—would have on hand.

Walking into that cabin, I remembered what it seemed so easy to forget—that Jean, too, was suspect. At moments that memory would come up as it came up now, and I'd draw back, watching him, seeing his curious mixture of litheness and awkwardness, his bulldog tenacity. Then he'd begin talking, and my mind would get drawn into what he said; I'd forget.

"Mark and I just expected to be here four days." He waved a hand at the iron bed, the flat-topped round iron stove, the table, the two kitchen chairs. The moment the screen door slammed after him he stripped off his coat as if that were standard procedure for entering his own habitat, draped it over the back of a chair, and began talking.

"All right. We begin with the idea that someone planned those tricks to make Jacqueline look, if not insane, at least suspicious. Let's tackle 'em one by one and see where we come out."

Eagerness lashed me as we sat down to his table. "This is what we should have started with: that fire in Jacqueline's bed. If we could find out how that was done—"

"Wait up." He had the notebook out again. Under his fountain pen, the stumpy thick handwriting appeared. "We've got to get things in order. One—that's probably the travel folders. Not tied up to Jacqueline, you'll notice. Anyone could have sent those to Fred. Two—I guess that would be Bill's cut-up shoes in Bermuda. Three—Bill's suit turns up in holes."

"That fire in the bed came next, I think."

"All right, four. Five—that must have been the wrecking of Fred's motorcycle. Six and seven—Myra's dress and Phillips's pajamas. Eight—Toby trips on a wire. No, that would be nine—Ed Corvo's motorboat was eight. Your bathrobe, ten. Pepper in your face powder, eleven. Eleven in all. No—twelve. Somewhere along there a magazine of Octavia's suffered mayhem, too."

I sat looking at the list. "Start with a belief in Jacqueline's innocence, and that list is the best bolstering you can have. They make her look—what Bill worried about—insane. Now they're part of murder. She couldn't hope to plead insanity and get *free*. She'd still be locked up in an insane asylum for years at least."

"Good girl. We talked about the folders—anyone could have sent them. The next is those shoes. All right. I was there in Bill's apartment in Duluth the night he packed for his honeymoon. I helped. Those shoes were okay then. I stuck 'em in myself."

"Then someone must have cut them up after they were packed."

"All right, we try to remember who could have gotten into Bill's suitcases. They were in the apartment until morning. Some of 'em in the bedroom, some of 'em in the living room."

"Who else was there besides you and Bill?"

"Fred."

"Not much use suspecting him anymore. Did he help pack?"

"A little, poor kid." That must be grief behind the stolidity.

"Anyone else?"

"There was a woman in every day to clean." His forehead pressed into bulges with the effort of remembering. "She was gone by then, though . . ."

The next was explosive. "Good gosh! Cecile Granat was there that night! She wanted to see Bill. She asked if Fred and I could beat it for a while—"

"Cecile!"

"When we got back after half an hour she was still there, having a drink. She went as soon as she'd finished it."

"If she was angry . . ." I was speculating down that road.

"What for?"

"Bill was getting married."

"Look, it's not quite the way you think. I'll tell you what she was there for. She'd been out at a party with Brad Auden. She wanted to ask questions. About Brad's wife. She didn't want to ask in front of Fred. Bill told me afterward."

"Oh."

"Yeah. Don't drag my mind from those suitcases. Fred bumped his toe on one and swore. That one was in the living room."

"So if Bill had gone out to fix the drinks, Cecile could have done her bit."

"We've got to chalk that possibility up against Cecile. No one else was in the apartment that night, I'm sure. Bill and I slept on the twin beds in the bedroom. Fred slept on the davenport."

He made a bracket opposite the shoe item on his notebook page and wrote in three names—*Cecile, Fred, Jean.*

"That last name is for your benefit," he reminded me. "Don't miss anyone. In the morning we took all that luggage over to Myra's. We left it there in one of the bedrooms upstairs while we were around Duluth doing the stuff we had to do."

I could remember Fred and Jean hauling bags upstairs; characteristically, Bill had mounted empty-handed.

Jean inked in more names in his bracket—*Ann Gay, Myra, Lottie.*

I protested, "Lottie wasn't there."

"Did you go out in the kitchen?"

Myra's Duluth house is as 1890-ish as the house at the Fingers— a huge brick "Italian villa," as it probably was called when it was built; it even has cupolas. Also, it has dark, long, narrow halls and a back stairs. I had to admit I hadn't been in the kitchen.

"Lottie was there, helping for the wedding. She's talked to me about it since I've been at the resort."

Lottie. Why should she always keep cropping up?

He added more names—*Bradley Auden, Carol, Phillips Heaton.* The last name seemed thicker, blacker than the rest.

"But I never saw him before—"

"Phillips Heaton." Jean repeated the name aloud. "He was there, all right. For once, he's where I want him. Myra had him neatly packed away in an attic bedroom. He was sulking. Didn't go to the wedding or any of the parties, but he was there. Lottie saw him plenty—in the kitchen. Easy for him to slip down the back way and mess up a few things in Bill's luggage while the wedding was going on. And—oh yes—Octavia. Let's not leave her out again." He added her to the list.

"It begins to look easy, how those shoes could have been cut." I brooded over the puzzle. "Bill didn't look at them until he found them ruined, and so many people had access to them. But how about the holes in that suit? That takes explaining."

"I wasn't so much interested when I heard the tale. How did it go?"

"Jacqueline said Bill had worn the suit in Bermuda. It was all right until it got back from the cleaner's. At first, Bill thought it was the cleaner's fault—"

"That whole thing might have been a bit of luck for the unknown wrecker. It might really have been the cleaner's fault."

"But there was that bottle of something that ate holes in Bill's handkerchief in with Jacqueline's manicuring things. Would those cleaning men have done that?—planted that acid there?"

"It doesn't seem likely, does it? What I'm wondering is something else. If that was acid in the bottle—suppose there was some other acid—one that would stay on a suit for a week without showing?"

I snatched at it. "An acid with a delayed action? Jean! Of course that must be it! Look, Jean, look at that list—the shoes, Myra's dress, Fred's motorcycle, Phillips's pajamas, the wire across the path, Ed's motorboat, my bathrobe, the pepper—those are all easy. *Anyone* could have done them. There are just two that make it look as if Jacqueline must be responsible—and those two are the acid on the suit and the bed that caught fire in the night, when only Bill and Jacqueline and Toby were in the house."

He was staring at the list. "That's right! I didn't see it!"

He didn't know about the bit of fluff in Jacqueline's manicure scissors, and I wasn't going to tell him. Anyone could have taken those scissors, too.

"You take the acids," I said. "I'll take the fire in the bed. That must have been handled by delayed action, too. I'm going to find out how."

That was what I was saying when the door opened to reveal Mark and Carol. They'd pretty well dropped out of mind; they seemed, as Jean said, so remote from what was going on. It was almost a surprise to see them grave and subdued, moving listlessly under the pressure of our sobering events.

"I heard you were at our house." Carol sat moodily on the bed. "We looked for you at the Fingers. No one was around but Myra, upstairs with that Octavia. Myra came down, but she was in the dumps."

"Dumps," I said. "That's a nice way to phrase it."

"Okay, you phrase it, then." She was edgy and distraught, sunk in what seemed to be some personal problem.

"She doesn't mean to—" Mark began, but she snapped at him.

"How do you know what I mean to be?"

"I'm not trying to make you cross, Carol." The boy seemed puzzled and apologetic toward her, hovering around like an uneasy cloud.

Carol, with her long legs extended, just looked hard at her feet in green anklets and crepe-soled saddle oxfords.

"We were just going." Jean was rising.

"We didn't come to chase you out," Mark offered, but Carol leaped to her feet.

"Don't you want your coat on, Uncle Jean?"

Jean had turned aside to Mark. "Did you call Captain Vorse?"

As Mark answered what was evidently a business query, I barely noticed Carol taking Jean's coat from the chair back, dropping it, fumbling for it, holding it for Jean until he took it from her.

"Gosh, no girl holds coats for me. And what was that 'Uncle Jean' stuff all of a sudden?"

She and Mark came out with us, then wandered off toward the lake. The moment they were out of earshot Jean reopened the subject they'd interrupted.

"I know the chemist at the Detroit paper mill. I'll call him long distance—he might know about those acids." He started toward the inn but then he stopped, turning to face me.

"No," he said slowly, "I'll go in to Grand Marais to put in that call. Ann, maybe I shouldn't have gotten you so mixed up in this."

A little clinging movement along my back, as if a butterfly crawled my spine. "You mean—"

"We all go around expecting a shot to pop off any minute, don't we? Anyway, I do. If the murderer gets to thinking we know too much, there won't be any doubt who'll go next."

WHEN I REACHED THE lodge, no one was downstairs, but in the hall above, Myra came to the door of Octavia's room, her finger in a gaily jacketed book. It felt ridiculous to hide what I wanted to do from Myra, but the last thing Jean had told me was to hide my activities from everyone. I wondered how I could get her out of the way or how else I could cover my being in Bill's room, working on that bed.

"Who—? Oh, Ann, you've got back." Relief in it. "I've been reading to Octavia. No one's been near the house except Carol and Mark, and they stayed only a minute." Weariness and strain were obviously wearing her thin again in spite of her efforts; blue mouth and eye shadows showed against the pallor of her skin. Through the half-open door I could just glimpse Octavia in a gray dress as hard to define as smoke, sitting with her back to the door, her head bent over something in her lap.

"I'll be back, Octavia," Myra said, and came out, closing the door. "I've always been so glad I was the one who—the one on whom Octavia could depend. But now—the rest of you are at least trying to find out who's done these terrible things. I feel house-tied."

I could summon a grim smile for that regret. "We haven't been what you could call successful so far."

"I've been trying to think . . . Cecile's running away, and then Jean asking those questions today—I don't see how Cecile could shoot Bill—he's too much her superior."

An attitude so outdated, it might have made me smile again if I hadn't seen an odd kind of truth in it. And there was my excuse . . .

I said, "We've been terribly inconsiderate, leaving you house-tied. Why don't you drive in to Grand Marais to stay with Jacqueline awhile?"

"I left Octavia alone while I went to the funeral. I hate to—"

"I'll stay here until you get back or someone else comes."

She stood hesitant, obviously torn; no question but it would be a relief for her to get away. She went back into Octavia's room and came out with faint surprise on her face.

"Octavia wants to go, too, for the ride. She says she'll stay in the car."

That was the first time I knew, directly, that Octavia could talk and did talk to Myra; I'd somehow thought she did nothing but the head-shakings.

From my window, I watched them leave in Myra's car, Octavia flitting so unobtrusively from side porch to car that I almost missed her. The moment the sedan had rounded the first pines, I was back in the hall where the doors stood open now on twilight. To make certain Phillips was absent I went to his room, where Toby's stripped crib still stood against the wall near the dresser; the sight of it momentarily erased my purpose; I felt, looking at it, as if its occupant, now gone, could never come back. I hadn't heard Toby's voice since she left.

In an instant, I was downstairs at the phone.

"Toby's aunt?" Mrs. Foster asked when I got the connection. "Why, yes, I remember. Have you found out yet who——? Oh, I'm sorry for you people. I can't think of anything else. Yes, Toby's fine. She's just getting ready for bed, but she'll come down." A cozy, normal, slightly sentimental voice, lulling panic. The receiver steadied against my ear. Then, banishing that particular fright altogether, Toby's treble.

"Are you fine, Ann? I'm fine. It b'oke."

"What broke?"

"Cecile. All b'oke."

She hadn't missed the likeness in that doll.

"That's too bad. How is Mickey Mouse?"

"He's fine. He didn't b'oke." Then quickly, with a childish resolution I could feel, "I talk Mama."

I said, "Mama isn't here right now. She'll call you in the morning." I promised recklessly; death or whatever else came between that promise should be kept.

"No! I yike talk Mama *now*!"

Then Mrs. Foster, anxiously explaining. "She's really all right. Not *very* homesick, except when someone calls up."

Not very homesick. In my ears as I hung up was Toby's wail, under and behind Mrs. Foster's words.

It was because I'd failed, Aakonen had failed, Jean had failed, that Toby had to be sent off alone to live with a stranger—like an orphan, like a war refugee. When I ran back upstairs, determination was a hand pushing me. No need for quiet, since I was alone in the house. My feet echoed from the stairs. But cautiously, I pulled the curtains shut before turning the light switch of Bill's room.

In the sudden light I crossed to the bed where the quilt had been pulled down to hide the scarring of the sideboard.

Kneeling, I pulled the quilt back, rubbing my finger over the blackened surface then exposed. All the char that would come off had been rubbed away from the wood; my finger didn't blacken. But the patina of the burn was unmistakable—the wood had been eaten in almost a quarter of an inch; the fire had spread over a length of three feet in a shape like the bottom of a circle—burned deeper and wider at the top of the board than at the bottom.

The fire, then, must have come from above the board, from the mattress. Swiftly I pulled all the covers back. The top of the mattress showed no sign of having been near fire. When I lifted it to see the underside, that, too, was unmarred. But it was a new mattress—an inner spring in pale green damask. The old one must have been burned and water-soaked so badly it was unusable.

The spring beneath wasn't new; it clearly showed the wide blackened circular scar where the fire had been. It was an old-fashioned spring with a surface of silvered double-wire mesh, closely woven, fastened at the top and sides to a metal frame. Underneath, strung along metal strips, were four rows of supporting wire coils, four coils in each row.

As well as I could, kneeling there, with the marks of the fire revealed, I recalled what Jacqueline had told me of it. She and Bill had gone to bed about eleven. The fire was after two. They were alone in the house, with the bedroom door locked and the key in the lock. There'd been no signs of anyone getting in a window.

That fire must have been set some way so it would break out in the night. Some sort of device . . .

Impatiently, I dropped the edge of the mattress which settled back over the spring with a bouncing plop. Wouldn't a time device call for wires? At least some sort of container. Certainly

Jacqueline would have seen anything like that. If she hadn't, Bill would. She'd said he'd searched. And what had he found? Two blackened matchsticks under the bed.

A slight sound behind me made me turn.

The bedroom door was open. Standing there, watching me, was Phillips Heaton.

15

NOTHING INSIDE ME COULD move—not my blood, not my heart, not my tongue. *Hide what you guess; hide what you do*—and here I was caught by the one person—I knew now—I least wanted to be caught by. I stood waiting for the forward-coming step . . .

But instead he stood still, slowly cocking the white head. The bushy eyebrows went up, and a smile appeared on his small mouth.

"I was certain Jacqueline hadn't come back."

He wasn't looking at me as he said it but at the bed, which was as it had been when I dropped the mattress—the covers thrown back, the charred sideboard nakedly exposed.

I opened my mouth to scream but shut it. Screaming might precipitate things.

And then I thought: *The cape, he isn't wearing the cape*, and some of the tightness inside me loosened—enough so I could speak with an effect of threat.

"What are you doing here?"

"I saw a light under the door. This is anybody's game now, isn't it?"

He was stepping lightly into the room, just far enough for the door to be gently closed behind him. My feet returned to enough mobility to edge me sideward toward the door, but apparently he didn't notice.

"So that's the line your investigation is taking, is it? The fire in the bed. Well, well. Interesting. Most interesting."

He reached the bedside; by that time I had my back to the door. My hand found the knob, and at the touch my pulse eased a little from the leaping and plunging that had followed that first freeze.

"You don't have to be afraid of me, my dear." The next soft words belied his inattention. "I'm interested in this thing exactly as you are. Fascinating problem. Let's see." The white head cocked farther. "The fire broke out in the night. Either Lord Heaton set it, or Lady Heaton set it, or someone else set it. Nice problem all around."

I bit my tongue to keep back a retort.

"Too bad, isn't it, that it will be practically impossible to find out how that fire started after all this time? Now, if we'd known at the time how important our little difficulties were to become— or if we'd had a well-endowed detective on hand—"

He meant me by that last crack, but I didn't rise.

"I'm almost sorry I wasn't here on the night of that fire myself."

"I noticed you were absent."

He had wits like a mountain goat. "Ah, you believe the fire was started by remote control? How did someone else—in Duluth, for instance—start that fire? Very interesting problem."

As I had, he pulled the mattress back to look down at the blackened bedspring.

"The fire was confined apparently to this, the side of the bed nearest the door. Bill, as a valorous husband, naturally slept on this side. That's the convention, isn't it? Your idea, of course, is that the fire was *not* started by the adored cousin . . ."

The words had slowed, apparently for thought. He stood for at least three minutes looking down at the bed in silence before he dropped the mattress, shrugging.

"I confess I don't see the answer. I'm afraid, my sweet child, that your dear cousin Jacqueline is going to spend a great deal of time in prison, pondering over her life. Although I quite definitely guess that Jacqueline is not guilty."

Something—I'd begun turning the knob, but my hand halted as he started toward me. This was bigger than personal fear.

"You said that as if you knew—"

He came on, spreading his palms in an unctuous wide gesture, palms down. "Know? *Guess* is better. Guessing doesn't seem so difficult—to an intelligent person. Very certain guessing."

The door was forgotten. So, almost, was the ability to speak. He just waited, watching me, amused, as a cat might watch an anticipation-petrified mouse.

"Then why don't you do something about it?" To my own surprise, my words when they did come were cool. This was a game he played.

The hands spread again, palm uppermost this time. "No proof."

"Then how can you know?"

"Psychology—the motive reasoned out—or shall we say intuition?"

"The motive—what is it?"

"My dear girl." It was deliberately provoking. "You just don't think. Haven't you realized, for instance, what a beautiful and wealthy widow Jacqueline would make—for a *third* husband?"

Hinting at Jean again.

I said harshly, "If that was the plan, Jacqueline wouldn't be pointed out as the murderer. People in jails and asylums don't marry."

He shrugged. "Well—if you don't like that idea, I have others."

"If you do know, you should be forced to tell."

The smile became more definite. "But that doesn't suit my purposes—no, really not."

Exasperation stung like a thousand bees. Before I could stop myself I'd said, "I can imagine one circumstance in which you'd know the murderer and it wouldn't suit your purpose to tell."

I was turning the knob again, but he made no threatening move; instead he chuckled cheerfully.

"You repeat yourself, my dear. You suggested a moment ago that you suspected me. I shall be able to take care of that. Have you forgotten my alibi for the night Fred was shot?"

He moved closer, and I quickly opened the door. Downstairs someone was calling my name. Jean.

"Ann! Where are you?"

"Here. Upstairs. With Phillips Heaton."

"With—What're you up to?" He got upstairs four at a time; his face when it appeared curiously foreshortened, as if it were squeezed in a vise. The eyes were two slits and the mouth another.

In the door of the bedroom Phillips was making a casual explanation. "We were looking into that little incidental matter of the burning bed. We got, I regret to say, nowhere. At least, I got nowhere."

"Not that easy," I said, and I felt vindictive. Alone I'd been afraid of him, but not now.

I said to Jean, "Phillips just told me he knows the murderer."

"He what?" Jean swung to face Phillips, incredulous. "Oh yes, the little lady is quite right." To him, too, Phillips put on the manner of deliberate, mocking provocation.

"Then *who*, for——?" Jean was moving forward, crouched, as if he might spring upon the man in the door.

Phillips raised a restraining hand. "Sh-sh-sh! No bad language. What I said to Ann was that I guessed. I have no proof—no more than you do. Without proof where would my guess get you?"

"It's darn well going to get us somewhere. If we know whom to suspect we can look for proof in the right places." Jean continued his advance, but he straightened. "See here, Phillips, this business is no joke. It's the job of every one of us to do what he can."

"I have done. I alone, I might point out." He was fencing, a light foil in a supple fist, against Jean, who wielded verbal brickbats.

"You're going to tell, or——"

To the implied threat, Phillips just stood silent, his eyebrows rising, the smile remaining on his mouth. In frustrated anger, Jean reached for him, shaking him; Phillips's cheeks got pinker, and his eyes snapped, but he let himself be shaken, limp, while the choleric blood thickened in Jean's face.

"You're not getting anywhere," I said. I could see that obstinacy only increased on the fat pink mouth. "There's a better way—Aakonen."

"Of course." Jean's hands dropped on the instant. He stood back, breathing heavily, glaring at the man he'd dropped. "Don't think you're getting away with anything."

Phillips, settling his tie, smoothing his hair, chuckled, looking slyly up from the corners of his eyes. "Come to think of it, a chat with Aakonen would suit me fine—tonight. You tell him I'm waiting for him. I'll be—yes, I'll wait for him by the fire downstairs."

That's where he was when we left him—sitting with an ostentatiously opened book on his lap, gazing at the fire, his face still occupied by that amused, well-satisfied smile.

We went to find Aakonen at once, driving to Grand Marais in Jean's car. On the way, I had to tell how little progress I'd made before Phillips interrupted me.

"I didn't do much better." Jean, too, tore his mind from our purpose to report on an earlier effort. "My chemist friend in Detroit couldn't give me an answer offhand. The acid that ate up the handkerchief—that would be easy, he said—sulfuric would do it. The delayed-action one was harder. He said he'd have to experiment."

"Did you tell him we need to know in a hurry? Did you tell him it might be something that would combine with gasoline or naphtha?"

A grunt from the dark face in darkness over the wheel. "Girl, I told him everything except my aunt Sarah's maiden name. He wanted to know what Bill's suit was made of, how it had been packed, had Bill noticed any unusual spots before the holes came, had he worn it in any unusual places, were the holes clean-cut, or was the fabric just weakened, and so on and so on."

"Wasn't he encouraging? Didn't he think some acid might work that slowly?"

"He was noncommittal. Said he'd call if he got anything."

I bounced with exasperation on the seat. "Can't anything be cleared up? I never saw anything like it! Wherever we turn only failure—blank walls!"

He grinned, but his face didn't light up. "You're telling me. And that reminds me—you didn't see my wallet around anywhere today, did you?"

Something that could have no connection; I relaxed dully.

"Apparently I've lost it. I—"

I quickened a little. "Anything important in it? Any—"

"Money. Ten or fifteen dollars. Insurance cards. The only thing that annoys me is—" He stopped, his square black brows drawing down. "If you don't mind, after we've seen Aakonen I'd like to drive around to the office."

"Was your office key in the wallet?"

"No, that's here on my key ring." He pointed toward the ignition. "I found my wallet gone when I went to put in that Detroit call. Had to borrow the money from Hanson. Lucky he knows me."

"Quite well, I imagine."

"Well, he's never had to carry me home to bed." That time when he grinned, it wasn't just his mouth.

FOR ONCE, WE WENT to the hospital thinking of Bill second. Since Jacqueline was there, Aakonen was sure to be. Miss Fleet's face splintered into a smile when we told her what we wanted.

"You've of course heard Mr. Heaton is definitely stronger. Dr. Rush said the change became apparent this afternoon."

Through the door she opened we had a glimpse of Bill, his face all in one piece again, the flesh adhering to his bones.

Aakonen came out, herding Jacqueline and Myra before him. Jacqueline, too, was changed; she couldn't have had much sleep since I'd left her the night before but she looked rested and eased, strong in a way I'd never seen before.

"It's just a matter of his getting well now," she said.

The big head with the vein across the dome gave a perceptible nod. "Tonight you should get some rest, Mrs. Heaton."

"Not yet," Jacqueline begged. "I don't want to go yet."

When we told Aakonen we wanted to talk to him, he sent Miss Fleet back to her desk and Jacqueline and Myra to the cubbyhole. Only Jacqueline and Myra. Octavia must be sitting out in the car, as she'd said she would. I'd noticed the sedan outside but, typically, had seen no one in it. Of course, Octavia might have slipped out for a walk.

"What is it?"

The big face seemed to wake as I told him of Phillips Heaton's statements.

"You say he said in so many words he believed the murderer *not* to be Mrs. Heaton?"

"That's about it."

"Hm. I will see Phillips at once." He started purposefully toward the door but he halted himself.

"No, I must wait here until Mrs. Heaton and Mrs. Sallishaw leave. I can see Phillips Heaton anytime tonight. Watching Mr. Heaton while someone else is in the room is a duty I will not delegate to anyone."

His face had fallen with weariness into folds like a Saint Bernard's, but latent strength lay under the tiredness.

Jean made a quick inquiry. "Do you know yet if the bullet taken from Bill was shot from the same gun that killed Fred?"

I thought Aakonen wasn't going to reply; he took minutes to consider before he did. Then slowly he nodded.

"The riflings show that, beyond doubt, the two bullets came from the same gun. *Not* Ed Corvo's gun."

"Still no sign of that gun—or the chalk or the cape?"

A headshake.

I asked, "What about Bill's things in his apartment? And he might have safety-deposit boxes. Are you sure he has no enemies?"

"We know he has an enemy," Aakonen said somberly. "What we do not know is who. His apartment, his office here, his safety-deposit boxes in Duluth—they've all been gone over. Fortunately his lawyer had power of attorney."

"Those policies"—Jean snatched at that—"they still in Fred's favor?"

A nod. "They revert to the estate if—"

I squirmed against that admission that Bill still might die. "Did his lawyer have no—?"

Aakonen spread his hands almost as Phillips had. "No threats, no lawsuits—"

"And Bill told that lawyer everything. He believed in hiring brains and using 'em." Jean left that with what looked like despair. "We aren't falling behind—it just seems that way."

MYRA OFFERED TO WAIT with Jacqueline and take her home. I went with Jean when he left for his office. But we didn't go directly to that office and what was to meet us there—or, rather, we did go directly but stopped on the way. At Hanson's, Jean swung the car to the curb.

"We stop here for station announcements. Apparently you forget about food, but I don't."

When we walked in Bradley was at the bar having a drink.

"Hallo, you here in town, too?" he asked. "You don't happen to have seen Carol around, I suppose?" He set his emptied glass down.

I sent memory backward. "We saw her late this afternoon—she was at the resort with Mark."

"She's out on some sort of expedition. She was supposed to come home for dinner and didn't. I called Mark, and he said she'd left the resort soon after six. When monkey business didn't turn up by eight, I got out on the highway and flagged a ride in. She must be around town somewhere."

Anyone missing now brought quick fear: *Is this another?* Yet Bradley seemed only perturbed.

I asked, "Did you call the Fingers?"

"No one there but Phillips—or so he said. He answered the phone."

"She's probably at some girlfriend's."

He frowned. "She has damn few around here. I've sent her to school in Duluth. What I guess is that she's had a fight with Mark and then went off somewhere to get him good and worried. Well, guess I'll look around town a little." He turned to limp toward the door. "Good night."

Jean stood watching him closely as he dropped the door behind him.

"Brad's more worried than he's letting on."

I shivered. "I'd be worried too if . . . But it's still early in the evening, and she's in a car—she must be all right."

We ate quickly, under that reminder of the peril in which we all stood. Within twenty minutes, we were out. We wanted to be back at the Fingers when Aakonen talked to Phillips. Jean's car drove up the main street and then into a side street marked with an arrow "Gunflint Trail." Halfway up that block he stopped the car before what, like the hospital, appeared to be an ordinary white dwelling but which bore a sign above the porch. This sign said "Heaton-Nobbelin."

"Town was overbuilt during the lumber boom," Jean told me. "Lots of offices in old houses." He led the way up a walk toward the black-windowed building.

When he'd turned his key in the lock and pushed the door open, an office smell came out—woody, varnishy, steely, inky— a smell so reminiscent of the insurance office where I worked that for a moment, I was recalled to all my ordinary life; it seemed the past few days must be a nightmare, the quick fears that could rise like flame seemed incredible. Then as I stepped into the hall, I was entirely back in the nightmare, fear leaping, muscles stiffening, my hands flying to grab Jean.

He was groping along the wall for a light switch.

"What the—?" Then the cords in his wrist, too, were drawing taut. Somewhere overhead there was a small scurry, as of a heavy mouse running, and then, clearly audible, a click.

After that, complete silence.

"That's Bill's office up there!" It came in a swift whisper. He was half crouched in the dark, silently moving forward. "No!" he whispered at me fiercely when I moved to follow. "You stay here! You can't tell what'll happen upstairs. Anyone could've heard us coming in. They'll be waiting."

"We ought to get Aakonen."

"And let whoever it is get away?"

"Then I'm coming along."

For answer, his elbow caught me in the stomach, knocking the breath out of me. In the dark I fell back, striking against something hard and wooden—a newel post. For a moment I clung to that post, gasping to get my breath; the second I had it I was following. But he was already at the head of the stairs, while I was at the foot.

There was the sound of a door being flung open, a slow silence, a click, a shout.

"Look out!" That was Jean shouting, but it wasn't Jean who was coming at me, pell-mell. The light from the now-opened door above was behind the flying figure, silhouetting it unmistakably.

Carol Auden.

She didn't stop when she saw me, although she gave a single sobbing scream. I held out an arm to block her passage. Jean was right behind her. She reached me, flinging the full force of her weight and her impetus against me, knocking me over. Together we tumbled down the few steps I'd mounted. Again my breath was gone. She was fighting me like a wildcat, scratching and pulling. When Jean dragged her away from me, she fought him as she had me and as silently; there wasn't any sound except the gasping, panting breaths, the thud of bodies.

She couldn't win against Jean; inexorably as the struggle continued he worked himself behind her, forcing her arms down to her sides, wrapping his arms around them at her waist. She became helpless in his grasp, still struggling but unable to make more than slight movements. On her face was the wildness of terror and despair.

Then suddenly and without warning, she sagged limply down against the arms that held her like a thinly stuffed rag doll.

16

JEAN EASED HER TO the floor.

"Carol Auden!" His amazement was the same as mine. "Can you tell me what she's doing, breaking into this office?"

"Water might bring her around." I had some breath back now and I saw that making Carol talk was the next practical step.

"Water—there's water in the back room. Wait—you watch Carol. I know where the light switches are." Jean padded swiftly down the dimness of the hall toward a back room. I bent over Carol, shaking her shoulder, but the shoulder remained limp.

Aunt Harriet occasionally fainted; it helped to rub her wrists. Water was running at the back of the house. I reached for Carol's wrist.

A fist was in my face—a fist with no limpness behind it. At the same instant, Carol was rolling like a booted football toward the door, catapulting herself to her feet. We'd left the door open. She was through it, the screen slamming, before I was out of my stunned surprise.

I yelled, "She got away!" By the time I reached the front door, feet were pounding behind me. From the foot of the porch steps I had a glimpse of a striped skirt flying like a flag at the rear of the house next door.

I ran, senselessly yelling, "Carol, stop!" Jean wasted no breath on calling; he was past me, reaching back of the house, lost in what seemed like a dozen sheds. When I found him again he was dodging in and around them, swearing steadily under his breath. We ran all the way to the end of the block, back to the other end of the block.

As we paused to stand, hot and panting, staring up and down a street that was murky at the middle and only dimly lit at the ends, a light flashed up in the corner house.

"Anything the matter out there?" A woman's nervous voice.

"Nothing in the world," I called bitterly back. "We're just having a game of run sheep run."

"Nerve!" The window slammed down.

The hum of car motors was all over town. Increasing, diminishing.

"She's away by now." Jean accepted defeat. "We left the office open. We'd better go back there and call Aakonen. He'll have to know about this. Maybe we can still catch him at the hospital."

"Carol, trailing her cloud of glory." Fact still had a hard time becoming reasonable for me. "It had to trail fast to keep up, the rate she was going."

No scurry met us now as we came back into the hall where light from above fringed into the shadows.

"I might just take a look around downstairs here before we go up." Briefly Jean switched on lights to look over what must once have been a living room but was now the habitat of a stenographer/bookkeeper/filing clerk. Behind that was his own office and to the left the wash-and-storage room in what had been the kitchen. He pointed to the back door, standing open, the key in the lock inside, the glass panel above it broken.

"That's how Carol got in."

We went then up the stairs toward the lighted room on the second floor—a long room the width of the house. The first thing I saw there was the safe against the front wall, its door hanging open, a green steel box on the floor before it, papers strewn like chaff around a threshing machine.

Jean nodded at my amazement. "That's what she was in, all right—the safe." He walked toward the phone on the long table desk.

The moment he did so, I was reluctant. "Wait. There must be some explanation. Because Carol was here rifling the safe, because she ran away—that doesn't mean—"

"Doesn't mean she's the murderer. I know that. Just the same, we can't let it slide."

To Central he said, "The hospital." Then, "Is Aakonen there? . . . Good . . . Please."

I said, "She can't hope to get away."

"She's got Brad's car—don't forget that. Hallo. Aakonen? This is Jean Nobbelin. Miss Gay and I ran into a little disturbance here at the office." Briefly he told what had happened, to the accompaniment of crackling questions. "All right," he promised, "we won't touch anything until you get here."

He hung up. "Just caught him. He was at the door, leaving with Jacqueline and Myra. Whew!" For once there was an excuse for the mopping handkerchief.

"The blinds are pulled—Carol must have pulled them. That's why the house looked dark on the outside." I was beginning that recapitulation of the obvious when I caught his staring.

What he was looking at was the floor in front of the safe. He walked toward the spot, bent, picked up what a sheet of paper had half hidden, and held out toward me a man's black leather wallet. Gold letters spelled his name on the back.

A scene flashed. "This afternoon, Carol offered to hold your coat for you. She dropped it—fumbled with it . . ."

He held the wallet open-side up. Three or four bills were still in the bill section; he folded the leather back from them.

"She didn't want the money. She wanted—this."

Almost invisible against the blue-black leather, the faint shine of inked numbers—3-7-4-8-6.

"That's the combination of the safe."

THE SLAMMING OF THE door below announced Aakonen's coming; we went to the head of the stairs to meet him. He'd come alone.

"Here I ought to be out talking to Phillips Heaton and I have to stop for this. I've got an alarm out. We'll have that Auden girl in half an hour. What was she after?" He wasn't wasting time or words.

"Something in the safe, apparently." Jean pointed from the door.

Aakonen looked at the disorder. "Owens went through that safe. Gave me a list. There was a note for six thousand dollars in that safe, signed by Bradley Auden. That must have been what she was after. But I—" He dropped to his knees to pick up the scattered papers.

I suggested, "If we could help—"

"No—look!" He rose slowly, his eyes fixed on a sheet he'd picked up. "Here is the Auden note—among the papers thrown out of the box. I do not understand it." As if helplessly, he held out the sheet to Jean.

I moved behind Jean. The sheet was a letterhead, with the Heaton-Nobbelin name at the top.

February 11, 1931

I promise to pay as I am able, or at the demand of William Heaton or his heirs, any part or the whole of six thousand dollars ($6,000).

> (Signed) BRADLEY AUDEN

Below were three notations:

Received $500 2/11/34 Wm. Heaton
Received $650 2/11/35 Win. Heaton
Received $300 2/11/36 Wm. Heaton

"I talked to Mr. Auden about that note." Aakonen seemed lost. "Mr. Auden said he'd had many expenses, due to his wife's illness lately, and Mr. Bill Heaton had suggested he let payments wait."

"That sounds reasonable," Jean answered. "Sounds just like Bill."

"But Carol Auden must have seen this—it was out of the box."

"Suppose this wasn't what she was after?" Jean made a quick suggestion. "If you've still got that list Owens made of what was in this safe, we could check against that. We've never had the office girl list the contents of that box—it was all personal stuff."

"The list is at my office."

While Aakonen went to get it, Jean and I spent the time gathering up the rest of the scattered papers into a neat pile. Amazement grew as I worked.

"Is there anyone in the world who doesn't owe Bill money?"

An annoyed rasp prefaced the answer. "You'd think Bill was the father of everyone in this town and for miles around it. Anyone want to start a business? Sure, he can get the dough from Bill. Anybody get sick? Sure, Bill will stake 'em to an operation. Kid want to go to college? Sure, Bill will get 'em summer jobs and loan 'em money the rest of the year."

"Are all his records of indebtedness in this box?"

"All? Heck! He holds notes on the grown-ups, but those college kids—he has a nice, fancy ceremony making 'em sign notes to keep up the story it's all a business deal. Then when they graduate, he sends 'em the notes for a present."

He swallowed, and the bulge of annoyance-tightened muscles around his mouth relaxed.

"I ought to know. I was the first."

WHEN AAKONEN CAME BACK, we checked each sheet of paper from the floor and the box against the list Owens had made, working down until all that was left was a packet in a rubber binder in the bottom of the box. When we got that far Aakonen halted, frowning.

"Owens divided the contents of this box into what belonged to Mr. Bill Heaton and into what belonged to you, Mr. Nobbelin. Out of what belonged to Mr. Heaton everything is now checked off. There is nothing missing."

"Then Carol didn't find what she came for!" The exclamation was mine.

"Gosh knows she can't have come for anything of mine," hastily from Jean.

"Unless it was the Auden note and she somehow missed it." Aakonen rested the list on the desk as his stubby fingers verified each check mark. "Yet how could she? And there is nothing else here which seems at all related to the people concerned."

Over his shoulder I read the names of the other debtors, all strangers.

Jean straightened. "It must have been something else she wanted—something not in the box."

"But you yourself say nothing else is touched. It must be that you frightened her away before she got what she wanted. But to make sure I will check through these papers belonging to you."

Jean objected, his face reddening and confused, but Aakonen wasn't to be stopped. One by one, Jean had to enumerate his possessions aloud for Aakonen to check from the list.

For the junior member of a firm, Jean hadn't done a bad job in setting himself up as an *easy* mark, either.

But nothing was missing from that list.

AS JEAN SCRAMBLED THE notes any which way back into the box, Aakonen's mind was already leaving.

"I am anxious to talk to that Phillips Heaton. Maybe this will become unimportant . . . Anyway, Carol Auden must soon be found. I will find out then what she was doing in this office."

He made a call but found out Carol was still missing. Grunting; he turned from the phone.

"I see nothing else here. I'll get on to the Fingers." But then he paused, his stubby hand going toward a wire basket on the desk.

"Mail. I wonder if any of this has come in since Owens was here."

"That'll be Bill's personal mail," Jean said. "Firm letters are opened by the girl."

Aakonen flipped down an envelope with the letterhead of a tailoring firm, one with the letterhead of an insurance agency. The last one he kept.

"From the First National, Duluth."

Jean moved to stand behind him. "That'll probably be canceled checks from last month. I just got mine."

"Checks." Aakonen brooded over the envelope. "I wonder . . ." His eyes flicked at me, then the thick forefinger moved along the flap. "At such a time as this . . ." It was half apology.

Rapidly he leafed through the checks. Then he said, "Uh," sorting one out. He took out another, another. The pack dropped in his right hand to the desktop as he frowned at the three he'd singled out.

I moved to stand with Jean behind him.

The three checks, each for a sum of twenty-five dollars and dated May 18, May 25, and June 1, were made out to Cecile Granat.

AAKONEN DROVE AHEAD TO the Fingers, Jean and I following in Jean's car. Aakonen had made no comments on the three checks. He had returned them to the envelope with the others. But my mind was busy.

"May eighteenth and twenty-fifth and June first. Bill was in Bermuda during that time."

"I don't need it pointed out." Jean was short.

"All for the same amount—as if they were a regular payment."

"Yeah."

"Dated a week apart. It looks as if—"

He yelled at me, "Don't talk about it!" He was swelling into fury, like a balloon being blown up, but with a strong effort, he got control.

"I'm sorry. It's just that everything I find out makes me sicker."

He was moody and restless all the rest of the way. Not until the car swung along the Fingers driveway did he emit a final growl.

"I hope Aakonen gets Phillips good and squeezed."

The night was dark; there must still have been a moon, but clouds obscured it. Dimly I was later to remember that as Jean circled the lawn and we passed the bulk and sound of the Fingers, I did notice a car parked at the east side of the house. But the wheels of my mind were grinding at their immediate concerns—Carol in that office, the checks, what Aakonen would get from Phillips, finding out how the fire had been started in that bed, the danger in which we all moved, the accelerating danger in which Jacqueline stood.

Two cars were parked on the driveway in front of the house—Myra's and Aakonen's.

Aakonen was waiting for us at the door. "I knocked. No answer."

The living room beyond was entirely dark. I was grateful for two solid men beside me as we pulled open the unhooked screen door and stepped inside. Jean found a lamp switch, and the room swam into shadowy existence. I looked around; no light in the kitchen or dining room.

"Myra and Jacqueline must have gone up to bed."

Phillips, too, was gone from the chair by the dead fire. Aakonen started for Phillips's room but as he passed the phone, paused to call his office. Carol hadn't yet been found. He was just completing the call when the door opened on Bradley Auden.

"I met one of your men, and he told me you'd be here." Bradley spoke to Aakonen; he was breathing quickly, shaken out of lassitude and unconcern now. "What's this about Carol being in Bill's office?"

As Jean reluctantly told him he stared at the three of us.

"That's impossible. Carol knew about that money I owed Bill—it wasn't any secret. I could have cleaned it up just by letting Bill in to thin out some of my wood stands that are too thick. She knew I could do that. I've talked about it. I can't understand it. The whole thing's crazy. Honestly, Ann, was she really—?"

I had to nod.

Aakonen spoke up. "What Carol was doing in that office is something we will know as soon as we find her. Now I want to see that Phillips Heaton."

Jean stayed with Bradley while I took Aakonen up to the room Toby and Jacqueline had had and which was now Phillips's. The door was closed, but Aakonen applied a gentle fist. Three other doors on the hall were closed, too—Jacqueline's, Myra's, Octavia's.

When there was no answer Aakonen pushed the door open. The room was dark until he got the light on to show the bed made up but empty, although Phillips had probably lain on it, because the spread was rumpled. A pair of mussed slacks was thrown on a chair back; pajamas lay on a chair seat; a shirt had been thrown on the floor near the window. Mechanically, I moved to pick up the shirt; I don't like clothes thrown on floors. But then I stopped; Phillips's mess was none of my business.

"Not here." Aakonen's low rumble voiced the obvious. "He must have gone out." The thick hand pulled out a heavy silver watch on a chain. "Eleven twenty-two. He should be back here soon. I will wait downstairs.

He walked back along the hall with the muffled clumps resulting from his efforts to be quiet. I switched off the light and followed. At Jacqueline's door I paused, laying my ear to the panel. As I did so Myra's door opened, and she came out in a bathrobe, her hair in a braid.

"Sh-sh-sh! I gave her two sleeping tablets to take. If she doesn't sleep she'll go to pieces."

Even through the wood panel it seemed to me I caught the regular flow of breath. I couldn't possibly know how important it was for me to open that door.

Myra had turned to Aakonen. "Is there anything—?"

He hesitated. "I just wanted a little talk with your brother. He told Miss Gay he'd guessed who did the shooting."

"Phillips did? But then why didn't he say who it was?" She moved back, staring at Aakonen. "He didn't say a word to me or Jacqueline when we got home. He's in his room, isn't he?"

"Not now."

She couldn't understand it. "Phillips is an owl but he's been sticking close to the house nights now." She shivered. "He was in the living room when Jacqueline and I went to bed."

She came downstairs to hear Bradley exclaim over the incident of Carol in the office. "There'll be some simple explanation," she consoled Bradley, who seemed close to distraction.

She and I made coffee while Aakonen again called his office, then the resort to ask if Phillips was there; he waited until Ed Corvo made the round. Cecile was in her cabin, Ed reported, Mark out somewhere hunting Carol. Phillips wasn't anywhere he could see. Aakonen went out after that to look around the boathouse and the barn. He came back to say both Bill's and Myra's cars were on the place; Phillips's couldn't be gone.

Hot coffee pulled Bradley together enough so that he borrowed Jean's car and left to continue what must certainly have been an aimless hunt. When he was gone, Aakonen looked the rest of us over.

"There is no need you should stay up." He settled himself definitely in a rocker as Jean left and Myra and I trailed up to bed.

In my room I walked wearily to the dresser, to stand looking at my reflection. Comfortable to know Aakonen sat so solidly downstairs; temporarily, at any rate, the house should be safe. I was rumpled and blown from fighting with Carol, but I didn't look nearly as torn as I thought I should. Phillips, Carol—those were Aakonen's problems now. But that fire in the bed—I still felt a nagging insistence that if I could figure that out, the answer would be valuable.

Jacqueline, I thought, was asleep on the scarred bed, but on an impulse I crossed to my own to pull back the cover and mattress. The spring on mine was a twin of the other, except that it showed no burn. Double-wire mesh on a frame. The mattress was thinner than the one on the other bed—felted cotton in a standard ticking—a good mattress thirty years ago.

Probably the fire had been started in a mattress such as this. I could do my experimenting in my own room. Here, at least, I wouldn't be surprised by Phillips Heaton. I squatted on my haunches beside the bed.

Suppose it were I who wanted a fire to start in that bed after I was far away? The only signs I could leave would be two burned matches on the floor. The sticks from two ordinary kitchen matches.

Friction was what lit a match.

Again I pulled the mattress back to ponder over the spring. Smooth wires. Smooth fabric covering the mattress. Still, if there were a restless sleeper above and the matches lay between spring and mattress . . .

Aakonen would see me, but on a spurt of excitement I went down anyway. He was still waiting in the rocker, his brows rising halfway toward the thick blue vein as I tiptoed down.

"Felt like a smoke before I went to bed . . ." I had a simple explanation ready. From the upended box in the black tin holder beside the kitchen stove I took a generous handful and came out holding the matches ostentatiously as I went through the living room.

"I didn't know any ladies here smoked." Faint disapproval.

"I don't smoke often."

He patted over his pockets, hauling out a pipe. "Where you get those matches?"

While he was in the kitchen I got upstairs. Two matches went between mattresses and spring, carefully caught in the mesh so they wouldn't fall through. Then with the mattress and covers back in place, I lay on the bed to twist and turn, got up to bounce the mattress with my fists, to move it back and forth over the spot where the matches were placed. When I lifted the mattress, the match heads were still perfect—a top cap of light blue, a ring of navy. They hadn't even abraded. One match stem was broken.

Two other matches, crosswise of the mesh this time, not bedded. Again I rolled and tossed, again pushed and bounced the mattress. I—not the matches—got the effects of friction; all they did was break. I tried a handkerchief above and below the matches, tried paper above and below, tried the matches on the metal frame at the side. Still no go.

When I sank on the bed again after an hour of effort, I was ready to admit I must be on the wrong track. You couldn't just put matches between a mattress and bedspring and expect them to ignite from the movements of the sleepers above. There'd have to be some sort of apparatus—something that would burn up, leaving no sign.

I've never been ingenious about gadgets. Trying to work them just exasperates me. As I sat, it seemed to me I was numb all over—mind, bones, muscles, skin. Failure again, more failure—were we doomed to go on like this forever, never finding out anything, completely overborne by the superior cleverness of the mind against us?

Slowly and dispiritedly, I undressed, tiptoeing down the hall, with my polo coat on over my pajamas, since I no longer had a bathrobe. From below came the faint aroma of tobacco—good tobacco; Phillips must still be out. The night chill had come down good and hard. It was warm under the polo coat, but fingers and nose felt the cold.

When I turned off my light, I saw that the clouds must be clearing; dim moonlight came in the window. Feeling cramped and stifled from my unsuccessful efforts, I threw the window up to let some air in before I locked it for the night.

Wind and water and forest kept their eternal, tumult of sound and motion. I stood a moment listening to the diapason. The chuckle of the river under the Fingers seemed very loud . . .

Then my ears seemed to sort out of all that noise one quiet, stealthy sound, unusual and near, as if something heavy were being drawn or rolled over grass—here, close to the house.

Instantly my head was out the window. I looked below and toward the back of the house. Then as I stood staring, I felt over my scalp the tingle of each individual hair rising.

Below, in the dim light of the three-quarter moon then riding between clouds, a car was darkly moving. Bill's one-seated car, its top still down. Evenly, slowly, it was approaching my window.

I couldn't see it clearly, but I could see this much—there was no driver in the driver's seat, no hands on the wheel.

The car moved, but there was no one in it at all.

17

I HAD ONE OF those moments in which I thought my imagination must be conjuring up visions that had reality nowhere, as if some spring in the universe had been broken. The car's hood was almost under my window now, moving smoothly, easily—terribly, as if it moved by its own power. No human being in it, none behind it . . .

I jerked so far out of the window that I had to clutch wildly at the sill to keep from falling. That shook me into some sense. Weights and balances still worked when it came to falling out windows.

Someone must have pushed that car. Released its brakes. The nose of the car was under my window now, and it seemed to be accelerating.

The lawn sloped. That was how Fred's motorcycle had been wrecked.

I ran. Aakonen heard my frantic plunging down the stairs.

"Bill's car!" I gasped at him. "The lake—"

He held out an impeding arm, but I was past him, out the door, across the veranda. The moon was edging behind a cloud; less light, but the dark shadow of the car was there at the end of the porch. Behind me a shout—Aakonen was at my heels, running in a diagonal to head off the car.

Again it seemed the machine had taken on the attributes of a live thing. It reached the flower bank and went down, gathering momentum as if it speeded to escape us. It had touched the beach when Aakonen leaped on its running board. I caught first at him, then at the car door, dragging my feet on the ground.

He threw himself forward, sprawling, over the door. The car seemed to be moving with unquenchable power; it had jerked as Aakonen caught it, but the drag of my feet on the pebbles did not slacken its movement. A hoarse exclamation from the man writhing over the seat in an effort to reach the emergency brake, and then the front wheels of the car were in water. Only another second before the whole car was in, staggering, wallowing, plunging like a giant beast in the pulling, pounding, leaping water.

Aakonen yelled in my ear, "Jump!" He'd twisted completely around in one swift movement. His face was toward me as he catapulted himself in a long arc from the side of the car into the churning water. I loosed my hands and immediately plummeted, feet down, into the bottomless deep, gasping, spitting, reaching for air.

No sight or sound of Aakonen in that roar and motion. I had to swim and swim fast. This was where Bill had said no swimmer ever went; this was where the chuckling river from under the Fingers flowed into the lake; I felt the power of its pull. Even then, even in the surging crash of water all around me, it seemed to me I heard the deep sucking ingestion of Bill's car by the lake.

But the lake wouldn't be satisfied by the car. It had me in hands that reached more surely than the Fingers of the shore reached; it wanted me, pulled me, sucked me away from shore. I fought it, beating against it with my arms, kicking it with my legs. Water washed in arching walls over my head; the arches crashed in a curve over me, smothering me, dragging me away. I could shoot up and away from that clasp, and the water would only rise to cover me again, to drag me, roll me, wrap me in its close, insatiable grasp.

Then something like an octopus tentacle had my arm, and I was lifted and thrown one last time.

"MISS GAY!" I WAS still being shaken. "Miss Gay!"

Aakonen.

When I opened my eyes, my arms and legs were still weakly and ineptly swimming on land. The moon was out again, and I lay on my back, with Aakonen bending over me. A path of light ran down the bald dome of his head, and water dripped from it on me. The harsh rasp of his breathing was louder and nearer than any other sound.

"I got you out of the current. You're all right now. You got to come with me. I don't dare leave you."

Urgent. With the help of his hands I got to my feet. My body swayed. He held me.

"Look. I've got to find where everybody is. I got to find who pushed that car."

Somehow I could stand again, make attempts to think again. Aakonen was running heavily, half carrying me with him. We were beyond the boathouse; the current had carried us that far to the west. Aakonen looked in the boathouse and around it, then on to the house. He just looked from the porch door into the living room, then ran over to the barn and around and through it. He was hunting. All I did was follow. Then he ran back to the house, left me by the dead fire to turn on lights in the kitchen, the dining room, the side porch.

"No one down here." His breath still rasped. Going upstairs, that harsh breathing was the near sound—that and the drip of water, the squish of water in our shoes. He held my hand as if I were a child.

My door first, open as I'd run from it. He turned the light on. Empty. Myra's door across the hall; Myra starting suddenly from sleep as the light went on, her bemused face rising from the pillow.

"What—?"

Aakonen panted, "Can't stop."

He pounded on Jacqueline's door, shot that light on.

Jacqueline there. Thank heaven, Jacqueline's dark head on her pillow, motionless. She was sleeping deeply.

He commanded me roughly, "Wake her!" and left me to dart across the hall to Octavia's room, which wouldn't open to him and on which he pounded as Myra appeared hurriedly beside him, pulling on her bathrobe.

"Mr. Aakonen, what's happened? Why're you—?"

"Explain later. I want to make sure your sister's in this room."

"Octavia," Myra called then, bewildered but obedient. "It's Myra, darling. Are you—?"

From the room beyond came what sounded like a frightened bleat; at that proof that Octavia was behind the locked door Aakonen immediately went on to Phillips's room and the bathroom.

Myra remained at Octavia's door, speaking soothingly until the door was opened; she went inside for just a moment, then appeared anxiously beside me as I still hovered over Jacqueline, who slept so soundly I hated to waken her.

"Ann!" Myra became even more startled as soon as she saw my state. "Whatever has happened? You're wet! Soaking! What—?"

I was wet. Good and wet. When she touched me I could feel how my flesh had congealed on my bones, I was so wet, so cold.

She shook me. "Heavens, Ann, you'll get your death of cold!" Without any more ado, she was hauling me to her room, stripping off my heavy, dripping coat, my pajamas, the stockings and oxfords I hadn't yet taken off when I ran out; she was pushing me into her bed, rubbing me harshly with towels until blood heat ran again against my skin. Aakonen stood in the door a moment— probably when I had no clothes on, but it wasn't a time to care. When Myra let up a little, his voice was coming up the stairs in a bellow.

Myra repeated, "Ann, can you talk now? What happened?"

I gathered myself together. "Bill's car went in the lake."

She stood aghast under this new blow. "You mean someone drove Bill's car into the lake?"

"No. It was like Fred's motorcycle. Someone must have pushed it so it started rolling of its own accord down the grade."

She just stood looking at me, spent. She whispered, "Is this going to keep on forever? It doesn't seem to me I can stand much more . . ." She moved away stiffly, mechanically. When she came back she had clothes from my room.

"You'll have to put these on," she said, but her mind was held by the other. "I feel as if I were besieged, the enemy all around . . ."

I, too, had had that sense of being besieged; I had it again now. Downstairs Aakonen was yelling, "Get out here! Round up the people from the resort!" He must be phoning.

In Myra's mirror, I looked like a dunked-and-half-resuscitated cat, my wet hair plastered to my head, my face thinned and sharpened by the struggle in the water. When I was dressed, Myra and I went, without speaking, toward Jacqueline's room, hearing Aakonen's bellow.

"Auden there? You know where he is?"

Myra said tightly, "He must be getting everyone together again." She paused at her sister's door. "It's Bill's car, Octavia," she said soothingly. "It's been wrecked. Try not to worry too much."

Octavia didn't answer; only her nose showed over the blanket.

Another inquisition to come . . .

Jacqueline was exactly as I'd left her, sleeping soundly. I went downstairs to tell Aakonen I was reluctant to wake her.

He just nodded at the request. "What did I come out here alone for?" he demanded savagely. "You tell me that!"

"Bill was fond and proud of that car. He'd had it for years," Myra said behind me, still listless. "After what's happened—we can be glad this time it's a car."

Aakonen had been holding himself like an arrow in a taut bow; as she spoke he stared at her, not breathing. Then he took in air until I thought he must burst. When he let the breath go it went in one tremendous gust.

Still he didn't say anything.

Myra went wearily on, "You'll have to get dry clothes on, Mr. Aakonen. You'll have pneumonia if you don't. I can see it's important to find who pushed that car, but—"

He said shortly, "One of my men is bringing clothes."

"Then walk. You mustn't stand still. I'll start the fire."

Obediently, as Myra and I worked with the fire, he walked, plodding up and down the long living room, end to end, bowed, as if he pulled a tremendous weight with each step, as if he were a plow horse pulling a deep share through black root-toughened ground.

IT WAS PERHAPS TWENTY minutes before the first car came—two men in it, one of them with the dry clothes. Aakonen waved us upstairs; we heard there the voices in hurried parley and the car's motor as it left again. Shortly after it left, another car came. Aakonen called us downstairs.

Jean and Cecile Granat were in the living room when we got there, Lottie, Ella and Ed Corvo, too, and a deputy I hadn't seen before.

Jean's eyes leaped to me. "*What* do you think you've been doing?"

Aakonen shouted at him, "No talking!"

"No talking?" Jean shouted back. "I want to know what's been going on here! Ann, you tell me! Where've you been?"

I pushed back limp, still-damp hair. "I jumped in the lake."

"What did you do that for?" He saw Aakonen's wet clothes in a puddle before the fireplace, as mine were in Myra's room upstairs. "Whose clothes are those?"

"Mine." Aakonen was suddenly more pacific. "Now, look, everybody, I want to talk to each of you alone. Jim, see there is absolutely no talking. I've got an alarm out for the others."

No mention of Carol. Hadn't she been found yet? I had just time for the quick wonder.

"Miss Gay, come out in the kitchen with me, please." He stood aside for me to pass him, closed the door behind me.

"Now. You sit there." He pointed me into a kitchen chair but he himself remained standing, leaning with one fist on the table. "How did you come to see that car go by?"

There was all that business of the matches. No use going into that.

"I fooled around in my room for an hour or so—I wasn't sleepy. Then I went to the window to open it. I heard the car moving down below. It must just have begun moving."

"Didn't you see anyone running away?"

"No. I looked, too. I nearly fell out the window."

"But someone must have been there. To release the brakes, if nothing else."

"Whoever it was must have gotten away before I looked. Perhaps heard me opening the window."

He took in air. "Was Mr. Bill Heaton's car parked there beside the house when you left here for Grand Marais this evening?"

I thought back. Jean and I leaving, Phillips by the fire. Jean and I walked to the resort to get his car.

"I didn't go around to that side of the house."

"Do you remember the car standing there any other time today?"

I couldn't remember anything connected with Bill's car.

"I don't even—The last I remember is that Jacqueline and I drove Bill's car into Grand Marais with Bill the night he was shot. But we came back out in your car. I entirely forgot—"

He groaned. "I had one of my men bring the car out and put it in the barn after we'd gone over it. Don't you remember anything of seeing it after that?"

"I remember that when Jean and I came back to the Fingers tonight, I noticed a dim shape beside the house." I hadn't looked to see if it was a car I recognized; I just remembered seeing a solid shadow I thought was a car.

He threw out his hands in a gesture of exasperation. "I cannot blame you. When I went out to look for Phillips Heaton, I noticed the car was there, glanced at it, saw Phillips Heaton wasn't in the seat, and then went by."

I sat up straight. "That's right! You said both cars were here! You must have known that was Bill's car!"

He explained wearily, "I do not know the habits of the family. I merely thought perhaps Mrs. Bill Heaton had run it out so it would be handy if she should be called to the hospital in the night."

I caught at it. "That may still be true. Someone might have seen it there—"

"I will ask Mrs. Heaton when I question her. Now to something else. I was waiting on the porch when you and Mr. Nobbelin got here tonight. We looked for Phillips Heaton—"

"Phillips!" I broke in. "He still away? Wherever can he—?"

"Yes. He is not here yet. After we had been to his room you stopped, coming back, at Mrs. Heaton's door—"

"I could hear she was asleep."

"Through the door?"

"I could hear her breathing."

There was an intentness in his eyes. "This sharpness of your ears—does it ever prove to be wrong?"

I shook my head in exasperation. "What are you trying to imply? That I didn't hear my cousin in that room? Why should—?" Then, like darkness closing in, I saw why he was so intent.

He hadn't, and I hadn't, actually looked in Jacqueline's room.

He said, "Before you came running down, I was on the porch awhile and once I walked out to my car. It would be just possible for a person from upstairs to have gotten out the side way without my noticing, but that person would have to be quick. I do not think you could have done it, because you *came* from upstairs when you ran out. Mrs. Sallishaw might just possibly have done it—she could have gotten back upstairs while you and I were in the lake. Mrs. Heaton, however—*she* could have been outdoors all the time, until just before we looked in her room!" He spread his hands helplessly.

I said frantically, "But you saw how fast asleep she was when we opened her door. She couldn't have gotten that fast asleep in a few minutes! And—and—" Wildly I cast about for any other aid. "Octavia—we didn't look in her room, either! She could have been out of her room all the time, too."

"I know where Octavia was when Fred was shot."

When I went back to the living room, I was in a sort of bleak despair. Why did Jacqueline always have to be so vulnerable? I started toward the stairs. From that time on, I grimly thought, I wasn't letting her out of my sight.

But the deputy called me back. "You stay here with the others."

So I had to take my place in the group. At least she should be safe now, with all these people below. In their separate chairs, Cecile, Lottie, and the Corvos were huddled in coats, as if they, too, had been dunked; all of them drew perceptibly away from me, Ed Corvo particularly looking at me with bright, angry eyes. Jean moved over on the davenport to make room for me beside him.

After me, Aakonen talked to Myra, but she was back in five minutes; the others followed her in short order. Mark was brought in by a deputy. His thoughtful face, still discolored by bruises, was thinned and haggard, and his long body drooped.

He asked, "Have you found Carol?" in a loud, inflectionless tone, as if he were deaf, before the guard had time to give his warning about silence. Mutely, I shook my head at him, and he sank into a chair, his hands loose between his knees, his head bowed.

Aakonen took him next but kept him no longer than the others. While Mark was in the kitchen, Bradley Auden walked in with Owens.

As Mark had, Bradley burst out, "Is Carol found? What's happened now?"

Aakonen took him after Mark. When he came back into the living room Aakonen was behind him. There was a curious air of quickening tensity over the room.

"Miss Gay, I'll have to wake Mrs. Heaton now."

I leaped to my feet as Aakonen said it; somehow I must prove Jacqueline had been asleep. Myra, too, was on her feet. "Don't startle her. It's terrible to be waked with a start as I was when you came into my room."

"What is it?' Jacqueline asked from deep in slumber when I shook her. Then she was in one instant wide awake, sitting in the bed, snatching for her robe. "Bill! They're calling for me!" She pulled the blue robe around her, tossing back her hair. "I won't be a second. I've got my clothes all—"

"No, wait." I pushed her back as she started rising. "It isn't Bill. Something else has happened. Another trick."

"Bill's all right?" She got only that much.

"Yes, Mrs. Heaton. At least, we have not heard from the hospital." Aakonen came forward to stand awkwardly by the bed. "Mrs. Heaton, you were at the hospital with Mr. Heaton—and me—all day long today. You will remember that."

"Oh yes, of course." She looked at him, waiting now.

"Then you came home with Mrs. Sallishaw around ten o'clock tonight. When you got home, did you run your husband's car to the east side of the house?"

"Bill's car? We were in Myra's car. She left it in front of the house so that if I had to go I could take that."

"When did you last see your husband's car?"

"When was it, Ann? Jean's been driving us—"

"Then you say you haven't touched your husband's car this evening."

"No. Of course I haven't."

Aakonen turned to look at me, then back at Jacqueline. "Will you tell me everything you did do after leaving the hospital tonight?"

"We came straight out here, Myra and Octavia and I. We left Myra's car in the drive and walked into the living room. Phillips was there."

She waited as if to be told she was saying the right things.

"Go on."

"Octavia went up to her room right away, and Myra made a pot of hot chocolate. We all had a cup. Phillips said—" She broke off to address me directly. "Ann, you know you have a perfect right to be in this room—I wouldn't think of minding."

"I was just—" I began. Aakonen was again cocking an eye at me. No use denying. I explained about my interest in the fire.

"Of course." Warm, eager color flushed up in Jacqueline's cheeks. "Did you—?"

I had to shake the head of defeat.

"But you will—we will. When Bill's safe I'll—"

Aakonen interrupted. "You and Mrs. Sallishaw and Phillips Heaton were drinking chocolate."

She went back to that. "I was cross with Phillips Heaton—he was nasty about Ann. I came up to bed, and Myra did, too. She told me not to mind about Phillips. I was desperately tired, and she gave me two sleeping tablets. I took them before I undressed so I'd get sleepy quickly. And I did. I went to sleep as soon as I was in bed."

"And after that?"

"Nothing until you woke me just now. Why—?" Her mind seemed to grasp then what I'd told her. "Ann, did you say another trick? What is it? It isn't serious, is it? No one else is—?" As if something pulled her up, she was rising to her knees in the bed, clutching the blanket to her breast.

"Oh no," I explained quickly. Aakonen let me explain.

"Bill's car," was her comment when I was done. "Bill liked it so much. But of course it's not important. He can get another car.

It's not as if—" But then she saw the significance. "Of course! This, too, was done by the murderer."

She sank back, looking from me to Aakonen. "It's like the other tricks. If you didn't see me here sleeping you couldn't know. It wasn't me." Her head went forward to her hunched knees in the blanket.

"No more you than anyone else," I told her firmly.

The dark head lifted, accepting. "I'll get up."

Without a word, Aakonen went downstairs, to return in a moment with Myra. The two of them went into Octavia's room but were there a bare five minutes. When Jacqueline and I got downstairs he was just finishing telling the group there what had happened. Two men stood at the door, one of them heavy and weather-roughened, the other slight and quick.

"Here I am, Sheriff," the small man said when Aakonen turned. "Diver here. Got my boat out front. Hell of a time for it."

Jean was on his feet, bewildered. "Good heavens, Aakonen, a diver can't move that car! You'll need a scow and a derrick. Even for Fred's motorcycle we—"

Aakonen ignored him, moving toward the newcomers with his ponderous tread. The three went out together.

"*A diver*," Jean repeated, incredulous. Then he whirled on me, and behind the black eyes, thought was racing. "Ann, you were along. What did Aakonen do in that car before it got into the lake?"

"We both tried to stop it." Nothing made sense. "Aakonen caught at it, but it wouldn't stop. I tried to drag my feet. Aakonen tried to reach the emergency brake, but then car was in the water, and we had to jump."

"He tried to reach for the brake . . . He's got a diver out . . . It's in the middle of the night . . ." The black eyes fled from face to face as if he were enumerating, as if he were storing up each person present. He stood stock-still, but someone else was moving. Toward him.

Bradley Auden. Bent, like a tight bow.

He whispered, "Aakonen's got a diver out. A diver could only . . . Carol."

Like a slow-motion picture, his body swayed from his feet in a circle, and he sank on the floor. He was almost like the puddle of Aakonen's clothes that still lay by the fireplace.

But it wasn't the body of Carol Auden that the diver brought up.

18

IT WAS AFTER FOUR in the morning when Aakonen finally came in to tell us.

The time before he came was pulseless, endless. Bradley Auden, after we revived him, was put in a chair beside Mark; as he sat there he looked like the ash of a man, like a burned cigarette that still loosely holds its shape before a touch scatters it to dust. Something else was happening in Mark: Mark was drawing in close to some inner steel framework, hardening, toughening, as if he were being beaten to strength.

The rest of us sat waiting in petrification, as if we were statues doomed to sit in timeless isolation.

That eternity ended on an opening door, on Aakonen striding in. He'd been wet again—his shoes, his arms. The khaki hunting coat was water-splashed. Inside the door he halted, to stand brooding over us as he had that day after Fred was killed.

Then he said quietly, "I will tell the rest of you what almost certainly everyone here already knows. From Mr. Bill Heaton's

car we have recovered a body—a body that was on the floor between the seat and the controls. That was why I could not reach
the brake."

Slowly, deliberately he ended.

"It was the body of Phillips Heaton."

FROM MARK CAME ONE sharp, wordless cry, as if he were a sleep-
walker blinking at light. Life seemed to creep to Bradley Auden's
body, too, flesh growing back on his bones, blood running. Over
the whole room there was a breath of movement . . .

Phillips Heaton. Gone, like Fred. Not a villain, but a victim.
No need to wonder now if his alibi might be a smooth trick like
the other tricks; no need to delve into his jealousies and resentments; no need for fright to rise when he stood in a door . . .

Phillips, Myra's brother.

She'd sat beside and a little behind me. When I turned to
look, I saw her mercifully gone, without a sound or a sign.

Her head was fallen to the side of the chair, her whole body
crumpled.

EVEN AFTER WE ROUSED her from the faint, she just kept bleakly
staring, and no strength came back to her body. At Aakonen's
command Jean carried her upstairs, and Jacqueline and I put her
to bed. We wanted to stay, but Aakonen brought up a deputy to
stay by the bed and ordered us down.

"I'm—all right," Myra whispered, but she looked like little
more than a drift of last year's leaves in that bed, and once when
Jacqueline touched her she closed her eyes, wincing.

Downstairs, Aakonen spoke. "I want each one of you to repeat to me when you last saw Phillips Heaton alive and exactly

what you have done since then. The rest of you listen for any small word you know is not true."

He was so tired, he seemed to sag together as he stood, to be shorter, wider, looser because of the depressing weight of weariness. Over the rest of us there was just one thought: *One more of us gone.*

By Fred's murder we'd been horrified, and after Bill was shot we'd been stricken into terror, but now we seemed in a state beyond fear or terror, as if the bombs had fallen time after time and we'd been cowering and afraid, but now we could only wait stoically for what came . . . for the next bomb to fall.

Into that anaesthetized terror Aakonen spoke again. "When Fred Heaton was killed, I named fourteen people who might have fired that shot. We now know that neither Bill Heaton nor Phillips Heaton held that gun. We know that Ed Corvo did not shoot Bill Heaton. Our circle grows smaller."

With slow deliberation he looked from face to face, and I looked with him. Jacqueline. Cecile. Ella Corvo. Lottie. Bradley. Mark. Jean. Me. Except for us there were only Myra, broken, and poor shrinking Octavia, and Carol Auden, lost somewhere. Bradley and Jean looked fixedly at Aakonen, but the others stared at Jacqueline . . .

"You will begin, please, Miss Gay."

Sound was odd in the room; it was like talking in a radio station's soundproof cubicle with the faces in which fear was deadened pressed against the glass, looking in, but with the microphones turned off so they couldn't hear a word. Into that thick silence I had to repeat what I had done that evening since Jean and I had left Phillips sitting with his amused and satisfied smile beside the fireplace.

When I was done, Aakonen waited as if someone might comment. No one did; the eyes still flickered toward Jacqueline.

Aakonen himself repeated first what he had learned from Octavia, then what Myra had told him. Octavia had gone up to her room the moment she and Myra and Jacqueline had returned from the hospital. She had, she said, stayed there.

"Octavia's door was locked on the inside when I got out of the lake. That's no proof, but—I must remember she has a good alibi for the night Fred was killed."

Clearly he had no belief Octavia had killed Phillips.

"As to Mrs. Sallishaw, she and Jacqueline Heaton went upstairs together, leaving Phillips by the fire. Mrs. Sallishaw says she took one sleeping tablet and was just dropping off when Miss Gay and Mr. Nobbelin and I entered the house."

He paused as if to judge. "I know Mrs. Sallishaw was upstairs when I got here and I know she was upstairs later. She would have had to be very quick to get down to release the brakes on that car. I do not believe she could have done it. Now you, Mrs. Heaton."

Jacqueline repeated her story. Again no comments, but the eyes were terrible to bear.

"You, Mr. Nobbelin."

Jean said that when he left he had gone straight to the resort. There'd been a light in the inn. When he'd found Mark gone from the cabin, he'd walked up to the main building. Ed Corvo was up, roused by the phone call asking if Carol was there. He'd stayed with Ed perhaps five minutes, then gone back to his cabin and to bed. Ed had wakened him to tell him to dress and wait at the inn.

Again the wait, again no comment.

"Mr. Auden, please."

Phillips had answered when Bradley called the Fingers to ask if Carol was there. Phillips had said he was alone; he hadn't seen him since. Bradley had been in town looking for Carol until a deputy's car had stopped him to tell him Aakonen wanted to see him and that Carol had been caught rifling Bill's office but had escaped. The same deputy had driven him to the Fingers. He'd borrowed Jean's car and left again. On the highway, he'd been hailed by Owens in another car. Owens had left the deputies in the other car to go with Bradley and had been with him since.

"That's right." Owens was uneasy. "I saw the car turning out of the drive here and hailed it. He didn't come back here to release the brakes on any car."

Of us all, Bradley was the only one who had a solid alibi for this murder.

"You, Mr. Ellif."

Mark spoke abstractly, almost dully. "When Jean and Ann left this afternoon Carol and I went and sat on the rocks, talking. About six, Carol left in her car. She said she was going home for dinner but she'd be back. Bradley called up after seven and said Carol hadn't come home. I was worried, but she'd told me to wait there, so I did. After a while Ed Corvo came around, looking for Carol. After that I went out on the highway, watching the cars go by, thinking she had to come pretty soon."

The deputy had found him there. He admitted he and Carol had quarreled a little. He didn't know why she'd go to hunt anything in Bill's office.

Aakonen prompted, "This quarrel."

A hesitation, then a careful statement. "It was about whether we should get married."

Bradley Auden stiffened. "She can't get married. She's just a kid."

Mark answered soberly, "That's what I think."

A wheel in my head began turning. It was Carol, then, who

wanted the marriage. She was tempestuous and sudden, but I wouldn't expect her to try to provoke a reluctant Mark into marrying her.

Again Aakonen waited; nothing was forthcoming.

"Miss Granat, please."

Cecile lifted her sullen withdrawn face to speak, without moving her body, held stiffly in the baby blue coat. "Phillips Heaton was at the resort talking to me this afternoon. He was going on and on, purring to himself, about why everybody did this, why they did that, how smart he was. He said he'd just made some lucky investments."

"You're sure he said nothing of what these investments were?"

"No, he just said I'd be surprised how much money he was going to have."

"He told Miss Gay shortly after that that he knew the murderer. Didn't he make any such statement to you?"

"No. Don't you think I'd have jumped at it if he had? Mostly he said how stupid everyone was. He said Jean was stupid, Ann was stupid, his sister Myra was stupid, Jacqueline was stupid, and especially Bill was stupid, who was supposed to be so smart. Everyone was stupid except him."

Aakonen had her try to give the conversation in Phillips's own words, but apparently she'd already given the gist of it. After he'd gone, she'd spent the evening tightly locked into her cabin, as she spent her evenings nowadays, reading magazines and listening to her radio. Ed Corvo had routed her, too, out of bed.

When would Aakonen speak about those checks? I sat waiting for it, but he turned away from her without a word on them.

"Ed Corvo, please." I sat up, opening my mouth to ask about those checks myself, but when I looked at Aakonen the tired, bulging eyes were fixed on me and he was shaking his big head significantly. He didn't want those three checks asked about— not there. And back of his eyes I saw the reason—he thought he already knew why Bill had given Cecile that money.

Unaccountably and perversely, I wanted to disagree with him. I saw Bill as he'd been until Fred was shot—tall and arrogant and—all right—wickedly masculine. But I couldn't believe that on his honeymoon he'd been paying Cecile twenty-five dollars a week because she was his mistress.

Then suddenly, I was certain. If Bill did have a mistress, he wouldn't pay her. He might give her things, lavishly, in chunks. But that small, regular payment wasn't in character.

I turned to meet Jean's eyes. What was he thinking? Something—it was right there under the surface of his eyes.

Lottie, Ed, and Ella contributed nothing; they'd been at the resort all evening apparently. When they were done, Aakonen's tired eyes again made the rounds, but he knew then he wasn't going to get anything.

"You can talk now," he said wearily. "I'm going to look around the house." He plodded toward the stairs.

Jean spoke quickly. "I suppose Phillips was shot."

Aakonen paused, halfway up the stairs. "In the back," he said.

Jean said slowly when he'd gone on, "Fred. Bill. Phillips. Someone seems to have it in for Heatons."

I could feel my eyes extending, seeing those people on the lawn, that significant afternoon of the Fourth. There'd been four born to the Heaton name; of those four only Myra now was left. Bill was still alive, but that wasn't by the will of the person who dealt death. But no again—there was still also Octavia, so hard to remember as a Heaton or anything else.

BEFORE I COULD THINK beyond that, Aakonen was calling down the stairs.

"Miss Gay! Will you come here?" It sounded angry and exasperated. As my foot touched the first step I remembered my resolve about not letting Jacqueline out of my sight. She came quickly at my beckoning glance, glad to get away from what that room had for her. As we went up Ella whispered significantly to her sister.

Aakonen stood in the middle of my room, glaring at an ashtray on the dresser.

"I thought I remembered I didn't find any cigarettes in your room before. Thought you were having a smoke?"

He pointed at what the tray held—matches, some of them broken. No cigarette ashes.

I explained my silly lie. "What I really wanted to do with those matches was put them between spring and mattress, then bounce on them to see if they'd ignite."

"Why didn't you say so in the first place?"

"It was so involved, and a cigarette was so simple."

"It isn't simple now. Don't you see, Miss Gay? You lied to me before—you said you had not been in Mrs. Heaton's room the night Fred Heaton was shot, yet I am certain that for some reason you were there. How can I believe anything you say?"

Jacqueline said quickly, "It's ridiculous to suspect Ann. You know she couldn't have released the brakes of that car tonight."

He shrugged. "I don't think she lies to protect herself. I think she lies to protect you. You can go now."

Yes, that was what he would think. If only I had proof that Jacqueline had been upstairs between ten o'clock and the time we waked her . . .

I asked, "Is there anything to suggest Phillips was killed up here?"

He answered shortly, "Nothing that I see."

"There must be something by which we could—"

When I didn't finish he turned impatiently to wait. "What?"

It was out of my own head I took the idea which was to produce one of the most damning of all the evidences against Jacqueline.

I said, "We've got to think. About the murderer. He was out there on the lawn tonight. Perhaps he killed Phillips somewhere else and dragged him to the car—"

I had what I thought my inspiration then. It lifted me to such excitement I shook Aakonen's arm.

"That's it! You looked at our shoes after Fred was shot. Dew had wet the bottom of that cape. Whoever killed Phillips tonight had to walk across grass. If you could find wet shoes—No, some of them have a right to wet shoes. But—Jacqueline, you got out of Myra's car on the gravel, didn't you?"

"Yes, I did."

I tugged at Aakonen. "Don't you see? If all my cousin's shoes are dry—she can't have gone out."

He came willingly after looking at the pumps which Jacqueline had on and which were dry. At the blue cretonne shoe bag which held all her shoes in individual pockets—it hung from her closet door—he took out a pair of white sandals. They were dry.

He took out a pair of black snakeskin oxfords. His back seemed to congeal. Wordlessly he turned, holding out the shoes. The soles were damp, and between sole and upper of one was a still-green blade of grass.

I stood waiting for something to happen, knowing to the bottom of my soul what it would be.

But it wasn't Aakonen who spoke next—it was Jacqueline— colder and harder than I'd ever known her.

"This is plenty!" She snatched the shoes from him. "Someone else wore those shoes—"

"The other women in this house are Miss Gay and Mrs. Sallishaw and Octavia Heaton. Are you—?"

"No. Of course not. I—" She held herself an instant quiet. "No, that's not the answer. Look—it isn't even necessary for these shoes to have been worn."

Aakonen had recaptured the shoes, but she went on. "Someone could have come in here anytime today, wet those shoes in the washbowl in the bathroom, and stuck in that blade of grass. Do you think if I'd known those shoes were wet I'd have let you come in here looking without one effort to stop you? Do you think if I *had* shot Fred and Bill—and now Phillips—that I'd point to myself as I'm pointed out now?" It had become an impassioned plea.

"Mistakes are what catch murderers."

"Can you call all the things that point to me mistakes?"

She was actually advancing on him, he retreating. I came out of stupefaction to join the attack.

"Look at Bill. It's my cousin's being there that's helped pull him through. Has she done one thing to injure him?"

"No, and she isn't going to." It was grim. He held out a large hand—the one that didn't hold the shoes. "Wait. I will have to think. Now. Here is the position. When you and Mrs. Sallishaw came upstairs sometime after ten, Mrs. Heaton, then Phillips was alive."

She nodded firmly. "Yes. We left him by the fire downstairs."

"Are these oxfords the shoes you wore today?"

"No. I wore the pumps I have on now."

"So the oxfords were here all day . . . Was there anything else in the room disturbed when you came back?"

"The bed."

I said quickly, "That was me, trying to figure out how that fire started."

"Nothing else disturbed?"

"Not that I saw," from Jacqueline.

He waved the oxfords at her, his face the shape of a groan. Then he turned away.

"You two go to bed."

He wasn't arresting Jacqueline then and there, but there was no triumph in our victory. His back said as clearly as words could, *Very little more grace is all I can give you.*

HE MUST HAVE DISPERSED the others, too; we heard people leaving. The deputy was gone from Myra's room. We went in to do what we could to make her comfortable. She'd drifted into a half sleep. It seemed criminal to leave her unattended. I went to the head of the stairs to call down, and Aakonen answered that he'd leave a man in the house all night; the man would have orders to look in on Mrs. Sallishaw occasionally.

Jacqueline and I went to bed in my room, door and window locked. In spite of her roused anger Jacqueline was asleep almost as soon as her head touched the pillow. It took me longer. After this last murder, after the finding of those wet shoes, it would be hard to keep Aakonen from acting, perhaps hard to keep some of the others from breaking into open accusation.

Yet after a while, I did sleep, not waking until late morning. Jacqueline was lying wide-eyed then, staring at the pattern of the ceiling cracks, her arms under her head.

She said, "All these days I've been trying to see who'd want to kill Fred and Bill and I can't, because the only motive I know applies to me. But I can see why Phillips was killed."

I sat up in bed, thoroughly shaken awake. "Why?"

"Phillips told you he'd guessed who the murderer was. And Cecile said he told her he was making some lucky investments."

"Of course. He was telling me the truth—he had guessed the murderer. He tried blackmail—and a bullet was his answer."

JEAN, BRADLEY, AND MARK were all in the living room with the guard when we got downstairs; they'd been there all night. Perhaps they'd dozed a little; it couldn't have been much. Their eyes were fatigue-puffed, clothes rumpled, faces uncouth, as men's faces always are when they've sprouted a stubble of beard.

Jean rubbed a conscious hand over his chin when he saw us. The other two, sunken in their chairs, just looked away.

Jacqueline and I went to the kitchen; breakfast was a necessity. But we were hardly there before the front door slammed, heavy footsteps sounded, and both Bradley Auden and Mark gave a hoarse shout, so that we ran to see.

Carol Auden stood inside the door between two men.

19

CAROL'S JAUNTY RUST-STRIPED DRESS was disheveled, her red hair a mop, her pointed face paper-pale, but her eyes were feverishly defiant.

"You can beat me and torture me and kill me," she announced melodramatically. "I won't talk."

Aakonen was there within the half hour, towering over her as she sat, small and crumpled, in one of the wicker armchairs, looking like a defenseless, tired child. Bradley and Mark had tried to question her before Aakonen got there, but now they jerked forward with restraining movements of their bodies, as if they wanted to grab her from the inquisition.

She admitted readily enough that she'd taken Jean's wallet. She admitted hiding the car up a wood road after she fled from the office. What she wouldn't admit was what she'd wanted in that office.

"You'll have to tell us sometime." Aakonen tried patience.

"Will I?" Hard going, but it tried to be pert.

"Why did you open that safe?"

"Call it curiosity."

"Were you looking for your father's note?"

She acted as if she hadn't thought of that. Her lips parted, and her hazel eyes widened. Then she burst into a storm of weeping as violent as she had been subdued.

"Don't ask me!" she wailed. "It isn't me! I had to do what I did. What I was doing was *all right*!"

"Miss Auden!" From Aakonen a shout with enough authority behind it so the crying stopped in mid-wail, breaking to a gulp. "Why were you afraid of being caught if what you were doing was all right?"

"Because then I—couldn't do what I've just simply got to do."

"You're not doing anything"—discipline seemed waking in Bradley Auden—"except go home and get to bed. You—"

Aakonen turned to the man who'd brought her in. "Where did you find her?"

"She was right there in one of them cabins at the resort. Asleep across one of the beds, with her clothes on. When I looked in and seen she was there I just about—"

"At the resort," Mark said dazedly. "She told me to wait for her. She came there anyway."

Aakonen asked her, "How did you get there?"

"Walked. I left the car and watched my chance to get across the highway when there weren't any cars. I knew Jean and Ann would tell." Her eyes roved over me, but no animosity showed.

A pause during which Aakonen just looked down at her. Then, "Did you come here to the Fingers last night—walking or any other way?"

"No. Why would I?"

"Did you see Phillips Heaton last night?"

"Him? I wouldn't care if I never saw him."

"Did you drive Bill Heaton's car out of the barn last night?"

She glanced then at her father. "What's he asking me that for?"

"Answer me. Did you have a gun in your hands last night?"

Fright rising at the increasing tensity of the questions. "No! I didn't—I didn't have any gun!"

Jean interposed, "She didn't have any gun when she ran from the office, Aakonen. Don't—"

"Perhaps you will be interested to know"—Aakonen's sharp gaze kept on Carol as if Jean hadn't spoken—"that last night there was another murder at the Fingers."

The girl's face froze. She whispered, "Another—murder?"

"Phillips Heaton is dead."

"Phillips—Heaton," she repeated weakly. And then she turned to Mark. "You were—"

She caught it there. Visibly her head circled on her neck; her father caught her as she went down.

THERE WAS NO FAKING in that faint; it was fifteen minutes before we brought her to.

When she did come out of it, she closed her eyes tight almost as soon as she'd opened them, and tears slid from between the lids. She didn't cry stormily now; she cried helplessly, silently, as if she had neither strength nor hope. When Aakonen after a while tried questioning her again, she made no sign even of hearing him.

Seeing her made me remember Myra; I'd completely forgotten until then that Myra, too, was fallen by the wayside. When I ran up to her room I found her asleep, but her breath and her pulse seemed so slight I went back down to say I thought we'd better call Dr. Rush.

Aakonen, with his eyes on the still-sobbing Carol, nodded his head.

Dr. Rush's verdict was the same for both. "Exhaustion and collapse. I'll leave some capsules. Keep them in bed."

"Carol—it won't be serious, will it?" That was Bradley.

"Nothing that rest and a relieved mind won't cure."

Jacqueline had waited with her own question until Dr. Rush had seen Carol and Myra. "Bill—is he doing all right?"

"Nicely."

"Then can I—?"

"No need for it today." He was brusque, looking around at those of us in the living room. "You people require a few too many of my services. I was up pretty early with Phillips Heaton."

Aakonen quickened. "That. What did you find?"

"Shot in the back. From not farther than four feet, I'd say. Bullet lodged against a rib. Got it for you."

Aakonen walked out with the doctor, to stand leaning over the physician's car door a moment, then, without a glance at the house, he got into his own car and departed.

"Thank God," Bradley said, "he isn't—he didn't arrest Carol. I don't know what I could have done for Marjorie if that had happened."

Thank God, *I* thought, that he hadn't arrested Jacqueline.

We put Carol to bed in my room, giving her the sedative Dr. Rush had left. Bradley called Auden, telling the maid there that Carol had been found and was resting, that Mrs. Auden was still to know nothing of what was going on. Then he came upstairs to sit beside Carol. He stayed there all the rest of the morning, watching her as the fitful sobbing slowed and stopped and she slept.

To Myra, too, Jacqueline and I gave the capsules Dr. Rush had left for her. When we waked her she just lay quiet, vague, and strengthless.

"Phillips," she said. "If we could have found him before the car went into the lake, he might have lived."

She dozed again after a while. When we left her Jacqueline was grim.

"We've got to look out for her—guns aren't the only way of killing people."

Sometime during the morning, Octavia had unlocked her door, because when we brought up a tray for her the door handle turned.

We didn't have actual evidence Octavia had been in this room when Bill or Phillips was shot, I thought, even if we did have it for when Fred was shot. But as I looked at the slight ridge made by her small body under the blankets, the body that seemed to cower even there, it seemed impossible this could be the source of the evil against which we contended. Only the smooth brown back of Octavia's head showed; she lay on her face with both arms around her head, unmoving, as we entered.

Jacqueline dredged up some difficult calm cheerfulness.

"Myra's not feeling well this morning, so Ann and I brought your breakfast, Octavia."

Pity for anyone so poorly equipped to meet any kind of life was in her eyes as she went on, "Wouldn't you like to dress when you've had your breakfast? I'll be driving in to see Bill, I hope. Maybe you'd want to come along."

A quick, almost convulsive negative movement of the head encircled by arms.

"Myra's in her room, and there'll always be someone else in the house, too," Jacqueline produced for a last reassurance, and we left her; there didn't seem much else we could do.

In the hall outside, Jacqueline sighed. "Poor Octavia. If Myra breaks down under this—I don't just dread it for Myra's sake. What'll become of Octavia?"

We went downstairs to Jean and the remote, reserved Mark. For several moments, no one said a word.

I tried to see where we were now that Phillips was dead. Two gone now. One fighting for his life in the hospital. Two more, Myra and Carol, pushed beyond the breaking point. Octavia and Bradley and Cecile and the four of us—we were what seemed to be left.

Would one of us, too, soon lie dead, with no sign to say who had come and gone? And in this small circle, *whose were the hands that carried so much blood?*

Again the feeling of helplessness and futility. The juggernaut of death seemed to roll unimpeded; nothing seemed to halt or hinder it. The telephone broke that silence.

Jacqueline answered, turning from it breathless and shaken. "Bill's conscious."

WHAT I SAID ALL the way in was, "Suppose—just suppose this is the break we've got to have? Suppose this should be the end? If Bill would only know who shot him . . ."

But even as I said it, it seemed an impossible consummation; I couldn't believe there could be an end.

Just as we reached the hospital Aakonen's car, too, skidded to a stop before the door.

"They called you?" he asked as if in disapproval. He went ahead of us but he held the door open behind him for Jacqueline to catch.

Dr. Rush was waiting at the desk. "Bill became conscious just after I got back. We haven't tried to question him. He recognized me."

"He can talk?" Aakonen hadn't even paused; he was plowing steadily on toward Bill's room, Jacqueline and I in his wake.

"He spoke my name."

The guard held the door open. Inside the room Miss Bolles looked up from the bedside.

"He's still conscious."

Jacqueline started forward, but Aakonen held her forcibly back.

"No. Stay there."

Dr. Rush backed us into the corner toward which Aakonen pointed.

Bill's face was alive again, still and graven, his head moving only a quarter of an inch when Aakonen spoke. But his eyes were open.

"Mr. Bill Heaton," Aakonen said, and emotion threaded it, gratitude.

"Aakonen." Bill's voice was an echo of itself, but it was a living echo, cognizant, inflected. A greeting as to someone he hadn't seen for a long time.

Aakonen said, "Don't try to make long answers. Someone shot you."

"Like Fred," the distant sorrowful echo came. Grief was what he'd waked to.

"Yes. You remember, then." The big face over the bed had softened but it was hardening. In a held pause, Aakonen half straightened the bulky shoulders in the hunting jacket.

He's going to ask now, I thought; *now's the minute.* I hadn't a glance to spare even for Jacqueline.

It came. "Mr. Heaton, just answer yes or no. Did you recognize who shot you?"

Another pause; quiet in the room so intense you'd think the movement of a finger would be heard.

A faint stir, as if the head on the pillow started to gesture the answer. But instead the weak voice came.

"No."

Beside me Jacqueline gave an uncontrollable gasp, and Aakonen stepped back as from a blow. Through my own body I felt what hadn't even been a hope receding like lost strength.

Any other answer would have been too good to be true. What had been happening couldn't end simply with a word. Yet we'd been keeping that chance in the back of our minds—the chance that Bill might know. Now there wasn't even that. As I stood there it seemed to me we had nothing as the result of all our efforts. Against what sort of force were we pitted? A force that could kill and kill again and leave us nothing, so that after days of work and hunting we would not have the slightest clue—only that fateful thinning of our ranks.

I had a sensation of being back in the grasp of the lake, of feeling we were all in its grasp—that the lake was tossing us, beating us against the sharp rocks of happening, that we were all helpless; taking what this outside moving force had decided upon for our lives and our deaths.

AAKONEN ASKED BILL A few more questions; they served only to establish that Bill knew what he said.

"Where were you when you were shot?"

"The Fingers."

"Was it long after you went out?"

"A while."

"Didn't you hear this person coming? You must have seen him."

"Black," Bill said. "All over. Black over his head."

The memory carried excitement; his head and shoulders moved as if he were going to try to get up, and Dr. Rush, who had moved to the opposite side of the bed to hold his wrist, held up a restraining hand.

Aakonen said quickly, "I understand, Mr. Heaton. You were standing in front of the five rocks. You looked up and saw someone standing quite close, so close the hand with the gun was within a few feet of you. The night was unusually dark, but you could see that the figure was dressed in black and had something black drawn over its face. You perhaps stepped forward—"

"Yes," Bill said.

"The person fired at once."

"Yes." Bill had sunk back, the stimulus of excitement gone. But before Aakonen could go on, he'd spoken again. "My wife."

"I'm here." She was away from me and at the bedside in one movement. The bleak desperation that held me didn't touch her; she was smiling, then shutting her eyes on spurting tears. "Darling, you mustn't talk. You—"

"Not dead yet," Bill said. It had satisfaction in it, and his mouth relaxed into something that might after a while become a grin.

He slept soon after that, and Dr. Rush asked us to go.

"You understand," he told us in the hall. "Mr. Heaton has made a perceptible improvement, but that does not mean he should be subjected to fatigue."

The door opened behind him to emit Miss Bolles's disembodied head.

"He woke right up," she said. "He—"

From the room the weak voice demanded, "Jacqui."

Dr. Rush threw up his hands. "I'm afraid, Aakonen, that Mrs. Heaton will have to be allowed in the room. I've known him since he was in diapers; I won't deny his request for his wife."

So Jacqueline, spouting radiance, went back to stay with Bill, which meant that Aakonen stayed, too—and did no other investigating.

Nothing done and nothing being done to clear up the murders. Alone in the hall, I stood so sunk, I could scarcely move. My feet did somehow take me to the waiting room cubbyhole, and while there I saw through the front window the orderly standing on the walk, smoking a cigarette. A man came by, stopped to talk, a conversation that lasted only a second and ended by the orderly having his hand violently wrung and the passerby running toward downtown Grand Marais.

The news that Bill was conscious was out.

And at that reminder that no matter how skillful the murderer had been, he'd had one failure, my teeth came together with a snap.

Over me, as over the others, death was poised. But until it got me, I was fighting.

A NEW INVASION WAS on at the Fingers; reporters and cameramen swarmed the place. The news of Phillips's death, too, was out. As I hastily swung Myra's car to land directly in front of the door, a scow with a crane on it was anchored some distance out in the lake; men on the scow were yelling orders at each other; along the shore more men yelled and milled about, and the cameras ground.

The moment I had my foot out of the car, two snappy males popped up like Jason's dragon-tooth warriors in front of me.

"Miss Gay, you swam out after the car, didn't you?"

"No, thanks," I said. "I swam in from it. Seems to have done me good." I felt hard and careless under my new impetus to use what short time I had.

"You know the body was in it last night?"

"Oh, certainly. We have bodies in almost everything these days. One in the bathtub this morning."

"Say, is it nice to kid poor hardworking guys like us?"

"Look," the other said. "All we want is a little local color. We got the facts. This Phillips Heaton, now. Millionaire sportsman. Grandson of old Rufus Heaton—"

"Millionaire sportsman," I repeated, and for a second I wished Phillips Heaton could hear it; he'd think that was awfully funny. But there was a third man with a wink in one eye and a candid camera in the other, and I could see Aunt Harriet staring at a front page, with my picture labelled, MILLIONAIRE SPORTS-MAN'S GIRLFRIEND GRIEVES.

"Oh no," I said. "You see, Phillips Heaton didn't have a dime. And he didn't like it. He'd gotten mixed up in something. We don't know just what. But it seems there's been information smuggled back and forth across the border. Something to do with certain prisoners interned in Canada . . ."

I was making it up as I went along—pure fiction. But that, in case you want to know, was the genesis of the story which was to ripple wider and wider in the newspapers; which had seven government agents snooping the woods, ending finally, in the arrest of a guide named Alex (short for Hermann) Duvernois (short for Schneider) and, through him, eleven men on the Canadian side of the border and four on the American side; and which was to send one man who had been strutting the national capital back to an unnamed foreign country—where he was not at all anxious to go—very quickly indeed.

Yet that ridiculous fiction has nothing to do with Jacqueline's story; I ended my part in it on the note of an opening door and a vicious jerk that pulled me from what was by then a knot of reporters, like a fish flipped from water.

"You idiot!" Jean said nicely through his teeth.

Unfortunately—or fortunately, as it turned out in the end—he went back to the reporters.

"There's not a word of truth in what Miss Gay was telling you. Phillips Heaton never knew a spy in his life."

I don't think those reporters had believed me. But as Jean spoke one of them asked softly, "What are you so hot about, brother?"

"There's no more connection—"

"We heard you." The answer was even softer, and the men melted, looking back, whispering.

Inside the porch Jean glared at me. He'd managed somehow to wash and shave. "Now, see what you—"

I still felt hard and careless. "Bill's conscious. He doesn't know who shot him, but even Dr. Rush says he's better."

Jean forgot the reporters. If he were the guilty one, I thought, he did an artistic job of going down to the bottom over the disappointment of Bill's lack of knowledge—and then an equally convincing job of being relieved over Bill's improvement.

Inside I found Cecile sitting with Bradley beside Carol. Myra was awake but lying limply in bed. Because it was long past noon, the most immediate concern seemed to be lunch; Cecile came down to help me. Bradley took his in Carol's room, on a tray; with no sleep and what else he had on his mind, he was teetering on the edge, and the first thing he did was knock the cup off his tray. Carol slept through the crash, but Myra tottered out from her room to see what was happening now. In spite of my protests, she insisted on going downstairs to see that a tray fixed just the right way got to Octavia, who lay headlocked on her face, as if she hadn't moved since Jacqueline and I left her. Some of the breakfast was gone, though.

"I can't fall to pieces," Myra told herself, dazed and weak but struggling to get herself together, as we came out of Octavia's room. "I can't leave Octavia to—Not that you're a stranger, Ann, but Octavia dreads anyone but me."

She insisted on coming downstairs to the lunch table, too, where we were joined by a Jean who had pulled into himself like a sulky turtle and a Cecile wavering between hardihood, distrust, and the helplessness that had come on her since she'd learned she couldn't run away. I admit I was ready to jump at a pinfall myself.

"All I think about"—Cecile leaned forward to tap ashes from her cigarette when the meal was done—"is getting away again."

We'd been keeping the talk on Bill's recovery as we ate, but she was back on the taboo subject now. "I'm just about ready to let Aakonen put me in jail. Nice, safe places, jails—no murders there."

As she spoke, a shutter in my mind flew open; I didn't allow myself time for second thoughts.

"That's right—something turned up when Jean and I were in Bill's office last night." I made it significant.

Immediate comprehension and warning in Jean's eyes. "Now, listen, Ann—"

I paid no attention. "Aakonen opened an envelope holding Bill's canceled checks for last month."

The full breast rose then and stayed high; fingers tightened on the cigarette.

"There were three checks which had been made out to you, Cecile. Three checks, each for twenty-five dollars, dated May eighteenth, May twenty-fifth, and June first."

Myra asked weakly, "Ann, what are you saying? Surely—you can't—"

But the baby blue eyes across the table weren't defenseless; they looked out of armor.

"So what?"

"I thought you might want to make some explanation."

"I don't."

Jean began, "Ann, can't you—?"

"No," I said. "I know what it looks like. Three checks made out to Cecile. I know how Aakonen thinks it looks. As if perhaps Cecile always got twenty-five dollars a week from Bill, but when he was away in Bermuda, where he couldn't deliver the money in person, then he sent checks."

"All right," Cecile. said. "He sent me three checks. Any reason why he shouldn't owe me seventy-five dollars?"

I didn't answer. She turned to look at Myra, who'd sunk back in her chair, with her white head averted; she looked at Jean, staring down at the knuckles of his interlaced fingers. For an instant, there was something on her mouth that reminded me of Jacqueline's mouth.

She said, "You think, Aakonen thinks, Myra thinks, and Jean thinks that there's just one reason Bill would give me money?"

"No," I said, and my skin prickled as if a storm were coming. "If I'd thought that, I wouldn't have said a word."

"You mean you don't believe—?" It was quick, but what came next was slow. "Of course. You're thinking from Bill's side."

"Cecile," Jean said, "let it slide. You don't have to talk."

"That's what I planned," she said, but something—could it be courage?—was in her tight hands like a weapon.

"You're right, Jean—I don't have to talk. That was my plan at first. That's what I was doing that day after Fred died when you surprised me in the woods. I was hiding the—evidence."

She smiled without humor. "I did a good job, too, didn't I? But of course you didn't know what to look for. Two envelopes. Two letters. One of them written by my mother. One of them from Bill."

It was me she looked at, unwavering.

"Then later Bill was shot, and I thought he was going to die. I knew how it would look if it got out about the money. I made up my mind then that if the time came I'd tell how it was."

She dropped the cigarette in her plate and folded her hands in her lap.

"Bill's supported me since I was fourteen. Ever since my mother died. He says he doesn't want me to—have to make money. I suppose"—it came with what looked like hard self-judgment—"I suppose he knows how I'd make it if I had to make it."

She stopped. The long dark lashes over the baby blue eyes lifted to Jean. Then she tossed the flaxen doll's hair back and looked at Myra, her mouth twisting with a curious mixture of humor and insolence.

"That's all, except for why Bill supports me. He does it because I'm his cousin, just as you are. He does it because I'm your sister."

20

MYRA WAS IN NO shape to take it. She asked wonderingly, "My sister? But Octavia is my only sister." And then her breath caught and her eyes flinched, as if she'd been struck in the face.

She whispered, "My father. Oh no!"

Everything went from Cecile's face except amusement; certainly there was no pity there. She leaned easily forward, shrugging.

"Oh well, a father isn't much to have in common. Not one who contributes a few germ cells to your existence and calls it a day."

"Myra, I'm sorry." That was my voice working of its own accord, not much help from my mind. "I'm sorry, Cecile."

And I was sorry, terribly sorry. Sorry this new humiliation and pain had to come to Myra, sorry for Cecile, sorry she'd had the birth she'd had, sorry she must carry the inevitable bitterness, sorry I had provoked this new disdain she had to suffer.

Cecile said, "That's all right—I've been waiting for it."

"I'm sorry, too." Jean was squeezing Cecile's wrist, and for once, a man was looking at Cecile with an entirely nice look in his eyes.

My first thought was that Cecile needn't have made that admission; she'd done it out of loyalty to Bill.

I HAD TO HELP Myra back upstairs to bed. She said only, "It's unforgivable of Bill to have brought that girl here."

When I got back downstairs no one was there; I think Jean took Cecile back to the resort. I started clearing the table, my mind on trying to see what difference this revelation of Cecile's might make.

I'd had a rush of sympathy for Cecile, but that was neither here nor there—I'd had rushes of sympathy for practically everyone involved, except perhaps Phillips Heaton—and now look where Phillips was.

Would Cecile start out shooting Heatons just because she was an ex officio Heaton herself? Cecile and her mother might have had plenty of reason for hating Charles Heaton . . .

Charles Heaton had been burned to death in a fire whose origin no one knew . . .

The bread plate which I'd picked up to carry to the kitchen tipped its forgotten contents on the table.

The fire had been in 1920. Cecile couldn't have been much more than four then. Impossible for her to have been responsible. But had anyone investigated what her mother was doing the night of that fire?

Suppose a hunger for revenge had been instilled in Cecile?

Phillips Heaton had spent the afternoon before he died with Cecile; I'd seen them on the beach at the resort—Phillips sitting with his arms around his fat seersucker knees. Had it been Cecile that Phillips suspected? In that case, Cecile's story about the investments must have been clever camouflage—Phillips would know he couldn't get much from Cecile.

"Someone seems to have it in for Heatons . . ."

I decided I had better tell Aakonen.

BILL'S CAR CAME UP out of the lake just as I was leaving. I heard all the way across water and beach the angry grasping sound the lake made as the car was lifted from it. The car moved in a slow semicircle over the water, hanging from a huge steel arm, to be deposited on the scow in back of the crane. Water poured from it; it looked battered and crippled.

Little chance of getting any clues from that car, I thought, after it had been all these hours in the lake.

At the hospital, Jacqueline was gone; Dr. Rush had sent her out to get lunch. But Aakonen was in the hall. As I told him of Cecile's contribution, he listened with his head down-bent. When I'd finished he kept on standing that way; no light of interest crossed his face.

"You were right to tell me," he said at last. "That Cecile is Charles Heaton's daughter I have known since she was born. It was gossip in the village then. That Mr. Bill Heaton was taking care of her—I am glad that is the way it is."

You suspected another reason, I thought, but I didn't say it.

That was the last comment he made on what I had told him of Cecile. When he went on, it was to give the warning that accelerated everything that happened from then on.

He moved forward, straight upon me. I backed until the small table of the waiting room hit the back of my legs. There was an ominous soberness about his face and his advance.

He said, "I am glad you are here. There is something I want

to tell you. Tomorrow morning there will be an inquest into the death of Phillips Heaton."

That. I should have remembered it would come.

"Miss Gay, I have no doubt that after that inquest tomorrow, I shall have to arrest your cousin for these murders."

No world under my feet, no solidity anywhere. The only entities were the words he said, screaming past me like vampires in flight.

"You mean you—it's come." That was my unrecognizable voice.

"Miss Gay, you will see I won't be able to do anything else. The jury will find that Phillips Heaton died at the hands of Jacqueline Heaton. Have you forgotten those wet shoes after she'd said she had not stepped on grass?"

"But she explained that. Someone else could have wet those shoes!"

"You can make that explanation at the inquest."

"But what else can we do?" New terror rising now. I reached for his arm, shaking it. "Jacqueline didn't do any of this shooting. No matter what other people think, can you let an innocent person be—?"

"Innocent?" he asked. It was as weary as death. "Miss Gay, there is only one reason why Mrs. Heaton has not been charged long before this—because I hate to arrest Mr. Bill Heaton's wife."

He was reminding me what he'd told me about Bill, and suddenly he was closer, his voice rough, begging.

"If there is anything you can do, do it quickly. I do not know enough about this kind of murder. I can't rest or sleep, worried always that I'm getting nowhere; perhaps even now another person is being killed. I can't let this go on. Every fact I have is against your cousin. Long before Fred was killed, everywhere she went, mischief followed. Fred was killed after he had provoked her. All the signs of his death point to her. The cape was hers. She was right there when Bill was shot. She could so easily have taken the gun. And then the shoes—"

He spread his hands in a wide, spreading, helpless gesture.

"There is little evidence against anyone else. The only person who could possibly benefit by the deaths is your cousin."

"She doesn't benefit by Phillips's death!"

"You know and I know why Phillips was killed. Because he boasted that he knew the murderer."

"But Phillips told me he knew the murderer wasn't Jacqueline!"

"For that, I have only your word."

"What can I do for Jacqueline if everything I say is disbelieved?"

"You admit lying to me twice."

I groaned. "They were such unimportant things."

He didn't answer. I rushed on, "What about all the other things? About Cecile Granat's being—?"

Another weary gesture. "Would Cecile try to kill the man who was her only support?"

No, in Bill's death Cecile stood only to lose. I plunged again.

"Mark. He had that fight with Fred. And Carol in Bill's office—you know she was up to something."

"Where does Carol benefit by Mr. Bill Heaton's death?"

"The Corvos, too. There was that trouble about the accident—"

"Miss Gay, the course you are taking now is useless. Phillips Heaton's death—that perhaps was not planned. But the rest was planned. That Fred should die first, that Mr. Bill Heaton should die—only one person benefits by the deaths in that order."

"But Bill didn't die!"

"No," he said, and his lips were folded in a straight line. "And I am here to see he does not die."

HE WAS ALLOWING APPEARANCES to take their course. He was done investigating. That was what he was telling me.

Even at the first inquest, the jury and the people had suspected Jacqueline.

I threw myself against his stand, battered myself against it. It was no use. He didn't want to arrest Jacqueline, for Bill's sake, but he himself had come to believe her the murderer. Out of some obscure reasoning, he told me this as a sort of last effort to help her out if help could be given.

His parley with me ended when Jacqueline came back from lunch to pause radiantly at the entrance to the cubicle.

"You should have seen Hanson's. Mr. Hanson was out on the sidewalk. The lunch room was full of Bill's crews. Celebrating. They've taken the place over: Was there ever such a glorious day?"

How could I tell her what sort of day it really was?

Silently I followed her down the hall, Aakonen persistent in our wake. Bill's eyes were open again, restless until Jacqueline got in. As a last resort I told him, too, what I'd found out about Cecile, to see if the disclosure would waken any suspicion in him.

What it woke was almost a normal Bill Heaton smile.

The weak voice said, "Good old Cecile."

I DROVE BACK TO the Fingers alone, leaving Jacqueline under Aakonen's hawklike watching, with Bill. I didn't think she'd have torn herself away even if she'd known how desperate her situation was.

Not just a matter of fighting until I went down. It was up to me now to see that tomorrow never came.

Couldn't we ever get a break? Hadn't that chemist, for instance, had time enough now to do his experimenting? And then that fire in the bed—somehow I felt that if those two which tied all that succession of tricks to Jacqueline, could be blown into thin air, then some of the weight of evidence would go with them. And if I could fasten those tricks to someone else . . .

Again I thought how incredibly adept this murderer had been. There had to be clues, if I could only see them. There had to be some other motive besides Jacqueline's, if I could only worm it out—perhaps from information I already had . . .

In the Fingers living room were Jean, Mark, and Bradley Auden, hammering away at the problem of what Carol had been doing in Bill's office. Mark had perhaps slept a little; he looked better, but Bradley didn't. Neither one was glad to see me, but Jean swung a chair around for me, and I dropped into it. An answer to any mystery was a step in the right direction.

"Carol inferred it wasn't for herself she was in Bill's office," Bradley was saying. "She has no close friends around here—none who'd have any connection with Bill. That just about narrows it down to her mother, Mark, and me."

He repeated that last. "I guess I've got to admit it's become three."

"I don't know what to say." Mark fumbled with words. He'd been fined down until almost nothing was left but his mathematical cleanness and precision.

"I haven't got anything against you, Mark, if we can get things straightened out. My wife hasn't even seen Bill for a long time—she's bedridden. It couldn't be for her mother Carol was in that office. Then me. That note of mine. Carol knows I could have cleaned that up. How she could—"

"It looks, then, as if it must be me." Mark's eyes had gone wide. "I've got to see through it. Carol must have made a mistake, someway, about me. I'm trying to remember what I've told her. I know I told her my father worked for Bill's father and was killed on the job. I lived with an aunt near Lutsen—my mother had died before. The day I finished high school one of the teachers told me to go see Bill Heaton. I guess you know Bill helped me through the engineering course. Then the day I graduated he sent me the notes I'd signed for the money he loaned me and a letter saying I had a job if I wanted it."

He stopped to sit breath-held and staring. "Good lord! If that could be it—Carol knew Bill helped me. I can't remember ever telling her he sent those notes back . . ."

He was out of his chair, leaping the stairs three at a time, the rest of us after him.

Carol was asleep, but he didn't stop; he shook her until she woke. "Carol! Wake up! We've got to know—"

She had to come up a long way, blinking dazedly as the light struck her eyes, looking from Mark to the rest of us, expectant. Then she shrank back, twisting to bury her face in the pillow.

"Go away! Can't you let me alone? I didn't take anything!"

"That's it! You didn't find anything! There wasn't anything to find!" Mark poured exclamation. "Carol, Bill made me a present of the money he'd loaned me when I graduated from college."

The shoulders in the bed had quit twisting, become very still. When she turned to lie face upward the hazel eyes were ominously quiet.

"You mean you don't owe Bill anything?"

"No—I mean, yes—I owe him a terrible lot. But not notes he holds over me."

She was slowly pulling herself upward, resting her weight back on her hands, staring at him. She'd forgotten the rest of us.

She whispered, "But you fought with Fred the night he was

killed. And then when Bill was shot—you let me tell a lie. It wasn't nine thirty when you left Auden that night—it was eight thirty. I did look at the clock."

"But I never looked to see what time it was. I thought I'd gone home earlier that night, but when you said it was nine thirty I believed you—"

"So I went on lying about the time." Her tone wasn't a whisper any longer; it was loud and angry. "I got started thinking why you might want to kill Bill and I remembered you told me he loaned you money for school—and your father was killed working for Bill's father—and you wouldn't marry me so I couldn't testify against you—"

The voice was rising. "I had to get those notes so you wouldn't be suspected—that's what I thought! And it was perfectly awful!"

Carol's words were now a shriek.

"I had to *sneak* and steal Jean's pocketbook and I was scared, and they caught me, and I fell down when I was running and hurt my knee and I almost *froze* to death in those woods, and all the time it wasn't *true*!" She lifted her nose, howling.

Mark was laughing, tears running down his cheeks, patting her back as he tried to pull her against his shoulder. "Carol. I'll never forget what you tried to do for me. It's all right now—you don't have to cry."

But she fought wildly against him. "I do, too, have to cry! I was such an *idiot*!"

Behind me, Bradley Auden gave a sudden bark of laughter, pushing past me, brushing Mark aside. Carol collapsed on his shoulder, and her father rocked and crooned.

"SO THAT'S THAT," JEAN said gloomily at the foot of the stairs. We'd both turned as if by common consent to walk away. "Like everything else. Maybe we know now why Carol was in that office, but does it shed any light on the murders? It does not."

"Except that we know now Mark had no alibi for the night Bill was shot."

"What's his motive?"

"Who else has one?" I remembered as I said it that Jean perhaps had as much reason as anyone, but the necessity to have someone working with me was too strong; I told him what Aakonen had said.

He stood looking at me, completely still. "Of course," he said slowly. "It had to come, with things going on this way." He sat down in the nearest chair, resting his face in his hands. "Oh lord, I feel as if I had wires around my chest and someone pulling on the two ends."

Then in a sudden transition to what looked like anger, he was up, pacing the floor.

"What was I given a brain for? There's got to be some answer to this—got to . . ."

I'd had one idea. "There's your chemist—"

He almost leaped at me. "Yes! If he had anything—"

Then he was at the phone, tearing the receiver from the hook. "Get me George Crowley at the Middle States Paper Products Company in Detroit."

He waited, with unquiet eyes and the flicking of muscles over his face showing that the hounds of thought still chased. Then the call came through.

"George? Listen, we're getting desperate. How about those acids? . . . I know, but—can't you give me any? . . . What if it isn't a week? Test 'em out now! We've got to know!"

He turned from the phone, spreading his hands as Aakonen had that morning.

"He says he can't tell whether a chemical will eat holes

through a suit at the end of a week until I've given him a week for the chemical to be on the fabric. He's trying out some. Some of the fabrics are already in holes. He's got to leave the others for a week and then see what happens when he puts them in naphtha."

"So even if there is an answer we won't get it in time."

"I've been working on the fire in the bed, too, in my cabin. If we could get at it from motive . . . We had a weak one for Phillips. Where's that now? Who else? Myra, Brad, Mark, Carol, Cecile, the Corvos—I can't see anything on any of them. You're out. I know I didn't do it—"

The phone rang, punctuating it. Jean answered.

"Who? . . . Oh, Mrs. Foster." He relaxed a little. "Yes, of course. This is Jean Nobbelin . . . Yes, it's true. Unbelievable but true . . . No, we still don't know."

The news of Phillips's death had reached Duluth. I moved to take the phone from him, but he fended me off.

"Sure, I'd like to talk to her."

I stood so close I could hear Toby's voice when it came on.

"I'm fine, Mama."

"This is Jean. You being a big girl? Mama isn't here right now."

"I coming you now." Even at my distance I heard the obstinate decision.

"But it's nice where you are. Lots warmer, and you have things to play with you wouldn't have here."

"I yike be Mama and Gramma," the small voice repeated, and I heard in it something lost and forlorn.

Jean let me talk to her then. I talked quickly, trying to tide over crisis. When I turned from the phone, we both said nothing for a moment. When Jean did speak, his voice had the oppressiveness of Aakonen's.

"Poor little chicken. If tomorrow happens . . . she'll have to suffer, too. As if she had any part in this mess . . ."

Myra called from upstairs and I went slowly up. She'd heard the ring of the phone. I had to tell her all about Toby. She lay wan and white, looking almost blankly over at me.

"Isn't this ever going to end?" she asked. I couldn't tell her, either, that it had to end.

She'd heard Carol's loud wails, too. "I'm glad that's explained anyway," she said, and I remembered what Bradley had said, that they'd once been in love. "I wonder how long since she's had anything to eat."

So I went in to Carol, now leaning back and smiling sleepily at Mark, who held her hands, and at her father, who limped along the floor, with his unlit pipe between his teeth. She was reserved with me but hungry. She'd like ham and eggs.

That's how it happened that I went down to the kitchen to light the kerosene stove which served as an auxiliary to the range and found there were no more matches in the tin box on the wall. Myra kept the staples in the pantry. I hunted along a top shelf until I found the carton. From an individual box I pulled the red, navy, and white cover, slipping the inner container with its matches into the tin holder. Mechanically I struck a match for the fire, kneeling before the stove.

But I didn't reach the flame to the burner; my hands halted.

In my right hand was the burning match, tipped to let the flame carry along the stick. In my left was the red, navy, and white matchbox cover. I'd scratched the match on the strip of sandy abrasive along the side.

Slowly the hand with the match moved until the flame was at the end of the box cover; gradually the flame ate into the cheap cardboard, and the cardboard blackened, red flame curling from

it, smoke curling. The cardboard curled back upon itself, disap-
pearing.

All of it.

The match burned my fingers; I dropped it on the burner
shelf. Slowly I rose, dropping the matchbox cover, too, of which
only a third was left. I stood watching it burn to a thin black ash.

I knew then how the fire had been started in Jacqueline's bed
by someone who wasn't there.

21

STRANGE NOW TO LOOK back on the incongruous happenings of those next few hours when the cords of circumstance were drawing so inexorably tight.

When I called Jean out to the kitchen to tell him about the fire, he went up in a flame as bright as the match. The next thing I knew, he had his arms around me and was kissing me, hard, and my whole interior became a ski slide on which something went down, *whoosh!*

The same instant, Bradley Auden asked, behind me, "Are those eggs——?"

His voice wavered and stopped, and what came next sounded completely confounded. "I have heard that romance flourishes in the midst of death." His mouth was twisted in an odd, rather unpleasant grin. "You better tell me——do I start shaking hands, or do I look the other way and pretend it never happened?"

I'd started pulling away, heat against my cheeks, but the arms around me held fast. Jean's intense black eyes were watching me as if Bradley Auden weren't there, and I saw in them something held back, disturbing.

Deliberately, Jean kissed me again before he let go. Then he turned to Bradley, his face not relaxing.

"The devil finds work," he said. "What did you come down for anyway?"

"Eggs," Bradley said. "Ham and eggs for my repatriated daughter."

He loosened up to be jocose and familiar when I was forced to admit the stove wasn't even lit. Then he saw the ash of the matchbox cover and poked at it with a curious finger.

"What *were* you up to?"

From then on, he watched me with a different surmise as Jean moved smoothly to sweep the ashes into his hand and wash them down the sink.

"It seems I interrupted Ann when she was lighting the stove, and she dropped the match on some paper. You know how a girl gets flustered."

"That looked more like a box."

"It was a box cover," I said.

He kept on watching me until I had the ham and eggs fried and toast made, but he went upstairs with them without any more comments.

"Bradley Auden," I said when he was gone. "Where does he come in on this?"

But Jean dismissed him. "Anybody'd have known something was up, with both of us blazing like neon lights."

"I'm going right in to Aakonen with what I've guessed."

I was halfway to the side porch when Jean jerked me back. "Don't be an idiot. Don't you see what you've got? A surprise. Something to spring at the inquest tomorrow. You're going to need fireworks to squeeze Jacqueline by."

He dropped me then to walk the kitchen impatiently.

"But it isn't enough. Heaven knows it isn't enough." He talked on, speculating, jumping to the attack from one side and another, rehashing what little we knew.

My first reaction to his stopping me was the suspicion that rose so swiftly now against anyone. Did he have any reason other than the one he gave for not wanting me to tell Aakonen?

But as he talked on, shaking a kitchen chair as if to shake from the inanimate object some answer to the questions he asked, I found myself, as usual, following him, beating my head against the things I couldn't know, feeling myself pitted against that force so much more adept than myself, so much more slippery—and all the time the need for haste rising as the minutes went by, rising like water up a riverbank in flood . . .

The grocery bus came. I had to tear myself away to buy food for dinner. The dead no longer ate, but the living had to be fed. The phone rang—this time Jacqueline. Bill was apparently asleep for the evening, and she'd been told to go home. She wondered if I'd come for her.

More time gone with nothing to show. Swiftly, I drove to Grand Marais, using Myra's car again, every mile a minute falling through my hands. I had to do something. At Grand Marais, I swerved the car into the Main Street, a vague idea beginning in my mind. When I passed Hanson's, it looked and sounded like a riot. Hanson was leaning good-humoredly against a lamppost in front. I slowed the car.

"Is that the same celebration for Bill?"

"Yep," he said. A bottle came through his front window; his eyes followed it with what looked like admiration as it sailed over his head and the car, shattering against the opposite curb. "They're all good guys. If they ain't got the dough today I'll get it next payday."

At the hardware store, I bought sheets of sandpaper and hurried on to the hospital where Jacqueline waited on the steps, radiant still. Beside her, in dark contrast, Aakonen.

He came down to open the car door for her.

"I have just learned something," he said. "My men have been working on Mr. Bill Heaton's car. No one pushed it before it went in the lake. No one released its brakes."

"No one?"

My mind sped back to night and the car moving by itself under my window. "But that's impossible!"

The large head shook. "No. I have just been telling Mrs. Heaton. The brakes were set. A chemical started that car—an acid. That was an old car—it had brake bands only on the two rear wheels—exposed brake bands. They were eaten through. It must have been an acid."

"Like Bill's suit," I said. The car that had come up out of the lake had had a story to tell.

"Exactly," he said significantly. "Like Bill's suit."

Couldn't there be any help in this? "Bradley Auden had an alibi for the time that car must have started—he was the only one of us who did."

The shoulders lifted. "Yes. He now becomes one of you."

HE TRAILED US OUT to the Fingers. He talked to Bradley upstairs for perhaps twenty minutes but came down alone, hunched and tired, to pause in the kitchen where Jacqueline and I had begun preparing dinner. He had gotten nowhere.

"You will remember about tomorrow," he said as he went out. As if there could be any possible chance of my forgetting.

"What does he mean about tomorrow?" Jacqueline asked. "Oh, I know," she answered herself, "the inquest."

And I had nothing but that small idea . . .

————

EIGHT OF US AT that last dinner—the dinner for which, with my idea forming like a slow-whirling eddy in my mind, I insisted Jean, Bradley, Mark, and Carol stay. I called the resort to invite Cecile; she wouldn't come alone even in the early evening, so Jean and Mark went for her. Octavia stayed in her room as ever, but we helped Myra down from upstairs.

Eight watchful people, with nerves vibrating like violin strings at a touch. The table was pleasantly set and the food good and the fire warm, but four of those people ate as if they feared the very food and kept themselves apart, not just from Jacqueline now, but from each other.

Of the eight, only Jean and I knew how perilously short the time was, but wasn't there some growing urgency, some new feeling of haste and necessity over the others also? Carol, pale and jumpy, not any too sure in her belief that Mark was innocent, Mark alternately eating and relapsing into abstraction, Bradley trying to hold himself quiet but with a leaping alertness in his eyes, Cecile behind armor, Myra pathetically struggling for strength to get her through the meal, Jacqueline ignoring animosity, watching me.

Jean, too, watched me, his eyes pulled in, as I feverishly, heedlessly talked about anything—Bill's improvement, the necessity for guarding him, Toby. Muscles in the back of my neck tightened until they were rigid and aching. No one else said much. Over my own voice, there was mostly that eternal chuckle and roar of the wilderness so constant, so insistent in its varied rhythms that it was an almost intolerable drumbeat. If I let myself listen to that thrum, I could break, too, break now at this table where people ate wood-broiled steaks and there was that waiting, growing intentness.

I spoke some of that thought aloud. "Here we are, eating steaks—good steaks. Last night one of us died. We're getting like people in London. We sit at our tables and wait."

No answer.

"Some of you think you know the answer, but you're wrong. Some of us have set out to prove you're wrong, but we haven't gotten very far, have we? There was Bill. He's supposed to be the new businessman, the type that builds up instead of tearing down. He believed Jacqueline didn't kill Fred, and look what happened to him—he went out and got shot like a lamb himself."

Jean spoke slowly then. "Some people get shot for talking too much."

I wound myself tighter. "Jean, the handler of men. Myra, the clairvoyant. And me, where've I gotten in spite of all the talents I boasted? Remember, I was the girl with the eyes and the nose and the ears . . ."

Suddenly the table and the faces that bent forward, watching me, were gone; I didn't see any of them.

Me with the eyes and the ears and the nose . . . Was that me repeating? Or was it an echo? When I came back from the dark, rushing chambers of blind thought, I blinked at light and the reserved, wary faces, and my hands pushed at the table edge, white knuckled. The little plan had whirled out and become big, falling over me like a waterspout.

"But I know of something I can at least try," I said. "There was once when the murderer and I were in the same room. He came into my room to slash my bathrobe and shook the bed to wake me. He'd put on something of Jacqueline's, or else he carried one of her pomanders, because I caught the scent of spice."

A gasp from Jacqueline. "You didn't tell me that!"

"No, I didn't want to. I was afraid. I'm not afraid now. I know this is a murderer who'd do just that—carry the spice and wake me. I'll show you why . . ."

My coat was thrown over the wicker davenport; from its pocket I got the sandpaper I'd bought at the hardware store. When I went to the kitchen for matches, Jean shouted at me, standing up to stop me.

"No," I told him. "I've got to do it." And he let me go.

Standing beside the table, I ripped a sheet of the sandpaper in two, laying half of it over my emptied water glass. Two of the matches I forced through the sandpaper as far as the heads. Then I laid the second half of the sandpaper over them.

"Look," I said. "This is a bed. The bottom sandpaper rests on the spring. The mattress is on top. Bill is asleep and he turns in his sleep."

My hand moved over the sandpaper, rolling it. I didn't even know it would work; I was risking what I'd guessed. Slowly I moved the sandpaper, and it wasn't long—a spark flashed; a thin waver of gray smoke went up, and then a black circle showed through the top paper. As intent as the others, I stood back to watch while the sandpaper blackened and curled to a substance-less thinness. When I flicked the ash with my finger the crumbled flakes fell into the glass.

Someone let out a long breath.

Then Jacqueline was hugging me. "Ann, wonderful Ann! You would stick until you got it."

"It would have worked slower than that in the night," I said. "But it shows how a fire could have been started by someone who wasn't there."

"We can call Aakonen right away—"

I pushed her aside. "That's not all. Jean has a chemist—a friend of his in Detroit—doing experiments. Any day now"—

this wasn't truth, but only Jean and I would know that—"he'll be able to tell us the name of the chemical that ate holes in Bill's suit after it had been on the suit for a whole week."

I paused. "Perhaps you don't all see what that means. It means that none of that long series of tricks will any longer be tied up to Jacqueline, because there were just those two that made it look as if she had to be responsible."

"Ann," Jacqueline whispered again. Over the others was that complete, intent, intense silence.

"Then that night the murderer was in my room. It was too dark for me to see, but not too dark for my ears and nose. There's something it seems to me I should be able to get."

In those seven pairs of eyes facing me, wasn't there more than watchfulness? It seemed to me I could feel it—the crouch, the poise of the wolf at bay. I tried to single out the wolf stare, but all the eyes were alight, all were intent, any one pair no different from the others.

"So," I said, "I want to play the game we played on the Fourth of July. Everyone who was here then except Fred and Bill and Phillips. And I'd like to have Lottie and the Corvos." I turned to Jean. "Would you get them?"

He asked, "Ann, do you know what you're doing?" His lower lids were pulled up so tightly he had almost no visible eyes at all.

I only nodded.

"All right." He left.

When he was gone the others stirred a little. Bradley Auden laughed, but it was forced.

"So that's what the burned cover was this afternoon. A matchbox cover. It's been annoying me ever since."

Carol shivered. "You wore my scarf that other day, but now I haven't any. I wished I had had one last night."

I went upstairs to get a scarf of my own. When I got back, Jacqueline was carrying one of the chairs to the opposite end of the room.

"Away from the fire," she explained. "Fire has a smell, too."

Then I had the rest of my idea.

"It shouldn't be here at all. It should be in my room upstairs, exactly as it was the night of the Fourth. I'll pull the curtains and lie, with my eyes covered, on the bed. Each one of you can open the door, walk in silently, stand awhile by the bed, and then shake the bed before you go away. That'll be the nearest I can get."

A gasp then from Jacqueline. "But, Ann—I don't like that! That's frightening!"

"I'll say *All right* after each one of you shakes the bed. If you don't hear that—well, you'll know who was in before you."

They all protested, circling around me. As they did so I just looked from face to face, counting them up. Everyone was there . . . No.

"Myra," I said slowly, "I'd like it if you'd persuade Octavia to do this, too. Not that she's under suspicion—I remember about her locked door—it's just to make the test more complete. You can explain."

She didn't like it, but there seemed a compulsion now in the room, as it were the common will that this should go through. She said at last, "I know you're doing this for Jacqueline," and went to persuade Octavia.

"Wait for Jean and the others before you begin." I gave a last suggestion and followed Myra upstairs.

Swiftly in my room I set the stage, drawing the curtains, shutting the place into soft gray dusk. The bedcovers were still thrown back as Carol had left them when she got up for dinner. I leaned back against the propped-up pillow, waking my senses.

From through the walls, the incessant lake and pine sounds came thinly in. I must tune those out. A door slamming below—that would be Jean coming with the Corvos and Lottie. A loud rumble—that would be Jean's anger over the change in plans. My toes tingled as if my feet were cold.

A faint scent about the bed that was Carol's, not mine. I must identify and discard that. Pine fragrance and lake dampness, the varnishy smell of wood, warm dryness of feathers in the pillow, clean smell of cotton. Identify and discard.

People came up the stairs in a body, a heavy charge. Then a hush and the door quietly opening; soft footfalls along the boards of the floor; a pause.

Faint and refreshing, the scent of spice. They'd sent Jacqueline in first. The bed moved gently.

"All right," I said. The footfalls receded.

A closing and an opening door. Heavier, wearier movements. Pipe tobacco, a slight limp. Bradley Auden. The bed moved.

"All right."

Lottie next, and after her Ella Corvo. They both moved in a heavy slide of garments and limbs, their scent one of cooking and damp awed perspiration; I knew then they could be ruled out as suspects; I never considered them again. Ed Corvo, however, I had to guess almost by elimination; he had no scent that I could catch.

One by one they came: Jean, Myra, Carol, Mark, Cecile, each one conscientiously playing his role. And as they came, a fearful wild elation grew in me. All around me, I could feel the tautness pulling tighter. That was what I wanted.

Octavia came last. I heard the faint footfall, but otherwise it was almost as if there were nothing in the room. No—some slight, sharp scent, hard to identify, and one I didn't remember.

If I could have recognized after all these days any faint reminiscent scent, any reminiscent movement, it would have been pure gain. And sure, I tried, but didn't actually expect to remember.

Kill or cure now. I knew very well what I was doing: I was building a trap, making the murderer think I was dangerous, making him feel I knew too much. I was so frightened, my skin was cold but I went ahead, anyway, making myself bait in the trap.

AFTER OCTAVIA THE DOOR opened with no attempt at softness.

"Okay, you've had 'em." It was Jean.

I sat up, pulling the scarf from my eyes. The light went on, and they all trooped in.

"There's something." I put it with careful vagueness, wrinkling my forehead in token of perplexity and thought. "I have to think. It seems to me there's some recollection—if I could just get it to the surface."

They were silent, watching me and waiting, as I swung my legs from the bed.

"I'll have to sleep over it, I guess. Try to dredge it up from my subconscious. If I wake in the night as I did then, out of sleep . . ."

As I walked toward them Octavia was still there at the back of the group, but she melted away. They all fell away a little, moving stiffly, as if their joints had rusted. Yet they accepted what I was doing, as if there were a doom over all of us, and whether I exposed myself dangerously or not made no real difference.

Bradley Auden, turning suddenly, almost knocked Myra over; she'd been visibly holding herself together only by force of will. She clutched at him to keep herself upright, her dark eyes completely bewildered and spent.

"It's dangerous," she said. "Can't you all see it's too dangerous? Ann can't do this." When no one answered, I did.

"Nothing's dangerous anymore. Don't worry, Myra. You ought to be in bed."

Jacqueline and I helped her get there. When we walked downstairs, the others were standing almost as helplessly as Myra in the middle of the room. They'd been talking, but at our appearance a dead silence fell.

Jean's black eyes lifted to me.

"Well, nothing I can do here, I guess." His hand went to his forehead in a crooked half-military salute. "I'll say good night. I hope some of us live to testify at that inquest tomorrow. Good luck with your subconscious, Ann."

Cecile was after him in quick panic. "Wait for me!"

Bradley Auden seemed to shake himself partially awake. "I'll see you get to the resort, Cecile. You, too, Jean and Mark—all of you. This is no time for anyone to walk through woods in the dark alone."

They borrowed Myra's car and went together, all of them, even the Corvos and Lottie piling in, hurrying as if they couldn't get away fast enough. Jacqueline and I stood on the porch watching them go.

Jean, I thought bitterly disappointed—he'd accepted the whole thing; he'd gone as easily as that. He, like the others, seemed suddenly to have become just a puppet, jerked by strings, peering out of a masked face with solitary, expectant eyes. Why hadn't he managed somehow to back me up?

As we turned inside, Jacqueline, too, seemed tacitly to accept what I proposed to do. We went about hooking screens and turning off lights—those ridiculous habitual night preparations which guarded against nothing—and she didn't say a word. She walked upstairs with me, still not saying a word, and came in with me to help make up my bed with fresh sheets and cases. When that was done, she turned to me silently, putting her arms around me, resting her cheek lightly for an instant against mine.

"Ann," she said, and her eyes were wet, but she turned and walked out, and the light went on in her room . . .

Four of us in the house, four women in a summerhouse in which entry was as easy as a slit screen: shrinking Octavia, Myra broken to uselessness, Jacqueline leaving me, I with my trap built . . .

I stood in it, knowing what it is to stand alone.

I couldn't back out now. I walked down the hall to the bathroom and came back, calling good night to Jacqueline as I passed her closed door, noting that Octavia's door was tightly shut and, no doubt, locked on the inside, stopping in to see that Myra was as comfortable as she could be made.

She roused to beg me again, "Ann, I don't like what you're doing. We ought to have one of Aakonen's men in the house. I shan't be able to sleep. I—"

"Nonsense!" I told her cheerfully over the turmoil in my mind. "No one will come. I'm in no danger."

I closed her door firmly and my own. No chair under my door tonight. Quickly, I made a survey of that room where the curtains were pulled and the bed waited . . .

But it wasn't waiting for me. That bed was going to be occupied by that pet of girls' dormitories—a blanket dummy. I was a reckless fool, but not fool enough to try sleeping in that bed tonight.

For the first time, I took thought of what I'd cut out for myself, and a cold finger seemed to press against the back of my neck and run delicately, icily, all the way down my spine.

To some extent, I'd been successful—I knew I had. I'd felt it in those people—the rising tension. Suppose I were the murderer behind one of those pairs of eyes—how would I rest tonight, wondering when that girl—that Ann Gay, who had discovered the secret in my trick of the fire in the bed—might wake in the night and remember?

Even if the murderer guessed, even if he was pretty sure that I remembered nothing, still he couldn't be entirely certain. And the night would be on my side, the long hours in which the murderer must lie expecting, waiting. The wilderness sounds would be on my side, because even away from here, where he couldn't hear the chuckle of the Fingers, the murderer would hear the urging crash and roar of the strong, insistent, hungry lake and the forest . . .

Suddenly those sounds seemed to burst into my own room, filling it, crowding it; in that instant I wanted so badly to run downstairs, to call Jean, to call Aakonen that it pulled me completely around, facing the door. Yet I'd known from the moment I set my hand to this plan that I couldn't ask Jean's help, couldn't call Aakonen, that that would give away the trap.

Pulling the belt tight on my roughly dried polo coat, I swung myself around again. Swiftly, I crossed to the bed, taking the extra blanket from the foot, pulling back the covers. The blanket I shook out and rolled the long way, placing a diagonal for legs, a curve, and then another diagonal. The end of the blanket lay on the pillow. My brown sweater must go over that for hair. I pulled the covers up, tucking them loosely in around the blanket until the similarity grew strong; that blanket might very easily be my body.

I went then to the closet for my sweater, pulled open the door—

My mouth opened, but suddenly a hand was over it, a rigid arm along my back. I didn't even fight. Was my heart stopped? I couldn't move.

Jean Nobbelin was in my closet, his arm grasping me, his hand over my mouth, his fierce dark grimace before my eyes.

I don't think I fainted. I just stood there with shock buzzing through my body, my eyes unseeing.

And then when nothing else happened, a slow aching. I waited, and still nothing happened.

My eyes came alive again at last enough to see the movement on his face—his lips moving rapidly but soundlessly. Incomprehensible movements.

Then the lips formed a word I'd seemed to see before—"Idiot!"

As if that were a key, I could recognize them all.

"*Don't yell, don't yell,*" were the almost soundless words on the lips. "You goof, did you think I'd let you do this alone? Did you think I couldn't see what you were up to?"

I did collapse then, sagging down against him. The hand went off my mouth.

"Of all the harebrained ideas!" The whisper was in my ear. "I could have shaken the everlasting—" Then a change. "Okay, where do we go from here?"

No strength to lift my words to a whisper. "You went with the others—"

"I came back. Snuck in here while you were in the bathroom." The black eyes were looking at the bed then, and his two hands squeezed, one at each side of my waist. "So you did know enough not to get in that bed."

My paralysis had been so great, I'd forgotten the bed. I quickened to what I still had to do, pulling loose from him to get a soft brown sweater from its hanger. Back at the bed I arranged it around the top of the blanket to give a rough semblance of hair.

"Hide. I've had the light on too long," I whispered. He flattened himself against the wall while I pulled the curtains back and the window open, while I stretched in the clear light of the window as if I yawned for bed. A bullet might come through that window . . .

But none did. I padded across the room to click off the light, kicked the slippers from my stockinged feet at the bedside, lay creakily down.

The room was in a dark gray haze—oxford gray. No moon—more a reflected lake haze. Through it I could just see outlines—the footboard of the bed, the dresser against the inside wall, the chair to the right of the bed, and beyond the window, Jean's bulk moving soundlessly toward me.

Slowly, against the creak of the spring, I got myself out of the bed.

He was whispering but so inaudibly I couldn't at first catch it.

"I've got my shoes off, too. Look, I'll get on the other side of the bed, behind that chair. The curtains won't hide you. We'll have to pull the dresser out so you can get behind that."

He'd taken command, and I saw the wisdom of his generalship. If he were behind the chair and I behind the dresser, that would put one of us on each side of the bed.

I suppressed a moan. "I didn't even think," I whispered. "They could have walked on either side of the bed. If I'd been here alone and on the wrong side—"

The bones of my right hand almost cracked under his answer.

Noiselessly, we moved on the dresser, which must be soundlessly raised, soundlessly moved forward, soundlessly lowered to the floor again. When the operation was completed I was dripping and weak, yet the dresser hadn't been heavy. It had creaked, but no more than a bed might.

"Now, you stay here behind this dresser." He thrust something long, smooth, and iron-cold into my hands. "That's the stove poker from my cabin. I grabbed it before I started back."

"What'll you have?"

"What would you have had if I hadn't come?"

Again I saw how reckless my planning had been. But I hadn't really planned; the thing had just grown. He gave my shoulder a last squeeze and moved away, his dark bulk receding so inaudibly it was uncanny.

The chintz-covered chair swallowed him, and then in the thick grayness of the room there was neither near sound nor near movement, except for the slight flow of my own breath. But, as always when the near sounds stopped, the loud, boisterous roar outside became immediate—the lake lashing against its rock rim, the wind rushing, with its sound of silken tearing, through the trees, the underground river sounding its endless gurgling mirth.

No change in that wilderness sound; it had inflections but no cadences; it softened and loudened but it was always the same sound, the same organ swell, diminishing to a fall of wind, increasing to its rise. An arrogant sound forever untamed. No words in it, but it urged. *Death waits*, it seemed to say, *but death always waits* . . .

Was it the wilderness that was making me do what I did now? Would I ever in any civilized place have had the courage to put myself as bait in a trap?

I thought of that unknown person I sought, somewhere outside this room in the night, and it seemed to me I could hear the urging of the wilderness in his ears, too. *Go now*, it could say. *Live your own life, take what you want in the killing; save yourself by killing. Yours isn't the weak way, the way of law; yours is the wild way. Take, get, kill . . .*

I stirred to get away from that terrible counsel, fastening my thoughts instead to the room and the peril in which I stood. Jean was there, but if the murderer came, he would come with a gun. If he dared to turn on the light as he came in . . .

The blanket roll in the bed was a ruse for darkness only. If the light went on, I had a poker, Jean nothing but his bare hands.

I shifted my weight to the other stockinged foot, and then my heart stopped.

The door was opening.

No sound, but the black wedge of wood moving into the deep gray dark. The door closing softly, and there were three in the room. Two soundless, crouching, and one moving softly, hesitantly forward . . .

The scent of spice.

Substance seemed to fall from my body, leaving it fleshless. The figure moved until it bent above the pillow.

"Ann, I've come to stay with you," Jacqueline whispered.

From behind the chair, a dark movement.

She must have touched the sweater then and known. She whirled. "Ann! Where are you?" A whisper still but beseeching.

Substance closed down on me again. Jean was across the bed from Jacqueline, waiting. I came out from behind the dresser.

"Here."

"You're—Of course! I should have known."

"Sh-sh-sh!" I said. She was whispering a little too loudly in her relief.

She caught at me. "I was frightened to death for you, waiting until I thought it was safe to come." She saw Jean then, starting.

"Ann, who's—?"

"Jean."

She gave a gasping, suppressed laugh. "It's a convention. Oh, Ann, I'm glad it is!"

Jean had gotten around the bed. "Get behind that dresser. Both of you. Jacqui, are you sure you weren't heard or seen?"

"I was as quiet as a—termite."

"If anyone was on the stairs—Well, if it's ruined, it's ruined. Anyway, you whisper too loud. Get back there."

He stationed us and was gone again.

Once more the inside quiet settled down, the hush under the wide, muted roar. Cold, but I stood doubly warmed. Once more no sound except the breathing, doubled now. Sometimes I thought I even caught the rhythm of Jean's breathing from across the room.

Jacqueline and I huddled side by side, easing our backs against the wall from the slow strain of standing. Minutes fell into the hush that was so deep you listened for the drop— minutes that lengthened ceaselessly. Minds waited; muscles waited; nerves waited for the sound and movement that did not come. The hush thickened; the deep gray of the room thickened; the roar, too, thickened, as if it might be growing closer, as if the wilderness itself might be creeping in upon us, the lake advancing on its side, the ranks of the forest advancing one pace and then another.

At first, I had heard every creak and settle of the log walls and the heavy floors, but as the night wore on, I no longer heard those sounds; I seemed to exist in a coma in which there were no sounds except that urgent bell of the wilderness roar. Three people waiting in a trap, listening to that bell . . .

But yet there was another presence, too. One that waited outside as we waited inside. Waited, debating, pulled and pushed, wondering if I were really enough of a menace so it must kill again. Wondering and listening to that urgent bell.

It was almost as if I had joined tongue to the wilderness, urging that outside inimical force to enter here . . .

My signal was the stopping of Jacqueline's breath.

It had come.

The door. That dark wedge at the door. Increasing. A dark form that was inside, a form that seemed to loom, gigantic in shadow. Like a shadow it moved, inaudible, detaching itself from the door. Then it paused. Poised, still, listening.

A long exhalation of breath—mine. I couldn't stop it. As if I knew it was for that the dark form listened. I breathed in as deeply.

The shadow moved again, became a part of the footboard of the bed, then detached itself from that, too, moving like a black wraith up the side of the bed.

Our side.

The shadow bent.

Jacqueline threw herself forward as a loud, exploding crack sounded. I was moving quickly, too. Something fell with a sharp clatter. The shadow whirled just as Jacqueline and I struck it, throwing it back upon the bed.

In that next confusion of desperate struggle, there was again no sound except our labored, panting breaths. Something was in my hand and against my face like unclean clinging fur. We seemed to be, not four people writhing and struggling, but twelve.

"Get the gun—" That must have been Jacqueline, gasping.

Jean—"I've got it."

A long sweeping movement. Impact. The shadow jerked once.

An arm I had been struggling to hold down became suddenly still.

"That's got it"—Jean. Harsh. Quick. "Get on the light."

I ran. The switch came under my hand. The room burst into light—blinding light in which my eyes swam black, in which there grew the reality of a dresser, a chair, a bed, in which Jean and Jacqueline bent over a black velvet cape with a hood, thrown, face downward, over the tumbled bed.

As I moved forward, Jean pulled the hood away from Myra Sallishaw's head.

22

THERE WAS BLOOD ABOVE Myra's temple and a blue bruise on the head that was so delicate it might have been carved by Lalique.

"She came to help. Worn out as she was, she came to help. She must have." I was at the bed, holding to the footboard.

Jean pointed. "That's Bill's automatic."

Beside the limp hand from which it had been wrestled lay what looked like a thin revolver. And in the bedspread over the rolled blanket, just about where my heart would have been if I'd been under that bedspread instead, was an irregularly round hole, its edges blackened and singed.

"*MYRA!*" JACQUELINE SAID. "BUT it can't be Myra who's been doing this murdering!" She was staring at the unconscious figure on the bed, bemused and lost. "She's been so good to me and she loves Toby . . . She's been so completely wrecked since Phillips was killed. So frail and pitiful—"

Jean had the thin wrist in his hand. "I guess we don't have to tie her up. She's out. Good and out. If I'd known who it was, I wouldn't have hit so hard. I guess we better get Dr. Rush."

Disconnected thoughts were running through my head; easy to piece things together after guilt is shown.

Myra's hair was white. The cape would be useful to hide white hair.

Myra had been quick to champion Jacqueline. But she'd been as quick in disbelief when anyone else was suspected—Ed Corvo or Mark or Cecile.

She'd said, "Imagine his keeping those!" when I found the travel folders in Fred's suitcase. I hadn't thought of those words from that day to this, but somehow they drifted up now as I stood looking at that hole in the bedspread.

The cape and the gun had been so successfully hidden. No one would know hiding places here better than Myra, who'd lived here or near here most of her life.

Myra, so cunning . . .

Into the confounded and shocked quiet in which the three of us looked down at her came that impervious, wildly elemental roar through which the chuckle threaded.

I remembered that the gray wolf of the forest has some of the manners of the aristocrat, too.

MYRA WAS STILL UNCONSCIOUS when Aakonen came with Dr. Rush. Jean had done the telephoning in a sudden wild triumph. He'd called Auden, too, and the resort. Jacqueline was forced to hold her hand over the mouthpiece to keep him from calling the hospital at that hour.

"Bill can know in the morning. He can't be waked up."

Ed Corvo was there first, an overcoat over his pajamas. Bradley, Carol, Mark, Cecile, Lottie, Ella—all were there soon in various stages of dress and undress, circling the bed, while Dr. Rush worked over Myra.

He grunted at Jean, "You're lucky you didn't hit any harder."

Jean glared at me. "My foot hit the poker on the floor. A heck of a lot of good it did giving *you* a poker."

I'd completely forgotten the poker; that must have been what fell with that sharp clatter.

Jacqueline was helping Dr. Rush, bending above the bed as Myra opened her eyes.

So the first words Myra said, in a faint whisper, were, "Jacqueline. What are you doing here? I can't kill you. That would ruin everything."

SHE MUST HAVE BEEN disoriented, thought she still bent above the bed, a bed on which somehow Jacqueline lay instead of me.

Then the still-wondering eyes traveled to Dr. Rush, to all the eyes fastened in judgment upon her. She came back to full consciousness instantly, struggling to rise.

She said with an echo of old crispness, "I'm Myra Heaton. What's been happening? I've been attacked. It must have been—"

"It's no good, Mrs. Sallishaw," Aakonen told her. "You were seen by three people—Mr. Nobbelin and Miss Gay and Mrs. Heaton—coming into this room. You fired at the blanket roll which was in the bed. You were wearing the cape. Mr. Bill Heaton's automatic—with a silencer on it—was in your hand."

"Mr. Nobbelin and Miss Gay and Jacqueline," she repeated. "Will you believe them, Mr. Aakonen? They'd do anything to make Jacqueline safe. It's a trick they've worked out."

As she said it she was fumbling in the bed from which Jean

had long since taken the automatic. Aakonen moved forward to stand beside Dr. Rush, his hand on a hip holster. Her eyes raised to that hand, got no farther.

Aakonen said patiently, "No, Mrs. Sallishaw. You gave yourself away in the hearing of everyone present."

He told her what she'd said to Jacqueline as she was recovering consciousness. Myra sat in the bed, humanity flattening out of her face, leaving it completely brittle.

Aakonen continued, "I am arresting you for the murders of Fred and Phillips Heaton and for the attempted murder of Mr. Bill Heaton."

She gave an ingratiating, rueful, bewildered laugh. "But I can't be arrested for murder," she said. "I'm Myra Heaton. Don't you understand? I'm *Myra Heaton*."

I saw in that instant how she really believed that true, how she had walked from her childhood in a charmed spell, believing herself somehow finer than other people, somehow invulnerable, somehow beyond law or guilt, because she was a Heaton—she belonged to the great of the earth. All her life as the trappings of Heaton prestige had fallen from her, and she had fought against recognizing or accepting the loss; in her own mind, she had remained what she believed herself to be—the royal and unapproachable daughter of a royal American line. Just like Phillips.

AAKONEN WOULD HAVE TAKEN her then, but Jacqueline begged, "Wait. I'd still be so glad if—Myra, you didn't have any reason for killing Bill—any reason for killing Fred. And your own brother—"

Myra smiled. "Of course. This is all silly. I must get to my lawyer in Duluth." She was sitting quite straight in the bed now, her white hair down her back in a braid, her bathrobe around her, the scarlet-lined folds of the cape I'd given Jacqueline still under her. Assurance was increasing.

She asked Aakonen coolly, "Have you forgotten I stood right here in this room with Ann when we both saw that figure near the Fingers where Fred was killed? I could hardly be in two places at once."

"I saw only a shadow," I said. "We agreed it might have been Mark coming home—"

"If it was about ten thirty," Mark agreed. "Fred didn't die then anyway. He was alive when I got to the cabin."

Jean put in quickly, "Don't you see? That's tricky, like the rest. She looked out and saw that figure, with Ann right beside her. She wove that in with what she was going to do. Aakonen, we found out about one of those other tricks—the fire in the bed. Ann found out. She—"

Myra stood up from the bed, smoothing her robe around her, standing erect, smiling; no sign about her now of the collapse she'd been displaying since the death of Phillips. The look on her face suggested that she enjoyed the flash of rapiers and was sure of holding her own.

"You found out how the fire in the bed *might* have started," she told me coolly, "but you didn't prove it did start that way or that I had any hand in it."

"Wait," Jean said. "This is all unimportant. It's details. What's important is the motive. Wait." The whips of thought dented his face as he went slowly, ploddingly on.

"It was all planned to look as if Jacqueline was responsible. That's the base. And Myra would have to benefit somehow . . ." His tone on the last words wore down fine and thin.

Myra took a step forward. There was a movement on her face

as if she could have thrown herself at him, clawing, to keep him from reaching what he hunted.

Then Jean said lingeringly, "Lord! I should have seen it. Toby—Toby's the key! With Fred dead and Bill dead, Jacqueline would inherit. But with Jacqueline in prison or an asylum, the money would be held for Toby. Jacqueline said once that if she went to prison, Ann would take Toby. But Ann couldn't take Toby if Myra had wanted her. Myra is Toby's grandmother, and Ann is only a second cousin. Myra would have had Toby and the money, too."

It was Jacqueline who broke that silence, taking a step forward.

"That would mean you hate me."

Two women confronting each other.

Myra knew then, of course, that she was done. She seemed to grow as she stood there, her height rising; I remembered how gigantic her figure had seemed when it walked into that room in darkness.

"No, you can't imagine that I'd hate *you*, could you?"

The syllables fell clearly, tightly. "*You*, who murdered my son. If it hadn't been for you, he'd have been in school yet—safe. He'd never have worked in that terrible mill. Pat was a Heaton. He should never have *had* to work. Hasn't a mother a right to avenge her only son? *Everything I've done, I planned on the day he died.* I hated Bill and his luck. I planned for you to marry him. I planned that Fred should die and Bill should die and you should rot in jail and my son's child should be mine, to take his place."

I'D SEEN HER STANDING through a long afternoon beside her son's coffin. I'd heard what she'd said to Jacqueline that day: "He must have married you to leave me someone."

This had been what she meant.

————

MYRA MOVED BACKWARD IN our silence, her face changing to a sort of triumph.

"You think I failed, don't you? I didn't. I'm proud of what I've done. Proud of the way I handled it. I had bad luck, but that wasn't my fault. Everything I did was done perfectly."

Jacqueline said, "Toby—you did at least love her."

"I wanted the child to be a boy. But a girl did very well. I'd have married you to Bill even if you'd hated him. But you didn't. That part was ridiculously easy. I also knew I'd have to hurry after that, before you had a brat of Bill's."

She'd thought even of that.

"It wasn't hard to get Fred to hate his stepmother. And after a little incident in his office, Bill was extremely sensitive about insanity."

She paused to look at us, her smile entirely like Phillips's now.

"I thought it was a pity people couldn't know how I worked those tricks. Some of them were easy. But the fire in the bed and the holes in Bill's suit—those were harder. Yet *so* effective."

"Not for good," I reminded her. I had seen through one of those.

"Guns make removing people very simple." It was still triumph. "All I had to do was wait for Fred near the boathouse stairs after I'd seen everyone safely to bed and the idea of a prowler was in Ann's mind. I'd known from the moment I saw the cape that it was a godsend, to hide my hair in the dark. I wanted Fred to know me—I had the hood thrown back. He walked to the Fingers with me. He thought his cousin Myra was the only friend he had. He didn't even see the gun."

Jean said, "Thank God for that."

"All I had to do was dress him up a little and hide the gun and the chalk. You'll never know where. I took the cape back to Jacqueline's closet and saw her scissors on the dresser. I thought then of her pomanders. But I was wrong to go to Ann's room to cut up her robe—Ann's nose is too sharp."

She did look then for a moment full at the wreckage of her plans.

I wouldn't have wanted to be alone in a room with eyes that looked at me as hers looked now.

She said, "Ann, you're too sharp. You were finding out too much. I thought when I shunted you off on Jean Nobbelin—I thought no young man and woman thrown together in these wilds would spend much time thinking. I must say you surprised and disappointed me. It would have been much better if you'd been out of the way."

"It isn't because you didn't try," I told her grimly.

"Bill was a disappointment, too—first when he wouldn't believe Jacqueline had insanely killed Fred and then when he wouldn't die. Of course, I hadn't taken sleeping powders that Saturday afternoon. I waited until Jacqueline fell asleep and Bill went out. The cape was so handy on the porch. But then I had to go for the gun—a misfortune, because Ann came home and Jacqueline ran out. I couldn't, you see, kill Jacqueline. The plan didn't allow it."

I could see that our rushing Bill to the hospital had given her plenty of time to hide the cape and the gun and be safely in bed by the time Phillips and Jean looked for her. But she was no longer talking about Bill.

"Poor Phillips," she was saying sweetly. "He'd been such a drag on me all my life, and when he came to my room and tried to start that new blackmail—" She shrugged.

Bradley Auden spoke then for the first time, quickly. "New blackmail?"

She stopped then, raising her eyebrows, smiling at him.

"Wouldn't you like to know?"

"Myra, I've wondered—" Bradley turned slowly then to look at the rest of us. "I've been trying to watch the house. I was out near the barn one night when Jean came home and almost caught me. I had to run. If I'd been caught, I'd certainly have been arrested."

Exclamation from Jean. "That was *you*?"

"I fell and twisted my ankle. Next day at the funeral I had to fall deliberately so I'd have an excuse for the swelling and the limp."

Myra paid no attention. "Poor Phillips, he was such a fool. No one in the house but Octavia and Jacqueline, Phillips and I, and I'd given Jacqueline sleeping tablets. I shunted Phillips off and went for the gun, wearing Jacqueline's shoes—much too big for me. I shot Phillips in his own room. It was very simple to drive the car under his window and slide him through the window so he fell in the car."

She looked at Aakonen and laughed. "My dear Sheriff; there was even some blood on Phillips's floor. I washed it up and dropped a soiled shirt over it. You didn't even find that out."

I'd walked toward that shirt to pick it up. By the time Aakonen had searched the room, the spot must have been dry.

SHE SAID REGRETFULLY, "I don't deserve the misfortune I've had. Bill's not dying—that was devastating. I did go to the hospital to finish the job, but I was too closely watched."

That was when Aakonen's face lit with a triumph that transcended hers. He hadn't made the catch, but one obstinate, determined thing he had set out to do he had accomplished. He'd kept Bill alive.

"I had a right to do what I did," Myra said stubbornly. "I was the head of this family. I've carried all the family burdens—Phillips and Octavia. I took care of them. I saw to it they both had good alibis for that first death."

When she spoke Octavia's name, I became conscious of a sound that might have been going on for a long time behind me—a faint sobbing whimper.

Octavia, forgotten to the last. No one had even thought to summon her. Yet when I turned she was there, her hand over her mouth, her dark eyes, frightened and sick, on Myra. She must have heard the sounds of conflict in her room and lain wondering—or was it fearing and knowing?—what was going on, until the necessity to see had grown greater than timidity, and she had crept here to the others.

When I looked at her, she spoke the first words I ever heard her say.

"What will I do?" It was still the frightened whimper of a child.

Yes, what would she do? What would become of her now? She who must have known—surely after Phillips's death at least—that Myra was the killer. How had Myra kept her from revealing what she knew? Then I saw the simple weapon. Octavia had just spoken it aloud. With Myra gone, there'd be no safeguard for Octavia.

Then with a flash I saw that Octavia, too, might be Myra's victim. Long years of being made to feel that her defect made her too loathsome for human sight. Jacqueline had said there were more ways of killing people than with guns.

While I stood seeing what Octavia's life must have been, someone else acted. And that person, out of all the people there, was Cecile Granat.

"Let's you and I go back to your room," she said, and her

voice wasn't kind—it was casual. She moved toward Octavia, taking her arm, and for a moment Cecile's face was open. Somewhere there was the face of a fourteen-year-old girl who was already outcast and wild, and whose mother was just dead, and who hadn't yet gotten that letter from Bill which she cherished so strongly she had hidden it in the woods to keep it from sight.

Cecile was also a Heaton. Heatons could be remarkably fine as well as remarkably evil.

Myra watched, indifferently, Cecile leading her sister out. She laughed a little. She said, "I'd like to see Cecile keeping it up as well as I have. I've always played my parts perfectly. Not one of you suspected me. When people started getting frightened and falling to pieces and wanting to run away, no one wanted to run away or fell in pieces more convincingly than I did. You had to trap me to get me. It's a pity that girls from the best families couldn't go on the stage when I was young. I should have been the greatest actress the world has ever known."

SOME DAYS LATER, ANOTHER section of the puzzle was filled in. Aakonen got a letter with a sealed enclosure.

To whom it may concern, the note in that enclosure read.

In case I am unhappily and violently removed from this mortal sphere, it would be the part of good judgment for the investigators of my demise to look closely into the activities of my sister Myra.

Myra's such an impulsive person. You see, she once had an affair with Bradley Auden—oh, quite a violent affair—and it continued quite some time after she married John Sallishaw. My father unfortunately took the wrong walk through the woods one night. It was Father's intention to do a little talking

to John Sallishaw the next day—dear Father did so hate hav-
ing his own pleasures appropriated.

So Myra, poor girl, had to burn Father up. I was drunk,
but not too drunk to see her tipping the lamp. I'd have gotten
out by myself if I hadn't tripped. Myra's rewarded me to the
best of her ability for my silence, but some day it may be handy
to tell her that this note exists—who knows?

It was signed with a flourish, *Phillips Heaton.*
I didn't see Bradley Auden's face when he heard of that note.

BUT THAT WAS STILL unknown on that dark Wednesday night
when Aakonen drove off with Myra handcuffed to a deputy in
the seat behind him.

Those of us left blinked at each other like a colony of underground animals that could hardly stand the light of relief that
possessed us.

I didn't know how I felt. I felt exuberant and wild and exhausted. I felt as if I could waltz to the moon and back. I felt as if
I could fall on the floor behind the davenport—that's where I
was standing—and sleep for a week.

Jacqueline was on one side of me, Jean on the other. We
seemed to have stuck that way.

Jacqueline said hazily, "It's all over. There won't be any more
people dying. Bill's getting better . . ."

Jean shattered bemusement by yelling, "We're free! We can
do anything, go anywhere! Tomorrow you can get Toby back!"

"Tomorrow?" Jacqueline asked, and suddenly she was laughing and crying. "Tomorrow isn't soon enough. Get your car."

It was four in the morning when we started that wild ride to
Duluth. Jacqueline talked the whole the way in.

She said, "All my life I've been unsure. I thought, suppose something terrible should happen, so terrible I couldn't stand it? I've always looked for people to help me bear things. But last night, waiting behind that dresser, I wasn't unsure at all. The worst that can happen to me has happened—waiting beside Bill, fighting for him not to die—that was the worst. And I stood it. I know now I can stand anything."

She said, "Toby knew all along. That's why she's so independent. She knows I'm strong. I'll support her like an unbreakable wall."

She said, "I'm never going to cling to Bill anymore. We're going to be different—we're going to be even."

AT SEVEN, WE WERE in Duluth and walking into the room where Toby slept in the crib Mrs. Foster had borrowed for her. There were streaks of dried tears on Toby's cheeks.

She lay without stirring when Jacqueline woke her.

"Mama," she told herself, and when Jacqueline took her up she cried softly, rubbing her nose back and forth against Jacqueline's neck, sobbing low and quiet as an adult sobs in grief.

A minute for the memory of a world gone wrong, and then a minute to accept that it had become as suddenly right. She jerked her wet face up from her mother's neck, beaming.

"Ann," she wanted to know, "you get me a blue chalk?"

We told Mrs. Foster everything as we hustled Toby into clothes and clothes into suitcases. "*But Myra!*" Mrs. Foster kept gasping. "Not Myra Sallishaw!"

I don't think she heard Jacqueline's heartfelt thanks. She did take the check Jacqueline gave her, but, from the way she was twisting it in her fingers, I wondered if it could last to get to the bank.

"WE'LL MAKE THE HOSPITAL by ten," Jean promised. We did. I'd even quit being tired by that time; I just felt mildly and drunkenly hilarious. Jean had been grinning all the way back from Duluth, as if something terrific and wonderful he could hardly wait for was drawing close.

"Central has been calling you the last hour," Miss Fleet told Jean.

He sat down to call while Jacqueline and I took Toby off to the washroom. When we got back, the grin was all over his face.

"Good old George Crowley. Seeing that we were so anxious, he hurried up his tests. It seems he believes a solution of potassium hydroxide—about a ten percent solution, he thought—would stay on wool tweed for a week without showing any ill effects but that at the end of that time the fabric would be weakened enough so cleaning would produce holes. It isn't acid that eats wool—it's alkalis. Remember that anytime you're up to tricks."

He preceded us down the hall but stood back to let us first into Bill's room. The guard was gone.

The head on the bed turned two inches this morning.

Toby ran. She asked in amazement, "Bill, you s'eep now?"

Bill gave such a convincing demonstration of strangling that Miss Boles leaped to his side.

"No, go away," he told her. To us, "Toby's here. That means—"

Jacqueline and I told him, trying to be subdued and unexciting but finding it hard going. He couldn't ask many questions, but when we got through, there weren't many questions left to be asked.

"Myra!" Bill was as confounded as we'd been. "I'd have sworn by my bottom dollar Myra was all right."

Jean had stood back but now he walked to stand beside me, the grin again all over his face.

"Bill," he said, "you've had the heck of a break out of this. I figure you've got a right to a little entertainment. Look what I've gone and done."

The full tide of his exuberance was on him now, and a faint warming excitement woke on the face on the pillow.

Jean faced me, the danger signals up in his black alarming eyes. I started backing up to the wall, but he grabbed me anyway and I let him. He kissed me—not politely. I started getting mad, but I had time to get over it before he pulled his face away.

Jacqueline was just staring; so was Miss Bolles.

The weak but unbroken voice from the bed said, "Make him marry you before he does much more of that, Ann. His father had nineteen children."

That wasn't just an echo of the Bill Heaton grin.

I remembered I never had liked tame and predictable men anyway.

"*You!*" I said at Jean. "Did you have this in mind when you sent that letter that got me here?"

Jean said blithely, "Sure." There wasn't any room for him to move closer—I was already backed against the wall. But he moved closer.

One of the most popular American crime writers of the twentieth century, **Mabel Seeley** was known as "The Mistress of Mystery." Critically acclaimed titles like *The Listening House* (1938), *The Crying Sisters* (1939), and the Mystery of the Year–awarded *The Chuckling Fingers* (1941) have placed her stories and characters alongside those of Agatha Christie, Dorothy L. Sayers, and Sir Arthur Conan Doyle. Among her many accolades and awards, Seeley was most proud of her service as the first director of the Mystery Writers of America. Born on March 25, 1903, in Herman, Minnesota, Mabel Seeley is best known for crime novels featuring female detectives who defied the stereotypes of the time as self-reliant and strong-willed Midwestern heroines.

Ready to find
your next great read?

Let us help.

Visit prh.com/nextread